L.J. Shen is a *New York Times*, *Wall Street Journal*, *USA Today*, *Washington Post* and #1 Amazon bestselling author of contemporary and NA romance. Best known for her angsty, dark books and barely redeemable alpha heroes, she writes fairytales with teeth and claws. She lives in a picturesque beach town with her family, pets and inner demons, and enjoys reading, travelling, cooking and spending time with her grumpy cat.

authorljshen.com

- authorljshen
- @authorljshen
- @authorljshen
- @authorljshen

ALSO BY L.J. SHEN

Sinners of Saint
Vicious
Ruckus
Scandalous
Bane

All Saints
Pretty Reckless
Broken Knight
Angry God
Damaged Goods

Forbidden Love
Truly, Madly, Deeply
Wildest Dreams
Handsome Devil

Society of Villains
Bad Bishop

TWISTED PAWN

L.J. SHEN

HODDER &
STOUGHTON

First published in the United States by Bloom Books, an imprint of Sourcebooks, in 2026
First published in Great Britain in 2026 by Hodder & Stoughton Limited
An Hachette UK company

The authorised representative in the EEA is Hachette Ireland,
8 Castlecourt Centre, Dublin 15, D15 XTP3, Ireland (email: info@hbgi.ie)

5

Copyright © L.J. Shen 2026

The right of L.J. Shen to be identified as the Author of the Work has been
asserted by her in accordance with the Copyright, Designs and Patents Act 1988.

Internal design © Sourcebooks 2026

All rights reserved. No part of this publication may be reproduced, stored
in a retrieval system, or transmitted, in any form or by any means without
the prior written permission of the publisher, nor be otherwise circulated in
any form of binding or cover other than that in which it is published and
without a similar condition being imposed on the subsequent purchaser.

All characters in this publication are fictitious and any resemblance to real persons,
living or dead, is purely coincidental.

A CIP catalogue record for this title is available from the British Library

Paperback ISBN 978 1 399 75253 4
ebook ISBN 978 1 399 75254 1

Typeset in Adobe Caslon Pro

Printed and bound in Great Britain by Clays Ltd, Elcograf S.p.A.

Hodder & Stoughton policy is to use papers that are natural, renewable
and recyclable products and made from wood grown in sustainable forests.
The logging and manufacturing processes are expected to conform
to the environmental regulations of the country of origin.

Hodder & Stoughton Limited
Carmelite House
50 Victoria Embankment
London EC4Y 0DZ

www.hodder.co.uk

AUTHOR'S NOTE

Dear reader,

Thank you for reading *Twisted Pawn* (Society of Villains #2).

While reading *Bad Bishop* is not necessary to enjoy this complete stand-alone, doing so will give you a better understanding of the world, its characters, and the relationships between the key players.

These characters also appear in my book *Handsome Devil* (Forbidden Love #3), which is a stand-alone. Even though you don't need to read it to enjoy Achilles and Tierney's journey, doing so will give you further insight into their story.

Some artistic liberties were taken when writing this book. For instance, in the Italian baptism scene. Some traditions were changed to reflect the cruelty of the Camorra and are in no way affiliated with the practice of the Catholic Church.

Finally, please note this is a *dark* story full of gore, violence, questionable sexual situations (including dubcon and CNC), and other sensitive subject matters.

Reader discretion is advised.

For a full list of the content warnings, visit here:
shor.by/HBBr

To the ones who never stopped believing, even when hope was the only thing left.

You are the knife I turn inside myself;
that is love. That, my dear, is love.

—*Franz Kafka,* Letters to Milena

When I saw you, I fell in love, and
you smiled because you knew.

—*Arrigo Boito*

SOCIETY OF VILLAINS TREE

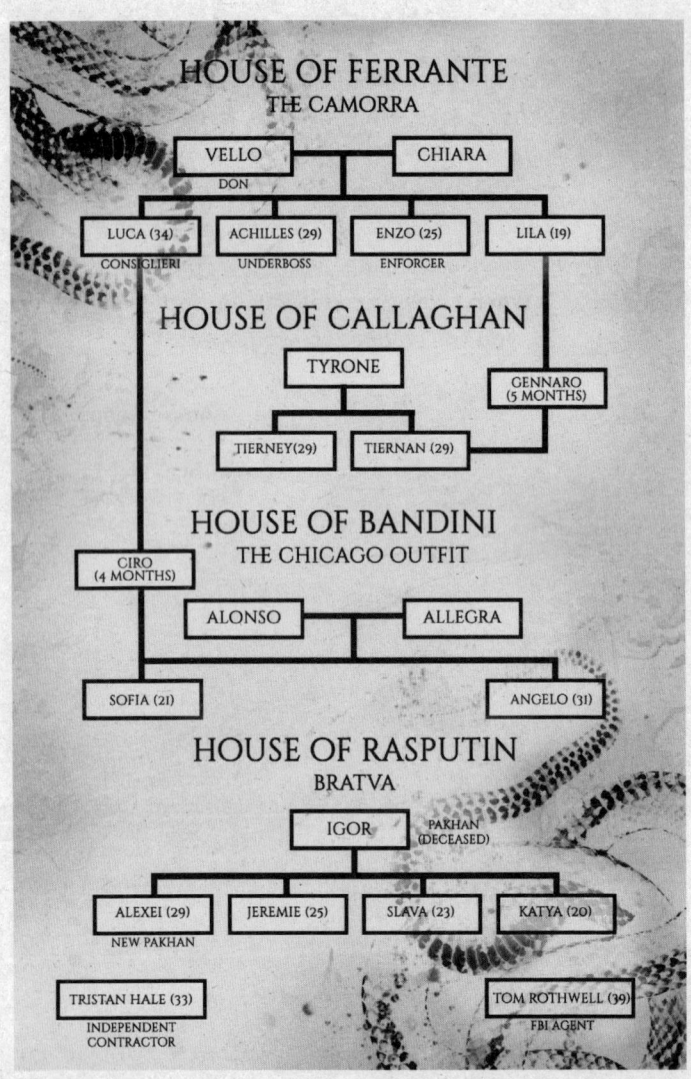

term: TWISTED PAWN

In chess, the pawn is the weakest piece, and is worth only one point. Historically and culturally, a pawn represents a soldier, a peasant, or infantry. Easily dispensable and widely underestimated.

PLAYLIST

(Best enjoyed when listened to in this order)

"NAnthem Vol 2"—N'to, Patto MC & Peste
"Sins to Sacrifice"—Az Apathy
"Precious"—Depeche Mode
"Psychos in Love"—Cheska Moore
"Halo"—Texas
"Skyfall"—Adele
"Fight"—Freestyle Concept (feat. Dope One, Clementino, Inoki, L-Mizzy)
"Ready or Not"—Fugees
"RUNRUNRUN"—Dutch Melrose
"Trauma"—Cheska Moore
"Harley & Joker"—notefly & BrillLion
"Black Eyed Boy"—Texas
"Roman Sky"—Avenged Sevenfold
"Static"—Sleep Theory
"Tainted Love"—Scorpions
"Temptation"—Union of Sound
"Closer"—Kings of Leon
"Say What You Want"—Texas

AFTERWORD

Death.

Don Vello knew it intimately. Personally. Fondly.

It was his trade. His passion. His destiny.

He wasn't scared to die. He and Death were too familiar for that. Old friends of sorts.

Besides, one cannot fear something so natural and inevitable, like the bloom of a flower midspring.

He had a few months to live if he was lucky. He needed to choose a successor. Now.

He thought he knew who it would be up until two days ago.

His second son by marriage, Achilles.

Achilles, the ruthless. The courageous. The untouchable. The *psychopath*.

The cruel offspring who exceeded his expectations.

Achilles had been different from the start.

Like his brothers, he had been baptized in Vello's enemy's blood when he was a newborn.

Unlike his brothers, he'd seemed to enjoy every second of the ceremony.

A small, stoic thing, he didn't thrash or whine as Vello lowered him to the baptismal font at Chiesa di San Pietro Martire. He slept soundly, cocooned in the place he considered home—another man's demise.

Vello had held him by his foot, watching as the child turned crimson.

The only part of his body the blood did not touch was his pink, smooth heel. Vello's wife, Chiara, placed her hand on his shoulder before the baby was dunked all the way. "No," her voice trembled. "Please. He needs a shred of humanity."

Vello disagreed but complied. The doctors had said his wife had something called postpartum depression. That he had to be careful with her womanly notions.

Women really were silly little things, weren't they?

No matter. He was pleased enough to accommodate her request.

He had planned to call the boy Achille. A good, strong Italian name.

It was his exposed heel that made the don add the extra *s*.

Achilles.

For not all of him was dipped in blood. He had one vulnerability. Now, he had to find out what it was.

Growing up, Achilles lived up to his name and showed unstoppable strength.

He was a fearless soldier and a fierce warrior.

He demonstrated such malice, even his own family feared him. He killed and mutilated. Never blinking, pausing, or hesitating to execute an order.

His mother avoided him at all costs, his siblings tolerated him out of necessity, and his father brimmed with pride, for his wife had been mistaken: Achilles did not seem to have one soft spot in his entire depraved existence after all.

Don Vello thought Achilles would do well as the don of the Ferrante clan.

But that was before.

Before he found out about his son's mortal weakness.

It came in the form of a copper-haired girl.

The daughter of a mediocre Irish mobster.

A thoughtless, reckless, *pointless* thing.

Tierney Callaghan.

The twisted little pawn was his Achilles' heel.

TWISTED PAWN XIII

A seasoned chess player, Vello had once upon a time thought he could get rid of the little whore. Make her an isolated pawn. Remove her from other key players who could help her survive.

But he'd been too late. The girl was ingrained too deep inside his son's system.

Vello heard footsteps approaching his office. Achilles, probably. He'd have to kill him after his last stunt. A sad state of affairs, but Achilles chose this path for himself.

Nobody betrayed the Camorra.

Not even the Don's son.

Vello sighed, pulling his drawer open and cocking his gun.

At least he'd still have Luca.

At least he'd still have Enzo.

At lease he'd still have his secret favorite son.

A second set of footsteps sounded from the hallway. Whoever was coming brought reinforcements.

He smiled to himself bitterly. Perhaps he wasn't the one to do the killing, after all.

Reaching a frail hand to his Battle of Waterloo chess set, he picked up a pawn, using it to knock down a king. His wife would know what it meant. She'd appoint the son most fitting to be the king of the underworld.

During his last moments on this earth, he marveled at God's cruel humor. How He'd molded man in his own image but gave him a vulnerability that never failed to seal his fate—a heart.

For even the greatest of warriors…

Surrendered to love.

Luca
Achilles
Enzo
Tiernan
il prediletto

even though it breaks rules...

PART ONE
THE HUNT

CHAPTER ONE
TIERNEY

PRESENT DAY
CHIESA DI SAN PIETRO MARTIRE, NAPLES, ITALY

"Fuck. Where is it?" I plopped onto the first pew of the church, rummaging in my Chanel bag for my pack of cigarettes. I didn't normally smoke. Then again, I wasn't normally thousands of miles away from home, in close quarters with the most powerful Mafia family in the world. Oh, and did I mention half its members wanted me dead? Fun times.

As if on cue, a large figure slid onto the pew behind me. An unlit cigarette materialized in the hand of an arm stretching across my shoulder. I plucked it from its owner with a scoff.

I didn't need to look to know who it was.

As clichéd as it sounded, I always felt his presence before I saw him. He'd been my shadow since we were fourteen.

I recognized the rhythm of his breathing in the dark, the temperature of his gaze on my skin, the pulse of his footsteps inside my own chest. He'd become an integral part of me. Something so deeply entrenched in my existence, it was another facet of my identity now.

Achilles Ferrante.

My enemy. My rival. My impending demise.

"Do you always curse like a drunken sailor in church?" His dry burr reverberated in the pit of my stomach.

"Only when I have to share it with you." I slipped the cigarette between my scarlet-painted lips, dunking my hand back into my purse to hunt for a lighter.

Achilles leaned forward, his lips skimming the shell of my ear. "Wanna know something?"

Goose bumps pebbled the back of my neck. Fifteen years later, and he still smelled of firewood, leather, and spice. "No."

"You look like a whore in that dress," he rasped, his voice dripping so much venom, I wouldn't have been surprised if the floor was slippery.

"One you can never afford." I flipped my hair in his face.

Despite my careless facade, his words landed like a bullet right in the center of my chest.

I wasn't a sex worker, but I had slept around with the wrong kind of men in the past. Men who were cruel to me. Men who had hurt me. It was the only way I could accept any form of affection.

But that was before the asshole had put me on surveillance two years ago. Now, I had to walk around everywhere with one of his soldiers. No more sex life for me. God forbid a girl enjoyed her favorite cardio.

"Sweetheart, if I wanted you, you'd be screaming my name so loud God's ears would ring."

"Sorry to disappoint, but even ladies of the night have standards."

"So you admit to being a whore?" The wooden pew creaked beneath the weight of his carved muscles as he edged closer. "Do you offer group discounts?"

"Why, are you planning to bring every facet of your disgusting personality?"

Finally, my fingers wrapped around the silver Zippo in my purse. *Bingo.* I stood up, careening on my too-high heels toward the atrium before he delivered his lethal comeback. I zipped past stained-glass windows and marble columns through the double doors, pouring into the sunshine.

Outside, the stairway teemed with guests. I searched for Mount Vesuvius beyond yellow and golden buildings surrounding the church but couldn't find it. I slouched against the wall, lighting up the cigarette and scanning the crowd. My heart was in my throat. I was tired of the stupid organ never staying where it was supposed to whenever Achilles Ferrante was around.

He wasn't wrong. My outfit for my nephew Gennaro's baptism *was* inappropriate.

It was a red minidress, far too short for anything that wasn't a nightclub. But you know what else wasn't appropriate? Baptizing a not-quite six-month-old baby in some dead criminal's blood. Yet that was exactly what the Ferrantes were about to do.

They were ruthlessly sadistic. Unfortunately, so was my idiot brother whose baby was being christened. Tiernan said he didn't mind Gennaro continuing his wife's family's tradition as long as the blood he was dipped in was of someone who deserved to die. Apparently, that someone was a rival clan's underboss and a child molester.

Tiernan was an atheist. Where we came from, we knew there was no God. We'd prayed to Him every night when we were kids, and He never answered. This would be the first time Tiernan set foot in a church. But I knew better than to argue logic with my brother when it came to his wife. What Lila wanted, he delivered. No questions asked. I felt no resentment or anger at the special treatment he gave my sister-in-law. I'd do anything for Lila, too. She was just that kind of person.

Kind. Wholesome. Perfect.

Speak of the devil, my brother was heading right in my direction.

"What the fuck do you think you're wearing?" He greeted me in his usual sociopathic fashion, barging into my line of vision and casting a large shadow over my frame.

Tiernan looked flawless in his Savile Row suit and slicked-back hair. He wore an eye patch after Achilles had scooped out his eye. But that was before he had married Lila. These days, they'd take a bullet for one another.

I shrugged, taking a drag of my cigarette. "A dress."

"*Bullshit*. People are staring."

"People always stare. The least I can do is give them a good reason to."

"Today's not about you, Tier."

I said nothing because he was right. But if I told him the real reason I dressed this way, we'd get into a fight, and I didn't want to ruin today for him.

"Isn't it time you act your age?"

"That's a rather philosophical question." I took a deep drag of my cigarette, letting the smoke hit the bottom of my lungs before fanning it sideways. "I find that you're only as mature as your responsibilities. I happen to have none. No family. No kids. No job."

No future, either, but I never let myself think about it too much.

"You can have a husband and a job in no time. Just say the word and I'll get it done."

I snorted at the offer. "I'm good, thanks."

"You need to cover yourself up."

"You wound me, brother." I pouted. "These legs are meant for flaunting."

"You know, there's more to life than pissing people off."

"I didn't wear this to piss people off."

I wore it to *warn* people off. I was the harlot, the jezebel, the Delilah of the family. Not wife material and definitely unfit for an arranged marriage. See, a couple of years ago, Achilles had convinced Tiernan that if my brother allowed him to pick a groom for me, this would somehow tame my feminine rage—that if I got hitched, I'd be happy and normal.

So now my mission was to make myself as desirable to

Camorrista men as a prostate examination by Captain Hook. Because no matter what, I'd never *ever* let anyone take away my liberty. Never again.

"Where's my nephew, anyway?" I changed the subject.

Tiernan jerked his chin to his right. I followed his gaze. His wife, Lila, stood at the foot of the church's stairs, a circle of women fawning over her. She was holding Gennaro—Nero for short—close to her chest.

Lila was a true beauty. Delicate features, pale blue eyes, and flaxen locks, all wrapped in a flowery pink chiffon dress. Nero, however, was the spitting image of us Callaghans. Same burgundy hair. Same green, shrewd eyes. A chubby-cheeked version of his father, swathed in a white christening robe. It was funny how the sweet little angel found solace in the devil and even managed to domesticate him. Because for the first time in his life, my brother looked…*happy*.

Nero gurgled and reached for his mother's loose curls, fisting a golden ringlet and twisting it between pudgy fingers. Lila giggled, kissing the tip of his nose.

I'd held Gennaro thousands of times. Bathed him. Changed his diapers. Sniffed him. Lila was generous about sharing her son with me, knowing how much joy he brought into my life. And yet, every time I saw them together, it felt like someone speared a rusty nail straight into my heart and twisted slowly. It was a reminder of everything I'd never have.

I yawned, my gaze shifting back to my brother. "Did you choose his godparents yet?"

"Yeah."

"Who?"

"Luca and Sofia." He cleared his throat, avoiding my eyes. "They chose us to be Ciro's godparents. It was only appropriate that we reciprocate."

"Right." I forced out a smile. "Etiquette is so important in the underworld."

Luca and Sofia were Lila's brother and sister-in-law. They were married, with a son close to Nero's age, so it made sense. But that didn't soften the blow. They didn't see me fit to be the godmother. And why would they? I was a mess. A *hot* mess, granted, but still a mess.

"Listen, Lila's nervous as it is. I need you on your best behavior," Tiernan growled.

I rolled my eyes so hard I saw suppressed memories. Like I'd ever do anything to hurt Lila.

"I mean it, Tier. No funny business."

"Yeah, yeah. I'll be a vision of elegance and propriety. Don't worry."

The clucking sound of wood hitting concrete entered my ears, and we both turned in its direction. Don Vello Ferrante slapped his walking cane over the stairs up to the church. My father walked by his side.

"It took them almost six months to baptize the baby," Vello growled. "This is unheard of."

"Lila didn't want to put Nero on a plane before he got his vaccinations," Tyrone replied.

"Who cares what Lila wants? *Per l'amor di Dio*," Vello spat out. "She's just a woman!"

"What's killing him?" I asked Tiernan, still watching the don.

"Not sure. But it better hurry the fuck up. Now if you'll excuse me"—Tiernan brushed past me—"I need to go bite off my father-in-law's head before he upsets my wife."

I flicked the remainder of the cigarette to a nearby bush, tugging the hem of my dress down. People shuffled into the church, pushing past Camorra soldiers who stood on guard.

Since procrastinating was my favorite hobby, I plucked my phone out of my purse and checked my messages.

An invitation to a wine tasting upstate with a senator's wife and her friends.

A committee brunch for a fundraiser.

A spa weekend with my good friend Frankie Keaton, the sitting president's wife.

I'd have to say yes to all of these engagements. Since I didn't have a real job, my task was to form connections my brother and the Irish Mafia could use. Tiernan paid me a monthly salary. I, in return, made police officers look the other way, county clerks speed up permits, and the port workers put aside goods the Irish later sold for triple the price on the streets.

After RSVPing my next month into mindless social obligations, I logged on to the encrypted messaging app, stopping on an unread message from a few weeks ago. My thumb halted over the screen.

> Unknown: Do the right thing, Tierney. It's your only chance at freedom.

Nibbling on the corner of my lip, I contemplated answering FBI Agent Tom Rothwell. He'd been on my ass for a couple of years now, trying to convince me to flip on the Ferrantes. But since I didn't have a death wish, I kept shutting him down.

He was an option in case everything went to shit. Hopefully, it'd never come to that.

With a sigh, I slipped my phone into my bag, turned around, and reentered the church.

In the span of a few minutes, the first few pews had filled up almost completely. Tiernan and Lila stood at the altar, next to the priest. So did Luca and Sofia, the godparents.

There was one almost-empty pew—the second one from the front, where Achilles sat alone. Since I'd rather bathe in acid than sit next to him, I hurried to the first pew and squeezed myself between Lila's brother Enzo and my father.

"Pumpkin." My father kissed my cheek.

"Tyrone." I coiled away, pressing against Enzo. The childish pet name grated on my nerves. I was twenty-nine. Besides, we weren't close enough for nicknames.

"Shame about the outfit. You don't need it to look beautiful." His eyes swept over me disapprovingly.

I didn't answer. I was never good enough for my father, and he made sure I remembered it. He had ignored me all of my adolescent years, and as soon as I came of age and he realized I was too difficult to marry off, he gave up on me altogether.

These days, we barely spoke and only saw each other when Tiernan invited us both over.

"Yo, Tier." Enzo slung a tan, muscular arm over the pew, giving my shoulder a playful squeeze. "Waddup?"

I liked Enzo. He was funny, kind, and outrageously hot. Our paths didn't cross often, but when they did, we could spend hours bantering and having a great time. He and Lila were the only Ferrantes I didn't actively want to push off a cliff.

"No complaints," I said. "You?"

"A few complaints." He tossed a piece of mint gum into his mouth, scratching his forearm absentmindedly. "Hunger, mainly. Been cutting carbs. Gotta maintain that eight percent body fat."

"Only a certified masochist would do that." I scrunched my nose. "Quitting pasta and bread would make me stabby."

"See, that's not a problem in my line of work." He grinned good-naturedly. Enzo was an enforcer. Stabbing people was his day job. You'd think it'd make him less lovable. You'd be wrong. "And the results are wild. You should see me under this shirt. I'm more shredded than sensitive documents President Keaton doesn't want leaking to the media." He rolled his tongue over his perfect teeth, giving me a cheeky wink. "*Allegedly*."

I snorted, shaking my head. "If you're trying to milk me for gossip about the First Couple, save your breath."

"So you're not denying that he did it. Interesting." He wiggled his brows.

I laughed. "What else is new?"

"Oh, let's see… I'm giving up pussy for Lent."

"Why?" Achilles chimed in. "The whole point of Lent is giving up something you *like*."

"Enzo, it's May." I frowned, ignoring the asshole behind us. "Lent is in March."

"*Next* year's Lent," Enzo clarified. "This year's done. Might as well enjoy the sex."

"Everything I know about your sex life, I've learned against my will." I chuckled. "Do I want to know why you're doing this?"

"Lost a bet with your brother."

"What'd you bet on?"

"I said you wouldn't wear something scandalous today. And he… well, doesn't have much faith in you." Enzo's whiskey eyes trailed down my bare legs.

"Even her brother knows she's a lost cause." Achilles tsked from behind me. "I made the mistake of trying to fix her once. Never again."

That was it. I'd had it with this asshole. I turned around sharply, spearing him with a glare.

"Can you be helpful for once in your life and evacuate your grotesque face from my vicinity?"

"Only because you asked so nicely, *Piccola Fiamma*." He stood up, buttoning his blazer with one hand. "As it happens, I do have business to attend to."

Achilles glided out of the pew with a grace that no hulking, six-four man had any business possessing, disappearing between Roman columns.

My nickname, *little flame*, wasn't born out of love. It was born out of hate. A reminder of everything we'd lost and everything we could've been if I hadn't gone and fucked it up.

That was what killed me the most. Knowing it was me who threw it all away. Who managed to take this beautiful, pure love this boy had given me and turn it into potent, burning hatred. I'd ruined our lives, and now he was making me suffer for it.

The organist began playing, snapping my attention back to the here and now. The chatter stopped. The priest, a frail white-haired man, stepped forward and began his blessings.

"Nel nome del Padre, del Figlio, e dello Spirito Santo."

Echoes of muffled screams ricocheted across the church's walls. Every back in the room straightened. The ominous music grew louder. The priest proceeded, ignoring the cry of panic and pain.

"Padre nostro che sei nei cieli, sia santificato il tuo nome."

Achilles appeared from behind the altar, holding a thrashing, disheveled man by the back of his neck. His captive's hair was sweat-drenched, his suit unkempt.

The underboss. The molester.

Lila instinctively pressed Gennaro to her chest. Achilles stopped in front of the baptismal font, pressing the blade of a sharp knife to the man's main artery.

"Venga il tuo regno, sia fatta la tua volontà, come in cielo così in terra."

The priest clutched his Roman missal to a point of white knuckles, training his gaze hard on the pages.

"Dacci oggi il nostro pane quotidiano, rimetti a noi i nostri debiti, come noi li rimettiamo ai nostri debitori."

Achilles slowly ran the blade across the man's neck above the font, slicing his carotid artery with a surgeon's precision. Crimson liquid gushed out, pouring into the hollow object. The thrashing and muffled cries stopped. All the while, Achilles stared at *me*, hatred burning through his pupils.

A river of blood sloshed over the fountain, filling it to the brim. The audience watched in silent shock. Achilles let go of his victim, and the lifeless body crumpled at his feet.

"E non ci indurre in tentazione, ma liberaci dal male. Amen."

Tiernan scooped Nero from his mother's arms and brought him to the font.

The priest took a shell, scooping some of the blood, and let it drip down Gennaro's head. His hair was the same shade as the blood. Nero gurgled happily, fingers reaching for the shell, trying to snatch it from the minister. More blood dripped down the crown of his head and onto his christening gown.

My stomach churned. Even though I grew up in the belly of the underworld, I wasn't a big fan of blood and murder. Plus, I wasn't a believer, but slaughtering someone in a church seemed especially sinister, even to me.

Suddenly, the rumbling purr of motorcycles sounded from outside the church. The engines roared louder and closer, making guests look at each other in confusion. It sounded like dozens of them were approaching.

Tiernan made a cutting motion with his hand, and the priest stopped talking. Silence fell over the church. The steady, quiet *drip, drip* of blood leaking from the baptism tub filled the air.

The church's doors blasted open. Women shrieked, jumping from their seats and grabbing their children, stuffing them underneath the pews for shelter. The men unholstered their weapons, charging toward the doors.

Twisting in my seat, I watched as two men in balaclavas tossed hand flares into the church and ducked back outside. The flares hissed and exploded. Red smoke detonated, thick and suffocating, covering the entire room.

The rapid fire of semiautomatic weapons rang in the air. Smoke scorched my eyes and filled my lungs. Screaming and blood blanketed the nave.

Shit.

I darted up from my seat, peering around, desperate to find Tiernan and Lila. My main goal was to save my family. I'd worry about myself later.

A large figure stepped in front of me, their face veiled by the red smoke. It snatched my hair at the back of my skull in a punishing grip and pushed me chest-down onto the floor.

My pulse roared in my ears, and I immediately tried to thrash and fight. "What the f—"

A designer boot slammed between my shoulder blades, tucking me so I was hidden under the pew safely. I coughed out smoke, fighting for my next breath. All I could see was the wingtip toe of the boots that hid me. They were spattered in fresh blood.

I was about to grab it and break his goddamn ankle when the figure crouched low and Achilles's face peered down at me through the red fog.

Scarred.

Terrifying.

Achingly beautiful.

Gone was the long-limbed sad boy who had crawled through my bedroom window every night to keep my nightmares at bay. These days, Achilles Ferrante was a warrior forged from violence and mayhem. Every inch of his face was marred with scars and burns, and the rest of him—from the jawline down—was covered in ink.

He gripped my jaw, tilting my face from side to side. "Hurt?"

I shook my head, unable to produce words as panic closed its invisible claws around my neck.

He yanked a second pistol from under his tailored blazer, placing it in my hand and curling my fingers over it. "Wait till I come for you, and don't do anything stupid."

I stared at him, furious and scared. I couldn't believe any of this was happening: that he had murdered a man in a church, that we were under attack, and that there was a huge possibility some of my family members were dead.

"Goddamn it, Tierney. I want your word."

My eyes darted around frantically. Where was Tiernan? Lila? Little Nero?

"Your *word*." Achilles grabbed my jaw, returning my attention back to him.

"I'll wait for you," I spat out. "Now get your filthy hands off me."

He paused for a moment, drinking my face in like it was the last time. The world fell to the periphery of our existence, and we shared a single pulse.

He tucked a stray flyaway behind my ear like he used to do before everything between us went to shit. For a fraction of a second, we were us again.

I opened my mouth to tell him the truth before it was too late. Before one of us died.

I'm sorry. I never meant to hurt you. And none of it was true.

Nothing came out.

A loud pop pierced the air. The person behind him got shot in the head and fell to the floor beside me. Haunted, lifeless eyes stared back at mine. Achilles stood up and was gone in a flash.

Enzo and my father were nowhere in sight. They'd joined the Camorra's efforts to push back the assailants. I tilted my head toward the altar, searching for my family again. Through the evaporating red mist, I found them huddled behind the organ, Tiernan protecting Lila and Nero with his body. He had his gun cocked and ready, aimed at the open doors.

He didn't join the other men.

As far as he was concerned, everyone else could die. His small family was his entire world.

A gunman in a balaclava and full combat uniform stalked inside, pointing his M16 at them. I squeezed one eye shut, aimed at the back of his head, and smoothly pulled the trigger. He dropped like a stone before Tiernan had the time to shoot him.

My brother's gaze skidded in my direction. He jerked his chin in thanks.

"*Run!*" My scream was swallowed by the echo of gunshots and weeping. "I'll cover you."

Carefully, I rolled my body the other way, peering through the gap under the pew at the entrance.

The men had enveloped the doors, acting as a human shield for the women and children. They'd seemed to manage to kill all the rival clan members who had entered the church and were now waiting for the next wave of attack.

This was a war declaration. By whom, I wasn't sure, but someone had decided to dethrone the Ferrantes as the leaders of Napoli's Camorra clans.

Anticipation made the air sizzle. The corpse next to me was still staring, and now that most of the smoke was gone, I could see the face clearly. It was the priest.

There was a bullet hole in his temple. His blood crawled along the floor in my direction, soaking the sleeve of my dress. I pressed my lips closed, swallowing down the bile bubbling up my throat. I flicked my gaze behind my shoulder. Tiernan, Lila, and Nero were gone.

I let out a shaky exhale. Knowing they were safe made it slightly easier to breathe.

I heard a galloping horse in the distance. It whinnied, coming closer, until its hooves touched the church's steps, click-clacking.

Clank.

Clank.

Clank.

Clank.

Through the curtain of red dusk, a black stallion materialized. It soared into the church like a mythological creature. Gasps and whimpers echoed across the walls.

I craned my neck to get a better look, a fresh wave of fear and nausea slamming into me.

Someone straddled the horse. The body of a man was strapped to it.

The man was headless.

A headless horseman.

Before I had time to digest what I was seeing, the horse advanced straight toward my pew, the corpse bouncing atop it. It was strapped in and erected by ropes.

As it got closer, I realized the body was booby-trapped. The torso of the corpse was naked, sewn across the chest and stomach in black stitches that looked ready to burst.

His gut was full of explosives. And he was headed my way.

I didn't want to die.

I wanted to live and find my own happiness.

I realized if I wasn't going to move from under the pew, I probably *would* die.

Achilles had made me promise I'd stay put and wait for him…

Fuck that asshole.

Rolling to my knees and elbows, I began army crawling to the front pews, away from the horse. I had one mission only—survival.

I didn't make it more than two feet before a rough hand grabbed the collar of my dress from above. It tossed me forward with force. I sailed from beneath the pew and across the room, my stomach burning with the friction. My shoulder crashed against the wall. Pain exploded everywhere. White dots filled my vision. I choked back a sob.

A body at least twice my size landed on top of me, pinning me to the floor. Achilles's masculine scent invaded my senses. He covered me from above, his forearms protecting my face, his legs locking mine in place so I was completely shielded.

I wanted to thank him but knew he'd taunt me if I said anything. The few times I'd tried to explain myself to him had been met with ridicule and cruelty.

A few moments passed before I realized the bastard was hard.

His cock pressed against my ass cheeks through our clothes, thick and long, threatening to rip the fabric between us.

I didn't know if it was the violence or me that brought him to arousal—probably both. I shifted, trying to escape the sensation of him. Not because it was unpleasant but because I couldn't bear to get turned on by the man who ruined my life on a daily basis.

"Stay fucking put," he growled.

"Tell your dick to stop harassing me, then," I bit back.

"Don't read into it." Chuckling, he ground against my ass, just to piss me off. "We're exes."

"Exes who never had sex."

"*Yet.*"

"*Never.*"

"Soon," he volleyed back with a lazy drawl.

"Get off me."

"No. But if you don't shut up, I'll get off *on* you just to teach you a lesson."

"I'm going to put a bullet in your goddamn head." He knew I'd do it.

"If I roll off you now, the next explosion is gonna get you. And it's coming," he ground out impatiently. "Do you want to die?"

I didn't. That was the truth of it. I wanted to live, even if I didn't have much to live for.

"What's it going to be, then?" he taunted.

"Fine, I guess you can be my human shield," I huffed. "Better you than me."

"Piccola Fiamma." His breath fanned the back of my neck, hot and whiskey laced. His heartbeat against my spine was slow and even. "I promise you, if someone were to take your useless life, it'd be me."

A powerful explosion erupted. Walls rattled, windows shattered, and sizzling heat engulfed us in a ring of fire.

Everything turned black, but I knew I'd survive.

Everyone had a guardian angel.

Mine just happened to be my stalker.

CHAPTER TWO

THEN

She was fourteen when they first met.

Had only been in the country for barely two months.

It was late, dark, and cold. Drunks shouted and laughed outside her window.

She didn't like New York at all. There were too many people and not enough trees. It was busy and filthy and terrifying.

And she hated sharing Tiernan, her twin brother, with other people.

Now, they had a father. He was tall and had nice teeth. He bought her nice clothes and pink sneakers and filled the fridge with food she could eat without even asking for permission.

She knew she should like him, but for some reason, she couldn't. Her tummy felt heavy, and not with food, every time he walked into the room.

Maybe she'd like him better if she understood what he said.

But Tiernan was the smart one. Her twin brother had learned English quickly. She only knew Russian and some American Sign Language she'd learned from a prisoner in Siberia.

The last six months had been a blur. She didn't remember how she and Tiernan had escaped the prison camp. She just knew they had and were meant to be safe here.

But she didn't feel safe. She felt like a guest in a stranger's home. She didn't know her father or older brother any better than her next-door neighbor.

They tried to be nice, but every time they looked at her, they exchanged sharp glances, like there was something wrong with her.

Of course there was something wrong with her. In fact, she doubted if there was one thing right *with her. But she didn't need the reminder that she not only felt broken but also looked it.*

They stared when they thought she wasn't watching, while she picked at the old scabs on her skin. One time, she managed to peel an entire layer of skin off her forearm using a butter knife. The pale, freckly skin rolled smoothly, revealing pink, raw flesh. She had smiled to herself because she'd finally managed to feel something after months of numbness.

Pain.

The next day, all the sharp objects in the house had magically disappeared, and Tierney was scheduled for a weekly meeting with a Russian-speaking therapist.

They must've filled in the blanks about everything that had happened to her in the work camp. Little did they know, even the worst they assumed wasn't half as terrible as what really happened.

Funny, how she didn't remember the journey here, but she did remember every second of her fourteen years in Siberia.

The abuse.

The torture.

The humiliation.

The pain.

The rape.

"They pity you," Tiernan had chided her in ASL, scowling. "Stop moping around, or they'll think you're weak."

Maybe she was *weak.*

She cried. All the time. Crying felt like giving her soul a shower.

But she didn't want to disappoint Tiernan, so she tried really hard to forget everything that had happened in Siberia. And the therapist, although nice enough, was very nosy. She kept poking around in things that were none of her business and only made Tierney cry more.

But none of it bothered her half as much as one simple fact: She was losing Tiernan.

To the Callaghans.

To America.

To the Irish Mafia.

When they moved here, she suggested they take the same room, but he liked the idea of having his own space, so now she had to sleep by herself. She wasn't used to it. In the work camp, they'd slept with dozens of prisoners. It had been smelly and filthy, but she had never felt alone, and there had always been body heat and noise around her.

Now, lying alone in bed, she felt so cold.

Her father had visitors tonight. She could hear them through the wall, knocking back drinks and talking. Tiernan and Fintan were included in the meeting. Tiernan even spoke a few times. She was secretly angry with him for adapting so quickly. He slid right into the family like he'd grown up with their father and older brother. He'd even adopted their stupid accent!

Tiernan and Fintan were invited to all of her father's meetings.

Not her. She never fit in anywhere. Like an old puzzle piece curled at the edges, no natural place existed for her in the family.

Sick with jealousy, she curled into a ball under her duvet and drifted in and out of sleep.

An hour later, she woke up slicked with sweat and with a scream in her throat. She had had a nightmare. Again.

They were on top of her.

Laughing.

Unbuckling.

Kicking.

Slapping.

Putting their things in her.

She thrashed and made a choking sound, fighting off her duvet before opening her eyes and remembering where she was.

She felt a presence in the room and stirred awake.

"T—Tiernan?" she croaked.

A shadow glided into the room, closing the door behind it.

Taller and broader than her brother.

Someone who smelled like burning wood and old leather, not Irish Spring and mint.

A boy.

Although it was too dark to make out his features, something told her he was more or less her age.

She rose to her forearms, her heart still thundering inside her chest. What was he doing here? What did he want from her?

She wanted to ask but couldn't. Damn her useless brain!

She blinked. He didn't. In fact, he didn't move at all.

He was so, so still. And so, so beautiful. Like those kids you see in glamorous American TV shows. His eyes were so dark she could see her own reflection in them. She wanted to drown in them and never come up for air.

He stepped toward her, clasped the edge of her duvet, and slowly slid it up her body. That was when she realized she was shivering. Her skin was covered in gooseflesh.

She wasn't scared. Maybe because she could still hear Tiernan through the wall.

Her brother would never let anything bad happen to her.

The boy rearranged the duvet over her, fidgeting nervously, then reached beyond her shoulder, picking up a book from her bed and placing it on the nightstand beside her. He refused to look at her now, eyes stuck on his shoes, like they fascinated him.

"I just...um, you seemed cold," he muttered.

She didn't understand what he said.

She wanted to thank him but didn't have the words. So she reached out cautiously and touched his cheek. It was warm and fuzzy, like a peach.

The boy sucked in a breath and flinched, like it hurt. They both stared at each other in shock.

What just happened?

She didn't hurt him, did she? Then why did he look like he was in pain?

Gulping, the boy stepped forward again, forcing himself within reach of her.

"D—do it again."

What was he saying? What was she supposed to do?

He grabbed her wrist and put her hand on his cheek, staring at her with wild, wonderous eyes.

She didn't know what was happening but didn't want to stop it either. The boy hissed, trembling into her touch. She didn't know it, but it was the first time he'd felt a loving hand.

Slowly, he leaned into her palm until he rested his entire cheek on it and closed his eyes.

Oh my God, *she thought.*

I'm touching a boy.

I'm touching a boy, and I don't want to throw up.

I'm touching a boy, and I don't want to die.

I'm touching a boy, and it feels even better than picking at my scars.

They stayed like this until her arm began to hurt and her palm began to sweat, but still she didn't want to let go. She had a feeling he needed her touch more than his next breath. Which was silly. She was a nobody. To him and at all.

"Chelovek," *she choked out.*

"Chelovek?" *he repeated, frowning.*

She nodded. "Chelovek."

He tucked a stray hair of hers behind her ear, smiling like a weirdo. He was glad it was too dark for her to see him blushing—and surprised he was capable of such bodily function at all. Heat flooded him, and he didn't know what to do with it. It was good heat. Not angry heat. The kind that tickled his stomach when his dad gave him a pat on the back. It didn't happen often, but when it did...his whole world tilted.

He didn't know what to do with all the tightness in his chest, so he leaned down and pressed his lips to her forehead. Butterflies exploded in his stomach, tickling the back of his throat as they took flight.

The gesture was so soft, so sweet, it made her head swim. No one had ever kissed her before. Not even her twin brother.

Her body had been violated, abused, and used so many times, by so many men, and yet she had never experienced a small, innocent kiss.

The boy stepped back and turned around, his steps heavy as he headed to the door.

No! *her mind screamed.* Please don't leave me.

"Nyet!" she blurted out, clapping a hand over her mouth in shock.

She had never spoken to anyone who wasn't Tiernan. Not her dad. Not her therapist. No one.

He froze midstride, turning around slowly, blinking at her.

"You no go." She pointed at him, too desperate to be embarrassed about her broken English. "You stay."

They studied each other. Neither of them dared breathe. Finally, he pointed at her desk chair with a question in his eyes.

She nodded.

Yes.

Please.

Stay with me.

Bad things happen when I'm left alone in the dark.

One day, when I find my words, I'll tell you about them.

He sat down, his eyes never leaving hers.

His stare warmed her skin. An extra blanket to shield her from the world.

They had no idea what this all meant. How their lives would coil around one another in a serpentine spiral of toxic obsession and desire that would throw the entire underworld off its axis.

All they knew was she was alone, and so was he, and together, the world seemed slightly less cold.

She closed her eyes and went back to sleep.

He didn't leave until the sun rose and chased away the darkness.

Protecting her from her own demons as much as from himself.

CHAPTER THREE
ACHILLES

ONE WEEK AFTER THE BAPTISM

My doorbell rang.

Again.

And again.

And a-mother-fucking-gain.

I pinched my cigarette between my thumb and middle finger, removing it from my lips as I examined the disemboweled body at my feet.

Oops.

I wasn't supposed to kill Tierney's hookups. Just rough them up a little. What could I say? I was only human. Mistakes happened from time to time.

Or in the case of Tierney's hookups, *all* the time. I currently stood at 100 percent murder rate when it came to the men she screwed. No, wait, *fuck*. Why was I so hard on myself? Make that 99 percent. I didn't kill that one shitbag, Angelo Bandini. Not for lack of desire on my part, but…still counts.

He was the son of the Chicago Outfit's boss. Offing him would likely spiral into an underground war. And while that sounded like a good ol' time, I had the Camorra's interests to think of.

I *did* relieve him of a few fingers. You know, to make sure he could never touch her again.

She didn't have many hookups to begin with. The bodyguards I put on her wouldn't allow her to stray. But every now and then, she managed to slip under the radar, shake off the men I'd assigned to her. I always found them—the assholes who touched my woman.

And when I did, I dealt with them accordingly.

A pang of disappointment pinched my chest. I'd been doing so good. I hadn't killed off-duty in months. Not to mention hung someone by their entrails.

The doorbell rang for the millionth time. I sighed.

I didn't have any friends, and my family tried to keep our communication to a minimum, so I had no idea who the unwelcome guest might be.

"You know." I rolled the body beneath me with the tip of my boot so it landed face up, so I could look him in the eye when I spoke. "This whole situation is as uncomfortable for me as it is for you. You think I *like* doing this? No. And you're gonna be a bitch to clean up."

My little spitfire didn't normally put the lives of nameless assholes at risk for an orgasm. Not since she realized I was killing them. Something must've veered her off track. That incident at Gennaro's baptism, maybe. Nothing awakened carnal urges quite like staring death in the eye. If only she'd asked, I'd have given it to her; I'd fuck her for hours, drawing out her pleasure until she couldn't walk straight anymore.

All she had to do was say the word. I'd have helped. I was a nice guy like that.

How did she manage to sneak this fuckboy into her apartment, anyway? I had three soldiers surveilling her ass at any given moment.

No matter. It wasn't like the prick was going to be missed.

Hamish Upton was an Ibiza-based, English DJ on a sabbatical. No family. Only a handful of friends. By the time someone realized he was missing, he'd be thoroughly digested by the hogs to which I would soon feed his remains.

I didn't have to make their deaths so violent and long, but I did it anyway. Because they always hurt her. A bruise here, a black eye there. All with consent, but consent meant little when you preyed on someone broken.

No one was allowed to hurt Tierney Callaghan.

No one but me.

The ringing ceased, and a sharp knock on the door sounded. I flicked the cigarette to the floor, crushing it with my boot. My place was normally pristine, but I let it go a little after I found out Tierney had hooked up with some rando.

And by a little, I mean a lot.

And by a lot, I mean I should probably look for another apartment and torch the entire building. Maybe even the neighborhood. The blood from carving Upton's body seeped into the cracks between the marble slabs and soaked the walls.

I'd killed him and brought him back through CPR three times to prolong his death before I bled him out. But once I did, I really drained him good. The place was a mess.

Honestly? So was I.

You should've given up after Angelo, Little Flame.

My unexpected guest decided to kick down the door with a loud bang. Good call. I wasn't going to answer. I grabbed a disinfecting wipe and ran it over my bloodstained hands as I calmly made my way from my office to the living room.

Luca, my older brother, the heir apparent, and the Dick of Monte Cuntsto, stood in the foyer. "What, pray tell, the *fuck*?"

He wore black slacks and a matching turtleneck, both Prada. Good-looking guy. Shame about the sodium-free rice personality. He was a fine man, Luca. Pragmatic, ambitious, and devilishly smart.

Unfortunately, his lack of personality and emotions made Dad really uneasy about handing him the keys to the kingdom.

Unfortunately for *him*, that is. Not for me.

"Got caught up in something." I disposed of the bloodied wipe in the trash of the open-plan kitchen, dumping beans into the grinder of my coffeemaker. "Coffee?"

Luca shook his head. "We don't have time. Dad set up an emergency meeting."

"Did he now?" I pushed a carafe into the coffee machine. "Who died?"

"I was just about to ask." Luca sniffed the air, scowling. He followed the foul smell into my office, returned after a few moments to the kitchen, kneading his eyelids with the pads of his fingers.

"Oh my fucking God."

"Somebody called my name?" Enzo swaggered into my apartment on cue, stepping over the unhinged door on the floor, unperturbed. He wore a nude, ribbed polo shirt, slim-fit chinos, and those stupid sneakers that came looking battered and old and still cost a grand. Pretentious little shit.

My baby brother stopped in front of a mirror on the wall, rearranged his already perfect hair, then winked at himself.

Unlike Luca, Enzo *did* have a personality. It was just an annoying one, but at least he still had it. He was the sunny golden retriever of the family. An outgoing, friendly, loved-by-all type of guy. Other than his cutting habit, he could almost pass as a normal person.

He was ridiculously handsome, but that was hardly a surprise. I was the only fugly motherfucker in the family. I wasn't born this way, but it was hard to look past the burn scars and uneven skin on one side of my face.

I swiveled from the coffeemaker, fully annoyed now. "The fuck did I do to warrant this visit?" I pointed between the two of them with a spoon. "In all my years in the city, you haven't visited me once. Now I get a two-person detail for a meeting?"

"Sangue Blu landed in Newark an hour ago." Luca tucked his

hands into his front pockets. "He's on his way to the Long Island estate."

Sangue Blu, "blue blood" in Italian, was Stefano Coppola, a Naples-based Mafia don and the man whose underboss I'd sacrificed at my nephew's baptism. Dante had molested a young girl on the Ferrantes' turf, so making an example out of him was necessary to put Coppola back in his place.

The Camorra consisted of clans. Eight different clans made the Secondigliano Alliance. We were the strongest and most ruthless clan in Naples, with Coppola coming in a far second.

The last couple years, we'd been busy pushing the Bratva back to its borders in America and neglected business in Naples. The Bratva was rapidly growing, and now they had a secret weapon—Tiernan, my brother-in-law and the pakhan's best friend.

Killing Coppola's underboss was a way to signal we were still the top dog in Secondigliano. Judging by Sangue Blu's swift and lethal reaction, in the form of blowing up a seven-hundred-year-old church along with its priest, he didn't share our opinion about the hierarchy in the city.

"Why's Dad humoring this nobody?" I scoffed.

"He's not a nobody," Luca said. "He's the son of the late Gianni Coppola. We've been losing our grip on Naples. He wants to cut a deal. It's better to squash this now."

"Not if he is asking for more turf in Secondigliano," I countered.

"We don't know what he wants yet," Luca reasoned.

"Hmm, guys? What the hell is that smell?" Enzo looked up from his phone, screwing up his nose in distaste.

"We need to haul ass to Dad's." Luca cocked his head toward where my door was five minutes ago. "Coppola's waiting."

"I ask that you join me in vigil to find the fucks I have to give." I turned my back to him, picking my espresso cup up and tossing it back like a shot.

"No, seriously, what's that funky smell?" Enzo asked again.

"We're going with or without you." Luca ignored our baby brother. "I suggest you join us."

"Why?"

"Negotiate."

"Bullshit. You don't want me there. I'll just blow shit up. I'll ask again—why?"

Luca shrugged, his expression, like his entire existence, giving me nothing.

At this point, Enzo wandered into my office to follow the stench. I rinsed my espresso cup, calmly setting it on the dish rack. Fine. I'd go to the stupid meeting. My social calendar was hardly overflowing. Best monitor the situation myself. My father was weakened by whatever the fuck was killing him, and Luca wanted this shit sorted so badly he'd be willing to give Sangue Blu the entire city of Naples, his firstborn, and a goddamn blow job.

"Let's hit the road." I plucked my biker jacket from the back of a dining chair.

Enzo reappeared from the hallway, looking visibly appalled. "Dude, are you insane?"

I wished people would stop asking rhetorical questions. Such a waste of time.

"How many times did you kill him?" Enzo jerked his thumb behind his shoulder.

"Two." *Three*. Why did he need to know, anyway? Was he conducting some kind of fucking empirical research?

"You promised no more recreational killing." Enzo ran his palm over his face, his smoke-soaked tone reaching DEFCON 1. "You promised you'd try pickleball instead. I freaking got you a ten-class pass at the country club. Betsy asks every week why your name's not on the schedule."

I didn't have a conscience. If God forbid one ever fell into my lap, I wouldn't know what to do with it. What I did have was one hell of a temper. And where Tierney Callaghan was concerned, the minute I knew someone touched her, I either had to kill them or kill her. And she was technically family, so that left me with option one.

Shedding blood quieted the noise. Slowed down my thoughts. It brought me calm no cigarette or drug ever could.

The eternal chicken-or-the-egg dilemma—was I a stone-cold killer because I was groomed to become one, or was it in my DNA to kill, just like my mobster father? Both nature and nurture worked against me. A perfect storm, and guess which motherfucker was the eye of it? Dead center. That's me.

"He's not innocent. He touched what's mine."

"Tierney?" my older brother sighed.

I jerked my chin in a nod. I'd only ever claimed one thing as truly my own.

All the rest—money, prestige, power, cars—didn't mean jack shit.

Luca and Enzo exchanged looks.

"You look like you've had a bad day," Enzo said, pushing off the kitchen counter and opening his arms. "Can I give you a hug?"

"Fuck off."

Enzo turned to look at Luca, who gave him an impersonal shoulder pat. "That's a no."

"Don't say I didn't try."

They thought I lacked control where Tierney was concerned. They couldn't be more wrong. I was nothing but the picture of bridled restraint. If I lacked control, we'd have been married with fifteen children by now. One for every year I'd known her. And there wouldn't be a filleted corpse in my office.

If I didn't have control, things would look fantastic for everyone involved. It was my very control that ruined lives.

"Let's go." I shouldered past them. "I've a shit ton of blood to clean tonight. Another twenty-one grams won't make much difference."

CHAPTER FOUR
ACHILLES

It wasn't just Sangue Blu at the meeting.

The round table was filled with the upper echelon of the Coppola clan. Stefano sat across from my father, who had donned some makeup to give his lifeless skin some vitality.

My mouth curled in distaste. My father pathetically clung to the last shreds of his existence. I'd kill him myself if I had any sense of altruism. But I needed him to crown me his rightful heir first. Do things by the book. My position couldn't be contested.

He'd be a fool to deny me the role. Enzo was too softhearted. Luca had the charisma of pencil lead. Another nameless Ferrante bastard lurked somewhere in the world, but that was just who he was—a bastard. If he was stupid enough to come forth and challenge me, I'd treat him to a butcher's special.

Sangue Blu was a medium-height man, athletically built, clad in formfitting cigar pants and a silky dress shirt. His dark hair was tied into a ponytail. He had a snakelike air about him, a combination of elegance and repulsiveness many ugly, powerful men wore.

"Achilles." He opened his arms. "Anything you want to say to me?"

The entire room eyeballed me, waiting for an apology for killing his underboss.

"Sure. The ponytail looks stupid." I grabbed the back of a chair, taking a seat. Luca and Enzo followed suit. I coiled my fingers together on the table. "Why are you here?"

Stefano's beady eyes danced with perverse excitement. He rolled his pinky ring with his thumb. "What, no pleasantries?"

"That ship has sailed. Now start talking before it fucking sinks."

"All right, fine." He rolled his eyes, the gesture dripping amusement. "I'm here to shake hands."

I narrowed my eyes. "Just like that?"

"Any day is a good day for peace."

"I slaughtered your underboss."

"Dante had it coming. He should've never touched that little girl. I'd have done it myself if you had waited a few days." He waved me off. "Plus, I blew up the church and took out fourteen of the guests before his body stiffened." Sangue Blu shrugged. "A sufficient payback in my book."

None of said guests were family or even high-ranking Camorristi. No women or children were hurt, either. Then again, he already knew that. That he chose to settle things diplomatically told me something was off.

"See, the circle of violence always ends in resolution." Stefano looked around the silent room. "I'd rather strike a deal before we both lose manpower and weapons. We all abide by the same system. What is the point of more bloodshed? In the end, what's the Camorra really about? Loyalty, alliances, power, and blood."

My father and Luca nodded. Enzo and I exchanged skeptical glares.

"Well, thank you *so* much for the uplifting speech." Enzo clapped his hands together, his enchanting smile on full display. "And I'm eager to proceed to the kumbaya portion of this evening, but if you're here to make a deal, you better wow our pants off."

"First order of business: I think we should work together." Stefano's impudent smile made me want to carve his mouth off. "How do you feel about selling me some of your coke? You have the best in the city."

That's because we sourced it ourselves. Visited our coca farms in an undisclosed location quarterly to supervise the process.

"We're open to it," Luca chimed in. "For the right percentage."

"Understandable. I'm sure we can find a number that works for all of us."

"Before we get into the numbers, our men in Naples are telling me you've been treading into some parts of Chiaia and Forcella." My father scowled. "Double-charging protection money and selling weed."

Stefano feigned confusion. "Who said that?"

"Cut the crap, Sangue Blu. I have eyes and ears everywhere," my father hissed out. "This is *our* territory."

"I mean no disrespect, Don Vello," Coppola cooed, "but it's a busy area. Lots of human traffic. Your people don't seem to keep up with the demand."

"Our supply is none of your concern."

"That's true, but if your customers want to buy more drugs, why shouldn't I sell to them?"

"You know exactly why. Retreat to your borders."

"Or what?" he drawled, kicking back in his seat. "The Ferrante clan rarely visits Naples. You're out of touch. Powerful, yes, but if you want to keep ground, you need a strong alliance with us. I'm willing to pay for your drugs and guard your territory for you. But you need to offer me something to make it worth my while."

"You want *us* to make concessions?" Luca asked.

"Peace isn't free." Sangue Blu shrugged. "I'm willing to pay you for drugs. What are you willing to do for me?"

"Not kill you," Enzo offered charitably. Coppola laughed.

"What do you want?" my father grumbled.

"I'll pay you ten percent commission for the coke we sell, no more than that," Sangue Blu said, bargaining. "And I want to buy it below market price. Three thousand euros per kilogram."

"That's less than half of what we charge our affiliates." Luca's eyebrows slammed together.

"I'm not your other affiliates. I'm the rising king of Naples, with an army twice your size. And as much as I want peace, I won't shy away from war." He pushed a cigarette between his lips, grabbing a Clipper from the table and lighting it.

"Thirty-five hundred euros per kilogram," my father said decisively. He wasn't wearing his oxygen mask, and for a moment, I saw the man he once was: The great Machiavelli Ferrante I lived to impress. "And you pay in advance. Final offer."

Shit agreement, but I'd deal with it later, when I had the throne.

Sangue Blu nodded. "I also want my incoming shipments in the port untouched. You've been raiding our goods for years."

"We'll see to that, but if we catch your men on our turf again, selling drugs or touching kids, we make an example of them," Luca said laconically.

"My soldiers will keep their drugs and hands to themselves," Coppola reassured us. "I want a guarantee you'll do the same."

"Don't worry," I snapped. "We don't recruit pedophiles."

"And the redhead I saw outside the church that day, while I was overlooking the operation." Sangue Blu slouched back, drawling slyly with his gaze locked on mine, one leg folded over the other. "I want her, too."

I stiffened, my entire body revolting and convulsing from the inside at the blasphemy that fell out of his mouth. The only thing keeping me from gouging out his Adam's apple with my fingers was the knowledge he deserved a slower, more painful death than that for this request.

"She's not for sale," I grumbled around the cigarette hanging from the side of my mouth.

Though I could understand why he'd jumped to that conclusion. Trust Tierney to prance into church looking like a high-class hooker and make everyone think she charged by the hour. That little red dress had less class than a cum stain on a motel carpet. The fact that I didn't rip it from her and cover her in the priest's robe was all the evidence my family needed that I had control where she was concerned.

I'd saved her that day, and I would save her life all over again.

Because she was mine.

To control. To ruin. To obsess over.

"Not just for fucking." Coppola rolled the amber liquid of his whiskey in his tumbler, puffing out a cloud of smoke. "I want to keep her. Marry her."

"Marry her," Enzo repeated, eyebrows hitting the ceiling.

"Yes."

"You want to marry Tierney Callaghan," he double-checked, probably hoping if he said it enough times, Coppola would understand how fucking stupid it sounded.

"The one and only." Stefano's smile just begged me to crush all his teeth into dust. "I did my due diligence. She has connections. Pedigree. A great piece of ass. What's the problem?"

"The problem is she won't consent to marrying a low-grade mobster," I deadpanned.

"Low grade?" Sangue Blu tipped his head back, laughing. "I am the son of a titan, just like you. As for the life I have to offer her…" He scanned the room to make sure he had everyone's attention. "I dug into her family tree. She's in the Irish Mafia. Like knows like, yes?" He licked his lips. "She'll feel right at home in my crooked kingdom."

Sensing I was about to kill and drain my second victim in twenty-four hours, Enzo piped up. "What about Katya Rasputin? She's in the market for a groom. Young. Hot. Bratva affiliated. You'll get way more connections. The Irish are small fry."

"I like fries," Stefano said. "And I like the redhead. She's the one I want. Not anyone else."

"She's not ours to give," Enzo said good-naturedly.

"That's not what I'm hearing." Coppola rubbed his lower lip contemplatively, his gaze flicking to me. "Word in Naples is Achilles is in charge of her matchmaking. Well, I'm a widower, wealthy, and willing. Now, deal or no deal?"

I opened my mouth to tell him to start running before I was interrupted.

"Give us ten minutes." My father stood up, wobbling over to the door on his cane, clapping my shoulder from behind midstride. "I'm sure we can work something out."

We filed into the drawing room. Luca closed the doors behind us with a soft click. My pulse hammered against my eyelids. I felt like I had five minutes to stop the world from imploding and zero fucking tools to prevent the inevitable.

I needed to remain calm if I wanted to come up with a plan.

Smoke. I should smoke. Or kill someone to take the edge off.

No. Enough killing for today.

Producing a cigarette from the soft pack in my pocket, I lit it up and sucked in a long drag.

Then I noticed Tiernan in the room. He was sprawled on an upholstered recliner, legs crossed and arms draped on the armrests with that steadfast, malevolent expression that made people turn inside out.

I recognized a psychopath when I met one because I saw one every day when I looked in the mirror. And Tiernan definitely fit the bill—dead eyes, flat stare, merciless air.

My father brought reinforcements.

He'd been waiting here for a while.

He knew.

I broke into a cold sweat, every fiber in my goddamn body trembling.

Fuck calm all the way off.

They'd already made up their minds.

This wasn't negotiation; it was intervention.

They were taking Tierney away from me. No. She was mine. *Mine*. Besides, she didn't want to get married. She loved her freedom. With me, she had a version of it. I respected her boundaries.

For the most part.

Fuck, *fine*, I had some room for improvement in the boundaries department. So what? At least I didn't make her marry or screw anyone.

Not even me.

"Sit down, son. This conversation is long overdue." My father gestured to one of the recliners. I walked over to it and sank down. Everyone else sat, too. I trained my face to its usual jaded expression while my mind went underwater.

"This is about the Callaghan girl," my father announced.

"Yeah, I did the math." I blew a cloud of smoke from the corner of my mouth. "What about her?"

"Coppola and her... It's a good idea."

"No."

The men in the room exchanged frustrated glances.

"You can't marry her, Brother." Luca clapped a hand on my shoulder.

"I know."

"What do you think you're doing, then?"

"Making sure no one else can, either."

"So it's true, what they say." My father gripped his jaw, drawing a labored breath. "You're still sweet on her after what she did to you."

"Wouldn't go that far." Some of the coldness returned to my voice. "It's a slight fixation. Totally manageable."

"You've killed all of her lovers," Enzo pointed out.

"And yet nobody ever found the bodies or conducted an investigation that led to our doorstep. As I said—*manageable*."

"Stefano Coppola personally came to me when he landed this

morning." Tiernan spoke for the first time, leveling an icy, one-eyed glare at me. "He asked me for her hand in marriage."

The silence that followed was so loud I was surprised my eardrums hadn't exploded.

"I'm going to accept," he finished.

"She won't agree," I growled, the coppery taste of blood flooding my mouth. If I'd bitten myself, I couldn't feel it. I was numb all over and yet in excruciating pain.

"She'll have no choice," Tiernan countered. "My sister rarely does what's good for her. Marriage will redirect her energy into something worthwhile—life away from the parties, loneliness, and fake friends."

"Yeah?" I leaned forward, tapping my cigarette into an ashtray on the coffee table. "Doing what, sucking some stranger's dick?"

"She's always wanted to live by the Mediterranean Sea." Tiernan ignored my words. "She'll live a life of extravagance and pampering. No pressure or expectations. Far away from the baggage and mess of New York. Coppola will be good to her. He has a small child. She'll have someone to fawn over. His first marriage was a love match, and his late wife had been happy." My brother-in-law looked almost defeated, and I knew why. Loving Tierney Callaghan was a messy business. I'd made the mistake of doing it once and barely survived to tell the tale. "Let her go. She needs this. It's time for her to be happy."

"How'd his late wife die?" I asked.

The room was quiet.

"How did she die, motherfucker?" My voice boomed, ricocheting over the curved, grand ceilings of my parents' mansion. "Do you know? Because I do. She was trying on a dress in a boutique when some asshole slipped into her changing room and shot her in the neck. Retaliation for a stolen drug shipment. That's how. She bled out for six hours before she finally died. You want that for your sister?"

"Coppola dealt with the clan responsible for the attack," Luca supplied solemnly. "Tierney will be safe."

"Spin it any way you like, but you're selling your sister to a criminal." I stubbed my cigarette out, smoke fanning from my nostrils.

"You did the same to Lila," Tiernan said matter-of-factly.

"Freedom." My jaw clenched. "I gave Lila *freedom* through you. You were her only way out, and I knew she'd have you wrapped around her finger before the week was out."

I'd been the sole supporter of my baby sister marrying Callaghan, and their marriage turned out to be the most successful human venture since sliced bread. But it was different. I knew Tiernan was incapable of hurting Lila the night he'd found her on the fountain and spared her life. It was the first time he'd shown mercy to any creature. A fatal human error I knew he wouldn't have made under normal circumstances.

Coppola wanted Tierney because she was beautiful and because she was *mine*.

"Stefano will give Tierney a wide berth," Tiernan drawled apathetically. "She wants freedom, and even if she can't see it right now, this is the closest she'll ever get to it. I'm not asking, Achilles. This match is happening."

My father flashed my brothers and Tiernan a loaded look, and they filed out of the room, giving us some privacy. I watched them leave, curling my hands into tight fists to stop them from shaking.

Dad waited until the door clicked shut before he turned to me and spoke.

"A don should wed a wife who is loyal, obedient, and self-sufficient. Someone to run his home and bear his sons while he runs his empire." He laced his fingers together. "The Irish girl is none of those things."

"I know." I clenched my fists tighter. Unclenched them again.

"Do you?" He studied me intently. "Because that means you cannot run around chasing a forbidden skirt. Settle down. Take a wife. Assume your role as the don of the Ferrante clan. This stalemate between you and Luca… You can end it right here, right now."

I looked up, curling my fingers around the armrests to stop the shaking. I couldn't believe what I was hearing. He'd been dragging his feet about choosing a new don for years. "Are you jerking my chain, or are you going to put this in writing?"

We all worked hard, but most men always found time to play. Not me. I didn't take a wife, girlfriends, lavish vacations around the world or semiprofessional golf tournaments. I didn't indulge in shopping sprees and weekends with 50K-a-night prostitutes to numb my nonexistent conscience. I worked, and then I worked some more. I forfeited my life to the Camorra and deserved nothing less than ruling it.

I deserved it more than Luca, who thought he was entitled to it because he was the firstborn.

More than Enzo, who had the personality of a friendly, enthusiastic puppy.

And more than that nameless bastard who was our half brother my father kept in touch with over the years.

"That solely depends on you," he said. "I'll give you the role if you give up this woman. Nothing good will ever come out of her. She's an exposed weakness. An Achilles' heel. Coppola knows it—that's why he's asked for her."

Right on all fucking accounts. I could never have her. Deep down, I knew it, too. Even if I could, she'd be my ruination. She'd undone me when we were teenagers. Completely obliterated my soul into shit. Fuck knew what she was capable of now that she was a full-fledged femme fatale. I'd be a fool to find out.

"Let her go," my father said. "And I'll give you my kingdom."

Swallowing hard, I digested this new reality into my system. This needed to stop.

The stalking.

The killing.

The obsessing.

Enough was enough.

No more tossing, turning, praying to a God who'd forsaken me before I'd taken my first breath. No more fixating, hating, shaking.

No. More.

Collecting myself back into the unfeeling monster I was, I threw my father an enigmatic look. "The Irish girl won't be an issue. If Sangue Blu wants her, he is welcome to her."

My father leaned forward, using the last shreds of his energy to pinch my cheek, kissing his fingers. "That's my boy. I always knew you were my special one."

Blood thundered in my ears. I stopped my hands from shaking by threading my fingers together.

"Are you sure about the Callaghan girl?" he asked.

"Positive."

"In that case, you wouldn't mind doing one last favor for me, would you?"

I had a feeling I very fucking much would, but it made little difference at this point. I arched an inquisitive eyebrow.

"Deliver her to Coppola personally. Show him that he's wrong. That she is not your blind spot."

A few moments later, we reentered my father's office, sat at the round table, and started the voting process. My father picked up his gavel. "Stefano, make our cut twenty percent. You'll pay standard, like everyone else."

"Do I get the redhead?" He grinned.

My father jerked his chin in a nod.

Coppola gave him a two-finger salute. "Twenty percent it is, then."

"All vote for the new order."

Every man in the room raised his hand. Every man but me. Coppola watched me closely, waiting for a crack in my facade, a shred of evidence to my weakness.

I pushed it all down, including the urge to warn Coppola not to hurt her in bed, like all the others did. Not my circus, not my monkeys. Tierney was a big girl. A big girl who knew how to work a gun and a knife like no one's business.

She's an addiction. A disease. A problem.

I raised my hand, my face blank.

My father slammed the gavel on the table. "We'll deliver her to you by the end of the month."

CHAPTER FIVE
TIERNEY

AGE FOURTEEN, THE NIGHT BEFORE THE ESCAPE

"We should wait for my brother," Tierney said.

She watched as Lyosha poured boot polish into a Styrofoam cup, using a twig to mix it with baby oil. Fire was crackling in the hearth of his father's office. This wasn't the first time she'd snuck in here, enjoying the warmth and a nice plate of food, but it would be the last.

Tomorrow, she and Tiernan would be gone.

If they managed to escape, Lyosha would lose them to freedom.

If they got caught, he'd lose them to death.

Either way, this was goodbye. She wished she could tell him she'd miss him. It was the least she could do.

"All right." Lyosha extended the tip of the twig to the fire, letting the flame catch, before pushing it back into the cup, turning his makeshift ink into soot. "Drink more vodka." He tilted his chin toward the bottle on the desk. "The first tattoo is supposed to be painful."

She did as she was told.

She loved Lyosha but not in the same way she loved her brother. She was never shy or flustered around Tiernan. She also could not look at her twin and see past the fact that he looked so much like her, with his burgundy hair and green eyes.

Alex...Alex was...pretty. She sometimes caught herself wanting to rake her nails through the opulent crown of his rusty-gold hair. More than once, she found herself studying his face with rapt fascination. The elegant slope of his nose. The perfect shape of his red mouth. His lashes, which started out dark but were lighter at the tips. His beauty pleased her, and he was the only boy other than Tiernan she trusted not to touch her, not to hurt her.

Which was probably foolish, seeing as the only reason she was here, in this camp, was because Alex's father carved her mother's pregnant belly. He had stolen the twins and left their mother to bleed out.

Foolish because she could never trust another human—let alone one with a penis—other than Tiernan after everything she'd lost here.

Still. Alex fascinated her. And if she weren't so broken, maybe she could have actually brought herself to like *him, like him. Not just as a friend but as a boy.*

Taking a swig of the vodka, she let the fiery sensation burn a path down her throat, passing it to Alex, who took a sip without removing his eyes from his handiwork. He was now pouring the ink into an empty toothpaste tube, his brows furrowed in concentration.

"Are you sure you know what you're doing?" she asked.

"No," he said patently. "But we'll figure it out. What's taking Tiernan so long?"

She knew the answer. Tiernan was making last-minute preparations ahead of their escape tonight. Stocking up on food, clean water, and gas, making sure he had the keys to the car they were about to steal and the maps to the place they were headed.

"I—I don't know." She forced herself not to blush.

Looking for a distraction, she trudged to the desk and pulled out the Latin book Alex used to teach her and Tiernan how to read and write.

"What are you doing?" Alex looked up.

"Looking for the quote we'll tattoo on ourselves."

"I already chose one for us," he said. "Audentis fortuna iuvat."

Fortune favors the brave. It was good but not good enough for her to etch it into her very being for the rest of her life. Tierney shook her head. "I want something else."

Alex made a face but didn't argue. He had a mild nature. Different from his father's. She flipped through the pages, keeping her tears at bay. Every few seconds, her gaze fastened back on Alex. It was stupid, but she was paranoid he could read her mind and know what was going on, that she was about to run away and screw him over.

He was threading some sort of needle into the motor of what looked like an electric shaver.

Her eyes landed back on the page and collided with words that struck her like lightning.

Oderint dum metuant.

Let them hate as long as they fear.

She gasped.

Alex stopped what he was doing and looked at her. "What?"

"I found the quote for us." *She recited it, holding her breath, craving his approval.*

Alex nodded seriously. "I like it. Where are we putting it?"

"Somewhere everyone can see," *she said.* "The side of our necks."

Tears rimmed her eyes, and this time, she couldn't make them stop even if she tried.

Alex scowled, setting the toothpaste tube and razor motor down on the desk. "What's wrong?"

She shook her head, wiping her face quickly. "Nothing."

"You never cry."

She didn't want to lie to him but couldn't tell him the whole truth, either. She settled for something in between. A truth, mistimed.

"I sometimes get overwhelmed with what...with the things..." *She hiccupped, letting it all out now.*

Alex barreled across the desk, snatching her by the arm and holding her arms firmly. "With what?"

"With the things that happened to me here," *she finished softly, gaze skating down to her feet. To the shoes that were too small, too old, too torn. She'd lost a toe a few years back. And she had lost other parts, inside herself, that were much more important than a piece of flesh.*

There was a part of her—not a small one, either—that wondered what the point was in running away. She could never outrun all the things that had happened to her. She could never escape the memories.

Alex knew exactly what she meant and jerked her into his body in a firm hug. He cupped the back of her head, his warm breath tickling her ear. "You need to forget all about those things, Tierney. Shove them to the back of your head, to a place where no one—not even you—can reach them, and you move on. You don't have a choice. The only way to survive is to deny what happened to you."

"But it's all I can think about."

"Tierney," *he barked, pulling away and holding her face in his hands. Alex never barked—rarely raised his voice—so the action anchored her back to the present.* "Listen to me carefully now." *His eyes held hers.* "You're going to forget every single thing that happened to you. You'll bottle it up and soldier through. Because you're strong. Because you're brave. Because you're a Callaghan, goddammit."

"Kiss me." *The demand was guttural, coming from a place deep inside her.* "I need to feel something else."

Something that wasn't angst and pain and despair.

"Not tonight." *He thumbed away a stray tear, then rubbed the arch of her brow tenderly.* "You're upset tonight. Tomorrow, if you still want me to kiss you, I will."

Tomorrow I won't be here, *she wanted to scream.* And you'll hate me forever for leaving you and taking your best friend with me.

"I won't regret the kiss," *she whispered.*

"But I will." *He tucked a piece of her red hair behind her ear.* "I will never take advantage of you, Tierney. But one day, when you're strong enough…" *He left the sentence unfinished.*

He reached down and pressed his lips to her forehead so softly, she had the oddest thought.

That he knew they were running away, and he still let them.

Sending them off with a gift more precious than matching ink.

A tattoo of hope.

CHAPTER SIX
TIERNEY

"Well, well, well. If it isn't my favorite blow-job artist."

Achilles stood in the doorway of my apartment at ten thirty in the morning, looking both smug and bored.

My stomach bottomed out. That couldn't mean good news for me, and I really wasn't in the mood for more of his abuse.

I barely managed to scrape myself off my bed today. Had spent the last couple days crying uncontrollably after my messages to Hamish remained unread.

Selfish bitch. You did this to him. It's all your fault.

I was usually careful with my hookups, making sure Achilles didn't know about them. I used burner phones, hotel rooms, and aliases. And I always made sure the encounters were few and far between and concealed any bruises with makeup. But the loneliness I felt after Gennaro's christening cut too sharp, sliced too deep, and I needed warmth. Another human body to drown in.

Hamish provided that, along with some manhandling that left me with a shallow cut on my cheekbone and a blue bruise on my neck.

"The answer is no," I said, keeping the terror out of my voice. "I don't want to hear about your Jehovah's Witness journey."

"Glad I caught you in a perky mood, Piccola Fiamma. I have some good news."

"You have an incurable disease?" I pretended to brighten up. "You're saying your final goodbye to people?"

He glanced down at me with the interest a panther afforded a mouse, an unabashed menace. For a moment, his gaze flicked to the cut on my cheek. His eyes darkened, like a light had been switched off behind them. "You gonna invite me in?"

"Not in this lifetime."

He shouldered past me, giving zero fucks, as per usual. I watched his back through the thin, black material of his shirt, the corded muscles of his arms, the two sleeves of intricate black tattoos. He had three crosses inked on the right side of his neck and an imprint of a kiss on his left side, the shape of my lips.

Back then, we thought the kiss was just the beginning. Not a parting gift to symbolize the end.

His gaze skimmed to the moka pot on my stovetop. "Hmm. Espresso Italiano. I'll have some of that."

"That's already spoken for, Achilles. Go get yourself a cup at the deli down the street."

He had a weird fixation with trying to make me make him coffee. I didn't know why. However, what I did know was that I'd willingly cut off my own two hands before giving him what he wanted.

I discreetly wiped my palms over my pants. I was scared of him, scared of what he came here to say, and scared to ask what he did to Hamish because I already knew.

My brother was family to him. I knew Achilles wouldn't kill me without a damn good reason, which he currently didn't have. But I also knew death wasn't the worst punishment. What he did to me now—the controlling, the bodyguards, the surveillance, the forced loneliness—that was the ultimate punishment.

"Everything okay?" Achilles catalogued my apartment, running a hand over the back of my credenza to see if the place was bugged.

"Yeah. Why?"

"I've been here for a full minute and you still haven't hurled any sharp objects at me."

"I'm reserving all my energy in case I need to claw your eyes out." I crossed my arms over my chest, popping one hip bone out.

"It's your lucky day, Little Flame, because I'm about to give you a great reason to."

I carefully schooled my face to look bored.

"I found you a husband."

Two seconds. Five words. That was all it took for my entire world to crumble at my feet.

I didn't move, let alone cry. Fuck that. He wasn't going to get the pleasure of seeing me break. I'd wait, like I always did.

"Is he tall? Dark? Handsome? Rich?" I purred.

"Relatively. Yes. I guess so. And very. Respectively."

"You're not handsome, Achilles."

But he was, to me. I didn't see the scars, the cuts, and the burns everyone else did. I saw that fourteen-year-old boy with the peach fuzz who tucked me into bed and guarded me all night to keep the nightmares at bay.

"Me?" He tossed a caustic look behind his shoulder, snorting. "No, sweetheart. I'd swallow you whole."

"You'd choke on me."

"I don't doubt it. But it's still not me."

Of course it was. It had to be. He wouldn't give me up so easily. Even if he hated me. He *murdered* men for touching me. How could he ever let me go?

I snorted. "Yeah right."

"I'll be delivering you to him shortly, so I suggest you start packing. I need his business, and he needs a wife."

My brain short-circuited. He was serious. It really wasn't him. But I couldn't... I mean, how did he plan to...

It felt like he stabbed my chest with an icicle.

"Wait, what? Achilles, *no*."

"Yes." He stopped in front of an Emilia Spencer painting on my wall, his mere tone giving me frostbite.

"But I thought—I mean, I—I…"

What *did* I think? That he'd defy his father to marry me? That he'd forgive me after what I'd done to him? Of course he handed me over to be someone else's headache.

"You didn't really think I'd risk the don title by marrying some lowly Irish slut, did you?" His brow crumpled in mock confusion, a sly grin twisting one corner of his mouth. "I thought we knew each other better than that."

His words were more painful than fists. Deadlier than bullets. They would leave scars that were beyond skin-deep.

"*Oh*." Achilles tsked, tilting his head sideways. "That's too bad."

I couldn't breathe. Couldn't move a muscle in my entire useless body.

"Don't do this," I warned, voice quivering.

"Already did." He was halfway out the door.

His back was the last thing I saw before I fell to my knees and let a raw shriek burst from my throat.

He finally did what he promised he would all those years ago.

He destroyed me.

CHAPTER SEVEN
ACHILLES

I needed to get fucked.

Urgently. Immediately. Indefinitely.

Not in the biblical sense. I couldn't touch another woman. Never really could. Not that I was a virgin by any stretch of the imagination. But I screwed women rarely, and always from behind, so they wouldn't get a front-row seat to the mess that was my face. Nobody deserved to see that. Hell, my own mother recoiled whenever we were in the same room.

Sometimes, I'd pretend to have a mistress. A regular hookup. Spread the word around. See if Tierney cared.

She never did.

She'd let that information slide off her shoulders as if nothing happened.

Fuck her and fuck her and fuck her.

Fuuuuuuuck.

She was so fucking beautiful.

So much I always held my breath the first few seconds when I came face-to-face with her.

Ah, shit. My head was a mess.

It was midmorning, hardly a good time for a stiff drink, but how did that saying go? The heart wants what it wants.

Mine wanted to go into cardiac arrest from alcohol poisoning.

My vision was blurry as I exited her apartment building and took the stairs down, charging to my black Ducati. I hadn't stopped shaking since that meeting with Sangue Blu. That was two days ago. I had to drink myself into a near coma before I showed up on her doorstep today to deliver the news. And guess what? I was going back to doing exactly that.

I mounted my bike and pushed on my helmet, flipping the kill switch. The beast roared to life beneath me. My pulse hammered against the side of my throat the entire ride from Hunts Point into Manhattan.

When I got to the Forbidden Fruit, our notorious nightclub and a Ferrante stronghold, I headed straight to the underground office.

Enzo was there, his red-soled sneakers stacked on the desk, texting. His eyes were droopy and his mouth agape as he stared at his screen. *Sexting*, more like. Who was the unlucky guy?

I had no idea why he wouldn't come out of the damn closet. It was pretty obvious his interest in women was nonexistent. Shit, I even tried pulling him out by fucking his (now ex) girlfriend, thinking he might've felt some kind of stupid gallant commitment to her. No dice. The little shit was still pretending to be on the market for a Mafia princess. Anything to appease Daddy Dearest.

But I was too wrapped up in my own shit to worry about my baby brother's love life right now.

"Out." I charged to the bar cart, plucking a bottle of whiskey. I slugged it back. My phone pinged with an incoming message.

> Dino: Carrie is coming down with your coke. Do you want her to stay?

Laughable. Even if I wanted to fuck someone—which I didn't—my dick never got fully hard for anyone other than Tierney. All I managed was a semi. And this, for all intents and purposes, didn't qualify as one of those.

My thumbs flew over the screen. No. Have her drop it here and leave.

"Hold on a minute. I'm wrapping up something. Carpe DM, *amiright*?" Enzo chuckled at his own stupid joke. "Seize the text."

"Out," I croaked, bracing my hand against the wall.

"Holy shit, Bro, how much did you drink? Your breath is flammable." Enzo's eyes were still glued to the screen, thumbs flying across it.

The room spun out of focus. I stared at my feet. *Fuck*. The last thing I needed was to drown myself in more alcohol and drugs.

The woman was a sickness. I needed to detox her out of my system. The thought of not being able to check on her; to slip into her bedroom when she was asleep, watch her chest fall and rise to the rhythm of her breath; to know what she was doing at any given time…

"Bro?" Enzo was up now, standing in front of me, peering at me with his dumb Bambi face. His phone was blowing up with messages, and he clutched it in his fist like he couldn't wait to get back to it.

"I said get fucked!" I hurled the bottle of whiskey at his head. He ducked. The bottle flew across the room and shattered on the door right before Carrie opened it, holding a bag of coke.

"Hiiiiii." She stuck her bleached head between the door and the frame, exhibiting a lip-glossed smile. "Dino said to drop this for you?"

Enzo spun his head, staring at me in disbelief. "You sampling the goods now?"

I'd never used drugs in my life. It was a rookie mistake and a surefire way to become an addict. But desperate times called for desperate measures.

"Get out, Enzo." I dropped my voice to a deadly whisper. "I mean it. Don't fuck with me right now."

"Fine, asshat, but I'm putting you on suicide watch. I'll be checking in every other hour. Goddammit." Enzo stomped to the door, bypassing the golden liquid on the floor. He snatched the bag of coke from Carrie, squinted to ensure it wasn't too laced with shit, then tossed it over his shoulder and into my hands. "Come on, CarCar. I don't want you in the firing line when this *stronzo* gets shitfaced."

CarCar? The lovable idiot was now giving the prostitutes pet names?

"Carrie." I dipped my pinky into the bag of coke, then rubbed it over my gums.

"Yeah?" she purred, probably hoping I'd fuck her. I tipped well, and had a nice, thick dick. Taken from behind, she could imagine I was anyone. Even someone human.

"Get me more coke. And another bottle of…" I squinted at my hand, realizing it was empty because I'd tossed the whiskey on my shithead brother. "…whatever the fuck that was."

I spent the next thirty-six hours snorting and drinking myself into a near coma.

CHAPTER EIGHT
TIERNEY

"It's for the best." Tiernan killed the engine of his Mercedes on the tarmac. We were parked on the edge of the runway strip at the private airport where the Ferrantes' company plane was about to take off. The formidable man inside was ready to take me to Italy, to a new fiancé I'd never met. I held back tears.

Pushing my Miu Miu shades up my nose, I refused to show weakness. "You know, Tiernan, history is full of men who thought they knew what women needed. Never ended quite as brilliantly as you think."

"You always said you wanted to live by the sea."

"I also said I wanted to choose my own husband." I tried to keep the shakiness from my voice. "Funny you forgot that last part."

Tiernan scrubbed his face, staring out his window. "Look, I know it's not ideal, but—"

"But you're too busy with your perfect little family and booming business to keep a close eye on your wayward sister." I curled my fingers around the door handle, a fresh wave of fury hitting my chest. "Totally understandable."

"You're off the mark. I'm trying to help you hea—"

"Don't patronize me, Brother. We're both fucked up. You're just hiding it better." I shook my head. "I'll see you at the wedding in two weeks." I pushed the door open and hopped out of the SUV.

Tiernan got out and rounded the vehicle, popping the trunk open and hurling out my suitcases. I'd only brought two, plus the tote bag on my shoulder. I had plenty of clothes. An unholy number of shoes, too. But I postponed sending them to Italy, still clutching on to the hope I'd be able to change Achilles's mind.

Tiernan rolled the suitcases across the tarmac toward the plane. I stared at his back, nauseous with dread.

I knew he thought he was doing the right thing by me. He knew I wasn't happy, leading a loveless, sexless life, with Achilles breathing down my neck and monitoring my every move. As far as he was concerned, this was an act of liberation, not punishment.

I had to marry Coppola. Defying Tiernan, the head of the Irish clan, came with a price tag I couldn't afford. My brother loved me in his own messed-up way, but I had no illusions about who and what he was.

Two Camorrista soldiers stood at the pulled-down airstairs leading to the airplane. When we reached them, they nodded at Tiernan, took my suitcases, and carried them upstairs. I placed a hand on the banister, trying to regulate my breaths.

"Don't do anything stupid." Tiernan grabbed the back of my neck, forcing me to look him in the eye. "You hear me?"

I wanted to shake off his touch, but the truth was, I brought this on myself. I went toe-to-toe with the cruelest man in the Camorra, and now I had to pay the price.

"What if Stefano is bad to me?"

"Achilles warned him off," Tiernan assured me. "But on the off chance he gives you trouble…just let me know and I'll break the lad's bones one finger at a time."

"Revenge is a pointless concept. What I want is to prevent the tragedy from happening, not plan a response to it," I muttered.

"You can hold your own," Tiernan said softly, and something inside my chest finally loosened.

Though his posture was slack and at ease, I knew he was eager to leave. Lila was still reeling from the baptism. He didn't like leaving her and Nero for longer than an hour anyway. He wanted to get back to her, and as much as I hated him in this moment, I still loved her.

"Go." I nodded, unable to bear the thought of Lila frightened. "Go to your family. They need you."

And then he was gone, the Mercedes driving out of the airport, disappearing in a cloud of dust.

It was time to face the music.

I entered the plane, numbly taking in the chrome-and-dark-accented cabin. I spotted Achilles at a round table with three of his soldiers. Two I recognized as Nico and Fabio, mid-rank members of the Camorra. The other one was Jeremie. Achilles seemed to take a liking to the Bratva heir, whom he had dragged as a collateral seven months ago during a gunfight. Didn't take a genius to figure out why. Jeremie was smart, quiet, efficient and didn't ogle me like I was dessert whenever he was assigned to chaperone me.

Either way, Tiernan told me Jeremie's time was almost up with the Camorra. Alex, his brother and the Bratva's pakhan, needed him back in Vegas.

Achilles wore gym shorts, a faded black *I'm not here to talk* hoodie with the hood flipped on, and a socks-and-slides combo. The picture of nonchalance. His brothers wouldn't be seen dead in this outfit, especially not showing their faces in Napoli. Luca and Enzo were all about appearances. Casual smart slacks, Hogan sneakers, and a well-tailored designer tee were their idea of dressing for comfort. But Achilles truly did not give a shit. Not about what people thought of him and certainly not about how he looked.

"Anywhere on this side of the plane." Achilles tossed a hand in his opposite direction, not bothering to look up from his game of cards.

Prick.

I slouched into a cream-colored recliner, popping my AirPods into my ears and scrolling through my messages. My girlfriends congratulated me on my speedy engagement, offering to plan a lavish bachelorette party. No one seemed surprised by the news I'd be getting married shortly. Everyone knew I was reckless and wild. My best friend, Frankie, even said, "I'm surprised this is your first marriage. Either way, you'll eat the man alive, leaving no crumbs."

But she had no idea who I was. She only knew the person I'd shown the world.

"Sixty seconds to takeoff," the pilot announced from the cockpit.

I tried practicing deep breaths, but even that small task seemed impossible.

The plane rolled across the strip, gaining speed, then took off. My stomach dropped. I didn't mind flights—not even flights in questionable, tiny airplanes—but I did mind this one. Because it was taking me to a future I had never signed up for.

Every second on this plane brought me closer to losing whatever I had left of my freedom.

I cleared my throat before speaking for the first time. "How long's the flight?"

No response. Achilles tossed a card into a pile, muttering something in Italian. The other men barked out a laugh. I closed my eyes and drew in a breath.

I wasn't prone to panic attacks anymore. I'd buried my past so deep inside my head, I no longer recognized it as a part of me. But whenever I did get them, they were bad. Achilles used to help me when we were younger. Hug me extra tight. Talk me through my emotions.

"Tell me five things you see. Four things you hear. Three things you can touch. Two things you can smell. One thing you can taste."

That one thing used to be his mouth. I'd reach on my toes and kiss him, and my anxiety would melt away like wax under hot water.

He wasn't that boy anymore. But I was still that girl.

The one who remembered the only safe place she ever knew was inside his arms.

The chatter in Neapolitan grew more boisterous. The men lit up cigarettes, pouring whiskey into tumblers.

I logged on to the Wi-Fi and googled the flight time. Nine hours. Okay, plenty of time to work with. I could find a way to convince him to turn the airplane around.

"Can you tell me where in Naples I'll live?" I asked evenly. Maybe if Achilles realized this was real—that he was really handing me over to be fucked by someone else—it'd stir something in him.

No response. I knew he heard me. *Asshole.*

"I hope you're not attending the wedding because I'm not sending you an invitation."

No answer.

"Does he know he's getting your leftovers?"

No answer.

My pulse hammered against every inch of my skin.

I needed to get his attention, and he was hell-bent on not giving it to me.

But Tiernan was right. I'd always been creative. The penny dropped when I realized I didn't necessarily need to get *his* attention. If I got his soldiers' attention, that'd be enough to piss him off.

I was wearing a summer dress—yellow with blue and pink flowers—with white ankle socks and a pair of Mary Janes. With a pout, I stretched across the recliner toward my tote bag on the side table, allowing my dress to ride up until my white cotton underwear was showing.

The chatter and laughter stopped.

"Can't find my AirPods," I sighed, wiggling my ass in the air, now on all fours on the recliner to reach my perfectly reachable bag. "Anybody seen them?"

I felt his eyes burning my ass like a good spanking.

Fabio cleared his throat. "You're wearing them."

"Oh. Silly me." I reached to one of my ears, popping the AirPod out and letting it fall to the floor. "Oops, so clumsy." I stood up and turned around, giving them a good angle of my ass as I bent down to pick it up. It wasn't the most sophisticated warfare scheme—but it was a bulletproof one.

Achilles decided he'd had enough.

He barked something in Neapolitan. His soldiers stood up and slinked to the back of the plane, leaving their cards behind.

"Show's over, Piccola Fiamma."

"No way. I've only just begun," I countered. I twirled on my toes, swiveling to face him and tossing my hair back. "Once they're back, I'm going to give your soldiers a show they'll never forg—"

"What do you want?" he said, cutting me off, sprawling in his seat. He rested his inked paw on his thigh, every inch of him deeply tanned and muscular.

"You know what I want." I kept the breathless panic from my voice. "I want out of this arrangement. I've never even met the guy."

"No." One word. Bored. Monotone. Controlled.

"Come on." I stepped forward, collapsing on the seat next to him. "I'll do anything. I'll move out of New York. Away from America. I'll even work for the Camorra!" I offered desperately. "You can use all of my connections. Even the Keatons."

"No."

My chest heated with rage and frustration. "There must be something we could barter." Gone was my game face and cool facade. I was desperate and didn't care if he knew. "Something that you want from me."

"There is something I want from you," his low drawl confirmed. "But it's too late to get it now."

His cool gaze swept down my body, top to bottom, his meaning clear.

Oh…

Of course. How had I not thought of that? Achilles never got over the fact we hadn't consummated our teenage crush. Back when we were together, he was too worried about my delicate sensibilities.

He'd barely touched me. I had to initiate every make-out session we ever had.

"Is this what you want?" I grabbed his wrist and placed his hand on my right breast. His rough palm pulsated heat through the fabric of my dress. My nipple tightened immediately. My heart stuttered but no longer from panic. I'd missed his hands on me. "Because I can give it to you, Achilles. I can make your wildest fantasies come true."

His free hand clenched next to his body, and his eyes, usually so black they carried the blue sheen of a raven's feathers, dimmed with yearning.

He always called me a whore, and in the end, I'd offered to become one for him. The sour taste of self-loathing exploded on my tongue.

But I didn't have time to mourn my pride. I'd save myself today so I could destroy *him* tomorrow.

I'd be his Delilah. Seduce, abuse, and abolish.

"You know you want to. Go on. Claim what's yours," I said, coaxing, guiding his hand from my chest, down my stomach, and between my legs through my dress. I squeezed them closed. "Me. On my knees. For you to do anything you want."

At the end of the day, it wouldn't matter. My only way of getting in bed with someone was to completely disconnect from my body to a degree we were two pieces of flesh milking pleasure from one another. Feelings and sex were completely different entities to me.

He leaned closer, his intoxicating scent taking over my senses as his knee pried my thighs open with its sheer power. Rugged fingers clamped around my thigh, his pinky brushing a hint of my panties as he squeezed my leg. His lips found the shell of my ear. "What I want to know is where you're hiding your weapon, since you've given us a striptease and I've yet to see it."

A smile tugged the corners of my lips. He knew me too well. I turned my head to whisper, "Give me a full-body check and find out for yourself."

"A fuck for a throne?" he asked flippantly, sitting back, his face dripping amusement. "You give yourself too much credit, sweetheart."

"A fulfilled fantasy for a small setback." I dragged a fingernail along his chest. "We both know your father isn't going to choose Luca. He hasn't yet, even though Luca played by the rules and married an Outfit princess to appease him. Luca is too cool, too safe. And Enzo? He doesn't have your bite. Your father will be mad, but he'll get over it."

I had no idea if what I was saying was true, but I always had the uncanny ability to bullshit my way out of a paper bag when needed.

"You know Don Vello so well?" Achilles sneered.

"I know human nature." I hitched a shoulder up. "And your father is human. A very flawed one at that."

He was quiet, which meant he was contemplating this, which meant that I *really* needed to drive the point home.

"You can have one night with me. To do whatever you want. All you have to do is turn this plane around."

"The weekend." His stance was lazy, but the devious glint in his eyes promised mayhem.

"I—what?" I wasn't sure I heard him correctly. My proposition was a shot in the dark. I'd never expected him to take me up on it. I didn't even know if I'd be able to move forward with such a barter if he agreed.

He drew his hand from between my thighs, collecting himself. "I'm not turning back the plane—not enough fuel. Plus, I have business in Naples until Monday. Let me fuck you through the weekend, and we'll square it off."

"Square it off?" I echoed numbly, proud of my steady tone. It betrayed nothing of what I was feeling inside.

"More or less. I can't take your virginity anymore—fuck knows there's no shred of it left—but I can still enjoy all the things I was too stupid and considerate to take back then."

I had to let his words slide over my skin without letting them penetrate it, or I'd go mad. I was close to madness anyway—being here, with him, having this conversation.

"And you'll let me go?" My mouth was dry, my pulse roaring between my ears. Achilles was an asshole but an honorable one. If he gave me his word, he'd keep it.

"You're mine from the moment we enter Italian territory until we leave it." He cracked his neck. "When we get back, I'll deal with my father. As for you"—he caught the ring on his pinky, swiveling it absentmindedly—"you'll pack a fucking bag, buy a one-way ticket out of North America, and I'll never see or hear from you again. We clear?"

I nodded, relief flooding me. I could do that. Moving away would be no hardship, aside from having to say goodbye to my brother, his wife, and my nephew. Nothing was keeping me in New York. "I give you my word."

"Good. Now be quiet and make yourself scarce until I call for you."

I slinked back to my seat and opened a *Vogue* magazine, burying my face in it. My thoughts were scattered, like pieces of glass from a broken vase. Where would I go? Ireland, probably. My ancestors' land. What would I do? I'd have some seed money. Enough to open a small shop. Buy myself a lovely cottage somewhere picturesque. Tiernan and Lila could visit me every summer with their kids. I'd be the cool auntie.

But first, I had to survive a weekend with Achilles, and I had a feeling that was no small feat.

I was determined not to blow this up. My future was waiting for me, and I was ready to finally meet it.

My freedom was worth it.

Even if the price was selling my soul to the man I hated the most.

The adrenaline crash made me doze off in the recliner. I woke up some hours later with my mouth gauzy.

Blinking my eyes back into focus, I saw Achilles and his soldiers sitting across from me. They were no longer playing cards. There was a suitcase open in front of them, and they were examining different luxury watches, no doubt stolen.

"How much time until landing?" I croaked out.

"An hour and some change." Jeremie popped his gum. He was messing with his phone, periodically smirking at something he saw on the screen. It was weird, watching this husky tank of a man exhibiting any emotion that wasn't annoyance.

Achilles flicked his wrist, checked the time, and stood up grimly. My heart sank all the way to my toes. "Up."

I rose to my feet and followed him to the lavatory. All eyes were on us, and I saw the derisive grins his soldiers flashed each other when I strode past them. They knew.

He waited for me to enter the bathroom, then locked the door behind us. It wasn't much bigger than a commercial airplane's, but it was fancier, consisting of veiny black marble punctuated with gold, a vanity with mirror, and a small shower.

"Thought we agreed the deal takes effect when we reach Naples." I rested my hip on the vanity.

"I said you're mine from the moment we enter Italian territory. That happened three minutes ago." He flashed me his phone screen, with a map of our plane traveling above a large body of water. "Want me to call air traffic control to confirm it?"

I shook my head. There was no need. He wasn't a liar. Just a dick.

He unholstered his gun, unloading the magazine and dumping it in the sink. "I'm clean."

"So am I."

"I know. I check your medical records quarterly." He tossed his phone on the vanity next. "Bend over and hold on to the sink."

Okay. So… We were really doing this.

I curled my fingers over the round marble sink nervously, pressing my hips to the counter. I stared up at the mirror in front of me. Because of the height difference, the angle didn't allow me to see his face. Only his torso, which was hidden by a hoodie.

He grabbed the hem of my dress and flipped it over my back, shoving it into one of my shoulder straps. There was something so mortifying in this gesture. My mind swam. He stared at my panties-clad ass for a moment, and I let him because I didn't have a choice. I gulped in a gasp as he grabbed my plain, white cotton panties from each side. His touch on my skin felt like somebody turned up all the lights inside me.

"You know, your underwear says a lot about you as a person."

"What do mine say?"

"That you're a *liar*."

He wasn't wrong. The Tierney the world knew would wear a black, lacy thong.

He pushed my underwear down in one go, letting it bunch around my ankles.

"On your toes." A rough palm patted my ass cheek. I swallowed back a groan.

I did as I was told, plastering my forehead to the cool counter. My ass and pussy were bare in front of him, up in the air.

"Spread 'em." He kicked my feet apart, and I did, as much as I could, anyway, with my undies still bunched at my ankles.

"That's enough," he released a mocking huff. "But good to know you're eager."

The insult landed square in my chest, but before I was able to stand up and tell him to go fuck himself, he pushed his shorts down and guided the warm, velvety crown of his cock between my folds from behind.

I froze at the invasion.

He didn't push inside. Just swirled the fat head in circles, tracing my folds, massaging them.

To my absolute horror, I was wet.

Wet because of the situation.

Wet because it was forbidden and wrong.

Wet because it was *him*.

Holy shit. No way. That couldn't be. It made no sense. I'd never been this turned on by anyone before, and he didn't even hurt me. I could usually only bring myself to climax when someone slapped or bruised me.

I wondered if he thought about my past when he was teasing me, and if so, I wondered if he cared. I couldn't allow myself to examine what was happening too closely.

I'd spent the last decade denying what had happened at that Russian camp. So much so that I didn't remember any of the abuse I'd suffered. The memories were hazy, sitting at the periphery of my mind, just past a secure wall I'd built, tall and strong, to shield me from them.

They felt like little weeds, desperate to claw their way in, to contaminate the lovely garden I now tended. Where roses and lilies grew neatly, alongside manicured shrubs. Of thoughts about shopping sprees and yacht vacations, and of admirers who only dared look but never touch.

I had managed to forget.

In order to live.

In order to survive.

But it came with a price. I had mastered the art of disconnecting my body from my soul when I got into bed with someone. I never made eye contact, never completely loosened up; I always kept the encounter on surface level. Enough to draw pleasure but not enough to penetrate the mental wall of security I barricaded my emotions behind.

The more Achilles teased my pussy from behind, the wetter I became, until I found myself grinding my nipples against the vanity, desperately seeking the friction as my vision blurred with lust.

Jesus, what was wrong with me?

The answer is too much and you damn well know it.

I couldn't wait to have his cock inside me.

When my pussy began making wet, embarrassing sounds, Achilles decided to guide his cock from my entrance up to my clit, spreading the wetness around. Despite my best efforts, I let loose a small moan, which I immediately killed with a lip bite. I felt his shredded six-pack quaking against the curve of my ass with a wry chuckle.

"You like that, huh?" he purred. "Do you always get wet for men who fuck you for favors?"

"I'm not—" I started lying, but then he pushed two thick fingers into me from behind, his dick momentarily springing between us and slapping my ass cheek. My core clenched against his fingers greedily, welcoming him in, coating him with my arousal. He spread his index and middle fingers inside me, stretching me to an uncomfortable and achingly delicious limit. Another moan escaped me, this time louder and accompanied by a shudder. *Fuck.*

Another mocking laugh.

"No weapon here. Let's check the next hole."

He withdrew his fingers from me and I heard the sound of his mouth popping as he sucked them clean. A fresh rush of heat rolled between my legs. I wanted him to drop to his knees and eat me out from behind.

In the mirror, I caught a glimpse of him spitting on his index finger. He guided it into my tight hole, spreading his saliva around the rim and slicking the area before pushing inside. My ass cheeks clamped around the assault, another groan of pleasure tumbling out of my mouth. It was both humiliating and arousing beyond belief.

He wiggled his finger inside me a little. "Hmm. Not here, either. Where is it, Little Flame?"

"Suck a bag of dicks," I moaned into the marbled surface. He slowly withdrew from my ass, letting my muscles pulse and clench around his finger, begging it to stay.

Next, his hand traveled up my waist and toward my bra. Simple cotton covered my modest tits.

His palm slid past the material of my bra, cupping my breast and toying with my nipple until it hardened. My entire body was humming, begging to be invaded. He trailed his hand along the band. His fingers halted on a small device tucked inside it.

Shit.

"Mini double-agent fixed blade?" he asked blandly.

"Urban edge," I corrected, as he carefully slid it from my bra and pocketed it in his shorts.

"Cute." He grabbed his dick, swirling its head against my opening again.

My mind and body rioted against one another. I was nauseous with anger at what he was doing to me, even if I did bargain my way into this position. But my body came alive, brimming with sensations I'd never felt before.

And because I couldn't take it anymore, not the desire nor the humiliation, I bit out, "Are you going to fuck me already, or can I take a nap?"

That made him push all the way inside me in one go and without any warning.

He was huge, and it was painful. I had no time to prepare for it. I squirmed and shifted, trying to accommodate him, the burn between my legs intensifying.

Because of course the bastard just *had* to have a glorious cock.

His balls slapped the back of my thighs. The tiniest groan escaped him—the sole sign he was enjoying himself. Instead of grabbing my waist like a normal person, he wrapped my long hair around his fist, tugging so his lips pressed the shell of my ear.

"Took me fifteen fucking years," he grunted, withdrawing and slamming into me again. "But I finally broke her."

He rode me like I was an unruly mare, with jerky, punishing strokes designed to show dominance. Each time he thrust into me, my clit hit the doorknob of the vanity, and I found myself rubbing against it.

My muscles shook. An ache grew between my legs, begging to be unfurled; I was going to come. I was going to come from a man who had taken me in vengeance. It surprised me because usually I needed my partner to hit me to get there.

We were both so screwed up, it was amazing we didn't make it as a couple.

Achilles yanked my hair, extending my neck. "Watch yourself get fucked by the man you tried to ruin," he hissed huskily. "Who's ruined now?"

He held the hem of his hoodie mid-torso so he could watch himself slamming into me. "Now that's a sight," he growled. "Not so feisty anymore, are you?"

"You're a dick," I hissed out.

"I'll take your word for it." I heard the grin in his voice, his abs bunching to a bulging six-pack under his ink. "After all, you're the expert."

He thrust harder, faster, making me bump against the counter again and again. I wanted to hate it. I wanted to hate *him*. But I was incapable of either.

I tried to conjure a sassy response, but all I could manage was desperately squeezing his cock for dear life.

I was close.

So close.

My mouth fell open, and I felt an orgasm seizing every muscle and cell in my body when he pulled out suddenly. Hot, sticky cum spurted onto the backs of my thighs. Then he pushed me down so my knees hit the floor roughly and pumped his cock to come into my hair.

The goddamn bastard. I was going to end him.

"What the fuck?" I scrambled up, pushing at his chest. He stepped sideways from me, flicked on the tap, and pushed his still-erect cock under the water, washing the traces of me from his skin.

"What kind of animal are you?" I cupped my hands under the tap, gathering some water I intended to clean my hair with.

"Don't touch it," came his dry retort as he tucked himself back into his shorts. "I want you to walk around with my crusty cum all over your hair. Remind you who's the bitch now."

"I didn't come."

"Yeah." He rolled his tongue over his front teeth in a devious smirk. "That wasn't accidental."

"Are you punishing me?" I seethed.

"Hey, I just had my dick in your cunt. I'm punishing both of us."

I closed my eyes and took a deep breath. I needed to not lose my shit and bite my tongue if I wanted to get out of this situation in one piece. Achilles was a psychopath. A real one. And unlike my brother, he wouldn't think twice before offing someone who annoyed him.

With a shake of my head, I pulled my underwear up and tugged my dress down. I didn't try to make myself presentable. There was no point. I was going out there looking like I'd been thoroughly fucked and like I didn't care one iota if everyone knew.

We exited the lavatory and made our way back to the sitting area. I headed toward my side of the plane when Achilles reclaimed his seat and slapped his thigh. "In my lap, Piccola Fiamma."

The prick was really going to milk every single second of this arrangement. But it was too late to back down, especially when I'd already started paying for my freedom.

I assumed my place on his thigh and scrolled through my phone, ignoring the curious gazes Nico and Fabio threw at me. Thankfully, Jeremie still had his nose buried deep in his phone, minding his own business.

I could feel the others' imploring eyes on my face, though.

"Anyone got something to say?" Achilles growled, staring down each of his soldiers with a wrathful glare. He yanked me closer, almost protectively. My back slammed against his chest. "Because I'd just *love* to hear what's going on in those empty heads of yours."

"Nope," "Sorry, Boss" was said in chorus. Jeremie didn't reply. He seemed above the bullshit. A true Rasputin through and through.

"Good," Achilles said slowly, his palm resting on my thigh. "Now look the other way before I claw your eyes out."

The soldiers busied themselves—one with a book, the other rearranging his Rolex on his wrist.

"Fuck's sake, Jer." Achilles popped a piece of gum into his mouth, not offering me any. "Whose thirst trap are you ogling on Instagram?"

Jeremie quickly turned his phone screen-down, but Fabio still managed to steal a glimpse. "Whoever she is, she looks Italian," he snorted.

Achilles shook his head seriously. "Then I hope for his sake he isn't planning on more than a quick fuck. Alex wants him back in Vegas."

Jeremie glanced up with an expression suggesting he wanted to off all of us for interrupting him, a glare so intense and full of evil, it might as well have been a war declaration.

Achilles was wrong. Whoever she was, he was going to keep her.

Even if the entire world had to pay the price.

CHAPTER NINE
TIERNEY

We landed in a small, private airport on the outskirts of Naples. Feeling self-conscious and more than a little used, I pulled my hair up into a hair clip to hide Achilles's artwork. There was no need to advertise what we'd been up to in the lavatory. Now that I had the time to digest the denied orgasm and mortification, I was plotting his slow, violent murder.

Only killing him wouldn't be enough. Too quick and impersonal. He thought I'd hurt him with my first betrayal? Well, he better buckle up because I had something much worse in store.

He'd pay for what he did to me. For *everything* he did to me.

A private air hostess lowered the stairway, and we poured out into the sweltering heat. A driver in a black Cadillac waited on the tarmac and drove Achilles and me to a hangar a few miles away. His soldiers stayed back, taking care of the cargo.

From my place in the back seat of the Cadillac, I spotted two sleek, black SUVs already parked inside the hangar. Two Camorra soldiers leaned against them. Both middle-aged, dressed to the nines, with large golden cross pendants on their chests.

I wasn't normally a fidgety person, but being smack in the middle of two Camorra families just looking for an excuse to off one another wasn't exactly a lifelong dream of mine.

Achilles unzipped the backpack between his legs and took out a gun. He checked the chamber, loaded, and cocked it. "Stay here."

"Like I have anywhere else to g—"

I didn't have time to finish the sentence. He'd already slid out of the car and slammed the door in my face.

Not one to sit around and wait, I reached for the door handle before hearing the automatic click of the vehicle locking from the inside. I flashed the driver a scowl through the rearview mirror. He shrugged. "Just following orders," he said in English.

I redirected my attention to Achilles and the men. He reached them, his gun concealed in the pocket of his hoodie, where his hands were casually stuffed. Words were exchanged. Achilles appeared standoffish and bored, whereas the men furrowed their brows, exchanging confused glances. I rolled down the window, hoping to hear the conversation, even though my grasp on the Italian language was minimal at best.

"*C'è stato un cambio di programma*," Achilles announced. *Change of plans.*

The men answered in a rush of heated words I couldn't decipher, but I did recognize some of the curses thrown in. Then one of them spat out, "*Siamo qui per prendere la rossa.*"

Rossa. Redhead. *Me.*

My heart doubled over. They were Coppola's soldiers, not the Ferrantes'. And they were here to collect me. I slouched in the seat, trying to make myself as invisible as possible. The angry, pissed-off men craned their heads to catch a glimpse of me in the car.

I reached for the asshole's backpack in search of another weapon, but there wasn't any. *Fuck.* I was decently trained in martial arts. Could probably fight them off if things went south. But if they drew a weapon on me, I was toast.

Achilles's voice remained calm as he spoke, which only seemed to aggravate them further. One of the soldiers—the bulkier man, the muscle—gave him an aggressive shove. Not enough to move him a millimeter but enough to piss him off. Achilles pulled his gun out and put two bullets between his eyebrows. The second man tried taking his gun out, but Achilles was faster, shooting him twice in the throat. They both dropped to the ground.

What the ever-loving fuck?

What the hell was he doing? *Fuck.* Could this man go through a twenty-four-hour period *without* reenacting the Red Wedding?

Achilles's soldiers materialized from the open mouth of the hangar. They got down to business wordlessly, taking care of the two bodies like nothing was amiss. Jeremie knelt and quietly collected bullet casings. Nico rubbed a spatter of blood with the tip of his shoe, pressing his phone to his ear as he barked orders. Finally, His Highness waltzed over to the passenger door and threw it open.

"Out." Achilles pushed the gun into his waistband.

I stayed put, arms folded over my chest. "Nice way to start our weekend sexcapade."

"Thought you wanted out of your marriage with Stefano." He grabbed my arm and yanked me out of my seat. "You're welcome, by the way."

I wanted him to negotiate a different deal with the don. Not to go on a killing spree and make everything worse for everybody. Vello was going to blow a gasket when he found out.

"Doesn't it screw things up in the Alliance even more?" I stood up and smoothed my dress over my legs.

"Don't look so fucking concerned. Watching my blood shed is your favorite hobby."

Achilles turned his back to me and strolled over to a parked freight truck. He stepped on a ramp, rolled up the door, and got inside.

A Ducati identical to the black one he had at home was parked there, facing us. He picked up two helmets from the floor and put one on. He mounted the bike and revved it up, riding it the short distance to me. When he reached me, he pushed a black helmet on my head and adjusted the straps under my chin with a rough tug. My hair clip fell to the ground, and he leaned down, picking it up and securing it over the hem of my dress. The small gesture made my pulse stutter in my chest. It was the kind of thing the old Achilles would have done.

He patted the space behind him in a silent demand. I climbed up, the place between my legs raw and throbbing, reminding me how rough he was when he took me on the plane.

"Heading home?" Jeremie asked, a skull bandanna tugged up his nose to protect himself from the fumes he was about to breathe. He was already pouring detergent over the bloodied concrete. Another soldier was wheeling in an electric pressure washer.

"Hotel. Gonna drop her off, then we'll head downtown for our first meeting. Stay close." Achilles flipped down his helmet visor. "I want six men patrolling her floor at any given time when she's out of my sight, armed to the fucking heavens."

"Yup." Jeremie tossed the empty detergent tank against a wall, fishing a blue Bic from his pocket. "She'll be in good hands."

"No one's allowed to touch her but me," Achilles growled.

"It's a figure of speech, Scarface."

"Don't like you saying the word *figure* when speaking about her, either."

How this jackass thought he was capable of handing me over to another man was a case for the FBI. I was surprised he let me get a manicure without killing my nail technician.

We took off, with me hugging Achilles's torso from behind. Because of the anatomy of the motorcycle, I was perched slightly above him, almost on top of him, and could feel every individual muscle in his back and stomach. His scent drifted into my system, mixing with the heady smells of summer and beach and mouthwatering dishes as we wove into the narrow cobblestone streets of the city. My hips involuntarily clasped around him, enjoying the heat of his body, the sturdiness of it, and every time we reached a traffic light, Achilles dropped one hand from the throttle, casually stroking the sensitive spot behind my knee.

We rode for a while, with him taking small side streets and hidden pathways of the city. I had a feeling he was throwing any Coppola people following us off our scent. If so, he'd succeeded because, by the time he merged onto a turnpike curving away from the city and onto a mountain, we were alone on the road.

He parked on top of a cliff overlooking the city. Killing the engine, he didn't take off his helmet or flick open the dark visor, which mirrored whatever he was looking at.

"Are you going to hurl me off a cliff?" I reached to unclip my helmet, pinning it between my arm and waist. "Because I'm sure open to it if it means not having to fuck you again."

He dismounted, turned around, and climbed back on the bike so we were facing each other. He grabbed my ass through my dress and slid me down so I landed in his lap. He was hard as a rock. His thick shaft pressed against my panties.

"Why'd you do it?" His tone threw me off. It was soft but still deadly. Another hint of the old Achilles I used to love.

"Why did I do what?" I playfully curled a piece of hair over my finger.

"You know what."

I did. I had tried to explain myself to him countless times, though I knew nothing would justify my behavior. It'd been over a decade, and I still mourned ruining the only good thing that'd ever happened to me.

I regretted what I'd done to him every moment of every day of every year of my existence.

But telling him that after he screwed me roughly just because he could and came in my hair was beyond the scope of my abilities. I didn't want to give him the satisfaction of knowing how much betraying him destroyed me.

I shrugged. "I didn't want you, and you didn't get the hint."

My throat burned with the lie. I knew I'd hurt him. Moreover, I knew the only reason he asked was because I couldn't see his face and what was written on it.

"Did you ever fucking care?" His voice was thick, muffled by the helmet and something else I didn't want to think about.

"No," I said coldly, pushing the word out to hurt him like he'd hurt me for the past few years. "Not really. At first, I was lonely, and you were a nice distraction. But afterward? You were deadweight. I needed to get rid of you. But you were so damn persistent." I rolled my eyes.

Another loaded silence and one with enough tension to be cut with a knife.

"Well. Didn't work quite as well as you hoped, did it?" he said, reaching between my open thighs and tugging my underwear to one side. "Take out my cock."

I looked around with uncertainty. "Here?"

"We're alone. Even if we weren't, it's not like you have a reputation to uphold."

Answering was only going to worsen my already-catastrophic situation. Best do what he said now and take my revenge later. I reached into his tented shorts, yanking down the waistband. His cock sprang out, cum dripping on his hoodie.

"Stroke it." He took my hand and guided my moves along the length of it.

I spat on his cock defiantly to moisten it, adding some phlegm into the mix of spit.

He laughed in response, fastening my fingers over it. "Brat."

I scowled at myself in the reflection of his black visor and knew he was staring as I jerked him off. His arms fell to his sides, and I pushed up his hoodie with one hand, tracing the tattoos of venomous snakes, skeletons, and cobwebs adorning his perfect form. Desire roared in my veins. It quieted every other thought inside my head. I wanted him, badly, and I didn't care the only way to get him was if he punished me for what had happened.

"You know, I paid your little shrink a visit when we were twenty-five," he said, his tone wry and amused, while I was pleasuring him. My spine stiffened as his cock grew thicker and longer in my hand. "Asked him what the fuck was wrong with yo—no, don't stop. *Keep going.*"

I tried to swallow a lump in my throat. Failed.

"Nice try." I picked up the pace on his cock, wanting to yank it off his damn body. "Therapists don't share information about their patients."

"Apparently they do when there's a gun aimed at their crotch," Achilles said conversationally. "It's amazing how persuasive I can be with a sour mood and a full chamber. Wanna know what he told me?"

No, I didn't. In fact, I never stuck around long enough to get a diagnosis from a therapist. I didn't even know which shrink he was talking about, I'd been to so many.

"Not particularly," I said, pumping him harder and faster, suddenly wanting him to come and leave me the hell alone.

"He said when a child suffers a big trauma at a young age, they often get mentally and emotionally stuck at that age. *Arrested development*. He put your emotional maturity somewhere between fourteen and fifteen. Said you'll stay this way until you work through your shit and accept what happened to you at the camp."

Tears clung to my lashes. I didn't want him to see me in a moment of weakness, so I breathed through my nose and tried to push through it, jerking him off faster.

Fucking come already.

"Oh, good. I'm ready for you now." He flicked my hand off his dick, then grabbed the backs of my thighs. "Get on top."

He was going to make me screw him after the things he'd said to me?

Why not? You just told him you betrayed him because he never meant anything to you.

I pushed my knees up and mounted him. He grazed my clit with the tip of his fingers. A shudder rippled through my entire body. His cock slid into me, my wet entrance accepting it eagerly—greedily—as he buried himself to the hilt. This position was so much better than the one on the plane because now he was hitting my G-spot, curled all the way there, without even moving. I trembled around him, a rush of heat coursing through my veins.

Don't enjoy this. What the hell is wrong with you? He just admitted to a gross breach of privacy with your former therapist.

He grabbed my waist and readjusted himself, tilting his hips up and hitting the sensitive spot inside me again. Another quake of pleasure rolled through my body, and I grunted.

"So fucked up." He brushed a thumb over my cheek, chuckling. "You've always been just as sick as me. Ride me, Tierney."

I did. I didn't even bother pretending I didn't like it anymore. I was fucking my archnemesis who loathed me, and I was enjoying every single second of it, even if he wrecked me. Because he was right. I was a mess and always would be. We'd tried to fix each other once, and look where it got us.

With each roll of my hips, he slammed deeper into me, hitting my G-spot. I controlled the pace and the movement, which meant I was now in charge, drawing pleasure from the situation whether he liked it or not. I wrapped one hand around his neck, the other tracing his abs as I moved on top of him. Hate radiated between us, potent and fierce. We were fucking, but we might as well have been fighting.

I was riding a criminal high, my inner muscles spasming around him, milking my pleasure from him. I could feel the first wave of orgasmic ecstasy washing over me.

"Hate you," I moaned, grinding my clit against his abs as I slammed down on his cock again.

"Hate you more, baby."

He grabbed my waist, hurled me up and brought me down to

my knees in front of the Ducati. My knees hit the ground with a thump.

"Nah, you don't get to come this time, either." He pushed the glistening head of his cock past my lips. I slammed my teeth together in anger. Achilles let out a growl, taking his dick in his hand and slapping my cheek with it. It didn't hurt, but it infuriated me, and to my shock, I felt my tears close to falling.

"Better open up, sweetheart. Fuck knows what other hole I'll choose to come in if you deny me."

God, I was going to destroy the bastard as soon as we got out of here. I didn't care if I had to hide from the Camorra for the rest of my life. But right now, in this exact moment in time, I didn't have any choice.

I opened up, tasting my arousal on his cock as he speared himself all the way in. I choked around his girth, his tip scraping the back of my throat. Tears began leaking from my eyes. It wasn't just from my gag reflex. The humiliation strangled me, and I hated myself for not hating this. For still being turned on by what he was doing to me.

"Hamish told me you have a degradation kink." He clawed the back of my head, fucking my face with vigor. "You know, before I killed him."

I felt his hot cum sliding down my throat, and it took everything in me not to bite his dick off. He fisted my hair, keeping me still as he emptied himself inside my mouth.

"Oh, *fuck*," he grunted, closing his eyes. "Just so you know, if you try to bite me, I'm breaking your neck and letting you fall off the cliff."

I internally screamed like a wounded animal. I didn't think I could hate anyone more than Igor Rasputin, but Achilles came damn close.

After he was done, he let go of my hair. I fell backward, my ass hitting the ground. My tears kept falling, and now I wasn't just angry and ashamed—I was reeling.

Pushing up to my feet, I turned around and stomped away, descending the cliff on the same pathway on which we'd arrived.

"Tierney," Achilles barked. "Back here. *Now*."

"I'd say *fuck you, asshole*, but I don't want to fuck you. Even at the price of being sold to Stefano Coppola."

"Where do you think you're going?" His voice echoed across the cliff, carried by the wind.

"I'll find my way to Coppola. Fuck off and leave me alone."

I stomped so hard my teeth chattered with each step, but I didn't stop. I heard the engine purring to life behind me, and sure enough, he zigzagged in front of me, stopping in a screech and blocking my path. The mere sight of him made me want to scream.

"Get on the bike," he snarled.

"Leave me alone."

"What's wrong with you?" he growled, hands tightening over the handlebars.

"What's wrong with *me*?" I stabbed my chest with my finger. "This weekend doesn't give you a free pass to treat me like trash. I have enough of that from you when we're home. I get it. I wronged you. You never got over it. No one forced you to stay in touch with me. Grow up. You're talking about my mental age? Yours doesn't scratch eleven. All you do is bully and belittle me, and when we fuck, you don't even let me come!"

"Thought you liked degradation." He was almost comically surprised.

"Consensual!" I screamed. "You don't just fuck someone's face without permission. What the hell is wrong with you?" Wiping the tears with the heels of my palms, I shook my head. "You thought you were doing me a favor?"

His face bricked over, and he didn't say anything.

"You're a shit lay."

His throat worked around a swallow. "I thought this was how you wanted it."

The catch in his voice almost calmed me down. *Almost*. Ignorance was no excuse for abuse.

"Are you ever going to forgive me for what happened?" The question scorched a path through my throat.

"I don't know."

The air pulsated with intensity between us, and my lungs squeezed around the little air inside them. I couldn't take being near him anymore. A part of me wanted him to kill me already. Finish me off. It wasn't like he'd left much to live for, anyway.

I shook my head. "Move."

A muscle jumped in his jaw. "I'll let you come next time."

"There won't be next time."

"Yes there will, and I'll do better." He paused, measuring his words. "And I won't…" He cleared his throat. "I won't mention my conversations with your therapists again."

"Therapists?" I roared. "*Plural?*"

Another beat of silence. What else did he do over the years to keep track of me? I knew he'd stalked me. Murdered men who'd touched me. Accessed my medical records. Was anything in my life my own? Untouched by his destructive hand?

"Wow," I exhaled, a humorless laugh escaping me. "All this monitoring and you couldn't even buy me a carton of milk every time I ran out. Rude."

"You don't drink milk," he said softly. "It upsets your stomach. You drink that almond shit that looks like spunk."

Was it normal that one moment I wanted to strangle him, and the next, I wanted to hug him? I didn't think so. But there was something extremely vulnerable about this man only I seemed to be privy to.

"I'll ask for permission from now on before I do…"—he cleared his throat—"anything."

"You thought I didn't want to come?" I narrowed my eyes.

He stared at his slides. "Yeah."

"Well, no. I like to come. A lot. I like to be bossed around and spanked, but I have some hard limits." I took a deep breath. Might as well tell him, as I was stuck banging him for the entire weekend. "No spitting, no calling me a whore, no edging." The first two items reminded me of the gulag. The third was a product of it. I did not like being deprived of food, shelter, or pleasure. "You always have to make sure I come."

"Okay."

"But… You can hurt me."

"Hurt you?" I knew he was studying me intently, working something in that genius mind of his. "Hurt you how?"

"You can…" I licked my lips. "Hit me."

Silence stretched between us for a moment before he spoke.

"No, I can't."

"Yes, you ca—"

"I can't," he said, cutting me off. "Hurt you. Not like that." Pause. "And you don't need that either to enjoy yourself. I watched you. You nearly came both times we were together."

He was right. I hadn't thought of that. I wondered what that meant. But then again, a part of me didn't want to know. Sex was an exchange of orgasms, nothing more, nothing less. No emotion attached to it. Not even with my high school sweetheart.

"And I want us to have a safe word," I said.

He nodded. "We'll choose a safe word. I won't do—"

"And don't ever call me a whore again." I cut into his words breathlessly. "Every single sex worker I've met is eons more respectable and worthy than your sorry ass."

Something dangerous rippled behind the helmet. No one talked to this man like I did. Probably how I got myself into this mess in the first place.

"Look, hop on the bike. I'll tone my shit down."

"No. Good sex is the bare minimum. I'm still pissed off."

He groaned, tossing his head back, shaking his helmeted head.

"Tell me what I need to do to get your ass in gear because there's no guarantee Sangue Blu isn't on his way here with an army of soldiers and enough firearms to conquer Rome."

This was the closest I'd ever gotten to negotiate a more bearable weekend with him. We both knew I was mounting that bike. For better or worse, my imprisoner was my only ticket to freedom.

"I want to shop till I drop while I'm here. On your dime. You're not keeping me stuck in the hotel while you tend to your business." I folded my arms. "And I want you to stop being mean to me. Stop mentioning our past. And stop denying me orgasms."

"Done, done, and done," he said. "What's our safe word?"

His question threw me off. I normally went for a boring and trivial word. *Banana* or *tomato*. Something that wouldn't come up as a part of dirty talk in the bedroom. But I didn't have to think long to choose our safe word.

"It's two words." I licked my lips.

I could feel his gaze through the helmet, intent and lethal.

"Ford Prefect."

The two words hung in the air between us like a sword.

"Thought you said we're not allowed to talk about our past." His tone was neutral, measured.

"It's not our past," I said. "It's a book character."

"Ford Prefect." He grabbed my helmet and slammed it against my sternum. "Got it."

I snatched the helmet with a huff and hopped behind him. Apparently, the conversation wasn't over after all because he twisted around to face me.

"I'm not fucking you again so soon." I screwed the helmet on my head and clipped it. "I'm implementing a three-hour rule between sex. You're not worth the UTI."

"I'm not going to fuck you again," he said, and after a moment, added, "Not now, anyway."

"Then what do you want?"

"Is it a crime to look at you?"

"No, but if it were, you'd still fucking do it."

I glared at his covered face with open hatred, confused and out of my depth. I felt naked and exposed under his concealed gaze, knowing he was able to read me so much better than anyone else.

Finally, I punctuated the silence by saying, "If I'm such an awful person and you can't stay away from me, what does that make you, Achilles?"

"Ah, that's an easy one." His thumb brushed over the throbbing pulse beating against the side of my neck. "A fucking fool who is, and always will be, addicted to you."

"You don't act like a lovesick addict."

"I never said I *want* to be addicted to you." He shook his head. "I'd love nothing more than to purge you from my system. You are a disease, Tierney. People are also addicted to meth. Doesn't mean it's good for them."

"If you have any trace of compassion for me, stop hurting me," I said quietly.

"I can't," he admitted. To his credit, he sounded rueful. Almost forlorn. "You hurt me. Not just then. Today. Tomorrow. Every day. Your mere existence makes it hard to breathe. I have to live every day with the fact you didn't choose me. And I can't stand it." He flicked the visor up, finally letting me see a glimpse of his eyes. They were red, bloodshot. "I can't quit you. I don't know how. And it's ruining both of us. So do us both a favor and fuck the hell off when we get back home."

CHAPTER TEN
TIERNEY

The seaside hotel we were staying in was patrolled by Camorra soldiers. I guessed he didn't want to take me to the Ferrante household, to avoid tipping off his father. Although I was sure that, by now, Don Vello already knew things had veered off plan and his precious deal gotten screwed over.

The dozen or so soldiers monitoring the hotel inside and out were all carrying, so I knew better than try to escape them, if and when Achilles left me alone. I didn't know why, exactly, I didn't want to die. I certainly had no particular reason to live. Maybe I just wanted to survive as a *fuck you* to all the people who had hurt me.

I was still reeling from our spat at the cliff, so when we reached the presidential suite on the highest floor, I quickly paced toward the fully equipped kitchen and fixed myself a drink. I chose a brandy on the rocks and knocked it back in one go.

Nothing particularly noteworthy stood out about the suite. I'd been to more luxurious hotel rooms, but this one seemed to have that enigmatic charm of a place that wasn't trying to compete with expensive hotel chains.

I stared at the marbled kitchen counter, still holding my empty tumbler, my back to Achilles.

I was thinking I should probably hop into the shower to wash off the long flight. And maybe take a nap. It didn't matter how many hours I slept on the plane, nothing beat a good bed after a long journey.

Achilles appeared by my side, snatched the tumbler from between my fingers, and to my surprise, filled it again, handing it back to me. "Drink."

My spine stiffened, but I decided, for once in my life, not to argue with him. Another drink would probably do me good. I took a generous sip, glaring at him suspiciously.

"All of it." He placed his fingers on the bottom of the tumbler, tilting it to my lips again. I swallowed it all. He grabbed the tumbler and placed it on the counter, then snatched my waist and hoisted me onto the marbled countertop. I let loose a squeak, surprised by the contact.

"What the hell do you think you're doing?" I huffed.

"Showing you that you don't need violence in order to come."

Flipping my dress up to expose my bare thighs, he dropped to his knees and positioned himself between my legs. Rough, hot palms pushed my knees apart, the back of my thighs dragging across the cool surface. A heady, pleasant feeling of drunkenness, exhaustion and lust swirled in my head. He'd gotten me drunk to have sex with me. He wasn't a good guy. And yet, I knew I would've consented to this if I were sober as a nun, too.

His palm slipped into my panties, stretching the fabric and pushing them aside. I bowed my back and searched out the heat of his touch some more. He brushed his finger over my slit, staring at it intently, and maybe it was the brandy, but I could actually feel myself blush. I hadn't thought I was capable of that bodily function anymore.

"I'd wondered," he mumbled, eyes transfixed on my pussy, "if you were a redhead all around…"

My breath stuttered inside my lungs shakily as I watched him. "I am."

"I can see that."

I decided not to ask him what he made of it. I shouldn't have cared. But he spoke, anyway.

"What a curse it must be, sweetheart. To be such a divine creature, so utterly seductive, and yet unable to feel a goddamn thing."

With that invisible arrow to the chest, his head disappeared between my legs giving me a long, satisfying lick. My fingers immediately threaded into his hair, and I arched, tossing my head back and moaning.

"This is the only time I will go down on you, Little Flame." His words reverberated inside my body as he licked and nipped at my pussy. "Just to make a fucking point."

Panting, I watched his head moving between my legs, felt the sensation of his hot mouth and wet tongue inside me, every fiber in my body coming alive. He sucked my clit, drawing circles around it with the tip of his tongue, adding two fingers to penetrate me when I bucked my hips forward in desperation.

I didn't want to come. Didn't want to show him that he was right. That he managed to do what no one else before him could—bring me to a climax without hurting me. But my body didn't ask for permission. It convulsed and trembled, my muscles tightening like a bow as an orgasm slammed into me anyway. The sensation unsettled me, ripping through my body head to toe. Before I could get down from that high, he grabbed me by the back of my thighs and hoisted me up, pushing me against a round dining table. My stomach was flush against the surface. He pushed his shorts off, using his cock to tease me from behind.

"Do it now," I growled. I didn't recognize myself in this desperation.

He pressed home, and I cried out, the sharp sensation robbing me of my breath for the first few seconds. He gave me a second to adjust, for my muscles to relax, and then he started moving.

Again, I tried reasoning with my body.

You can't come from just penetration. You need him to spank you. Slap you around. Maybe choke you a little. This is just the way you're wired.

"Slap me," I growled.

"No." His voice was smooth. Measured.

My fingernails raked the wooden table. "I'm not asking—I'm ordering you to."

"If anyone here will be taking orders, it'll be you." He picked up his pace, slamming into me harder without actually hurting me.

Dammit.

"This is boring," I said.

He picked up his pace some more, now screwing me so hard the table moved with each thrust and me with it. "Tell that to your pussy. It's trying to choke my cock to death convulsing around it."

I was so close to orgasm, it was frightening. How did it happen? What sort of trickery was this?

"Stop this now."

"You have a safe word." He slammed into me again. "Use it."

But I didn't want to use it. I just didn't want him to know that he won.

"Ugh." I thumped my forehead against the table, letting it happen—letting my body take this pleasure and make it its own, and damn the consequences.

The second climax was just as earth-shattering as the first, making my teeth chatter as it blew through my nervous system. When he withdrew from me, I could barely keep myself upright.

I wobbled up after a few moments, examining my surroundings through a haze.

"Fuck." He chuckled low, patting his pocket for his cigarette pack. "I hope your spine is better than your resolve because it took me five seconds flat to break you and make you come. How easy." He shook his head, lighting himself a cigarette with a derisive smile.

I watched him amble toward the open doors of the balcony without a care in the world and realized belatedly that the windows were also open. People could've seen us. I was being sloppy, providing him no challenge. I just let him bulldoze in and prove to me that he'd managed to do what no other man could before him.

"Don't look so smug," I answered. "Your father will probably kill you when you get back."

"Oh, you're not that important." He settled on a chair in the sun, tilting his head up and closing his eyes. "But desperation looks good on you, Piccola Fiamma."

Something was off, but I couldn't pinpoint what it was.

I crawled to the shower, flicking it on and turning the water to extra hot. I stood under the spray for a full ten minutes before it came to me.

Reaching between my legs, I patted my carefully trimmed slit, then slipped a cautious finger, checking my sore insides. My suspicion was confirmed.

Achilles hadn't climaxed.

He gave me my pleasure—the two orgasms that were robbed from me in both our sexual encounters—and he left unsatisfied.

It was the first time a man had given me something instead of taking something away from me.

And it made me want to claw myself to shreds.

CHAPTER ELEVEN
ACHILLES

"Yo, Scarface." Jeremie fell into the seat next to mine.

"Sup, Vodka Breath," I replied.

"It's your father again." He slid my vibrating phone across the table.

Not a shocking development. He would call, wouldn't he? I'd killed two of Stefano's soldiers, ran off with his bride, and was currently restructuring every single border he and Sangue Blu had agreed upon in their meeting, breaking all of our clans' promises. I'd barged into Sangue Blu neighborhoods, taken over the areas his dealers worked, and threatened every motherfucker in my territory who dared pay Stefano protection money at gunpoint.

I spent the past twenty-four hours reminding the Camorra that the Ferrantes ruled all of Naples. No exceptions. I was making healthy progress setting things back in order here in Naples, but my mind wasn't in the game. Not fully, anyway. Instead it was affixed to a long-legged redhead with emerald eyes and a husky voice who had managed to burn through sixty thousand euros on my credit card in less than twelve hours.

Tierney was revenge-spending, while I was out here tempting fate and starting wars for her freedom. Last night she made a show of slathering the 3K-La Prairie eye cream she'd purchased all over her feet, explaining that walking all over me had given her blisters.

She didn't let our weekend arrangement douse her flame—on the contrary, after our exchange at the cliff, she was extra sassy, extra poisonous, and I'd even let her steal one of my guns without saying anything.

I trusted her with a pistol more than I did all my soldiers combined, anyway.

I made sure to visit her every three hours on the dot wherever she was—a mall, a restaurant, our hotel—to fuck her. I wasn't missing out on any of my hard-earned pussy, especially when it was this fucking good. I even woke her up in the middle of the night every three hours for a feeding. Sleep was for the weak and could wait until I returned to New York.

The first two times since getting to the hotel, I didn't even bother with my climax. I was so fucking laser-focused on making it good for her that I forgot all about myself. Only my shitty lies afterward made me claim some of my pride back. Hopefully, she didn't notice I didn't finish.

What was I supposed to say? *Hey, Tierney, sorry I couldn't make you come. Next time I'll try not to cream my pants the minute you look my way?*

So, yeah. The first couple times, I used her degradation kink as an excuse for my poor bedroom skills. Guilty as charged.

Now, I made her come, plenty. Never went as far as going down on her again—she wasn't going to see me on my knees on a regular basis—but I did make sure she was purring like a cat, humming with a satisfied smile before I found my release.

"Leave it," I told Jeremie, standing up from my seat at the coffee shop and shoving my wallet into my pocket. The call went to voicemail. "Where's Tierney?"

"Via Toledo." Nico flicked his cigarette to the sidewalk.

I grabbed my phone and pocketed it. "Text her that I'll be there in fifteen minutes and to wait for me on her knees in a changing room."

I didn't communicate with her directly when we weren't together. That would require unblocking her number, and I wasn't going that route, no matter how many times my dick was inside her.

"Now your brother's calling me." Jeremie arched an eyebrow at his phone as we exited the coffee shop and headed toward my Porsche.

Speaking of people I blocked. But that was a recent development. I'd blocked my entire family for the weekend.

"Which one?"

"Luca."

"Enzo's calling *me*," Fabio said. "Shit's hitting the fan. You gotta sort it out."

And I was going to. I'd face it all once I got home.

But for now, I was going to drown in her.

She wasn't waiting on her knees or in a changing room when I walked into the high-street boutique twenty minutes later. I was surprised she was even on the same continent, with the level of her defiance. She was wearing some sort of black corset minidress that made me want to kill everyone in the store for seeing her in it and the designer just for funsies.

"Oh, good. My errand boy's here." She shoved two sequined dresses into my hands with a scarlet smirk. Everyone at the store stared in shock, well aware I was Don Vello's son and one nasty son of a bitch. "Dark green or purple?"

She'd look good in a fucking trash bag, but I'd die before admitting it out loud.

"Sweetheart, the only thing I want to see you in is a coffin."

"Hmm." She trailed a pointy, black fingernail along my chest. "The fact you admitted to being obsessed with me kinda takes the sting out of the joke."

The only joke in the room was me, who kept talking a big game and still cleaning up her mess on the reg.

"Take 'em both," I said dryly, trying to push the realization I'd probably never get to see her in them to the back of my conscience. Far, far back. She *was* moving away and dropping off the face of the earth after this. I'd personally make sure of it. For her safety—and my own.

"If you insist." She tossed a third dress into my hands, reaching for a fourth on a rack laden with gauche frocks.

It was time I shoved something into that smart mouth to shut it up, and one of my organs was more than happy to volunteer as tribute. I tossed the gowns into a passing saleswoman's arms and muttered to her in Italian to have the eyesores waiting at the cashier, crowding Tierney toward the changing rooms wordlessly.

I wasn't mad at her. She was just doing what she did best—looking like sex on legs and acting like a teenager to piss people off. I was mad at myself for shitting all over the Camorra's entire operation for a taste of forbidden pussy.

Now, that's not to say I wouldn't do it all over again given the choice, but a man could acknowledge the sin he was committing and still fucking do it.

"Has it been three hours yet?" Tierney purred, refusing to cower. My big frame inched her slowly into a dressing room.

"And two minutes and thirty-seven seconds," I confirmed, flashing her my phone screen, where a countdown started every time I zipped myself up and stepped away from her.

She let loose a throaty laugh. "You're pathetic."

"I know." Hey, at least I had self-awareness going for me.

"And you don't care?" She elevated an eyebrow, taking another step backward.

"Not enough to stop this, no." I ate the space between us. Her back collided with the changing room's door. "I told you to wait for me on your knees."

"Did you, now?" She grabbed the collar of my shirt, yanking me closer with a provocative grin. "I try my best to block out the noise of men speaking to me."

No other woman ever gave me shit like Tierney did. No other woman ever defied me, fought me, dragged me out of my comfort zone. And no other woman ever would. I'd have to make peace with the fact my future wife, whoever she was, would bore me to death. And that every time I'd sink into her, I'd think of Tierney Callaghan. Until the day I died.

I raised my arm past her shoulder and pushed the door open. She collapsed backward, and I caught her by the waist before she fell, locking the door behind me simultaneously. She pressed her palms to my chest, gasping. "Nice instincts."

"Probably should've thought of that the time you tried to kill me."

"Can't blame a girl for trying." She hitched a shoulder up, pressing her back to the wall and arching her core against my ramrod-straight cock.

"How much is the dress?" I ran a finger along the velvet fabric between her tits.

"Eight thousand euros." Her smile was like a loaded gun. "Why? Are you starting to regret our littl—"

I bunched the material in my fist, ripping it from her body in one go. She gasped in shock as the flimsy thing fell at her feet. "On your knees."

She complied. Not because she was submissive, but because she knew she held all the power whenever she and my cock were in the same room.

Tierney unzipped my charcoal slacks, laughing derisively when my cock sprang out like a jack-in-a-box, a pearl of precum glistening the slit. She grabbed the base and took me into her mouth, swirling her hot, sweet tongue around the crown, squeezing the tip into a slit to scoop my precum, teasing me mercilessly.

Was there anything this woman didn't do mercilessly? I doubted it.

She palmed my balls—scraping them with her pointy fingernails, half-teasing, half-threatening, flattening her tongue against the underside of my cock and gliding it all the way down until she sucked my balls. I curled my fist, driving it to the wall with a low moan.

Of course she was good at sucking cock. Of fucking course. I was starting to see the error of my ways. Breaking up with her for trying to kill me was a disproportionate overreaction on my part.

I mean, was it really warranted? She only did it once. Everybody deserved a second chance.

If you give her another chance, she will *kill you and probably use your skin to make herself a new Birkin.*

That little stroll down memory lane doused the fire in my loins. Not enough to make my dick shrivel up in distaste—that would require some level of logic I didn't possess when it came to this woman—but enough to piss me off.

"That's enough," I growled, angling her head down and pushing my entire length into her mouth, making her choke and gag on it so that everyone in the store knew what we were doing. "Now take it like the good girl you'll never be."

She grinned through the discomfort, her red-rimmed, emerald gaze clashing with mine defiantly. Even on her knees, she was a fighter. She was always beautiful but especially when she cried.

Tierney bobbed her head back and forth, sucking the living fuck out of my cock, and I knew I wouldn't last more than a few seconds. More ammo for her to taunt me with, no doubt.

I still remembered the days when a single tear shed from her would send me tearing through the streets, rearranging faces and setting shit on fire.

A part of me missed those days. Caring about something, some*one*, definitely helped my psyche since my day job included killing people left and right.

Ramming my shaft past her stretched lips angrily while fucking her face, I felt the edge of her throat closing in, her gag reflex trying to pump me back out of her mouth.

I wondered if she knew what she looked like when she had sex. How lifeless her eyes became. How unmoved her expression was. No matter how hard I made her scream, no matter how good I fucked her through the mattress, an inherent hollowness lived in her features when we were together that reminded me we were screwing, not making love.

I only had twenty-four hours left before this trip came to an end and one more thing I wanted to do before we said goodbye.

I wanted to remind her of everything she'd lost and make her choke on much more than my dick—on regret. For everything that could've been if she wasn't so goddamn cruel and stupid.

Because I wanted much more than her body. Always had.

I wanted every piece of her heart and every last crumb of her soul.

CHAPTER TWELVE
TIERNEY

I had too much to drink.

That statement had been true about three glasses of wine ago.

Now? Now I was positively hammered.

I'd been holding up great the entire weekend, fucking Achilles like it was my job and I was vying for the employee-of-the-month bonus. I kept things light, casual, and toxic. I pushed my meltdown on the cliff into a drawer in my mind, where I also kept all the shopping site passwords I never remembered, pretending it never happened.

Normally, I abided by the one-drink rule to stay in control. But tonight called for liquid courage. I was trying to distance myself from what appeared to be the best date I'd ever had.

Was this a sick joke? Knowing Achilles, it was the only humor he was capable of.

On our last night in Naples, he'd decided to take me on a dinner date under the stars. The seaside restaurant offered outside seating, cozy ambiance, delicious pasta, and divine wine. The sound of the waves crashing against the shore cocooned me into relaxation, and I was loose-limbed from a chain of orgasms, a rigorous shopping spree, and hearty food.

After a weekend of showing me exactly what I was missing in the bedroom department, he was now determined to exhibit he was also capable of being a top-notch partner. A good fuck was a rare find. Good husband material? A mythical creature. Yet somehow, he turned out to be both.

The entire evening, he'd been attentive, soft-spoken, and in an agreeable mood. A total one-eighty from his surly, venomous self.

We bonded over neutral topics—food, vacation spots, our mutual hatred for the Red Sox.

Now he was just staring at me. Quietly. Contentedly Like a husband watching his wife, in a way that was both warm and familiar.

He seemed too pleased. Too sweet.

I knew it was a mind game. A way to make me squirm. I just didn't know his angle.

"So." I broke the disarming quiet, drumming my fingernails along the side of my wineglass, making the crimson liquid swirl and dance inside it. "Let's talk about your stalking tendencies."

I clung to our shared loathing like a lifeline. Hate fucks were familiar territory. Heart-to-hearts…not so much. And I especially didn't want to lower my hackles in front of someone who had every intention of kicking me out of his life tomorrow morning.

"I don't have stalking tendencies," Achilles said evenly. "I only stalk you. It's not a tendency. You're an anomaly."

I ignored the heat spreading across my chest. Stalking was *not* a healthy form of flirting. Even I knew that. I crossed one leg over the other. "Whatever. How often do you check on me?"

"Physically or remotely?"

I choked on my wine mid-sip, coughing into a napkin. "How do you check on me remotely?"

"Through your chaperones." He waited a heavy beat, studying me. "And through the camera I installed inside your apartment."

"There's a camera inside my *apartment*?"

"And a tracker on your phone, which allows me full access to it." He produced a cigarette from his soft pack, puffing it into life and hiding behind a cloud of smoke. "Which reminds me. Can you please stop texting Hamish? It's bad form to be doing that mere seconds after sucking someone else's dick. You're going to give me a complex."

The delicious heat in my chest quickly morphed into an inferno of rage, spreading into my veins like poison. The anger wasn't just directed at him but also at myself. I thought I'd been savvier than that. I had a strip of black tape on my laptop's camera, a VPN, and made monthly checks of my apartment to ensure it wasn't bugged.

Achilles read the embarrassment on my face and smirked. "You couldn't have found it in a million years. I was precise and strategic about where I put the camera."

"And where is that?"

"In the eye of the resurrection painting Lila gifted you for Christmas." Achilles winked, finger-gunning me. "Jesus's always watching you."

I didn't even *like* that painting. I only hung it because I knew how much it meant to my sister-in-law.

"You're going to hell."

"Was headed there with or without you."

"I should put a knife into your chest for that alone."

"If it makes you feel any better, you've done so much worse." He exhaled sideways, taking a slow sip of his wine. His first and only glass. "To answer your question, I check on you several times a day. I like to know you're safe. I like to know when you get home. And…"

"And?" I prompted, tilting my head sideways.

"To check you don't have nightmares."

"I don't. I mean…not anymore," I ground out. Again with this stupid, *stupid* pang of sympathy. I'd been so good this entire weekend, keeping it at surface level with him. And now *this*.

"No." He grabbed the wine bottle, topping off my glass. "But that's because you're in denial about what happened. Find a good therapist when you settle down at your new place. Fuck knows you need one."

"Well, if it isn't my knight in shining bulletproof vest." I crossed my arms over my chest, sitting back. "Don't pretend to care." My snark was my shield. It protected me from real conversation, which might lead to honesty, which might result in—God forbid—vulnerability.

He put his smoke out, scowling at the ashtray. "If I didn't care about your happiness, you'd be married to me by now, popping out babies left and right. I spared you."

"You'd marry me after what I've done to you?"

"In a heartbeat." His gaze, dark as his soul, held mine from across the table. "Nothing would kill you more than sucking my cock at the end of every day and making my dinner."

He was right. I was pretty sure if he made me marry him, I'd poison him.

"You almost forced me into marriage with a stranger," I accused. "How is that better?"

"It's not." He looked deep in thought, rubbing a finger along his chin. "I wanted to hurt you, to punish you for not choosing me. If Stefano caged you, I could live with myself knowing you were miserable, just as long as I didn't have to witness it every day."

An unfamiliar feeling clogged my throat. Intense sadness for what we'd become.

"I speculated you were the groom." I smiled, feeling tears burning my eyes again. *Goddammit*. I'd spent the last decade numb to everything around me. How could he undo so much in one stupid weekend?

Achilles smiled back. "We'd have made a terrible couple."

"A recipe for disaster." I agreed. "Harley and the Joker."

He shook his head. "You're no sidekick, Piccola Fiamma. You're the main event. Always were."

A tear slid down my cheek, and Achilles reached and scooped it with his index finger. For the millionth time, I loathed the simple fact I couldn't tell him the truth about what had happened that fateful day.

That it wasn't that I didn't love him.

I loved him too much.

I knew his only chance to get the happiness he deserved was by getting rid of me. I was faulty. Broken. So I made the decision for him.

And spent the last eleven years going from hating myself for making it to hating him for punishing me for it.

"How's your timer going?" I cleared my throat and looked away. Achilles never let anyone stare at his face for too long. He didn't like his scars and made a conscious effort not to be in the same room with his nephews, Nero and Ciro, worried he'd scare them.

"Didn't put one on this time. I wanted us to have one real date. No deadline."

"Why are you doing this?"

"Torture you, mainly. Is it working?"

"Yeah," I admitted. It hurt to see this side of Achilles. Laid-back and almost friendly. It was easier to think about him as the asshole who'd killed all my hookups and monitored my life in retaliation for what I'd done to him when we were teenagers. Now, I was reminded that there was more to him than a cold-blooded murderer. "Can you take me home?"

He stood and offered me his hand.

We walked out of the restaurant looking like a normal, loved-up couple.

The one we could've been.

It was a ten-minute walk back to the hotel, and I insisted we make it by foot. I needed to reorganize my thoughts and hoped the fresh air would sober me up.

Achilles chivalrously matched my sluggish pace, slowed by my three-inch heels and half a bottle of wine. It pissed me off that he was so agreeable.

Three Camorra soldiers trailed us, quietly surveilling the area.

This was our last few hours together. After tonight, I had to split and move away for good, leaving my entire life behind. We'd agreed on it, but I still struggled to imagine myself without my family, friends, and social circle.

By the time we reached our presidential suite, I was no more clearheaded than I had been ten minutes ago. He closed the door behind us, and I used the opportunity to pounce on him, jerking him close so we were flush against each other.

"Fuck me like a whore. It's what I deserve." I hoisted my legs up and vined them around his trim waist, pulling him even closer. His cock pulsated between us through our clothes.

This was my out. My off-ramp from all these pesky feelings he stirred in me.

"It's so cute when you pretend you can fight me." He clasped my jaw with one hand while he ground his shaft along my center. Goose bumps cascaded along my skin. "Like a kitty trying to take on a tiger."

I met him halfway, thrusting my hips, as we dry-humped against the wall deliciously, slowly enough to drive each other mad. I looped one arm around his neck, my other hand trailing his sculpted chest.

"Careful, Achilles. This kitty has claws. They might leave scars."

"You always do, sweetheart." His mouth latched onto the side of my neck, his straight, white teeth sinking into the sensitive flesh. "And I'll wear them like a badge of honor."

He devoured my neck, running his hot tongue along my pulse, nibbling softly, while I rode him through our clothes, running my fingernails along his back and leaving dents.

I darted my tongue out, tracing his stubbled jawline with the tip of it. I reached between us, unbuckling him with one hand.

Up until now, he'd only taken me either from behind or with a helmet. He never let me see his face, and we never kissed. His boundaries were clear, but I wanted to smash them to dust. I wasn't sure I had any hard limits anymore when it came to him.

His cock leapt free from his black boxer briefs. I ran my palm along the heavy shaft, thumbing a drop of precum and rubbing it. He groaned, his minty breath fanning over my face. My tongue traveled upward, tracing the edge of his bottom lip. His mouth, God, his *mouth*. I only had a hazy memory of what it tasted like, but it was delicious, like every dark fantasy I'd ever had. Mouthwatering and forbidden, conjured from the most depraved corners of my soul.

He froze and pulled away from me.

"F—Ford Prefect," he choked out.

CHAPTER THIRTEEN
TIERNEY

The words exploded and filled the space between us in a fog of smoke.

I reared my head back, confused. I didn't expect him to use the words. They were supposed to keep *me* safe, not him. Pulling away, I licked my bottom lip shakily.

"Are you… Did I…do something wrong?"

"No kissing." His nostrils flared. "I…can't."

I nodded, swallowing hard. "Okay. Yeah."

He caught my waist and turned me swiftly so my stomach was flush against the door. Flipping my dress up, he reached between my legs and dipped two fingers inside, spreading my wetness inside me. I was soaked and ready for him, riding on the edge of a dark spell only he could put me under.

Achilles kept every promise he'd made on that cliff. He flicked my clit, pushing the heel of his hand against my slit to form tension. I arched into his touch, throwing my head back, tears clinging to the tips of my lashes. His lovemaking seemed wild, intense, and chaotic, but I noticed how he took cues from me, how he withdrew when my pants became slower, shallower. How he pressed forward and gave me more when my breath hitched and my pulse picked up beneath his touch.

You don't need violence.

You don't need pain.

All you need is someone who would dedicate his entire being to giving you pleasure in the moment.

He brought me to my first orgasm before he entered me from behind.

An unpermitted moan tumbled out of my mouth. He grabbed my waist and stepped back while still inside me, walking me toward a TV stand across the room so I could bend over for him completely. Then he started pounding into me, fast and deep. My second orgasm hit me so hard I barely noticed him pulling out and finishing inside his palm behind me. Achilles groaned, striding into the bathroom and returning a few moments later with his pants immaculately zipped and two bottles of water in his hands. He handed me one. "All good?"

I pushed my dress down my waist and took the bottle from him. "Yup."

Jesus, why was I feeling…why was I *feeling*? Sadness, of all emotions, if you could believe it. But I wanted to kiss him again. I wanted his lips on mine. I wanted his forgiveness after remembering he could be soft when he wanted to be.

"Tierney."

"Hmm?"

"Look at me."

Rolling my eyes, I unscrewed the bottle cap and took a swig, giving him my back and swaggering to the bedroom. "Achilles, I don't have time for this sh—"

He grabbed my shoulder and swiveled me around, panting hard. Now he was staring at my face, not hiding what was plainly written all over it. Since the first time we'd broken up, I hadn't seen any kind of emotion on his face, and I forgot the effect it had on me.

"You're upset," he growled.

I snorted. "No."

"Why?" He ignored my denial.

Because you didn't kiss me. Because you bring me to an orgasm without hurting me, which never happened before. Because this entire weekend makes me feel like I'm a loose thread pulled at the seam, unraveling into oblivion, and once you stop tugging me apart, I'll be left bare and vulnerable and devastated. Because I'm confused, even though I shouldn't be. You're still the same man who'd kill me before he'd let himself admit that he's in love with me.

"*Why?*" he repeated, grabbing my face in his rough hands, his forehead pressed into mine. I inhaled him. Watched those scars I put on his face. And told him the truth.

"Because I can't blame you for not forgiving me. I haven't forgiven myself, eith—"

He crashed his lips to mine, grabbing the back of my neck and smushing our faces together. I yelped in surprise. Eleven years of hunger, desperation, and frustration poured into this kiss, which started more feral than any fuck I'd ever participated in. Our teeth slammed together, making him split his lower lip in the process, and blood leaked from the broken skin. I scooped it with a groan, my fingers twisting in his onyx hair and tugging him close. His tongue punishingly stroked the inside of my mouth, licking every corner to satisfaction. We kissed like the world was ending, pouring every single emotion we'd bottled up for years into that kiss. I rubbed my body against his, clamped my mouth on his tongue and sucked it like it was his cock.

We stumbled into the bedroom, still locked in this breathless kiss.

I released his lower lip with a pop, the salty taste of his blood flooding my senses and drugging me into a lull. "Fuck me," I demanded.

He was already hard and easing me onto the mattress, pressing the hard planes of his body against me. "Only if you don't break the kiss." He fused his lips with mine once again.

"I hate you," I moaned into his mouth. A reminder to myself, not to him.

"I hate you, too." He slammed into me, going deep, right at an angle that hit my G-spot. "So much sometimes it hurts."

And yet, we didn't break the kiss once. Not when I came, and not when he did.

Three hours later, we lay spent in sheets that reeked of sex.

"Tierney?" His voice entwined in the darkness like that was where it belonged.

"Yes?"

"I forgive you."

CHAPTER FOURTEEN

AGE FOURTEEN

At first, the boy came every week.

Then, every other day.

Finally, he started coming every night.

She knew he wasn't supposed to be there because he smelled like the subway: diesel, brake dust, takeout, and sweat.

He introduced himself as Achilles. Wrote his name in Russian on a piece of paper, which she tucked under her pillow as if he were a wish.

She told him her name was Tierney. He didn't need to write that down. Every fiber of her was etched into his memory like a bone-deep scar.

He brought her gifts. Italian pastries and CDs he'd burned with his favorite songs. Satin scrunchies for her delicate red hair, and two thick pocket-size books—the Oxford Russian-English Dictionary, *one for him and one for her.*

They leafed through the dictionary and pointed at words they wanted to say to each other. Getting to know one another was like peeling an apple slowly, paring the skin in one whole thread.

Slow. Careful. Oddly rewarding.

The raw anticipation of finding out what the other was going to say, the careful flip of the pages, the somersaults their hearts did in their chests made them forget the world outside of Tierney's bedroom.

A world where he was a stone-cold killer and she was the odd, broken girl her father and older brother were too cautious to approach.

One day, she pointed at a sequence of words.

"I am so sorry I still can't speak English."

He frowned at her, shaking his head and flipping through the dictionary to find his own words.

"I'll wait forever to hear your voice."

They grinned at each other, and she felt herself blushing all the way down to her little toes. He, too, felt like something inside him moved and shifted, rearranging itself in a way that made it less hard to breathe.

Their knees touched as they sat crisscross, and suddenly, he wanted to kiss her. Kiss kiss. *Not those quiet pecks on the temple he gave her before he slipped away into the night when they said goodbye.*

He had a dream, and it was a silly one, but he couldn't help it. He dreamed that this girl would make him coffee every morning. His mother made his father coffee every morning. And though there was no love lost between his parents, every morning was a quiet moment, of intimacy and camaraderie, when Chiara placed a steaming cup of coffee in front of Vello, and he nodded solemnly, accepting the gesture, as though it was a shake of hands, a hug, a statement that whatever this was, they were in it together.

They were almost fifteen, but he worried Tierney wasn't ready for that yet. All kinds of rumors flew around about what they did to her in the work camp where the Bratva kept the twins. Achilles made sure to punch whoever spread them, but they still gnawed at the corners of his mind.

Plus, he didn't know how to kiss. How to kill—yes. How to kiss—no. Even if he knew, what if all she wanted was friendship?

He pointed at more words, pushing down the foreign, all-consuming urge in him to touch her.

"I can't wait to hear all your amazing thoughts."

She put a hand on his knee, and a shot of pure pleasure zinged from his leg straight to his penis. The latter grew and stiffened in his pants, and he was fucked, fucked, fucked because there was no way he could keep his hands to himself for long, but he wasn't going to lose his only real friend, even if he had to chop off his own cock.

"I can't wait to share them."

A few months later, he crawled through her window, bruised and bloodied. His lip was split, his eye was swollen, and there was a gash along the entire right side of his face. His hands trembled so hard he couldn't gain control over them. She didn't ask any questions. Just ran a warm, wet cloth over the injuries on his face, standing between his legs as he sat on her bathroom counter. She did it again and again until the blood tired of spilling.

Achilles whimpered each time the fabric kissed an open wound. He didn't normally allow himself such blatant displays of vulnerability, but he knew, deep inside, that she didn't think less of him for hurting. Just like he didn't think less of her when those nightmares made her thrash and scream in her sleep.

"I did a terrible thing tonight," he croaked.

She shook her head violently. "I no care."

"I do terrible things every night," he corrected himself.

She gave him a sympathetic look.

"I ate a human heart, still beating, as I stared the man I killed in the face. All to impress my father."

The initiation.

Her stomach dropped.

"I...I feel like..." he began to say, then retched all over her. Threw up his dinner on both their clothes. He stared at her in horror. She stared back, calm and collected. She stroked his head. He whimpered in disbelief. "I'm—I'm sorry."

"Shh. You okay, Achilles."

If he needed to vomit on her to cleanse himself, she'd gladly let it happen.

Hell, if he needed to kill her to quiet the demons dancing inside him, she'd be a willing victim.

She'd do anything for him.

Even let him go if it meant he'd have a better life without her.

"Chelovek." Tierney kissed the split skin under his eye, gently brushing his hairline with her thumb. A fissure of pleasure rocked him from head to toe, pressure settling at the base of his spine. She was physically coated with his vomit, and she'd never looked so beautiful because she didn't even care.

"What does it mean?" he croaked. It had only been a few months since they'd met, but her grasp on English got better each day.

Tierney stepped from between his legs and brought the dictionary to him, leafing through the pages before stubbing a finger on the translation.

Human.

She called him human.

No one ever did.

Everyone thought he was a monster. His family. His schoolmates. The Camorra. He'd become one out of necessity, but he lived for those stolen interludes, the pockets of normalcy with Tierney, when he was just a teenage boy.

"Y—you think I'm human?"

She put a hand on his cheek. Kissed his forehead. He blushed.

"My dad… He says my ruthlessness is good. That I'll be the next don because of that. I'll be the most important man in the underworld." He was desperate to impress her.

Dunking the pink cloth into the bucket of warm water, she squeezed it and brought it to his wound again. He grabbed her wrist. She froze, her huge green eyes taking over her whole face.

"Promise you'll always be mine," he demanded, his voice void of the softness that came so easily to him whenever they were together. "I can't survive this life without you."

She nodded. She didn't understand exactly what he asked. But she wanted to give it to him.

Because he seemed like the only person in the world who understood what she was going through.

"Mine." He plastered his forehead to hers, heaving, breathing her in. "Only ever mine."

Several months later, Achilles brought over a book: The Hitchhiker's Guide to the Galaxy.

"It's a funny book, so you'll want to keep reading," he explained as he took his usual place next to her in her bed. She'd been having trouble with reading and writing, and he wanted to help her without making it obvious that he was doing so.

They still hadn't kissed, but in his fantasies, they did much more than that.

Even as Tierney's grip on English became better, even as she grew out of the childish frills and graduated to Golden Goose sneakers and cashmere cropped tops and designer leggings, he still had no doubt she was his.

Tierney was loyal to him. She loved him fiercely, possessively, her eyes glistening with the same lethal high he felt when they were together.

"I bring popcorn." She elbowed him, grinning.

"Bring some Coke, too. Oh, fuck, and something sweet. Chocolate, maybe."

Her smile was so big it almost split her face.

"Why are you so happy?" He laughed. It was addictive. Laughing. Smiling. Being casual.

"Because I understood every word you said."

"Oh yeah?"

"Yeah." She beamed.

"Well, let's see if you understand this..." He licked his lips. "One day you're going to be the mother of my children, Tierney."

Her smile collapsed, and she scurried to the kitchen, but he thought he saw her blushing.

Maybe she wasn't ready...? Of course she wasn't. She wasn't even sixteen, for fuck's sake!

Nice going, *stronzo*. You'll scare her off at this rate.

She returned with a bowl of popcorn with Reese's mini peanut-butter cups and Hershey's Kisses tossed in. They melted over the popcorn, making it stick into gooey clusters. He read the book to her out loud. Some jokes and words he had to explain. Most, she understood. She enjoyed the dry humor, like he thought she would. They blew through that series so fast, they barely slept that week.

When they finished the last book, he asked her who her favorite character in the series was.

"Ford Prefect," *she said without missing a beat.* "He is cool, like to party, and know how to survive. I want to be like him."

He couldn't imagine Tierney Callaghan wanting to be anyone else. She was a once-in-a-lifetime experience. So unique, so brave, the mere thought of her brought him to his knees.

"You're better," *he blurted.*

She gave him a heavy-lashed, meaningful glare. The kind his brother Luca told him to watch out for when he wanted to kiss a girl.

Then he remembered he'd rather die than lose her.

And for the first time in his murderous, psychotic, fucked-up life, he got cold feet.

CHAPTER FIFTEEN
ACHILLES

Fucking Tierney was a mistake.

Breaking all my rules for her? A catastrophe.

Forgiving her? The worst thing I could do for both of us. Because the hate was the leash that kept us away from each other. That reminded us this was a bad, bad idea.

I was a wreck. A mess. A goddamn disaster in a suit.

Wait, no. I wasn't even wearing a suit. What the fuck *was* I wearing? A pair of black denim jeans and a designer shirt ripped at the armpits Tierney had bought me on one of her shopping sprees. The shirt was neon green. She said it made my eyes pop.

My eyes are dark brown.

What the *fuck* was I doing?

Whatever it was, I needed to undo it, fast. Erase our entire weekend but especially last night.

So what did we have here? Let's see. First, I humiliated both of us by revealing I'd been speaking to all of her therapists (possibly more than she ever did). Then, I slapped her with my cock hoping she'd like it. Spoiler alert: she did not. Next, I confessed my obsession to her, proceeding to screw her like a rabbit in three-hour increments. I'd started a war with Sangue Blu without consulting my family. Rearranged the territorial borders of the Camorra Alliance. Went against Don Ferrante's orders, thereby betraying my clan. An offense punishable by death if I weren't the don's son.

All of this was fixable. *Maybe*. Somehow.

But one mistake wasn't—kissing her.

Feeling her lips against mine, remembering what they tasted like, and falling all over again.

I woke up with a sour mood and a headache. Tierney tried to be civilized with me, but so far I hadn't given her much to work with.

The entire flight to New York was spent giving her the cold shoulder. After a few hours of silent treatment, she finally caught on and retreated into herself, flipping through her fashion magazines and messing with her phone. A good development, as it allowed me to have a mental breakdown in the privacy of my own head.

My family had been trying to get ahold of my ass for the past forty-eight hours, threatening me with violent death. I wasn't worried about facing them. I was worried about not being able to keep tabs on her anymore. Of spending the rest of my life not knowing what she was eating, if she had nightmares, and whether I needed to kill someone who took out his aggressions on her in bed.

If she'd married Stefano, at least I'd have been able to keep an eye on her. Yes, Stefano would have gotten to fuck her, but I'd have been able to see her in Naples. Check that she was all right. That she was eating. That she was happy.

Once we landed, Tierney pushed her shades up her nose and uncrossed her legs, standing and thumbing her phone, probably to call an Uber. The urge to spend just a few more minutes with her—*alone*, without my soldiers—shredded every last trace of logic in my brain.

I stood and snatched her tote bag. The suitcases were left behind. She didn't need them, now that she was leaving for good.

"I'll drive you home," I growled.

"Thanks, I'd rather crawl on broken glass than spend another second with you." She smiled cheerfully, shouldering past me and stomping her way down the stairs.

"Wasn't asking." I made my way to the Porsche Cayenne on the tarmac. The engine was already running, and I knew one of my soldiers had made sure I had freshly brewed coffee waiting inside.

"Are you for real?" she called after me. I ignored her.

Seeing as I held her bag hostage, she slid into the passenger seat in my car, albeit with enough huffing and puffing to best an army of Karens. "Your behavior is bizarre."

Fair assessment. But not one that warranted a reaction.

"You know…" She clipped the seat belt on, reaching to reclaim her bag from me. "If this is a cry for help, you're going to have to be louder because nobody seems to give a shit."

We drove off into the midmorning New York traffic.

"Would you say something already?" she groaned. "This is probably the last time we'll see each other."

My head was killing me.

Fuck, fuck, fuck.

She couldn't go.

She *had* to go.

If she stayed, I wouldn't be able to protect her. Not from Vello, not from Sangue Blu, and not from myself. The walls of hate needed to be brought back up. It was our only chance at survival.

"I don't want to leave," she croaked, her body still pressed to the window as far as humanly possibly from me.

But you have to.

And I knew just how to make her.

By reminding her how much she hated me.

CHAPTER SIXTEEN
TIERNEY

"I don't want to leave."

As soon as the words slipped past my lips, I wanted to shove them back into my mouth.

He didn't deserve my words, and he sure as hell didn't deserve my vulnerability. Last night, he kissed me like the world was ending. Today, he wouldn't even look at me. The whiplash made me want to scream.

Plus, it hardly mattered. Achilles always had all the control in our relationship. If he decided something, I'd have to go along with it. Failure would be punishable by death.

Achilles didn't acknowledge my words, reaching for the glove compartment and popping it open. He took out his sunglasses case, retrieved his shades, and put them on.

"Make sure you have a fake passport, a couple burners, and enough cash to last three months," he said coolly.

"Don't worry about me. Wherever I go, you won't be able to get to me." I gave him a saucy side-eye.

"Nowhere far enough in this galaxy that I wouldn't be able to find you, Piccola Fiamma." He floored the accelerator, wrist draped atop of the steering wheel in a stance I found distressingly sexy. "But Coppola will try to retaliate."

"Against me? Why?"

"Because he knows what happened and probably reached the wrong conclusion that I care about you."

"I'm a big girl." I parked my sunglasses on my nose.

"Still a girl." He flicked his signal and turned into my Hunts Point neighborhood. "This is a grown-up game. Just do as you're told, Tierney."

He was unbearable and for no good reason at all. Yesterday was good. Even healing in some way. He told me he'd forgiven me for what had happened between us. Sure, I was pretty certain he'd done that because he saw how torn up I was about things. But why was he like this right now?

"Did something happen between last night and today to make you this insufferable?"

"Yeah." He smirked, giving me a mocking once-over. "I sobered up."

My face flamed with heat, and I turned to my window.

Two more minutes and you're out of his car and he's out of your life.

Fuck this two-faced dipshit with his hot-and-cold games. I was happy I'd never see him again.

"What, no comeback?" he teased.

I didn't answer, not trusting my voice not to break.

A few moments later, he parked in front of my building. I unclipped the seat belt, seizing my bag from between my feet.

"You're welcome for the ride," he had the audacity to say. But by this point, I'd regained my composure.

"Big of you." I flashed him a careless smile, hopping out of the car and slamming the door shut. I propped a forearm against the open window. "Wish I could say the same about the rest of you." I tilted my chin down to peer at him through the screen of my sunglasses, giving him a long, meaningful look.

"Thinking about my dick before we've even said goodbye." He sprawled back, his phenomenal abs traceable even through his shirt. "Love that for you."

"I hope I never see you again."

"You'll see me every time you close your eyes and touch your cunt for the rest of your life."

"Only if you left me with an unfortunate souvenir." I barked out a laugh. I didn't really fear an STI, though. Achilles was hygienic to a point of sterility.

"Don't worry, sweetheart. I came everywhere but inside that cunt of yours to make sure you don't get pregnant." He lowered his sunglasses a fraction, giving me a wink. "Couldn't run the risk of siring a redheaded bastard."

His words felt worse than being slapped in the face. Because every bad decision I'd made in my life somehow looped back to this—I couldn't have his children.

Losing my control and whatever was left of my composure, I rushed over to his side of the car and spat directly in his face. It landed square on his cheek. He stared at me icily but didn't wipe it.

"You shouldn't have bothered," I bit out, every bone in my body shaking with rage. "I can't get pregnant, Achilles. I have no uterus."

Leaving him with the secret I'd kept from him for fifteen years, I turned around and stormed away.

CHAPTER SEVENTEEN
ACHILLES

Drive, motherfucker. Don't look back.

I hit the accelerator and forced myself not to glance in the rearview mirror.

I couldn't fucking breathe.

"I can't get pregnant, Achilles. I have no uterus."

Things clicked into place.

You dumb fucking FUCK, how could you have missed all the signs?

In all of our time together—and the time after, when I was stalking her—Tierney never behaved like someone on their period. She never stocked up on tampons, never had cramps, never experienced a discomfort, an ache, a mood swing. I chalked it up to her being her—flippant, badass, untouchable.

I didn't have to wonder when and how it happened. I knew.

In that damn Siberian camp where she grew up.

I'd wanted to hurt her one last time, to have the last word. Craving to show her I could live without her.

The worst part? It was obvious that I couldn't. But turning around and apologizing for being a dick was the last thing she needed. I promised her freedom, and the truth was, she deserved it.

I'd meant what I told her last night: I *did* forgive her for what she'd done.

But I hadn't forgiven myself for the way I'd responded to it.

She deserved better than me. Whether or not she'd choose that for herself was another story.

My only consolation as I took the I-495 into Long Island to face the music was that we both got what we deserved in the end.

She got her freedom.

And I got a life of pure, unadulterated hell.

CHAPTER EIGHTEEN
TIERNEY

Two hours later, I sat on the edge of my coffee table, staring at the drywall I'd hammered into pieces and the now-not-so-hidden camera I'd ripped out and tossed on the floor. I did flip Achilles the bird before dismantling the device from the Jesus painting.

I hoped he caught it.

I tapped a flip phone against my thigh, squeezing the device for dear life in my fist. I'd been hiding it in the kitchen of Fermanagh's, the family-owned pub under my apartment, exactly for an occasion like this. Fermanagh's wasn't tapped, bugged, or wired with any Camorra devices.

Logic told me not to do what I was about to do.

Pride told Logic to go fuck itself.

I flicked the phone open and punched in the number I'd memorized months ago, just in case. Pressed the phone to my ear. Listened as the line connected.

Toot too—

"Rothwell." A curt, no-bullshit voice clipped out.

Drawing in a deep breath, I curled my fingers into my palm and pressed until blood gushed from the skin. "It's Tierney."

A hum of satisfaction escaped the federal agent. He had a massive hard-on for the Ferrantes. Bringing them down was his career goal, and he was one hell of a go-getter.

"It's about the flowers," I drawled.

"Where are you calling me from?" he asked evenly.

"A burner."

"Call a friend and ask them to meet you at your regular nail salon. Walk in there with them an hour from now. I'll wait at the back."

He wanted to make sure no one suspected I was meeting him. No doubt to protect his investigation, not me. From the little I knew about Rothwell, he was more ruthless than all the mobsters I'd met combined.

"I'm bringing a USB containing receipts." I hung up the phone and tossed it across the couch, closing my eyes. When I opened them, I studied my surroundings one last time, knowing I was never coming back to this place.

Once I got my bearings, I grabbed my real phone and texted my friend Jessa to join me for a mani-pedi.

Sure, her response popped up immediately. I'll fetch some coffee. Can't wait to hear about your Italian wedding!

Said Italian wedding seemed a lifetime away. One weekend with Achilles changed everything. Most of all, me.

My next phone call was to Sam Brennan, an underworld fixer Tiernan had on retainer.

"Yes?"

"Sam." I stood up and strode to my walk-in closet, pulling out a duffel bag. "Are you in Switzerland or the States?" He split his time between both.

"Boston." His pronunciation of the word left no room for doubt it was his hometown. "What do you need?"

"A fake passport."

"A good one?"

"Yeah. It needs to pass inspection for an international flight. Several, maybe. And every governmental system it'll be run through." I unzipped the duffel, tossing in clothes I needed. I stuck to basics—nothing flashy. Things that'd be comfortable to be on the run in.

"How soon?" he demanded.

I snorted. "Yesterday."

"All right."

"And…Sam?"

He didn't answer. Just stayed silent. I gulped. "Please don't tell anyone you're doing this for me or my new name."

"I don't work for the Ferrantes." He quickly did the math, his tone dry and oddly comforting. "I'm an independent contractor. As such, I have loyalty only to one person—myself. Call me from a burner in about two hours." He hung up.

My next move was to withdraw as much cash as I physically could, but I was going to do that after a shower.

I needed to wash away Achilles before I started my new life.

CHAPTER NINETEEN
TIERNEY

Despite nurturing a reputation as a high-maintenance hellion, I was still the same girl who grew up in a modern-day gulag. It took me less than five minutes to shower and brush my teeth. I slipped into a pair of jeans, sneakers, and a black top before screwing on a baseball cap and calling my bank on my way downstairs, notifying them I'd be withdrawing $10,000 in cash—the maximum most people are allowed to extract. I needed more than that, of course, but I had a good idea how to get it.

While at the bank, I asked the teller to transfer the rest of my funds—$30,000 and some change—to Tiernan's account. My brother had plenty of cash handy, and while I wasn't a big fan of asking for favors, this wouldn't even register as a loan because the full amount I was about to ask him for had already been deposited into his account.

Forever the control freak, my brother's name flashed on my phone screen before I fully stepped out of the bank, heading toward the nail salon across the street. I slid my finger along the screen, tucking my AirPods into my ears.

"The fuck have you gotten yourself into now?" he greeted, sounding more tired than angry.

To be fair to him, I did, in fact, veer off-script. Three days ago, he'd left me at a private airport, thinking I was off to live my best mobster-wife life. I was supposed to be in Naples now, choosing new curtains for my mansion.

"I undid the catastrophe you got me into," I said unapologetically. "I'm a single woman now."

The silence that followed told me he acknowledged he was wrong in handing me off to Coppola. "Tier—" he started.

"I don't have time for a heart-to-heart. I need thirty K in cash, but I guess you already gathered that."

"Why are you in the *States*, Tierney?"

"Change of plans. Achilles decided to let me go if I promise to move away and leave everyone alone."

"And Coppola?"

"Don't know, don't care." I pushed the rolled cash into my waistband. "He's Achilles's problem, not mine."

"What did you do to make him change his mind?" The edge in Tiernan's voice told me he already knew and wasn't above killing both of us for it.

"You're a red-blooded male. I'm sure you'll figure that out."

He groaned. "Do you need anything else? Other than cash and some fucking self-respect?"

"No, I got it all covered."

Knowing better than to ask me for any specifics on the phone, he said instead, "I'll have the money ready in thirty minutes. Meet me at my house."

"Give me a couple hours."

"I'll call Dad to come say goodbye."

I rolled my eyes, biting back a snarky reply. Tyrone was one person Tiernan and I had never agreed on. While he'd sired us, I'd never felt close to him. After Tier and I ran away from the camp at age fourteen and found our father, Tyrone explained he thought we were dead when his archenemy, Igor, had kidnapped us, carving my late mother's belly open when she was thirty-eight weeks pregnant. But I always thought it was peculiar that Tyrone knew his babies were taken—dead or alive—and hadn't ripped the world apart to find us.

And considering our so-called brother, Fintan, had betrayed us last year, resulting in Tiernan slaughtering him in a gruesome manner, I couldn't understand my brother's fixation with the Callaghans. As far as I was concerned, Tiernan was my only blood-related family.

"I'll try and get there before six," I said.

"Lila will be heartbroken."

"You'll come visit me once I settle down." I killed the call, spotting Jessa across the street. She waited for me outside the salon, holding two iced coffees and gossiping in a high-pitched voice on her phone. I waved at her with a wide smile. "Ready to be pampered?"

"Girl, *always*."

Showtime.

CHAPTER TWENTY
ACHILLES

"A disappointment." My father raised his walking cane, using it to smash my kneecap. I pressed my lips together, nostrils flaring, refusing to as much as groan. I was held by Fabio on one side and Nico on the other while Don Vello beat the shit out of me. It'd been twenty minutes, and so far, for a half-dead man, he was doing a pretty decent job.

"*Giuda!*" His cane smacked my abs next. My whole face was swollen, bleeding, and cut, and I still had to figure out how to stitch my own goddamn back when this was all over. "*Traditore.*" My father spat phlegm in my face. "I should put a bullet in your head and get it over with. Sacrificing an empire for a *fica*. You pathetic piece of shit."

"Do it," I snarled, blood trickling from the side of my mouth. My head lolled bonelessly. "Fuck knows I would."

Growing up, my father scarcely hit us. We were no strangers to his fist, but we needed to royally screw up to earn it. It had been a decade and a half since I'd last felt his wrath.

He was a surly *stronzo*, one without an ounce of compassion, and the only reason he spared our baby sister, Lila, from his fists was because he knew we'd kill him if he ever touched her.

"If you knew it was wrong, why'd you do it?" he roared in my face. Or tried to, anyway. He was frail and weakening more every day.

Though it was impossible to justify my actions, I did put some thought into it on my drive to our Long Island mansion. *But, Daddy, I wanted this pussy since I was a teenager* seemed like a nonstarter, so I went for a half-truth. Well, a quarter-truth.

Really, it was less than one-eighth true. It wasn't a complete lie, though.

"You negotiated a shit deal. One I'd have to agree to abide by once you kicked the bucket," I drawled in boredom. "Stefano doesn't deserve his stolen spots, doesn't deserve a discount on our supply, and doesn't deserve the redhead. It wasn't about her. But in the spirit of full transparency, fucking Coppola's bride was no hardship." I jerked a shoulder in a shrug. "Would do it again, provided the chance."

If my dick is still working after these beatings.

I hoped to hell Tierney was far, far away from this place by now. On a plane, sipping champagne, planning her new and exciting life. I hoped she was weaving a game plan in that gorgeous head of hers. Knowing Tiernan, he padded her pockets with cash and a few fake ID's to ensure she had everything she needed to start over. I stopped short of hoping she met a dashing gentleman in first class. A man headed in the same direction who'd take her on dinner dates every single week and wouldn't freak the fuck out because she kissed him.

Yes, I wanted her to be happy…but not *that* happy. I was still the only man for her.

Maybe if she was in a lesbian relationship…

Nope. Scratch that. No girls, either.

Anyway, where was I? Oh. Yes. Getting the shit kicked out of me by my father.

"You don't get to decide what's right and what's wrong for the Camorra." He sent a sharp knee straight into my ball sack, and finally, I fell to my knees, though I still didn't make a sound. "That's for me to decide."

"Empires sink all the time, old man," I hissed out. "Look at Pompeii. Did you really think I'd let you sink the kingdom we all built together?"

The soldiers were still holding my hands behind my back. I spat blood on the floor. So much I had to run my tongue over my teeth to ensure they were still there.

"You idiot, I *built* this empire."

"On mine and my brothers' backs," I retorted heatedly. "We get a say, too."

"Stefano is fuming. He rounded up all his soldiers and is planning an attack on us. Something big."

Vello sent another kick, this time to my sternum, rattling every bone in my body. That *did* make me groan, which apparently brought him satisfaction because he finally sighed and grabbed his gun from his mahogany writing desk, flipping the action open and loading the magazine.

"Nico, Fabio, sorry you had to see this."

"No problem, sir," Nico murmured from behind me. "We won't breathe a word about this."

"I know. Because this is where your journey ends." I heard the pops of gunshots through a suppressor as my father killed the soldiers who held me down. They fell on either side of me with loud thumps. "Have someone clean this up and spread the word Nico and Fabio went rogue in Naples." My father tucked his gun into his holster.

I grunted in confirmation.

He stepped forward and offered me his hand. I stared at it in quiet resignation.

"Did you fuck the redhead out of your system?"

"Yeah," I lied, taking his hand. He hoisted me up.

"Good. Good." He patted my scarred cheek. "Where is she now?"

"Far away, if she's smart," I muttered around what felt like a bucket of blood in my mouth.

Through half-shut eyes, I saw him smiling down at me, his psychopathy on full display. "Well, we're about to see how smart she is, aren't we, son?"

CHAPTER TWENTY-ONE
TIERNEY

Supervisory Special Agent Thomas N. Rothwell leaned against an ancient microwave on a cheap Formica counter, ankles and arms crossed, the picture of stoic brutality.

He looked completely out of place yet perfectly at ease.

The man had jet-black hair cut neatly and dark-blue eyes framed by thick-rimmed Clark Kent glasses. He had a jawline Hollywood heartthrobs could only dream of and the body of a Greek god.

Rothwell was the kind of handsome to make women stupid and men feel threatened. I'd tried luring him into my bed over the years—he was one of the few men I knew Achilles wouldn't be stupid enough to kill—but he appeared to be faithful to his one and only love: his job.

He acknowledged my presence by flicking his gaze my way and tucking his phone into a pocket, elevating a dark brow.

"Thomas N. Rothwell." I tasted his name on my lips as I swaggered in his direction, tipping my ball cap like a cowboy. "That's quite a mouthful. What does the *N* stand for?"

"None of your business." He brushed stray lint off his immaculately pressed shirt. A white-collared Gieves & Hawkes, if I wasn't mistaken, and I was never mistaken when it came to luxury brands. He'd paired it with tailored Dior chinos and Jimmy Choo leather oxfords. No visible logo on any of these items. Old-money telltale.

"Tell me, Mr. Rothwell." I dragged a teasing fingernail along the center of his muscular pecs. "Did the Federal Bureau of Investigation announce a budget overhaul I've missed? Last I checked, FBI agents—even senior ones like yourself—can't afford a seventy-two-hundred-dollar getup for a day in the office." My black nail traced noticeably sculpted abs, stopping at his thin Hermes belt, also logo-less. "Make that eighty-two hundred." I offered him a flirty wink.

He flicked my hand off, not a muscle in his entire face twitching. "See my previous answer."

"Refresh my memory?"

"None of your business."

Oh, he was good.

But I was better. And I needed to put my point across before I left this godforsaken place.

"You know, I've done my research on you. God forbid I put trade secrets in the wrong hands and accidentally harm my own family."

He stared at me with an eerily calm expression that sent a chill down my spine. He refused to humor me by asking what I found out. Just as well, as I wasn't about to keep him guessing.

"A bachelor's in computer science from MIT and a master's in legal studies from Cornell put you on the fast track into the J. Edgar Hoover Building. You were tailor-made for the FBI. Almost like you sought them out. You've been with the bureau for twelve years, and the only way you're going to leave is in a coffin."

No response. Just the disinterested glare of a man who found me as appealing as yesterday's microwaved dinner. I continued.

"You're the best in your field, and putting Don Vello in prison will be your golden ticket to promotion. Senior Executive Service, right? You want this, bad. You work twenty-five hours a day. No wife. No girlfriend, either. Also—and please don't take offense—very few friends, if any. You like your grandma, I'll give you that. But other than Jean Rothwell, the only person I could find whose name you included in your will, is already dead." I tapped my pouting lips, frowning. "Makes you wonder where all this motivation and hunger are coming from."

He glared at me, unimpressed. "You done?"

"Almost," I said cheerfully. "I am *very* interested in giving you the Ferrantes' heads, but I have a few hang-ups."

"Shoot."

"You can have Vello, Achilles, and Luca. But you're leaving Enzo, Lila, and Tiernan alone." I drew a line in the sand. "In fact, I will need it in writing that none of this blows back on my brother's family."

"I'm not interested in the Irish or the woman." The hard-ass crossed his arms over his chest. "I can give you guarantees they'll be safe. But Enzo's going down with his brothers. He's the enforcer, Tierney. Got a lot of blood on his hands."

I squinted at the tiny square window in the nail salon's kitchenette, tsking. "I'm afraid I can't help you, then."

"Of course you can." Tom pushed off the counter, hands tucked inside his front pockets now. He stepped into my personal space, a waft of his unapologetically masculine scent—musky leather, bourbon, and something clean and fresh—invading my senses. "You're driven by vengeance, and you've been wanting to see Achilles pay for his sins for years now. I can make that happen." His voice dipped low, burrowing under my skin and digging into the crevices of my conscience. "Give me information on the Ferrantes, and I'll give you his head. You'll get full immunity, a new identity, and security around the clock."

"There's only one problem with your plan," I said.

"Enlighten me."

"My love for my family has always outweighed my hate for my enemies."

"Enzo's not your family."

"He's Lila's. She loves him. And I love her. If you can't carve

Enzo out of this deal, I'm walking out this door right now." I swung my thumb to the front of the store.

Tom clutched his jaw. Clean, square fingernails. But I knew better than to buy into his slick-and-proper exterior. The bogeyman lay underneath. Someone quiet and frightening who thrived in the dark. "Give me two minutes."

He threw the back door open and disappeared to make a call. I pulled out my phone, checking my messages. My mind drifted back to Achilles. I was sure his day was as chaotic as mine if not more, after the stunt he pulled in Naples. And because I was a softhearted idiot, a pang of guilt pierced through my chest.

He made you choke on his cock. Slapped you with his dick.

Okay, but I actually *liked* those things. Just thinking about them made my thighs clench around nothing and fantasize about a repeat.

Truth be told, our weekend together wasn't what brought me to this moment with Agent Rothwell. Yes, he used me as his sex doll for forty-eight hours, but I initiated the deal and, with over twenty orgasms under my belt, was more than a willing victim. No. What made me sell Achilles and his father to the feds was the last decade of my life and the way he used it as a weapon against me—stalking, murdering my lovers, and calling all the shots for me.

Tom pushed the door open again, bathing the small room with sunlight. He closed it behind him. "You think Enzo'll turn against his family for immunity?"

"No chance." I folded my arms over my chest.

"Then the best I can do is look the other way when we come for them and let him run."

"Will you chase?" I squinted, studying him.

"Not for the first three or four days." Tom checked his phone for the millionth time before pocketing it. "I can stall them, but I can't stop them. As I said…" Tom lamented slowly, as though I was a petulant child, "Ferrante Junior has a rap sheet longer than a Dostoyevsky book. He is a murderer. Now that I secured your brother and his wife's freedom, how about we get down to business?"

It was time to fess up. I was the chink in the great Ferrante wall of security. But all you needed was one hole in a dam to drown everything. Though the alliance between the Ferrantes and the Callaghans was fairly new, I'd kept tabs on their business for years. I knew every dirty secret about their operations and had evidence to back them up.

"I'm leaving the country in the next few hours." I twisted off my ball cap and shoved it into my back pocket. "So the USB will have to do."

"Where're you headed?"

"None of your concern. Whatever you need, you're going to have to get it before midnight. Which reminds me—I have a few loose ends in need of tying. I better go."

He couldn't stop me, since the FBI had absolutely zero ammo on me. I was as clean as a whistle as far as they were concerned, so any information I had was going to be given voluntarily.

"Are you in trouble?" he asked.

"I *am* trouble, Agent Rothwell." I grinned from ear to ear. "Don't worry about me."

He raked his gaze over my face, pulling out a business card and a pen from his pocket and jotting something. "There's a safe apartment two blocks down from here. After you're done taking care of your travel arrangements, meet me there. We need statements and recordings to go with the evidence. I trust I don't need to tell you this conversation never happened."

I saluted him.

"Oh, and, Tierney?"

"Yes?"

"The USB." He opened his palm. Rummaging through my back pocket, I placed it in his hand. It was full of evidence I'd collected over the years of the Ferrantes' wrongdoings. Of course, I omitted every single bad deed done by Enzo and Tiernan.

"Straight to the apartment," Tom reminded me.

"Yessir." I half turned, about to return to the salon.

He threw a glance at my shiny black nails. "Go for short, colorless nails. Less distinguishable. And change the color of your hair, or they'll find you in two seconds flat."

He disappeared before I had time to thank him.

CHAPTER TWENTY-TWO
ACHILLES

"Was it worth it?"

Luca strolled into my en-suite bathroom, parking a shoulder against the doorframe. His gaze found mine in the vanity mirror's reflection as I put down the surgical staple I'd been using to put myself together.

Groaning, I spat blood into the sink. "Absolutely."

"Glad you think so." He tucked a cigarette into his mouth casually, lighting it. "Because she sold you to the feds."

Whatever forty minutes of straight-up beatings from my father didn't do, these six words managed to achieve. I gripped the edges of the sink, willing myself not to fall to my fucking knees and weep.

The pain was more than skin deep. It cut past all the human organs and etched itself into my very soul. The same way it did when they removed the bandages from my face when I was eighteen and I heard my mother mutter, *"Now he has a face to match the monstrosity of his actions."*

This deep, carnal brokenness that felt like the earth was pulled from beneath my feet.

Then came the rage. The anger. The insatiable need for revenge.

I knew exactly who *she* was.

And I could only imagine what she'd told them.

The worst part was, I couldn't even blame her. I'd spent the last eleven years destroying her life to come to terms with mine. Now that she was no longer on American soil, she felt safe enough to return a favor.

You're going to prison for the rest of your life, dipshit, her voice teased inside my head.

"Source?" I grabbed the surgical staple, using it to clamp my open wounds. It hurt like a motherfucker, seeing as I had no body fat to cushion the flesh.

"Tyrone." Luca blew smoke skyward. "Dad's been paying him under the table to keep an eye on the Irish since they got in bed with the Bratva. He doesn't trust Tiernan."

Nor should he. Tiernan's loyalty lay with my sister and my sister only, followed—not closely—by Tierney and Alex, the Bratva's pakhan and his childhood friend.

But goddamn, that was low of Tyrone.

Wait, why the fuck was I mad at Tyrone when his daughter was about to throw me into prison?

"How'd Tyrone find out?"

"Bugged Tiernan's place." Luca sidestepped a pool of my blood. "Don't tell Tiernan about it. He's still an outsider," he warned.

Unlike our soldiers, Luca and Enzo knew exactly what went down in Naples with Tierney during the weekend. Now they thought I couldn't be trusted with a fucking paper straw.

"How much has she given them?" I grabbed the antibiotic ointment from the counter and lathered my injured areas with it before reaching for a bandage.

A glint of pure malice lit in Luca's eyes as he watched my broken figure, something I'd never seen there before. We were the two competitive siblings, the ones fighting for the don position. Enzo had never showed real interest in taking over in any serious way.

Luca had shown good sportsmanship thus far.

Not anymore.

"A USB containing evidence. Fuck knows what. She didn't specify."

Fuck. This was bad. But maybe not *that* bad?

SSA Rothwell was going to need much more than random screenshots to pin us down. He needed witnesses on the stand, and his only source was now on another continent. Plus, we had every high-ranking federal judge in our pocket.

"And Tiernan?" I tried to swallow the lump in my throat.

"Trying to fix the latest mess his sister created." Luca pushed off the doorframe when he saw my hands were shaking too badly to apply the bandages. He quietly took the roll from me, wrapping it across my midsection. He kept his eyes on the bandages as he spoke around the cigarette in his mouth. "His friend at the bureau told him Agent Rothwell won't leave Tierney alone until she flips on us."

"A little hard to do, considering she hightailed it to a country with no extradition treaty with us," I muttered.

I was happy she was on the other side of the world because whatever was happening next wasn't going to be pleasant. For her. For us.

"She's still in New York," Luca said.

"What?" I roared, my abs contracting, making one of my stitches rip. Blood oozed from it on cue. "Why the fuck?"

"She wants to give a statement to the feds." Luca glanced at his watch. "Tiernan's restraining her in his house, negotiating a pardon with Dad on the phone. If you get out of here now, you can probably catch her."

"If I catch her, I'll kill her."

She's betrayed me before, when we were eighteen, and it took me this long to forgive her.

I'd never forgive her for what she did today, though.

"If you don't pick her up and deposit her at our father's, the Camorra will," he said matter-of-factly. "Are you ready for her to be treated the way we treat a female traitor?"

I was out the door before I even put a shirt on.

The ride from my apartment to Tiernan and Lila's suburban mansion should've taken an hour.

It took thirty-three minutes.

My baby sister answered the door, shoving herself into my path and blocking the entrance. She was a hundred pounds on a good day. I didn't even need to touch her. I could practically blow her out of my fucking way. And right now? I was tempted to.

"Achilles," she said my name, her voice, sweet and breathless, new to my ears. She gasped at my busted face. "What happ—"

"*Move.*"

That wiped the concern from her face. "So remember how you said I can always count on you in case I need a favor?"

"No."

"Well, *I* remember, and I beg you to—"

"Look, I appreciate your loyalty to the skank who's trying to put your whole family behind bars. But if you don't move your ass right now—"

"Please finish this sentence." Tiernan materialized from the hallway, sliding between me and his wife, shielding her with his large frame. "I've been dying to unscrew your eyeballs from your face for a while now."

"What happened to you?" Lila tilted her head from behind his shoulder. "You look awful."

"As opposed to my usual dashing face?" I drawled. "Listen, either you two move out of my way, or I'm bringing reinforcements. We both know how the Camorra handle a snitch." My mouth quirked. "I was gentle with your sister this weekend. My soldiers, however, would tear her limb from limb."

"Shit. That reminded me." Tiernan snapped his fingers, pointing at me with a good-natured smile. "I forgot to give you this."

He swung his fist and sent a stunning punch straight to my

nose. I heard the crack of my cartilage dislocating. Blood gushed out of my nostrils.

I did deserve it, though.

It took me a few seconds to swing back from the pain. And then I saw it behind Tiernan's shoulder. A flash of flame-red hair. My heart skidded to a halt. I didn't think I'd ever see her again. The need to strangle the life out of her made every nerve ending in my body twitch.

I had no idea how she and my sister became best friends. Lila was a softhearted romantic with frilly dresses, a sweet nature, and an inexplicable love for the color pink. Tierney was a filthy siren, half dryad, half goddess, who dedicated her entire existence to defying and destroying.

"Nobody's handing anyone anything. We're taking separate cars to your father's place and getting this shit sorted." Tiernan grabbed his jacket from a hanger. Imma, his maid and my childhood nanny, emerged from the depths of the giant-ass house, placing her hand on Lila's shoulder.

"Vieni con me, bambina mia." The housekeeper tried steering my sister away from the door. Lila threw Imma's touch off. She turned to her husband. From this angle, I could see the hearing aid hiding beneath the mass of her golden curls. She clutched her husband's face. "If I hear they touched a hair on her head, I swear to Christ, Tiernan, I'll shoot you again, and this time I won't miss."

"I know." He leaned down to kiss her mouth. He smoothed her hair away from her face. I'd have rolled my eyes if I didn't know it'd hurt like a motherfucker with my new shiners. "I promise you, *Gealach*, she'll walk out of this unscathed."

"Promise her the moon next. It'll be easier to achieve," I scoffed.

I was going to kill this woman, and I was going to make a spectacle out of it.

"Bring her out," Tiernan barked behind his shoulder. Two Irish soldiers escorted Tierney toward the door. They held her arms back, and my knee-jerk reaction was to pounce on both of them and break their necks. Then I remembered who she was and what she did to me.

"Missed me?" Tierney flashed me a dazzling smile.

I wiped the blood from my nose, giving her my usual don't-give-a-fuck expression. If she expected verbal sparring, she was mistaken—that ship had sailed when she'd stabbed me in the back. I spat at her feet. In response, she thrashed, trying to break the confines of her captors' arms and launch herself at me.

The soldiers tugged her back, dragging her into Tiernan's Mercedes kicking and screaming.

Before they pushed her head inside, I managed to call behind her back, "Watch out for her hair. It's still full of my cum."

CHAPTER TWENTY-THREE
TIERNEY

"You're going to tuck tail, shut your mouth, and let me do the talking."

Tiernan finally opened his mouth after a silent drive to the Ferrantes' mansion. I thought he'd read me the riot act as soon as we got in the car, but he didn't speak a word, which put me on edge.

My twin got out of the car, rounded it, and grabbed me by the back of the neck like I was a wild animal, guiding me across the winding pathway toward the grand double doors.

When I confessed to him over coffee that I spoke with Agent Rothwell, my brother went ballistic. I'd expected this reaction but not that he'd hand me straight to the Ferrantes. A few minutes after my confession, Tiernan got a call from Don Vello himself, demanding my head on a platter.

Someone snitched, and I didn't know who.

Considering Tiernan and I were alone in his backyard when we discussed it and that I didn't tell another soul, it left me wondering if Tom Rothwell was a dirty fed getting a paycheck from Vello.

It didn't make much sense, but who else could it be?

"What do I need the Camorra's pardon for, anyway?" I bit out, trying to shrug Tiernan's touch off my neck. He gripped me harder in response as he let himself into the mansion and led me up the curved stairway to Vello's office.

"If you don't get pardoned, you'll spend the rest of your life running. Vello *will* catch you, even from prison." Tiernan gave me a less-than-pleasant shove up the last stair. "And when he does, death would be a sweet, unattainable fantasy."

A chill ran through me. Tiernan kicked the door to Vello's office open, dragging me into the lion's den by the arm.

I'd been here before, when Tiernan negotiated his marriage to Lila. The office, like the man, was vast and imposing. Heavy mahogany desk, upholstered velvet settee, and a gold-plated mirror gave the room a dramatic flair, all bracketed by pictures of the Ferrante family. A legacy of violence, cruelty, and tradition.

Behind a chessboard with gilded, hand-carved pieces sat Don Vello Ferrante.

To his right stood Luca and Enzo. To his left, Achilles, the now-errant son. He looked like he'd been beaten to near death.

Terror twined around my spine. I was deep in enemy territory with no one but my brother to count on.

Going to Rothwell had been an impulsive mistake. I could see it now. I wanted to ruin Achilles's life, but I just might pay for it with my own. Moreover, handing him to Rothwell didn't feel half as good as I'd thought it would. Yes, a part of me loathed Achilles for all he'd put me through, but another part would forever remember him as the boy who gave me my first earth-shattering kiss.

"Tiernan," Vello greeted, not even sparing me a look. "Sit."

My brother assumed the seat in front of Vello, planting me on the one next to it.

For once in my life, I found myself shutting up despite myself.

"I respect you, Tiernan." Vello tossed an unholy amount of what looked like painkillers into his mouth and flushed them down with a tumbler of bourbon. "You're a decent husband to my daughter, accomplished in your field, and for the most part, you stay out of my lane. Your sister, however, is another story. Considering she's just landed us in a world of pain and possible imprisonment, I cannot allow her to leave this place outside of a body bag."

Fear twisted my gut into a tight knot. I'd come here against my will, counting on Tiernan to make things right. My twin brother had always been the smart, quick-witted, calculated one. But what if his calculation was wrong this time? What if these were my last few moments on planet Earth?

I knew Achilles would be happy to do the honor after what I did to him. Judging by the busted-up face, our weekend together cost him much more than the throne.

"The unwarranted hysteria is unbecoming." Tiernan crossed his legs, leaning forward to flick open Vello's cigar box and help himself to one. "No one's going to prison, and no one's leaving here in a body bag." He allowed a pregnant pause, grabbing a cigar cutter and pinching the tip. "Unless any of your men touches my sister, in which case, I'll have no choice but to kill them."

Vello narrowed his eyes. My brother continued. "Tierney gave Rothwell a USB containing next to nothing. She's not going to the safe house to meet him. He can do jack shit with out-of-context text messages that may or may not be fabricated. Rothwell doesn't have any more case against you than he did yesterday morning."

"How do we know she won't go to him?" Vello flicked his gaze to me, snarling.

"I'll be her guarantor. I'll personally escort her to the airport."

I kept my expression neutral, the heat of Achilles's unrelenting glare burning a hole through my cheek.

"I don't trust her not to come back and fuck shit up," Luca drawled.

"She won't." Tiernan puffed on his cigar, stinking up the place just for the provocation of it. "We've reached an understanding. Tierney was rightfully upset after your brother made her his *prostitute* for the weekend." The word seared my skin, branding it. "For this alone, you're lucky I haven't started a war. Anyway, she's over it now and ready to move on."

"Just to set the record straight, your sister threw herself at my feet and begged to be fucked," Achilles said evenly, his eyes never wavering from mine as he spoke. "Didn't you, Tierney?"

I slammed my teeth together, swallowing down a venomous remark. Now wasn't the time to sass back. I needed to get out of here.

"You've lost your privilege to talk directly to her," Tiernan announced to his brother-in-law. Guilt rolled through me. They were so close before our trip to Naples. "For the duration of this conversation, everything you say and do goes through me. Understood?"

Achilles sneered. "You can't keep saving her forever. Sooner or later, you'll lower your guard and someone will catch her."

Tiernan turned to Vello. "We're wasting time here. She needs to get on a plane before Rothwell gets his hands on her. He'll try every loophole in the book to drag her into their headquarters and make her sing."

Vello shook his head. "I'm sorry, son. I can't let her walk away free. She's a traitor."

"Here's what's going to happen." Tiernan uncrossed his legs and put out the cigar in an ashtray. "If you don't pardon my sister, I'll gather up every Irish and Bratva soldier on this continent and conquer every single Camorra territory on the East Coast. Now that Alex and I are in business, I have the means and the manpower. Don't give me the motivation, too."

Tiernan and Vello stared down each other. The silence in the room felt loaded like a gun.

"You won't dare," Vello hissed out finally.

"*Try* me."

Apparently, Vello didn't want to do that. He blinked first, his gaze skittering toward me, his mouth coiling in open distaste. "I suppose we could make it a lesson."

I doubted he could teach me anything worth learning but kept my mouth shut. My brother was putting a lot on the line for me and not for the first time.

"What'd you have in mind?" Tiernan asked.

"She should take the knee and kiss the ring." Vello pushed up from his seat, using his cane. "Swear loyalty to the Camorra before she leaves."

I barked out a sarcastic laugh.

To my shock, Tiernan nodded. "That's fair."

My head whipped to him. *"What?"*

"Do as he says." Tiernan stood.

Vello rounded his desk, leaning against it in front of me. "On your knees," he snapped.

"Like father, like son, huh?" I sneered. *"No."*

"I see you chose violence today," Enzo said mildly. "Maybe reconsider? Your head's too pretty to roll on my floor."

"I choose violence every day." I hitched a careless shoulder up. "And I'd rather die than cower to this asshole over here."

"*Tierney*," my brother snapped. "Get it over with."

The silence cascaded along my skin like knuckles a second from delivering pain. I looked between every pair of lifeless eyes in the room. They were really going to make me do this.

Pushing a scream down my throat, I forced myself to slide down my seat until I was eye level with Vello's crotch. Every inch of me trembled with anger and humiliation. I couldn't breathe I was so furious.

"Kiss the ring, Miss Callaghan, and all will be forgiven." He extended his hand toward my face. He had a pinky ring—worn out, with something in faded Italian engraved on it.

My knees scraped the lush carpet, and memories from the gulag poured into the front of my mind. My ears buzzed as mounting pressure rose inside my head.

Bend the knee.
Open that mouth.
Take out my cock.
Yes, that's right, Irish slut. All of it.

The cold bronze of the ring bumped against my lips, urging

me on. The noise in my head intensified, and the small girl that lived inside it—the one I left behind in Russia—let out a shrieking scream.

I opened my mouth and bit off his finger, clean with the damn ring.

"*Puttana di merda!*" Vello held his wrist with a yelp, jerking his hand back. He staggered to the floor, slithering in pain, a venomous snake who'd just gotten a taste of his own medicine. His finger was hanging loosely from his hand. I spat his blood on his face and pushed to my feet.

I stumbled backward, heaving, my back crashing against my brother's chest. He shoved me behind his back, his pistol already drawn and aiming at his brothers-in-law.

"*Move.*" Luca pointed his gun at my brother, his eyes telegraphing fire. "That's twice she blew her chance at redemption. Get out of my fucking way, or I'm taking you with her."

"Go ahead." Tiernan didn't budge. It actually surprised me, and I swallowed back tears. I knew my twin brother was madly in love with his wife. He adored his new life with their son and had even formed a brotherhood with the Ferrantes. His loyalty rendered me speechless. "Make your godson an orphan."

Enzo helped Vello to his feet, tossing his father's arm over his shoulder as he escorted him outside to be medically treated. My heart was in my throat. The taste of Vello's blood sat heavy on my tongue.

"She's a traitor," Luca said.

"She's my *sister*," Tiernan reminded him.

Achilles stood in the corner of the room. His rage was quiet and dignified. His gun was cocked but aimed at the floor. "Let her go," he told his brother.

"What are you talking about?" Luca threw him a scowl. "She's sending you to *prison*."

"Let. Her. Go." Every word was rasped lethally, quietly, and with deathly determination. Slowly, Achilles turned to his brother, fixing the barrel of the gun on his head. He clicked the safety off.

"You won't." Luca snarled.

"In a heartbeat." Achilles's voice dripped malevolence.

"*Fuck.*" Luca lowered his gun, exhaling sharply. "Dad's gonna kill you."

"I'll deal with him." Achilles turned his attention to Tiernan, still holding Luca at gunpoint. "Callaghan, get your cunt of a sister out of here before my charitable mood sours. Deposit her at the airport and make sure she goes far, far away. And you"—his gaze landed on me—"next time I see you, I'll kill you. Make sure I don't see you ever again."

CHAPTER TWENTY-FOUR
ACHILLES

"Damn, that was one hell of a bite." Enzo took a swig of his protein shake. "I'm surprised you let that mouth anywhere near your dick, bro."

"Luckily I'm up-to-date on my tetanus shot," I muttered, pacing my parents' living room, waiting for my father to reemerge after getting stitched up by the family doctor.

"Yeah, some luck you've got there." Enzo let loose a rancid burp.

"Bro, those protein burps are lethal. Stop drinking these shakes around us," Luca grumbled.

"I can't help it, okay? I have to hit my protein goal and that means a shake every three hours. This physique doesn't just happen." Enzo gestured to his admittedly sick form. "You are what you eat."

"If that were true, you'd be a bag of dicks," Jeremie said, eyes hard on his phone as his thumbs flew over the screen, per usual.

"Jeremie," Luca barked. "Get the fuck out of this room, and never speak to a Ferrante like that again."

Jeremie complied without even looking at any of us, shrugging off Luca's shit-ass attitude. Enzo quirked an eyebrow at Luca. "Someone's in a sour mood."

"You shouldn't let him speak to you like that," Luca said, just as my father entered the living room. His left hand was bandaged into a tight fist. His pinky was gone. The doctor had to remove it. In the end, he'd learned the lesson Tierney had taught me years ago—that she was an untamable force, born to defy whoever tried to clip her wings. I had nothing but respect for her. She had more courage and fire than all the mobsters I knew combined.

The room fell quiet as Dad assumed a seat on a plush recliner. Enzo stood and lit a cigarette for my father and handed it to him.

He took a long drag, closing his eyes. "I'm sending an assassin to deal with her."

"A paid wet worker?" Enzo flipped his pocketknife in the air. "*Rude.* Why not one of us?"

"You're needed in New York, Luca needs to go clean up the Sangue Blu mess your brother has created, and Achilles made it clear he would follow this woman to hell." My father rolled his cigarette between his thumb and index, staring into space.

"All Achilles needs is to escort her there," Luca drawled. "But he needs to be the one who kills her because he's the one who screwed all this shit up."

"It's not as simple as all that. She's family," I contributed to the conversation.

"A family member who handed your neck to the feds before your cum dried inside her," Vello clapped back.

"Lila won't be happy. And Tiernan will likely start a war bigger than the one waiting for us in Naples," I countered calmly. Things were complicated as it was without throwing a murdered socialite who was in bed with the feds into the mix.

"Every war has its casualties," Luca said tonelessly. "Tiernan knows that."

"Would you have let him kill Lila if she went to the feds?"

Enzo visibly shuddered. "I'd kill anyone who comes near her."

"Tierney's not Lila. Our sister minds her own business," Luca parried. "And if Tiernan has an issue, he can take it up with me."

I stroked my chin, working this in my head from all angles. I usually enjoyed wet work. Killing quieted the noise inside my head.

Tierney, however, was a different matter altogether. But that's precisely why I had to take this job. I needed to kill the one thing more powerful than my lust for the crown—to eliminate the only person who could be an obstacle on my way to world domination.

She was my Achilles' heel.

But I wouldn't let her bring me to my knees. Not again.

"How do we know we won't raise FBI suspicions by offing her?" I asked. "Killing her would cut through all of the preliminary red tape that's stopping Rothwell right now. He'd get access to our computers, phones, documents. Search warrants would be issued. Maybe even a few arrests."

"We're going to get rid of her offshore," Dad said decisively. "No body, no crime."

"I still think it's less of a headache to incarcerate her somewhere far away," I argued.

"If you don't want to take her out, I'll do it." Luca unbuttoned his cuff links, rolling up his sleeves. "Naples can wait a few days. It's not like Coppola's going anywhere."

"Why would I not want to take her out?" I huffed.

"Oh, I think we all know the answer to that question." Enzo rolled his tongue to the side of his cheek and curled his fist, mimicking a blow job.

"Either you put her down humanely, or I'm sending Tristan Hale to do it." My father turned to me. "He'll make a show of it. You know his style."

Hale was an assassin for hire. A private contractor. And a very twisted son of a bitch. No, thank you.

"I'll do it," I said flatly. Fuck it. I'd done worse and for much less.

Tierney Callaghan wanted me dead.

I wanted her, *period*.

Seemed like neither of us were going to get what we wanted.

"Don't let me down again," my father warned. "You hear me?"

"Loud and clear."

"This is your last chance, Achilles. If you don't kill her this time..." My sire leveled an emotionless look at me. "I'll kill you both myself."

I believed him. If I couldn't do it this time, I'd be a liability the Camorra couldn't afford.

On my way out of my parents' house, I pulled out my phone and unblocked her number. The last message she'd sent me, from eleven years ago, popped up immediately.

> Tierney: Please, would you just let me explain myself? I'm begging you.

I knew she was going to get rid of her smartphone before boarding a plane, just as well as I knew she was downloading all her data right about now, just in case. Tierney was a smart, seasoned Mafia princess. I had no doubt I'd catch her—just as I knew she'd make it challenging.

> Achilles: I'm giving you a 24 hour head start, then I'm coming for your throat.

Two blue lines decorated the screen.
My heart nearly beat out of my chest.

> Tierney: Why'd you let me go in the first place?
> Achilles: No one deserves to kill you more than I do. I wasn't leaving it to chance.

The truth was, I thought Vello might give her another chance. He didn't. Now I had to eliminate her from our cat-and-mouse game. No matter. It was all becoming way too messy anyway.

> Tierney: So you're assigned to deal with me.
> Achilles: Yes.

> Achilles: It will be relatively painless.
> Tierney: He was going to send Tristan Hale after me, wasn't he?
> Achilles: Yes.

She was typing for a while, but nothing came through. The screen darkened before my phone flashed again.

> Tierney: Thank you. And if I manage to catch you before you do me, I promise to make it painless, too.

I watched her last message, my throat catching. So it had come to that. One of us was finally going to kill the other.

> Achilles: May the best person win.

CHAPTER TWENTY-FIVE

THEN

She'd become the belle of the ball seemingly overnight.

The most popular girl at her high school. Hottest cheerleader on the squad. Watching her from the shadows—something he did often once he realized their time together wasn't nearly enough for him—made him both proud and feral with possessiveness.

Her accent was now so flawlessly American no one could ever guess she'd set foot outside this country before. She'd reached full bloom, and he could finally see who and what she was under the thorns that hid her.

Tierney Callaghan was witty, fashionable, and mysterious but also kindhearted.

He'd watched her stand up to bullies on behalf of the quiet kids, discreetly pay for other people's lunches, and always speak her mind, even when her opinion differed from the mainstream.

Boys were enamored with her, begging her for a chance. She rejected all of them.

"I have a boyfriend," she announced proudly each time some poor bastard mustered up the courage to approach her. "He lives in Long Island. You don't wanna mess with him."

Achilles knew he was the boyfriend, even though he was still too chickenshit to kiss her. They did everything else, though. He took her to the movies, snuck into her room every night, bought her flowers and gifts, and listened to her vent for hours. She did his homework for him. Stitched up his wounds and kissed them better. Never judged or berated him for what he did.

She was untouchable. Goddess tier. And under his protection.

One night, she was invited to a house party where she'd gotten drunk. It was the first time she drank alcohol. It was just two Solo cups, but it made his stomach churn with worry and protectiveness.

He watched from the window, behind manicured bushes, as she gobbled up the neon-red liquid, ready to pounce when needed. He wasn't leaving anything to chance. He'd let her have her fun but keep her safe in the process.

Eventually, at eleven, the host announced she didn't want to get in trouble and sent everyone home. Tierney staggered on her too-high heels out the pretty colonial house, zigzagging into the night in her apartment block's direction.

He stayed four or five paces behind, stuffing his hands into the pockets of his bomber jacket, lowering his head to stay incognito. They'd texted all night and she promised him Tiernan was going to pick her up, but of course, Tierney being Tierney, she didn't want to bother her brother.

It was fine by him, though. He never trusted that fucker with her precious life the way he did himself.

They were almost at her building when she turned around sharply out of nowhere and tossed her arms in the air. "Why don't you kiss me?"

It took him a moment to get his shit together and realize she knew he was following her. And that the part that bothered her wasn't the fact that he did but that he still hadn't kissed her.

Tierney parked a hand on her waist. "Well?"

"I—I—uh." Very eloquent, Achilles. Great fucking job. Please join the debate club, you verbal wizard, *he thought.*

"And don't tell me it's because you're not attracted to me." She stubbed her finger in his face, stepping closer. *"Because I see the way your pants*

tent every time I touch you." Pause. "Which is A LOT." Another pause. "God, you're really bad at social cues, huh?"

He wanted the earth to open up and swallow him whole. "H—how long have you known I've been following you?" he stammered.

"Since the first day I met you?" She stopped herself from snorting incredulously. Something about the warmth in his eyes completely dismantled the frustration she'd built over the months and years against him. "You're not as discreet as you think, but don't change the subject."

He wouldn't dream of it. He decided early on he'd give her the truth. He respected and cherished her too much to ever lie to her.

"I—I thought you wanted to be friends."

"That's the last thing I want!" she cried out. "I want us to be together. I want to consume every fiber of your soul and body. That's what I want."

"Y—you do. I mean, you are," he choked out. "I was just scared you'd reject me."

"Why would I reject you?" She raged, grabbing the collar of his jacket, wanting to shake him. "I spend every free moment with you and refer to you as my boyfriend. What more do you need?"

"I—I can't lose you." The very thought sent a violent shiver down his spine. She wasn't a crush or a high school sweetheart or any of that crap. She was his life. Plain and simple. The only good thing about his day.

"Is it because our families would never let us be together?" She put a hand on his cheek, tilting his face down to look at her. "Is it because your father would never accept me?"

"N—no. I don't care about any of that. I only care about you."

"I only care about you, too."

His face was ablaze. Not even his natural deep tan could hide what she did to him.

But ultimately, she was braver than him because she took the step necessary to eat all the space between them. Their bodies collided, molding into one frame. She ran her fingers through his hair a delicious shade of chestnut brown she wished his children would inherit when he found another girl—a *whole* girl—to marry and have children with. She *couldn't have him forever. But she could have him tonight. And tonight would have to be enough for her.*

He trembled against her flesh, and she wanted to die, die, die, knowing he'd one day marry someone else.

She did it again, testing her power over him as if she'd discovered a new magic, this time running her fingers along the side of his face. Another quiver rocked his body, making him stagger back.

"Chelovek." She brushed the tip of her nose against his, taking his cheeks in her hands, and breathing him in. The look on his face broke her heart into a million pieces. He looked panicked, almost in pain. She wondered if it was because she was touching him or because he was being touched at all. She guessed it was a bit of both. He was starved for human affection. She closed her eyes, forcing herself to pull away. "If you don't want to kiss, we don't have to. I was just kidding," she whispered, stroking his face. She had an odd sensation, like her heart was swelling, becoming much bigger than something her rib cage could ever contain. "Well, half kidding. I'd love to kiss you, Achilles, but I'm willing to wait. We've both been through so much and I never want to..." She swallowed. "I never want you to feel like you have to do something you don't want to. I'll call you tomorrow." She kissed his cheek gingerly and shot him a nervous smile, her facade slipping.

No one ever managed to peer past the mask she put on when she faced the world. No one but Achilles. He saw her for who she truly was. And he loved her all the same.

He stared at her pleadingly, desperate for something he didn't have words for. She turned around and walked away. Her knees were jelly.

Keep walking, *she told herself.* Give him his space.

This was the part where he'd grab her waist and kiss her silly. A passionate, all-consuming kiss that'd put every Hallmark movie to shame.

It didn't happen that way.

In reality, she took the first, then second, then third stair to her building. When she reached the fourth, she heard a loud thump. She turned around. Achilles was at her feet, planted face down on the sidewalk.

"What happened?" she gasped.

"I tried to kiss you, but then you turned around too fast, and..." He didn't have to finish.

She rushed down, falling to her knees, just as he rose up. Their heads knocked together. She laughed. He sucked in a breath. And then he put his lips on hers, both of them on their knees.

It was their first kiss, and as such, it started clumsily. The pressure was too soft, then too hard. When they opened their mouths, their teeth clashed, and they grinned into each other's lips. She was the first to taste him, but once he had a taste of her, the monster he kept so tightly leashed around her broke off its chains. He grabbed the back of her neck and jerked her close. His arousal throbbed through his pants, and she ground against it on pure instinct, grinning as he let loose a wretched grunt. His tongue explored her mouth, and she linked her hands over his shoulders, moaning into his mouth.

"Is this okay?" He broke off the kiss for a second, dropping his gaze to watch the space between them as her sex rubbed against his penis like she was trying to light them both on fire.

"Yeah," she panted. "Oh God, yeah."

Their lips fused back together.

Tierney's happiness at finally being kissed by him was quickly replaced with an urgent fireball of a knot between her thighs. A delicious, warm pressure she needed to unfurl.

They kissed and ground against each other until their lips were raw, their mouths dry, their breath a little sour.

Achilles stood up first, helping her to her feet with gentle hands. He kissed the back of her hand and grinned. "Will you marry me?"

"Now?" She giggled, but inside, her flame had been doused. She'd heard Don Vello had great plans for his favorite son. He wanted Achilles to marry underworld royalty. Someone from a sizeable organization, like the Outfit or the Bratva.

"Not right this second, but as soon as we're eighteen," he said.

"But your dad—"

"He'll be fine," he said, cutting her off. *"I'll deal with him. He cares more about heirs than about pedigree anyway. I'll figure it out."*

Another thing she couldn't give him. Heirs to continue the Ferrante legacy.

"No one's ever gonna believe you're my girlfriend." He wanted to shout it from the damn rooftops. *"I'm a weirdo loner at my school and you're Little Miss Popular."*

"Then how about some proof?" She pulled out her burgundy lipstick, applying it to her luscious lips, and pressed an open-mouthed kiss to the side of his throat. "Here. Something to remember me by."

"This sounds like a goodbye," he accused.

She shook her head. "We rarely know when will be the last time we see someone we love. So I want to make sure every time we say goodbye, I make you happy."

"You wanna make me happy?"

She nodded. "More than anything."

"Then promise me one thing."

She stared at him expectantly.

"That we'll always be honest with each other."

"Always." She already knew she was going to break the promise. She couldn't tell him why they couldn't marry. The shame was killing her.

"Truth?" Achilles asked.

"Truth." Her voice trembled.

"You're the only good thing about my life."

His next stop from her doorstep was a tattoo parlor down the street. He inked her kiss to his neck, a reminder he belonged to her and always would.

At sixteen, it was his first tattoo, and he didn't know it yet, but he'd spend the next decade inking every last inch of his body, chasing a thrill that would never come again.

On his way back home, he pushed away the tiny bit of doubt that always bothered him.

The fact that her eyes never smiled when she did.

And that her laugh seemed to die as soon as she was sure no one was watching.

That every time he spoke about the future, she retreated to a place in her mind where he couldn't reach her.

And that she felt very fucking temporary, for something he wanted to hold on to forever.

CHAPTER TWENTY-SIX
TIERNEY

I tossed my phone into the trash halfway through my journey from Long Island to DC. Tiernan dropped me off at JFK, but I knew better than to get on a flight there.

Achilles could find anyone anywhere. He put bounty hunters to shame. I'd seen him in action. If I knew him well—and I did—he'd already assigned several soldiers to every international airport in the tristate area to watch who was coming and going. Pure instinct told me to delay my departure by a few hours and cover my tracks with some unexpected detours. Paying a visit to my BFF, Francesca Rossi-Keaton, aka, the First Lady, was just what the doctor ordered.

She had a luxurious apartment in DC with presidential security, exactly what I needed right now. It would give me a few hours to recalculate my route, examine my options, and fly out of an airport that wasn't necessarily on Achilles's radar.

"What kind of trouble did you get yourself into now?" She opened the door when I reached the skyscraper penthouse she used whenever the White House got too crowded. I muscled past her, tossing my backpack onto her leather couch. I'd had to ditch the duffel when I realized the Camorra was after me. The less baggage, the better.

"I need a few things from the convenience store downstairs. Can one of your bodyguards fetch them?"

"I guess..." She slanted her head sideways, her face etched with concern. Frankie and President Keaton had three children, even though she was my age. They'd started young. Well, she had. He was way older than her.

I knew I was considered an attractive woman, but Frankie? Frankie looked like a Disney princess.

"What's going on?" Her bright-blue eyes took over her face, framed by dark lashes to match her curly, long, dark hair.

"I need to disappear," I said shortly, and because I knew where this was headed, I added, "And no, Wolfe can't help me get out of this one. I just need your help."

She nodded. "Okay, anything."

I sent one of her bodyguards downstairs to buy hair color—black—large cheap sunglasses, and scissors. I couldn't pass the latter through airport security, but I needed to have one weapon with me at all times.

Francesca applied the dye to my hair, and while I waited, I went through her closet, picking black, bland clothes and stuffing them into my backpack. I then slid into a shapeless pair of pants and a matching long-sleeved shirt. Frankie washed my hair in the sink, scrubbing my temples clean of residual color. When I looked in the bathroom mirror again, I looked like Morticia Addams. It was jarring. My hair was a part of my personality. I'd never changed its color before. But I had no choice.

"You're freaking me out." Frankie planted a fist to her mouth when we sat in the open-plan kitchen in front of a plate of lasagna she'd microwaved for me. I wolfed it down. "At least let me give you some cash."

"I have more cash than I can carry." I flashed her a thankful smile. "I'll send word when I arrive at my destination to let you know I'm okay."

"Is this about the Ferrantes?" she demanded, delicate brows furrowing. "My family is in the Outfit. One word and I can fix—"

"No, no." I put my hand on hers. I was done messing with the Ferrantes. If Achilles came for me, I'd kill him. But I was no longer on a revenge spree against the Camorra. "It's nothing you need to worry yourself with. I'm okay. I promise."

I spent the night holed up in Frankie's DC apartment, studying maps and researching where to go with my new passport. Thanks to Sam Brennan's connections, I was now Louise Fisher, twenty-four, an American born in Connecticut, taking a sabbatical from her boring marketing job.

Ireland was off the table. It'd be the first place Achilles would look for me and was small enough that he could find me. Tiernan liked the idea of Thailand—big, far, and full of islands you could disappear in. However, my gut told me not to go with anything Tiernan had suggested. I trusted my brother with my life, but something, or *someone*, in his vicinity leaked information. After all, Vello found out I went to the feds somehow.

No. I needed to be the only person to know where I was going.

At three in the morning, I narrowed it down to somewhere in mainland Europe. I could rent a car and drive freely between countries, allowing me to be one step ahead at all times.

At around four thirty in the morning, I decided the European country I was going to start with was Italy. It'd be the last place Achilles would believe I'd go for obvious reasons—it was his home turf. And I wasn't going anywhere near Naples. Too many Camorrista eyes. Now, Northern Italy? That was another story. I swung my gaze to the grandfather clock across the room. Twelve hours down, twelve more to go before Achilles started to hunt me. I appreciated him giving me a head start but also despised him for underestimating me, assuming I'd be easily tracked down. One thing I was sure of: even after all we'd been through, I knew he'd still keep his word and avoid searching for me until my time was up.

I flipped open Frankie's laptop and checked the flights going out of Dulles International Airport to Italy. One was leaving in four hours. I purchased a ticket, putting in Louise's information and paying through Frankie's secured credit line.

Then I opened a new email and sent a cute little message to my number-one fanboy.

Two and a half hours later, Louise stood with her backpack, ball cap, and brand-new raven hair at the airport and boarded a plane to Venice, Italy.

CHAPTER TWENTY-SEVEN
ACHILLES

I stared at the clock as the last seconds of Tierney's twenty-four hours ran out, then stood from my seat. My apartment probably still reeked of Hamish's corpse, but my senses were now sharpened toward one goal—extinguishing my little flame.

Clicking my phone to life, I logged in to my email app and read her message again.

From: catchmeifyoucan1999@gmail.com
To: aferrante@ferrantecorp.com
Subject: Remember When...

Remember when you taught me English, Chelovek? I never told you, but my favorite word you taught me was incandescent. Glowing with intense heat. It reminded me of you. And I think, maybe, it reminded you of me, too.
Little Flame

I pocketed my phone, the corner of my lips crooked in a half smile. Did she think she was the cat and I was the mouse in our lethal game? I wouldn't put it past her. Tierney had always been an unpredictable creature. It was one of the reasons she held my attention in a death grip.

Now, to find her.

She needed a good forged passport, not some fed honeypot, so I knew Sam Brennan was the one to issue it. He was the best in the business and one of the only people in the country to forge the kind of identification that'd flawlessly pass an automatic counterfeit detection system. She'd need to go through a shit ton of those to get out of the United States and travel between countries. Just as well as I knew the Irish motherfucker was a dead end. Boston's infamous fixer wouldn't sell out a client to me, no matter the price.

I also trusted Tierney not to smuggle herself past borders in the trunk of some car. Getting caught was not a chance she'd be willing to take.

Sloppiness wasn't in her nature.

That left me to do some legwork. Luckily, I never shied away from a challenge.

And I knew just where to start looking.

"You sure there's no better way of finding her, boss?" Carmine, my soldier, whimpered three hours later in my makeshift computer lab. "There are, like, twenty thousand women in this database."

"Twenty-three thousand," I corrected. "And all I'm hearing is that you need to work faster."

I set up thirty laptops in my parents' drawing room, putting a soldier in charge of each, with Jeremie overlooking the entire operation.

Contrary to general belief, I didn't take a liking to Jeremie because he was a good soldier or a decent man. He was neither; the tank-sized Russian was as obedient as a kidney stone.

See, when Alex, Jeremie's brother, started nagging us to send him back to Vegas not even a month after I took him as collateral, I wondered why the rush. Jeremie was good at fighting, but so was every other shitbag on Alex's payroll. Jeremie, I'd quickly understood, possessed a unique skill Alex was in need of: *hacking*.

The night Jeremie had broken into Luca's security system and erased forty minutes of footage from his bedroom camera, the penny dropped.

Jeremie was a hacker.

A fucking good one.

Thank you, Luca, for being a shit husband who probably fucks his mistresses in his wife's bed.

Jeremie had the ability to bypass the cybersecurity software of individual airlines, but even more importantly, he could access the government agencies that received travel data in real time. This meant I didn't need to go on a wild-goose chase, searching for Tierney's grainy CCTV footage across the country—I could simply find out what alias she was using and see where she was headed.

"Jeremie, how far in are we?" I clapped the Russian's back. His glacial irises landed on my hand like it was dirt. I kept it there just to piss him off. He returned his attention to the laptop. "Thirty-two percent in. So far, no matches."

If Tierney had a passport that could get her past airport security, that meant one thing—identity theft. The passport had to mimic an existing one, which belonged to a real person. Presumably, a real person who fell victim to a security breach and was female, between the ages of eighteen to thirty-two, lived in the tristate area, and was white.

Twenty-three thousand people fell under this description. We went through every single one of them.

A picture of Tierney was plastered to the side of every laptop in the room as my soldiers browsed through face after face that resembled my little flame.

"It'd be easier if we just hacked into Sam's computer," I grumbled, scanning the slouched shoulders and concentrated looks of my soldiers as they went through every passport of every idiot who had their security breached the past few days. Brennan would choose a fresh victim, no doubt. One who fit Tierney's description enough not to raise suspicion.

"Sam's computer is secured through the nose." Jeremie clicked away on his computer, flipping through photos. "Besides, where's the fun in that?"

I stood up straight, weaving through the mass of bodies as I peered at screens.

An hour and a half later, we hit pay dirt. One of my soldiers snapped his head up excitedly. "I think I got her!"

Jeremie and I stalked over to him. On the screen in front of us Louise Fisher stared back, a fresh-faced woman from Connecticut. She had dark hair but otherwise held a striking resemblance to Tierney—same green, upturned eyes; same wide, graceful mouth and aquiline nose, and the bone structure of a supermodel. She even had a similar dusting of freckles across the bridge of her nose.

Fuck me sideways and call me Suzie.

"What do you think?" I elbowed Jeremie.

"I think." He grabbed the laptop from under his arm, setting it on the nearest couch, his fingers moving at the speed of light as he minimized a hundred open tabs and running systems. "You need to pack a bag because you're flying to Venice."

CHAPTER TWENTY-EIGHT
TIERNEY

I landed at Venice Marco Polo Airport in the early hours of the morning and cabbed it into the city, paying in cash. I needed to disappear in a large body of people and use Louise's ID as little as possible, if at all.

Flying under the radar was crucial to my operation. I only had one fake identity, and once Louise Fisher was compromised, I'd be screwed. She *would* be compromised. It was only a question of when. Which was why I wasn't staying in Italy long. The more countries I skipped, the less of a trail I'd leave behind.

I'd spent my flight researching the smallest, dodgiest hotels in the city. I didn't want Louise to check in to anywhere that required an ID. Where I landed was a small motel on the mainland near Mestre. It wasn't a motel, per se. In truth, it was more of a whorehouse. One that didn't require more than sixty euros per night to host me.

Tension ate at me as I treaded the stained brown-carpeted floor of the corridor, down to the last door. It looked so flimsy; I could probably kick it down myself. Swallowing a ball of nerves, I jiggled the key inside the keyhole, struggling to turn the ancient lock. Finally, the door whined open. I walked inside and locked it behind me.

The air stood still; the stench of cigarettes, cheap perfume, and sweat coated the back of my throat. A dark duvet covered the queen-size bed. The rest consisted of a small bathroom to my right, two stained recliners, and a small, round table under a shoebox-size window. The noise of old bedsprings groaning and excited moans seeped through the walls.

Shaking my head, I paced to the window—covered by a stunningly ugly yellow curtain—and withdrew the fabric an inch, peering outside.

A narrow, greenish canal stared back at me, as well as the orange building next to us. A balcony faced my room directly. If push came to shove, I could probably jump onto the balcony and pick the lock. I'd just about squeeze through the small window, but a man the size of Achilles wouldn't.

For the first time since we'd started our cat-and-mouse game, my heart rate slowed to a reasonable speed.

I parked myself on the edge of the bed, flipping my burner open and turning it on. A text message popped up on the screen.

> Call me.

It was Tiernan. My heart dropped again. *Shit.*

I called his number, pressing the phone to my ear. He answered immediately.

"You in Italy?"

I closed my eyes, willing myself not to fall apart. He wasn't supposed to know that.

Well, that didn't take long.

"I am," I croaked. "Did he find me?"

"That's the rumor," Tiernan tsked. "He's taken the private plane to Venice."

"How'd you find out?" It couldn't be Achilles who told him, because he knew Tiernan would warn me. Still, bastard had the nose of a bloodhound.

"Jeremie told Lyosha." And Lyosha told Tiernan. The pakhan had always been loyal to his Irish friend.

I rubbed my face, feeling like I hadn't slept in years. "Okay. So he found out the name I traveled under. But I've been paying for everything in cash since I got here and just checked into a hotel without ID."

"Don't get too comfortable," Tiernan ordered. "Get armed and get out. Continue east. Keep skipping borders. Jeremie won't defy Achilles when he asks him to find you, but he can't go around breaking into every government database in Europe."

I clutched my head in one hand, wondering if I should've gone back to Tom Rothwell and accepted the FBI's protection. It wasn't like me to surrender control, but Achilles was a merciless enemy and not one I could throw off easily. For all I knew, he knew exactly where I'd checked in and was halfway across the city on his way to me.

"Okay, I have to hang up." I swallowed.

"Do you need me to wire you money?" Tiernan asked. He sounded cool and collected, like his sister's life wasn't on the line. I'd only ever seen him fall apart once, and that was because of Lila.

"No, I'm good for now. Give my love to Lila and Nero."

"Stay safe."

I killed the call and went into the bathroom, tossing cold water onto my face. I wasn't sleepy—I was wide-awake, alerted by the sheer terror of knowing I could get offed any minute now—but I needed to think clearly.

Achilles was nearby. But knowing just *how* near he was would determine my next steps.

I grabbed my backpack and went downstairs, pouring myself into a sun-drenched Venice.

Reconnaissance. I needed to feel out my surroundings and strategize accordingly.

I took the bus to Santa Lucia, two stops from my motel, and crossed the Ponte della Liberta.

Once I arrived at my destination, I blended with the schools of tourists, heading toward a street littered with shops until I found an internet café. Keeping my head low, I proceeded to the last stall. The PC was ancient and cruelly slow, and the entire setup was in Italian. Still, I managed to check the schedules for the Ferrantes' private plane through a flight tracking website. According to the site, he had three more hours in the air.

My body sagged with relief. I still had time. Not a lot but enough to throw a few wrinkles in his path to me.

Tiernan was wrong. I couldn't outrun Achilles Ferrante. He was too smart, too patient, and too methodical. What I could do was kill him. I'd still spend the rest of my life hiding from the Camorra, but no man knew me as thoroughly as him. No other man could find me.

I logged on to my new email, knowing full well he could track me through my IP, just as well as I knew there was nothing he could do about it until he landed.

From: catchmeifyoucan1999@gmail.com
To: aferrante@ferrantecorp.com
Subject: Hi, asshole.

I didn't have to wait long.

From: aferrante@ferrantecorp.com
To: catchmeifyoucan1999@gmail.com

Hello, Louise.

I mustered all of my bravado not to pass out on the keyboard, even though the desire to throw in the towel was strong. The adrenaline crash was bound to hit me sooner or later. I couldn't remember the last time I'd slept and didn't know when the next time would be. How long could I keep this up?

How about a duel? I offered.

I didn't have a gun, but I could ambush him with another weapon. If I played it smart.

Sure. I'll duel with you. When and where?

Licking my lips, I craned my neck to make sure no one was coming in or out of the café.

Piazza San Marco. 3:30 p.m.

It was a crowded place, leading to both main streets and private alleyways. Endless opportunities.

It's a date.

I logged out of my email, deleted the history on the browser, and walked out of the internet café. Next, I went back to the taxi and bus station, returned to the mainland, and got into a Leroy Merlin—the closest thing in Italy to Home Depot—where I stocked up on three Swiss knives, small sharp scissors, and a zip tie. From there, I went to Piazzale Roma, where I checked out the area and possible escape routes on foot.

I stopped at a café and downed two espressos one after the other. After emptying my bladder in the restroom, I headed to a souvenir shop across the street, leafing through Venetian masks. I chose a *piuma volto intero*—a full face cover—made of papier-mâché. It was white, with a golden eye mask and feathers framing it.

Flicking my wrist to check the time, I saw it was almost three o'clock. I slinked out of the store and headed to the center of the square. I wanted him to see me.

I was bait, and he needed to bite.

Too bad he was about to find out I was pure poison.

Tourist season was at its peak and Piazza San Marco was full to the brim with street performers in Venetian masks. Enough that my sporting one didn't raise any eyebrows and allowed me further anonymity.

Achilles was going to show up here. And when he did, I was going to lure him somewhere and finish him off.

Then I was going to run far away from this place.

And never set foot in Italy again.

CHAPTER TWENTY-NINE
ACHILLES

A driver waited for me at the private airport on the mainland. It was just like Tierney to choose a convoluted place that was a bitch to navigate. He drove to the nearest point with water taxis, and I boarded one to Piazza San Marco.

Once at Piazza San Marco, I entered a souvenir shop and got a mask. I'd be disappointed if she didn't do the same. Tierney was whip-smart, even under duress. The tourist attraction was wired to oblivion with CCTV, and both of us intended to commit a grave crime.

I chose a jester mask in burgundy and gold. An homage to her Joker and Harley reference. I didn't mind her knowing who I was. It'd probably speed things up, and I was needed in Naples, anyway. The clusterfuck with Coppola wasn't going to unfuck itself.

I didn't really believe she'd managed to get her hands on a gun in the few hours she was in Italy, but I didn't put it past her to try and kill me in some other way. I'd beat her to it, but I wouldn't be happy about it.

In fact, I would never forgive myself. But it was either her life or mine, and I'd be a fool to spare her when she'd indicated numerous times she wanted me dead.

Donning my mask, I strolled out of the store and into the open square.

My phone began ringing. My father's name flashed on the screen. I answered, calmly surveying my surroundings through the mask.

"Have you found the Irish slut?"

A muscle in my jaw jumped at the slur, but I swallowed down my ire. "Yup."

"Good. Because we're sending Jeremie back to Vegas."

"Who authorized this transfer?" It sure as fuck wasn't me, and Jeremie was directly my inferior.

"Alex, and I don't have the time nor inclination to scrimmage with the pakhan. We've got enough on our plate with Coppola."

"And Jeremie agreed?" I moved deeper into the square, heading toward its center, to be in plain sight. Tierney *would* make a mistake. Not because she wasn't smart but because she wasn't a trained assassin. I'd done this song and dance a hundred times before.

"Jeremie is the Rasputins' problem, and I don't give a shit what he has to say about this," my father announced.

"What's he giving us in exchange?" I asked.

"The sister, Katya." He paused, waiting for a reaction that didn't come. "Twenty. Very pretty, I hear."

I made a grumbling sound, my eyes zeroing in on a long-limbed woman standing under an arch of St. Mark's Basilica. I'd recognize that ass, those legs, her posture from space, while blindfolded.

"I want you to marry her, Achilles," my father said on the line. "The Russian girl. Kill Tierney, make Katya your wife, and take the throne. You can have it all if you just do as I sa—"

I killed the call and pocketed my phone.

Tierney was wearing a Venetian mask and was armed to the fucking teeth. I spotted two Swiss knives and a small pair of scissors through her skintight clothes.

Smart girl.

It was a shame I had to kill her, but rules were rules. You didn't fuck with the Camorra and live to tell the tale.

Stuffing my hands into my jacket, I cocked my gun inside my pocket, strolling in her direction. I relished the moment she realized it was me. The way she tensed, like a small, jittery rabbit about to take flight. She turned south, taking quick steps out of the square. I closed the distance between us but kept my pace easy.

She didn't make the mistake of peeking over her shoulder. That would cost her time she didn't have. She kept moving with purpose and, when we entered a residential street, she picked up speed.

I was gaining on her, and she knew it because, soon enough, her brisk walk broke into a jog. She must've studied these streets prior to our little duel because the small, narrow roads kept emptying the farther we progressed, twisting and convoluting into clusters of orange-roofed buildings.

Another sharp turn. This time, as soon as I followed her, it forked into two darkened alleys. Both dead ends—one leading to a garage and the other to what looked like the back of a restaurant. I paused, knowing it didn't really matter which option I picked. Unless she somehow got her hands on a gun, she wouldn't walk out of here alive.

I chose the restaurant's rear. She probably hid behind the dumpster. I took my gun out and reached into my boot to remove the suppressor. Screwed it on. Stepping into the shadows, I trod behind the bin, gun first. A sharp, suffocating pain wrapped around my throat from behind, jerking me backward.

Son of a bitch. She'd hidden in the trash can and was now strangling me with a…zip tie?

At least she invested in a good one. The material threatened to tear through my skin clear to the bone. I felt special. She chose the best. For *me*.

She cut off my air supply, digging the zip tie deeper into my skin until it broke and bled. Any other person would've been toast in this situation.

Emphasis on *any other*.

Rather than try to lurch the cable off my throat, I squatted and pushed my feet up, throwing her entire weight off my back. Tierney flew across the alleyway, back slamming against the wall. I reached her before she had the chance to scramble up, tearing the mask from her face and aiming my gun at her while she was still on her knees.

"We have to stop meeting like this." She grinned up at me, darting her tongue out to lick blood from the corner of her mouth. Despite myself, I found my lips twitching. She had a great sense of humor, even when she stared death in the eye.

"Who told you it was a good idea to show up to a duel without a gun?" I asked softly.

"Please, no lectures. Just get it over with." She rolled her eyes, spitting blood sideways. She must've bitten herself when I threw her off me.

"Up." I grabbed her by the throat with my free hand, jerking her to her feet. I placed my forearms on either side of her shoulders, pinning her against the wall. "Throw your weapons on the ground. *All* of them."

She tossed her backpack aside, pulling out her pockets. A small pair of scissors and a Swiss knife fell out.

"And the other Swiss knife in your waistband," I prompted.

Groaning, she complied.

God, she was so fucking beautiful. Even without her signature red hair. I'd missed her face. I hadn't seen it in forty-eight hours and realized it had been entirely too long. Now to go the rest of my life without seeing it…unfathomable.

"You know, for whatever baffling reason, I still want you to have a relatively painless death, so I'll put a bullet in your head. Straight and simple."

She thrust her chin out. "Aw. You spoil me, Ferrante."

"Turn around."

Better to kill her while she wasn't looking. I didn't think I could handle seeing her eyes the last nanosecond before I took her life. They'd chase me to the grave and beyond.

"In a second." She reached to grab the collar of my black shirt, twisting it in her fist. "First, let me do this." She flung off my mask.

Then she leaned forward and kissed the shit out of me.

My lips opened in surprise, giving absolutely zero fucks the mouth pressing against them was attached to a woman who sought to actively kill me.

Break off the kiss, my mind screamed.

Shut the fuck up, my dick replied, swelling in my combat pants.

No, no. I was definitely stopping this. Just one more stroke of a tongue, to figure out what it was I was tasting. A hint of espresso, mint gum, and a touch of—

She rolled the tip of her tongue over the roof of my mouth. A shudder rippled through me.

I didn't care how many men she'd been with (though I *did* count them—fourteen). And I didn't care that she hated me. Those kisses? They were mine.

These men fucked her. But me? I *touched* her.

Her fingers twisted in my hair, nails scraping my scalp. The kiss turned frantic as our tongues waged war on one another. I pushed my knee between her thighs, spreading them, and she dropped one hand, snaking it to the small of her back.

Then she shoved a knife deep into my thigh.

I felt it pierce through every layer of muscle in my quads until it hit bone.

Fuuuuuuuuuuuuuuuuuuuuuuuuuuuuuuuuuuuuuuuuuuuuuuuuuuuuuuuuuuuuuck.

Fuck, fuck, fuckity fuck.

To her surprise—and my own—I didn't break the kiss. I was milking this shit until the very last minute. Tierney ripped her mouth from mine, glaring. I offered her a *yes, bitch?* smirk. She was still holding the knife by the hilt, the triumph draining from her face as she realized I wasn't going to fold and release her.

"That's right, Piccola Fiamma. Twist that knife. You've aways been good at hurting me."

She scowled, her surprise morphing into fury. "Why the hell are you so smug?"

"You could've stabbed me anywhere and didn't go for the heart. Is this a love declaration, baby?"

She reached for the gun in my hand. I twisted sideways to prevent her from grabbing it, then stepped back, the knife still stuck in my thigh.

Realizing she couldn't overpower me, she turned around and started running. I sighed in amusement, pointing the gun at the back of her head.

Pull it, motherfucker.

My index finger readjusted against the trigger. I reminded myself she'd stabbed me not even a minute ago. Tried to kill me—twice now—and sold me out to the feds.

Pull. The. Fucking. Trigger.

She stumbled and heaved, the adrenaline and exhaustion getting the best of her, and when she rounded the corner, she stumbled and fell, diving to the ground with a desperate shriek.

I lowered the gun and limped my way to her. Her eyes flared in horror at the sight of me. She slithered away from me on her forearms, a pathetic, defenseless creature.

"What's wrong?" I demanded.

"If you wanna shoot, shoot, don't ta—"

"What happened to your leg?"

Her gaze skittered from my face to her foot. She swallowed. "I—I think I sprained my ankle."

"Where are you staying?"

Her face hardened. "Like I'm gonna tell y—"

"I can execute you right now if I want to. Where are you staying, Tierney?"

She hesitated, her eyelashes fluttering, suspended between panic and desperation.

"In this fucking century, please." My leg was killing me.

She gave me her address. I knew the place. A whorehouse, a ten-minute distance from here. I kneeled on my good leg, scooping her and her stupid backpack in my arms and limping in that direction. We were going to take a water taxi at our state, which meant I was about to press a gun to someone's temple in broad daylight. Fucking fantastic. The woman really had a knack for throwing my life into the eye of the shitstorm.

"W—what are you doing?"

"The fuck does it look like?" Her question was valid, though. I had no business helping her ass. She should be bleeding in an alleyway.

"You have a knife in your thigh."

"I've noticed."

She wrapped her arms around my neck, and I fought the urge to kiss her, focusing on the pain in my leg instead.

"You're here to kill me," she reminded me.

"I know."

"Then why are you doing this?"

Because I've had enough of my own bullshit. I'd rather die than hurt you. And I don't fucking care. I don't care that it's not mutual and never will be.

"Shut up and let me think." My voice was dry, cold. "And if you'll be a good girl and stop trying to kill me, I'll let you seduce me again."

CHAPTER THIRTY
ACHILLES

The good thing about lodging in a whorehouse was that nobody asked any questions when I carried a busted-up Tierney into the place with a goddamn knife stuck in my body.

I stopped at the reception desk, flinging a few hundred euro notes in the clerk's direction, asking for ice packs, a first-aid kit, a shit ton of warm towels, antibiotics, a suturing kit, and pressure bandages to be brought to our room. "Grappa, too." I growled the final instruction. Fuck if I was going to take that knife out without anything to numb the pain. "I'll pay double if you bring everything within the hour." I rapped my knuckles over the cash. They got to work immediately.

Once we entered Tierney's room, I placed her on the bed and elevated her injured ankle, wrapping it in a cold, damp towel. It didn't look sprained, just a little swollen.

Thirty minutes later, the clerk arrived with everything. I iced Tierney's ankle first and popped a couple of Tachipirine in her mouth, making her wash them down with the grappa. She looked like a train wreck—a far cry from her glamorous self.

"When was the last time you slept?"

"Naples."

Four days ago, then. She was running on fumes.

"Go to sleep."

"I don't need—"

"Pipe down and do as you're told for once. That pretty mouth of yours almost cost you your life."

She protested, but I retired to the bathroom, locking myself inside with the grappa and medical kit. I sat on the edge of the bathtub, covered my face, and stifled a groan. I wasn't going to kill her, which meant I'd need to hide her. I'd deal with it. But first, to get that blade out of my thigh.

I tore my pants off with a pocketknife and examined the wound. Deep but mainly muscle. I grabbed the hilt of the Swiss knife and took a swig of the alcohol. I had no way of knowing if it cut through any nerves or important arteries. Bleeding out was also an option. I had to take my chances. I grabbed the towels and a disinfecting spray and got to work.

As I slowly pulled the three-inch blade out of my thigh, I asked myself if I regretted the night I opened Tierney's bedroom door all those years ago and let myself in, voluntarily tangling myself in her web.

The answer was no.

I didn't regret it one fucking bit.

Even if I died in the next few minutes.

At least I'd gotten to hold her.

CHAPTER THIRTY-ONE

AGE SEVENTEEN

He hated most months, but December took the damn cake.

First of all, he had to spend Christmas with his family. His mama always stared at him like he was going to kill someone at the dinner table. Like he was inhuman. His fault, really, for surpassing all of his father's expectations and becoming a well-oiled killing machine.

All he'd ever wanted was to be loved, and he'd been stupid enough to hope that if he just executed enough enemies and carried out enough dangerous tasks, he'd win his father's affections.

Secondly, and more importantly, he knew Tierney loathed December.

His girlfriend partied too hard, drank too much, and by the time he dragged her home from a party or a hangout, she was too plastered for him to do more than give her a chaste kiss on the lips.

Was he doing something wrong? Dammit, if only she would tell him what was bothering her, he'd fix it. He'd find a way. Even if he had to dedicate his life to making things right.

They still hadn't had sex. He'd waited for her to initiate, treating her as delicately as you would a soap bubble. If she needed more time, he'd give her that. Hell, he'd let her lose her virginity to his best friend if it made her happy, even if he had to watch.

Thank fuck *he had no friends.*

Tierney was a good, understanding girlfriend. They'd kept their relationship a secret because he knew his dad wouldn't approve of him dating her. She never gave him shit for it, never asked where he'd been, never complained when he disappeared for days at a time, because his father needed him to kill someone, dump a body beyond state lines, or handle stray drug shipments.

She tended to his wounds when he got hurt, was always ready with her arms open for a hug, and always talked him through his emotions, listening to him for hours on end.

The fucked-up part was that she kind of became a mother figure for him. She kissed his boo-boos. Threaded her fingers in his hair. Made sandwiches for him. Cleaned those pesky bloodstains from his shoes. She pulled him out of his dark thoughts after he killed, grabbing a book they both liked and reading his favorite scenes out loud.

She'd become so much more than a girlfriend, and he was terrified, because every time he talked about the future, she changed the subject.

The night she turned seventeen, they lay in her bed. He was holding her tight, kissing her temple, contemplating the future.

"I hate my birthday." She soaked his shirt with tears that night. December was the month in which the Bratva's pakhan, Igor, carved her mother's stomach open and pulled out the twins, kidnapping them after he left her for dead. "It reminds me of everything I lost before I was even born."

"Next year, I'll change that for you," he promised, stroking her hair.

"How?" she murmured into his neck, lips pressed to his tattoo of her kiss.

"Your birthday gift will be an engagement ring, and we'll start our own family. I'll never let this happen to our children. To you."

She froze in his arms. The air stood still.

"I'd forfeit my life to save yours," he assured her, stroking her beautiful hair, the color of rich red wine. "Dad will fall in line. You'll see. He thinks I'm the best with the knife and the gun, so he wants me to have a lot of heirs. When he sees you're the only one I want, he'll come around."

"It's that important to him?" She cleared her throat. "Heirs?"

He snorted. "It's all he talks about. Me giving him grandchildren."

"I heard he wants you to wed someone from the Outfit."

"Don't worry about it. I'll fight him on it. I'd rip my entire family apart to keep you, Tier."

"Achilles…" She squirmed in his arms.

"Yes?"

"There's more to this life than me, you know."

It was the stupidest thing he'd ever heard, and it made his stomach churn so badly, he vomited twice as hard as he did the night he ate a human heart.

Because he had a feeling Tierney was about to break his.

It was Tierney's eighteenth birthday, and his palms were clammy.

He had to face the music: tell his father he would not be entering an arranged marriage to strengthen the Camorra ties with whoever the fuck they needed to form an alliance with these days. It might land him in a world of pain, but nothing would hurt more than losing her.

He chose a ruby for her engagement ring. It reminded him of her hair, but more than that of her indomitable spirit.

He got into his car and drove to her new house in the suburbs, knowing full well her father and brothers weren't there. Tyrone and Fintan were visiting family in Ireland. They largely ignored Tierney's existence. Only Tiernan cared, and while he loved his sister in his own screwed-up way, he wasn't the type to celebrate with a cake and fucking beer pong.

Tiernan was out on the streets, pushing the Albanians out of Harlem. He was Achilles's age and twice as violent and vicious.

Achilles killed for his family and honor. But Tiernan? He killed because he fucking loved it.

Because she was alone, he'd decided to come early. He couldn't stomach the idea of her sitting there all by herself.

He rounded the corner onto her street when he noticed flames dancing in the Callaghans' open windows.

No. Not windows. Window. Tierney's.

He screeched to a halt and threw the driver's door open, sprinting down the street. Fire had already devoured her curtains and the edges of the wall.

Shit. Tierney would be there, in her bedroom.

He kicked the door down so hard it flew off its hinges. Tucking his mouth and nose into his shirt, he stormed inside. The first level was smoky and scorching hot but no fire yet. He had the good sense to run to the kitchen faucet, tear off his jacket, and soak it in water before donning it again. Then he took the stairs three at a time and headed straight to Tierney's room.

He knew Igor must have been behind the fire. The pakhan. That damn fucking monster came to finish the job on the twins' birthday.

Achilles was going to kill him.

It'd be the first thing he'd do as the new don.

Declare war on the Bratva and obliterate it for what they'd done to his girlfriend. No, to his future wife.

The fire seemed to be coming from her room. He'd have to walk through it to reach her if she was still inside.

He didn't hesitate.

Covering his face with his forearm, he plunged inside. The fire pounced on him as if it were a living, breathing thing, nipping at his sodden jacket like a rabid animal. A spike of agony shot through his body everywhere he was exposed—face, ears, hands. The flames branded him, etching scars onto his flesh like pointy teeth.

Would she love him scarred? Ugly on the outside as he was on the inside?

The answer was irrelevant. Because he'd still love her, and he'd never let anything happen to her.

He found her curled on the corner of the bed, facing the wall, her back to him. The flames didn't touch her. Like they knew she was made of the same elements. He scooped her up, his hands trembling so hard, he could barely feel them, and placed two fingers to the side of her throat.

She had a pulse.

It was faint, but it was there.

The little clean air he had in his lungs swooshed out in relief. He ripped off his wet jacket and covered her with it entirely. Then he picked her up, pressed her to his chest, and turned back to the door only to find he couldn't see it past the flames.

To get out, he had to get through.

Inhaling a lungful of smoky air, he pushed forward, running into the fire.

He was burning alive for her and he couldn't give half a shit. His entire being was focused on one thing—saving her.

As he charged down a stairway that crumbled beneath his boots into dust, giving in to the heat, he felt his skin pruning, curling at its edges, morphing him to look like the monster he'd long ago become.

The scent was unbearable. Like the back of a butcher shop.

His face. It was ruined. He knew without looking in a mirror. But it was his lungs that nearly failed him. They scorched so hot, the smoke inside them so thick, he couldn't see himself making it past the door.

Do it. Not for you. For her.

He'd heard of parents finding Herculean strength to protect their children but had called bullshit on it. He now believed it. He'd probably inhaled too much smoke. Suffered burns too deep for recovery. But he was past pain and discomfort. A force of nature, he hugged her tighter, protecting her body from the heat and flames; God forbid her pristine skin suffer so much as a blemish. Down the stairs and out the door, where he collapsed onto the hail-caked front lawn, rolling back and forth to extinguish the flames on his body.

She lay next to him on the grass, and he kept yelling to her. "Baby. Please. Please! Show me you're alive."

The broken sound coming out of him was pure polluted smoke, not voice. "Truth? You want the truth? Here's the truth—even if I die…even *if—"* He coughed again, his lungs giving out. No. He'd say it, he had to. Just in case she could hear. *"It was worth it. You were worth it, Tierney. All of it."*

She was so still and so pale, he was ready to rip his lungs from his body to give them to her. Then her chest constricted, and she sucked in a desperate breath.

Only then did he let himself pass out and succumb to his wounds, the swirling red lights of the fire trucks and ambulance dancing behind his eyelids.

CHAPTER THIRTY-TWO
TIERNEY

I woke up in a dark room feeling like I'd been run over by a fire truck.

My muscles were tight, my bones heavy, and I was pretty sure my ankle throbbed like it had its own pulse.

The ancient air conditioner coughed out stale air, the scent of cigarettes and mildew so sharp it hit the back of my throat. I stayed still, piecing together the last twenty-four hours in my head.

I was in my motel room in Venice. I'd hurt my leg but didn't break anything. I'd crashed into deep sleep—ten hours minimum, judging by the darkness outside. Achilles found me, treated me, and spared me. *For now.* He'd carried me here, but he didn't let me escape. I didn't know what his plans were, and I'd be a complete fool to sit around and find out.

Carefully, I rolled sideways on the mattress. The silhouette of a colossal male greeted me. *Achilles.* By the way his chest rose and fell in a steady rhythm, he was dead-ass asleep.

Now let's make him more dead and less asleep.

If only it were so simple.

I couldn't stand up and trot around the room, searching for a weapon. That'd wake him up. I guess I could tiptoe my way out. But he'd 100 percent be on my ass in three seconds flat. No. I needed to off him and get it over with. If I blew this chance, there wouldn't be another.

Maybe he intended to let me go. But the fact that he was still here didn't bode well for me. Life had taught me that counting on anyone's charity was a dumb idea.

Lying flat on my back, I stared at the ceiling and ran a mental inventory of potential weapons in the room. He'd gotten rid of all of my daggers in the alleyway, but I knew he slept with his Glock tucked in his waistband. I also knew I was a damn good thief. Spending the first fourteen years of your life living in a work camp that rationed chickpeas does that to you.

I slowly reached for his waistband, holding my breath so as not to make a sound. My fingers curled around the back strap of his firearm. The gun must've ridden up while he shifted in his sleep because it was already halfway out, lying on the mattress. A sigh of relief rattled in my throat. Inching it all the way out, I watched his face, expecting his eyes to snap open at any moment. But then the weight of the metallic weapon rested fully in my palm, and his eyes were still shut.

Fuck me. Okay. *Phew.*

The suppressor wasn't screwed on. Not ideal, but I'd make it work. I cautiously rose to my knees, careful not to make the bedsprings squeak. I stared down at his sleeping figure, clutching the gun with both hands. Aiming for his head, I flicked off the safety. A click rang in the air.

Do it, you idiot. What is wrong with you? Save yourself.

Nausea coated the back of my throat. What the hell was I waiting for? Why couldn't I pull the damn trigger?

"Do it."

The words snapped me into reality. Achilles's snakelike gaze locked on mine in the darkness. A nocturnal predator homing in on his prey.

I swallowed hard, still aiming the weapon at him.

"Go on," he coaxed, his voice steel wrapped in velvet. "It'll solve both our problems."

No. It wouldn't solve my most pressing one: that I'm still in love with your psychotic ass.

A sob ripped from my throat. I lowered the gun and dropped my head between my shoulders.

I couldn't do it.

He scooted up so his back hit the headboard and gently pried the gun from my hand. I heard him thumb the safety on. Something about the finality of the sound made me collapse onto his chest. And that was when the waterworks started, tears streaming down my face. I was heaving, choking, gasping for air.

"Why can't we kill each other?" I slammed his chest with my fists.

"You know why."

Because all my best memories were with him.

"No, *no!*" I shook my head. "You've ruined my life."

"I did." There was no hint of apology in his voice. "But I'm done getting even."

I clawed at his dark Henley, waffling between trying to kill him one last time or drowning in his addictive touch. I just needed a distraction…a buffer between me and all the feelings that flooded me.

My hand snaked under his shirt. Warm skin and chiseled abs. That simple touch sent an agonizing bolt of desire up my spine. I needed him inside me, consequences be damned. I climbed onto his lap, latching on to a vein in his neck and sucking it greedily.

"*Cazzo*," he groaned. "Be careful."

I looked down. Oh shit. I'd poked his stab wound by accident, breaking it open. Blood coated the bandage around it, which needed to be replaced. He wasn't wearing any pants. Just briefs. "Oh, sorry."

"For stabbing me or for kneeing the stab wound?" The smile in his voice made me melt.

"Hmm, both?"

He gripped my chin and smashed his lips on mine. Our tongues twisted together, and I planted my knees on each side of him on the mattress, grounding onto his erection. I loved the sounds I milked from the great warrior Achilles Ferrante. Helpless, barely controlled grunts of pleasure each time my pussy rubbed against his cock through our clothes.

"How's that ankle?" he murmured into our kiss.

"Better," I lied, not wanting to stop this.

"Good." He gave me a rough shove. I bounced on my side of the bed, falling to my forearms. He mounted me and tugged my panties down. He must've taken off my pants sometime when he tended to my ankle. "Been wanting to do this since we were teenagers." He used his thumbs to pry open my thighs, running the tip of his nose along my slit, bottom-to-top until his lips clasped around my clit. I grabbed a pillow and pressed it against my face, arching as I muffled a scream.

"You've done this before," I mumbled into the pillow.

"I wasn't concentrating on anything but making you come," he admitted.

It was appealing. His honesty. His boyishness. His ability to open up without embarrassment.

He swirled the tip of his tongue along my clit, sinking his middle finger into me, to find me completely drenched. I squirmed, wanting both to ride his finger and to escape the tingly, building pleasure.

"Fuck, you taste good." He added another finger, and then a third, fucking me while sucking and nibbling on my clit. I met his leisured, teasing thrusts with frantic enthusiasm, bucking my hips, my entire body begging for more. The man ate pussy like Michelangelo sculpted naked dudes, reaching masterpiece level of perfection.

"God, I—" I began to moan.

"Mmm. Pussy's perfect." He grabbed my waist and flipped me to my knees. The pillow I pressed against my face fell to the floor. "Now let's taste your other hole."

Achilles thumbed my ass cheeks open and plunged in, swirling his hot tongue against the rim before spearing it all the way through, to a point of half penetration.

Stars exploded behind my eyelids.

His fingers were still inside my sex, driving in and out quicker now, and I was so full of him, pleasure and pain swirled together in a perfect storm. I buried my face in the mattress to stifle my moans, my ass pushing against his face, begging for more. His fingers went deeper, faster inside me, his rough knuckles brushing my clit. I was going to explode.

My pussy clamped down on his fingers, desperate. My orgasm spread across my body like wildfire. Shivers swept up and down my spine.

"My turn." He bit the side of my ass softly, giving it a casual slap. My knees gave in and I fell to my stomach on the bed with an exhausted groan. My limbs felt like overcooked noodles. But Achilles couldn't care less as he scooted on his knees up my body, the swollen head of his cock nestling between my legs. "Gonna fuck you nice and good now." His breath skated across the side of my neck, his hand snaking over my shoulder and squeezing the front of my throat. "And if you're a good girl, I'll even let you breathe."

With a yank on my waist, he brought me to kneel on all fours. Before I could register what was happening, he slid into me, planting one leg over the mattress as he began slamming into me from behind. Our moans filled the room, soaking the walls.

"Shh, now. No one said you're allowed to enjoy this. Every time you make a sound, I'm going to squeeze a little harder," he murmured in my ear.

He was finally giving me what I wanted—violence, degradation, depravation—and I knew exactly why. Because he wanted to remind me he didn't need all that to make me come hard.

The pressure on my throat was delicious, addictive and drove me faster to the brink of an orgasm.

Something warm and wet plastered to the back of my thigh from behind. I didn't have to look to know his stab wound had opened completely and blood gushed out. He noticed, too. Crimson leaked all over the sheets and our bodies, dampening my flesh, entering my pussy. Still, he didn't stop, only fucking me harder, cutting off my air supply whenever I got mouthy, and letting me breathe again when I quieted down.

We were bathed in his blood, fucking like two mad people, and I never wanted it to end.

I angled my ass up in the air and closed my thighs together, relishing the friction. He turned me inside out, making me forget the mess we were both in. I dripped cum, and he dripped blood, and the sheets were a mess of pink and red.

"I—I have to come," I choked through his grip on my throat. I couldn't help it.

"Who are you coming for, Piccola Fiamma?"

"You."

"And who do you belong to?"

"Y—you." I tried stifling another moan of pleasure, my body tingling with goose bumps and pre-orgasmic shivers. "I belong to you, Achilles."

It was the truth. Depressing as it was, I could never want another. Just as well, as I'd decided to swear off men after all of this was over.

"Damn right you belong to me." His hand slid from my throat to my clit, his hot mouth covering the side of my throat as he trailed kisses on it while playing with me. "And don't you ever forget it."

I inhaled sharply, an explosion of pleasure detonating in my body. My knees gave in and I fell stomach-first to the bed.

Achilles came inside me, probably remembering our last farewell conversation, where I told him I couldn't get pregnant.

"Mine." He collapsed on top of me, crushing me to the mattress.

"Yours," I breathed. "Till death do us part."

Because that seemed to be the only way we could ever quit each other.

CHAPTER THIRTY-THREE
ACHILLES

"Where'd you get the clothes?"

Tierney plopped on the dilapidated armchair next to mine, rubbing the strands of her damp hair with a towel, fresh out of the shower. I wore slacks, a tailored black shirt, and my wingtips. My thigh wound was newly bandaged underneath, though the sheets still looked like we'd slaughtered a family of five between them.

Lighting a cigarette, I cupped my hand to protect the flame before passing it to her. She leaned to clasp it with her teeth, her cheeks hollowing as she gave it a good suck. I lit another one for myself. "My driver delivered my clothes."

Her face fell. "That means he knows where I'm staying." She stood up and hugged herself, striding to the tiny window.

She was tripped out. Paranoid about being found and anxious about what I'd do to her. I couldn't blame her, everything considered.

"He doesn't know why I'm here," I volunteered, "and neither of us is going to stay long enough for anyone else to find out."

"How's your dad doing?"

"You took his finger."

She sucked on the cigarette, nodding to herself. "Good."

I concealed my smile with a thick cloud of smoke.

She did that thing again today. The same bullshit she pulled in Naples, with her eyes glassing over when we fucked. It was a real shame she retreated somewhere else every time she had sex. If she were fully present in the act, she'd draw much more pleasure from it.

"Are you going to kill me?" She didn't bother swiveling to face me when she asked the question.

"I think we both know the answer." I took another drag.

"Your dad will kill you if you don't."

"If I were scared of death, I'd choose another occupation. Sit down. Let's figure it out."

She turned around, taking the place across from me. I drummed my fingers on the armrest, watching her. "How much money do you have?"

"Just shy of seventy K."

"I'll give you a million if you follow my plan."

Her eyebrows flew up. "And what's your plan?"

"You cross three borders in the next week, settle in Prague, and never show your face in America again."

She licked her lips, staring down at her hands. "Why Prague?"

"I know a guy who can hook you up with a clean passport. You'll be able to open a bank account. Rent an apartment. Start over."

"And what'll you tell your dad?"

"That I killed you," I said frankly. "You'll need to disappear from the face of the earth and not contact your brother for a solid year."

I was going to kill that motherfucker Tyrone with my bare hands as soon as I touched ground in America for what he'd done to his daughter. But even then, I'd have to make sure there weren't any other moles in the Irish and Russian operations that could rat her out. For all his shrewdness, Tiernan sure was fond of questionable dipshits. Between his deadbeat father and Russian pakhan, he kept dubious company.

"A whole year? Why?"

Because your own father fed you to the wolves, and I need to make sure you'll be safe.

But telling her that would just cause her more heartache and angst. She'd been through enough.

"I need to sort shit out on my end," I said vaguely.

She ran her finger along her lower lip. "You're really not going to kill me?"

"Trust me, no one's as surprised as I am. I've been wanting to do it for years."

In theory, at least. I'd been wanting to throttle that pretty neck until she went limp. I'd imagined her pulse fading under my fingertips countless times. But the truth of the matter was, when push came to shove, I couldn't fucking do it. And I'd had plenty of opportunities.

"And you'll leave me alone?"

I extinguished my cigarette, respiring the thick smoke through my nostrils. "Yeah."

It occurred to me there'd be no more casual verbal sparring, no glares across the room. Her pretending to hate me. Me pretending it didn't fucking kill me. This was it. If I wanted her alive, this would be our last interaction.

She tapped her lips, contemplating this. "Why three countries?"

"Buffer. The more you move around, the harder you are to track down."

"Are you sure? Tiernan said Jeremie has insane hacking skills. What if—"

I cut her off. "Jeremie's not gonna be the one looking for you. He's going back to Vegas."

"He is?" Tierney's eyebrows shot up. "How did Alex manage that?"

"Bartered him for the baby sister."

She frowned. "What would the Camorra do with a twenty-year-old wom—" Her expression smoothed over as she answered the question in her head. "*Oh.*"

"Oh." I flashed her a rueful smile.

"Who's she going to marry?" She was bone white. Didn't take a genius to know why. I was the next in line to get hitched after Luca. And I wanted to become don. She'd put two and two together.

"Yours truly."

For the first time since we'd broken up, I saw a pang of jealousy piercing through the woman who owned the very fabric of my fucking soul.

Years of parading women in front of her, of taunting her by dangling every piece of ass I tapped in her face, just so we could end up here.

"I suppose congratulations are in order." She tried to recover, plastering on a wobbly smile.

"Don't."

"Don't what?"

"Pretend like there'll ever be anyone else for me."

She opened her mouth, then thought the better of it and closed it. Whatever she wanted to say wouldn't matter in the grand scheme of things.

For the first time in her life, the great Tierney Callaghan was rendered speechless. Pity, as I never craved her words more.

I stood up and kissed the crown of her head, thinking it was a damn shame it was too late.

"Follow my plan." The order was clipped, cold. "Or both of us are dead."

CHAPTER THIRTY-FOUR
TIERNEY

I chugged two bottles of water as soon as I stumbled out of the motel, trying to push the nausea down my throat. I was numb head to toe, injured ankle included.

Achilles was getting married. It had never occurred to me that he would. Technically, there was no reason for him not to—he had a banging body, a fat bank account, and that dark, simmering energy that made women drop their panties. Why the hell not?

Well…because he was Achilles. *My* Achilles. The only woman to ever chart for him, for better or worse, was me.

I realized how shitty that sounded, even in my head, as I tramped my way to a car rental place where a vehicle was waiting for me. Achilles made all the arrangements—maps, transportation, another fake passport, the routes I should take—to get me out of here and to safety. I should definitely have been more grateful than I was, but I couldn't stop thinking about him screwing the faceless Katya Rasputin.

Soon to be Katya Ferrante.

Igor's daughter.

The one I'd never met, since she hadn't been sent to the Siberian camp her brothers were subjected to.

A fresh bout of bile traveled up my throat, threatening to spill out.

I had zero recollection of walking to the rental place, so it was a good thing I didn't have to fill out any paperwork. Achilles said to just dump the vehicle across the border and pay for my next ride in cash. Maybe I was growing into someone resembling my age, because for once, I decided to listen.

The car they gave me was a white Dacia Sandero. One of the most popular cars in Europe, hence entirely unremarkable. Muttering my thanks, I slid into the driver's seat and took out the maps Achilles gave me from my backpack. I was heading east, to Slovenia. I punched the address into the GPS device and started my journey. My next stop after Slovenia was Austria—Vienna—before finally arriving in Prague.

It gave me some time to marinate in my own thoughts. Thoughts I'd managed to push to the periphery of my mind because I was too busy surviving.

An hour into my drive, I couldn't take it anymore. Achilles said not to contact Tiernan for at least a year, but my emotions overrode my logic.

I took out my burner and called Tiernan. The damn phone didn't have a speaker option, so I had to hold it to my ear. He answered on the first ring.

"Jesus fuck," he spat out. "I've been worried sick. Where have you been?"

"Achilles found me."

"I gathered."

"And…" I sucked in a breath. "He let me go."

He smacked his lips. "That's the least the motherfucker could d—"

"You can't tell anyone I gave you a sign of life," I cut him off. "There's a mole around you."

"No one will know," he conceded. But I knew it wasn't true. He'd tell Lila. That was okay with me, though, because Lila was the last person who'd snitch.

"All I wanted was to let you know that I was okay and not to kill Achilles when he comes back and says he offed me."

"Bleeding fucking Christ," he muttered. "You should hang up. The longer we talk, the more likely—"

"Wait," I blurted out.

"Yeah?"

"Katya Rasputin..." I trailed off.

"What about her?"

"What do you know about her?"

I'd die before admitting to him I was jealous. But I was. The thought of Achilles putting a baby in that woman, watching her give birth, pouring the tiny amount of love he had in his heart into that baby made me sick and feral with jealousy. It ripped at my skin. I couldn't bear it.

"Not a ton." Tiernan's voice took on a bored lilt. "She's nineteen, maybe twenty. Goes to college somewhere in New England. Keeps to herself."

"Is she pretty?" My voice was unnaturally thick.

"The fuck should I know?"

"You've met her plenty."

"I don't look at women who aren't my wife," he scoffed. Then, sensing my urgency, he blew out a breath. "But I guess she's not terrible looking. Nothing to write home about but not appalling. She isn't Lila." I rolled my eyes at the pathetic longing in his voice. "And... She isn't you, either, sis," he finished.

"You would say that, wouldn't you." Tears filled my vision.

"I'm an honest cunt, for all intents and purposes."

"That, you are."

"We need to hang up befo—"

"Achilles is set to marry her."

There was a pregnant pause. "So I heard."

"Do you think she'll make him happy?"

I wanted him to be happy, but I didn't want him to be happy

with another woman. It made me feel like my stomach was ripped apart by hungry wolves.

"I don't think Achilles can be happy with anyone who isn't you."

Whether he said it out of loyalty to me or because he meant it was irrelevant. It was exactly what I needed to hear in that moment.

Pressing my lips together, I plastered on a smile so he could hear it. "I love you, Tiernan."

"Take care." It was an order, not a wish. "And if you need anything, call."

He hung up.

It took me four hours to drive to Ljubljana. It was a straight shot, no bathroom breaks. I drove with the same urgency Tiernan and I had when we escaped the work camp at fourteen. Like my ass was on fire.

Once in Ljubljana, I finally did something that wasn't obsessing over Achilles's upcoming nuptials—and that was to pee my own weight. As soon as I stopped at a gas station, I ripped out of the driver's seat and ran to the restroom and peed my life away. When I stared down at my panties, bunched around my thighs, I noticed white dots of Achilles's cum staining the fabric. That, along with the dull, stretchy pain between my thighs reminded me that we'd screwed each other's brains out not even six hours ago.

While he *knew* he was betrothed. He could've said something before I jumped into bed with him.

Would that have changed things?

Honestly? No.

It wasn't a real marriage and they weren't a real couple. And maybe this obsession went both ways, because something told me I would always jump Achilles's bones given the chance, no matter the circumstances.

It made me understand other women. The side pieces who preferred to take something over nothing, even if it broke their hearts and abolished their honor.

Oh my God, what was wrong with me? He was right. The first thing I was going to do after renting an apartment and buying a car was getting a therapist. Maybe two. Maybe six.

Exiting the restroom, I stocked up on water, energy bars, and gum at the convenience store. I walked out, leaving the car behind, knowing full well no one could track me down at this station, seeing as I was hidden under a ball cap and in a huge black hoodie I'd stolen from Achilles. It still smelled like him, and I was mad at myself for wasting his scent when I should've rationed it. Kept it in my backpack for the next time I needed a hit.

I made my way to the nearest main street, hopped on a bus, and didn't get off until I spotted a busy flea market along the river. There, I approached an elderly man with a casket hat and suspenders. He sat at an empty booth, trying to sell ancient-looking books and records without any success.

"What kind of car do you have?" I asked in English.

He didn't look up from his books, rearranging them on the small table. "Why you want to know?"

"I'll buy it from you for double its price."

That grabbed his attention. His gaze shot up to meet mine. "Renault Clio."

"How old?"

"Five years."

I nodded. "What's that, like, sixteen thousand Euros?" I took a wild guess, but I wasn't too worried about paying triple the market price. Money wasn't an issue. Between Achilles and Tiernan, I'd have plenty of it.

"Something like that." His eyes swept over me curiously.

"I'll buy it off you for thirty-two thousand. Cash." I stuck out my hand.

He looked around us, probably wondering if this was a prank. "I can't leave my things here. I... The paperwork..."

"Don't need it." I shook my head. "Take the money, give me the car, and don't ask any questions."

He stared at me in disbelief before nodding. "Yes. I agree to this deal of yours, strange girl."

An hour later, I was driving in a stranger's car toward Austria.

The drive to Vienna took four and a half more hours, and by the time I arrived, I was way too exhausted to keep on going. I wanted to eat, drink, use the bathroom, take a shower, and get a good night's sleep. Now that I knew Achilles wasn't after me—that he was actively throwing people off my scent to help me hide—I could do all that. In theory.

In practice, as I checked into a hotel in Hietzing—a far cry from the seedy motel in Venice—all I could do was go through the motions. Bathroom. Shower. Room service. I chewed my food robotically without even realizing what I was eating until the plate was half-empty and my stomach gave out. Then I curled into a ball on the bed, weeping quietly, rocked by the realization that the love of my life was about to marry someone else.

CHAPTER THIRTY-FIVE
ACHILLES

I was going to stalk her one last time.

What could I say? Old habits die hard.

Just to make sure she'd made it to Prague safely. That should take two, three days max. Nothing that'd throw me off schedule.

I'd made it this far keeping her alive—no small feat considering the giant, red self-destruct button she insisted on punching to death on a daily basis. I didn't need to rush. My problems in New York and Naples weren't going anywhere.

My old man had won. Even though I didn't kill her, Tierney was dead to the world. Out of sight but never out of mind. I was going to marry whoever the hell this Katya woman was, and the Ferrante legacy would live to see another day.

Somehow, granting my father his precious, warrior grandbabies didn't seem as appealing as it had been when I was a teenager. My desire to impregnate a complete stranger was low, and signing away my hypothetical children's futures to the Camorra seemed like a terrible idea, even to my conditioned ass.

Tierney took off with the car I'd rented for her. I'd rented a small Fiat for myself, following close behind. I wore a ball cap and a dark, long-sleeved shirt. She wouldn't notice me, because she wouldn't be looking for me.

And this time, once I saw she was settled, I *would* turn around and go away.

We drove into Slovenia, and when she ditched her first car at the gas station, I waited patiently for her to get on the bus before following it. I then waited across the street while she bargained with a merchant at the flea market, before joining her on her next four-and-a-half hour drive from Slovenia to Austria.

I wasn't worried I'd lose her, as I'd placed a tracker at the bottom of her backpack, but I'd never dropped a target before and sure as fuck wasn't planning to lose her.

On our way from Slovenia to Austria, my father called. I put the phone on speaker and tossed it onto the passenger seat, eyes glued on the road.

"Is it done?" he demanded. No small talk. Straight to the chase.

"Yup."

"You sure?"

"You're asking me if I'm sure that I killed someone?" If a tone could kill, the *stronzo* would finally be dead.

"I'm sorry you had to do it, son. It was a necessary evil." He wasn't fucking sorry, so I ignored that statement.

He continued. "The good news is you can now return home and we can start the preparations for your marriage with Katya."

"I'm headed to Naples to sort out the Coppola shit first."

That wasn't a lie. I *did* intend to go to Naples and deal with Sangue Blu. Especially considering he'd been retaliating by slaughtering our soldiers, young and old, pushing them into pools of acid.

I would do it. *After* Tierney was nice and settled in Prague. I was on her timeline, but she was making good progress.

"I assigned Luca to deal with Coppola."

"Coppola is my beef. And I think we have enough leverage to push him out of our borders."

"Considering you just shorted him a bride and six soldiers, it'd be political malpractice to send you down there."

"Relax, I'm not going to kill the guy." *At first, anyway.*

"What *is* it that you plan to do?"

"Talk."

He bristled. "A lot is riding on this. You gonna clean up the mess that you created?"

"You can bet your last dollar on it."

The line went quiet for a beat before he cleared his throat. "She's definitely dead, yes?"

"The fuck are you insinuating, old man?"

"*Bene, bene.* My hotheaded son. How you ever became such a good warrior with this temper of yours, I'll never understand."

I killed the call, hoping to shit my father would take my word for it.

She needed that new passport, and she needed to lay low.

Or we'd both be dead.

She checked into a luxurious hotel in Vienna at half past midnight, casually walking into the glitzy lobby with a backpack and a thirty-dollar getup.

I was in awe of her strength, with her quiet resilience and no-nonsense attitude. I knew she was hurting, but she hid it well. I was glad she chose somewhere nice, where she could get a decent meal, sleep, and amenities.

The minute she disappeared inside one of the elevators, I approached the receptionist and asked for the room next door to hers. An obscene bribe and a veiled death threat later, I had the digital key to the neighboring suite. Unlike Tierney, I wasn't going to sleep. I was going to stay alert and make sure no one else was coming for her.

At seven in the morning, I heard the door to the room adjoined to mine open and slid my laptop back to my bag. I followed her downstairs, taking the next available elevator. I watched as she whisked a coffee to-go and a plain croissant from an overpriced shop at the hotel, tossed her digital key in the checkout box, and slid into her car. I did the same, and we both started on our way to Prague.

We arrived at Old Town, where Tierney walked into the coffee shop I'd sent her to. So far, she'd done everything according to my instructions—a good indication she was serious about keeping us both alive.

Through the window, I watched Jakub, my old buddy, hand her a new passport. They shared a pleasant conversation. Pleasant for them, not for me. I wanted to stick a knife in his throat for smiling at her.

Stop flirting with my woman, I wanted to hiss out.

Did I care that he was gay and happily married to a guy named Steve? No. Not one fucking bit.

From there, Tierney proceeded to open a new bank account. I waited outside the HSBC branch and tossed breadcrumbs for pigeons, keeping one eye on the door. Finally, she walked out of the bank and straight into a real estate office across the street—also a contact I'd given her.

This is where you part ways. You see that she enters her new apartment, and you leave.

I gave her explicit instructions regarding the apartment I wanted her in—highly secured, with 24/7 surveillance, but not in a huge-ass skyscraper with enough human traffic to cover any wrongdoer's footprints. I even went the extra mile and gave her a list of properties I deemed suitable.

My balls were in my throat the entire journey following her from the real estate office after she entered her rented car. I released a queasy breath when she stopped in front of one of the buildings I'd flagged for her. Eight stories. Twenty apartments. Highly secure.

Tierney and the seedy-looking real estate agent poured out of their respective vehicles, and I parked but didn't kill the engine.

The real estate agent said something to her, touching her arm—I REPEAT, TOUCHING HER ARM—before dropping a set of keys in her palm, then jerking a thumb behind his shoulder. With that, he turned around and walked away.

Wait.

What the fuck?

Why wasn't he going in with her?

More than likely, the answer was he needed to show another property, pick up something, or—Jesus, I dunno—take a shit and would be back shortly.

But there was a slight chance this was a setup.

I was leaving nothing to chance when it came to her.

Killing the engine, I slid out of the car and followed her into the building.

Luckily for me, she decided to take the stairs. If she'd taken the elevator, I'd have been searching every individual floor, which would cost me precious time.

I trailed behind her, stopping at the edge of the stairway when she reached the second floor and stuck the key in one of the doors.

Leave the door open, baby. You're expecting that real estate agent shitbag, remember?

She shoved the door open and walked inside, leaving it ajar.

Thank. Fuck.

Pushing off the stair rail, I followed her inside. At this point, I knew I had to make myself known. She'd be pissed, but hopefully she'd understand. Hey, I was just trying to help her out.

I stepped into the sunny and spacious apartment, bare of furniture. The windows were open, and a summer breeze swept inside. Tierney had her back to me, staring out at Old Town Bridge Tower. Her now-black hair danced in the wind. A waft of its flowery, clean scent entered my nostrils and my knees went weak.

It seemed like the coast was clear. Still, my heart thrummed wildly in my chest.

I took another step forward.

What the fuck do I say?

Hi, Little Flame, I know I made a big stink about never seeing you again… Well, surprise!

Or: Oh, hi, Tierney. Fancy seeing you here. How about another quickie?

Suddenly, she turned around. Our eyes locked.

She looked…scared.

Why wouldn't she be? You were sent to Europe to kill her, idiot.

"Achilles…" Her mouth dropped in shock.

I opened my mouth to say I wasn't here to hurt her, just to ensure no one else did.

But before I could do that, a quiet, deadly *pop* of a bullet muffled by a suppressor sliced through the air.

Tierney's body dropped to the floor. Her emerald eyes were still wide-open, staring at me with terror, as blood trickled from the back of her head.

WHAT THE FUCK?

Fuck, fuck, fuck, fuck, fuck.

I careened toward her, falling to my knees, holding her limp head between my hands. Blood vined around my fingers, spilling onto the floor.

"No!" I roared. "Little Flame…no… I ca—can't… You have to stay. I'll do anything… I promise…just…please… I can't do this without you."

I plastered my forehead to hers, a savage cry ripping from my chest. With one hand, I took out my phone and called the 112 emergency line. In my other, I gripped her head wound tightly, trying to stop the blood loss. Oh fuck, oh fuck, oh fuck. I couldn't breathe. Not that there was a point doing so if she wasn't around.

But on the off chance I could save her…

Fuck. I couldn't lose her.

"She's dead," a robotic voice growled above my head.

I looked up.
Red purge mask.
Voice muffler.
Combat gear from head to toe.
Tristan Hale was standing in front of me, holding a gun.
The motherfucker just *killed* Tierney.
My Tierney.
The love of my life.
His seconds left on this earth severely decreased.
He better start fucking running.

PART TWO
THE CHASE

CHAPTER THIRTY-SIX

THEN

She woke up in a hospital with tubes in her veins.

Groggy, aching, and feeling like her lungs were full of lead.

The memories rushed to the forefront of her mind.

The alcohol. The despair. The fire. Achilles.

The only thing she'd ever wanted was for him to be happy and thrive. And somehow, she couldn't even get this right because, instead of eliminating herself from his life in a way that wouldn't make him struggle with a decision, she'd hurt him. Maybe even killed him.

What if he died?

What if she's caused permanent damage?

She ripped the needles and tubes from her veins. Pushing up on wobbly knees, she staggered to the door. Her vision was blurry, and she bumped into things.

"I—I need to see him," she whimpered, even though she was alone. "I have t—to make sure that h—he's okay."

Once in the hallway, she flung her shoulder against a wall to support herself.

He'd saved her.

She'd tried to commit suicide, set her room on fire, and he'd saved her. Idiot! She was supposed to save him from herself. From a life with a barren wife and a family that'd forever resent him once they found out her secret.

"Whoa. Easy there, tigress." Tiernan rushed toward her from the other side of the hallway, steadying her with his hands. "You need to be in bed."

"I need...need...to see him. Take me to him."

"See who?"

Like everyone else, Tiernan wasn't aware of her relationship with Achilles. She made sure of it. She didn't want Achilles to get into trouble with his family.

"Ach...Achilles," she coughed out. "He saved me. He should be here."

He opened his mouth, about to argue, but something in her expression told him she wasn't backing down. "Go rest. I'll find him for you."

Achilles was being treated just down the hall. She and Tiernan stopped outside his room, where two Camorra soldiers stood on guard.

"Let her through." Her brother jutted his chin at his sister. "She's the girlfriend, apparently," he muttered in annoyance.

"Don't care if she's the fucking pope," one of the soldiers spat sideways. "No visitors unless Don Vello says so."

Tiernan's expression clouded. "What if I tell you the next time I have to repeat myself, your windpipe is going to be used as my fucking—"

"Let her in," Luca ordered from the darkened room. He stood up, waltzing over to them. "But first, I want a word."

He reached the door, lowering his head to whisper in her ear. "Privacy."

"Tiernan, leave," Tierney snapped.

Her brother's hooded eyes promised to shed blood at the slightest provocation. "Fine, but remember I'm around the corner, Ferrante. And very trigger-fucking-happy to take you and everyone in your family tree down."

"Well aware."

He left. Luca still stood in her way, blocking the entrance. He was huge, handsome, and well dressed. But so impersonal and dead that he reminded her of a shark.

"How're you feeling?" She knew he was asking just to be polite.

"Been better."

Luca's cold gaze swept along her face, sending an ice cube down her spine. He wasn't supposed to know she and Achilles were together, though she guessed he had a good idea now.

"Is he...is he okay?"

"He's awake, if that's what you're asking."

"Can I see him?"

"You can, and you fucking will. Because once you get in there, you are going to break off your little affair whether you want to or not."

Her eyes widened. She knew, of course, that it was the logical thing to do. That Achilles deserved better. But with everything he'd done for her, it was hard to imagine doing this to him.

"B—but we love each oth—"

"Stop right there." Luca clapped a heavy hand over her shoulder. "You're a smart girl. You know as well as I do this shit won't last. Don Vello won't let it. He has big plans for Achilles. He sent me to tell you this is over. So it is over. Either you break it off, or I'll break you. Now, which is it going to be?"

She stared in his vacant, merciless eyes and knew he'd kill her without so much as a blink. Luca Ferrante was just as cruel as Achilles, but unlike Achilles, he'd never shown a trace of humanity or emotion to her.

And he wasn't wrong. They were doomed from the beginning. A Romeo and Juliet of the underworld.

"I'll let him make that decision." She stuck her chin out.

"If he picks you, I'll kill you myself," Luca said. "And while you don't give two shits about your own life, he does. It'd break him like nothing else. I advise you to think carefully."

She nodded, stifling a cry. "I'll break it off."

"Good girl."

"I never meant to hurt him, you know."

"Sweetheart." Luca palmed her cheek, giving her a pitying look. "I don't give a fuck."

Dizziness took over her as she wobbled inside the room. Her vision became white and spotty, and she collapsed onto a chair in front of his bed to stop herself from fainting.

She blinked into focus. Slowly, her vision returned, but she wished it hadn't.

Achilles was no longer the gorgeous, chiseled boy with the shy composure and bottomless brown eyes.

He looked...terrifying.

His face was partly hidden by bandages, but whatever was visible was marred with red, swollen scars.

He was awake and alert, studying her reaction to him wordlessly. She wanted to cry, to beg for forgiveness, to run away.

She did none of those things. Just took his hand and brought it to her lips. Kissed it gently, scared to hurt him.

"Are you okay?" *His voice was scratchy.*

That was all it took for her tears to start falling. It was just like him to worry about her until the very end.

"Yes. Are you?"

His disfigured lips stretched into a smile. "Take a wild guess."

She was going to break it off. To save him from her. And to save them both from Don Vello. Luca made it clear she'd never be accepted into the family.

"I started the fire." *Her chin vibrated.* "I...I wanted to die."

"You wanted to leave me?" *he croaked.*

She said nothing.

"Even though you knew it'd kill me?"

Silence.

"They say people who commit suicide are selfish."

She'd heard that before, and she did not agree at all. If being altruistic meant suffering an agonizing existence every second of every minute of every day of every year for the rest of her life, then maybe self-sacrifice was overrated. She'd never meant harm to anyone but herself.

"I—I knew your father would never accept m—"

"That's for me to worry about, not you."

She pursed her lips, staring down at her bare feet. *"You didn't even tell your family we were together, Achilles."*

"You knew I'd save you." He ignored her words.

"Yes."

"And you still did it."

She thought he'd be too late. He'd arrived hours earlier. She thought she'd planned this so carefully to spare him…

"Yes. But, Achilles—"

"Let me guess, instead of telling me what you were worried about, you drank yourself half to death, as usual, then tried to off yourself instead of fucking TALKING TO ME."

She flinched. He was right. But she was still new to loving someone. She'd never done it before.

"I thought I was doing you a favor," she whispered.

He snorted derisively. *"How do I look?"*

"W—what?"

"How. Do. I. Look?" He enunciated each word.

"You…" She looked away from him, not because she was disgusted but because his face was a reminder of what she'd done. *"You look like the love of my life."*

"The TRUTH," he roared.

"You don't look good," she admitted. When she chanced another look at him, she saw the unwavering cruelty in his expression. The one he gave everyone but her until today. *"You look…you look bad."*

"Funny." His lips twisted in a bitter curl. *"You look just as gorgeous as the last time I saw you. If not a little pale."*

She hung her head in shame. She wanted to just tell him the truth. That she wanted to die because she couldn't be the woman he was destined to marry. Vello would never ever let them go through with the wedding. And even if he did, Achilles would feel betrayed. No offspring. No heirs. If Achilles didn't have children, he'd never become don. And that was all he'd ever aspired to be. It was his dream.

Maybe he'd have stayed with her anyway. He was a good man. But he'd take a mistress. Another woman who could bear his children. And those kids would run between her legs in Camorra weddings and funerals, a constant reminder she wasn't good enough.

But it was too late now anyway. Luca was going to rip the world to shreds if she didn't break up with Achilles. He'd made it clear.

"*Tell me why you almost killed me,*" *he demanded.*

"*I…*" Tell him the truth. Tell him how much you lost in Siberia. Open up to him. "*I don't know.*"

"*You don't know?*" *He was so shocked, it came out as a whisper.*

"*I guess I…*" *She pushed each word out of her mouth like it was poison.* "*I guess I just needed to get rid of you somehow, and that was as good way as any.*"

He stared at her, shocked.

"*You got too clingy.*" *She forced herself to shrug.* "*And I knew you'd save me. I kind of hoped…*" Say it. Just say it and get it over with. "*I kind of hoped you'd die saving me.*"

He closed his eyes. "*We're over.*"

This hurt her so badly she couldn't breathe. She felt the words in her bones. They scorched through her. She squirmed on the chair.

"*I'm so sorr—*"

"*Don't,*" *he snapped.* "*I don't want your pity.*"

"*Achill—*"

"*Don't feel so bad, Piccola Fiamma,*" *he cooed.* "*Once I get out of here, I'll ruin your life, too. That way we'll be even. Now, truth?*"

"*Truth*" *she found the courage to whisper.*

"*I will always fucking love you, but I'll spend every waking moment of my life making sure no one else ever does.*"

And with these words, he condemned her to a loveless life, allowing no one to take his place.

CHAPTER THIRTY-SEVEN
TIERNEY

Beep. Beep. Beep. Beep.

The steady rhythm thunked against my skull.

Pain.

I was in so much pain.

And cold.

All the way down to my bones.

The air was dry. Static. Still.

I tried to pry my eyes open, but my eyelids were too heavy.

Beep. Beep. Beep. Beep.

Where was I? Was I safe? Was I home? Did it even matter?

Beep. Beep. Beep. Beep.

I slipped back into unconsciousness, letting the darkness swallow me whole.

Sometimes I heard voices even though my eyes were closed. They always sounded like they were coming from above and I was underwater. I didn't trust my own ears, especially when, one night, I heard the door to my room creaking open. I felt a shift in the atmosphere, the temperature dropping, like a nocturnal animal just entered my domain.

Then a brush of cold, callused knuckles over my jawline and a voice I'd recognize anytime, anywhere, under water or dirt. Dead or alive. A voice I had known since before it even spoke to me—of a beautiful monster who did very ugly things.

"You have to stay alive, Piccola Fiamma, so you can kill me like you promised." The words were spoken softly, unhurriedly. "I'm holding you to that. Don't let me down, Little Flame. I'm waiting on the other end."

This was a lie.

A coping mechanism.

My heart trying to piece itself back together.

It was the morphine. The drugs. My temporary insanity.

I forced myself back to sleep.

Hours, or maybe days, later, I woke up again.

This time, I managed to open my eyes. Everything still hurt like a bitch but in an abstract, indescribable way. They'd probably pumped me full of enough painkillers to kill an elephant.

Peering around, I registered a generic hospital room painted in soft blues. Lifting my head was a big no-no. I wasn't even going to attempt such foolishness. My skull was weighed down by a headache and about ten pounds' worth of bandages. I slanted my gaze until my pupils hurt, searching for signs, to see whether they were in English or Italian.

The last thing I remembered was being in a motel room in Italy with Achilles. He said he'd let me go.

He lied.

I mean, clearly, or I wouldn't be here, would I?

I didn't know why the pain from his lying was greater than the pain in my body, but it somehow was. Maybe because no matter how far we'd fallen, we'd never lied to each other before.

Other than that time Luca threatened to kill you.

My eyes finally landed on a sign under the mounted TV, but it was too far for me to make out the words. I *thought* it was English, but that didn't make any sense. Whatever happened to me happened in Italy. So why would I be anywhere else?

The door whined open, but my now-giant head with the big-ass bandage pressing onto my jaw and forehead was still nailed to the pillow and I couldn't see who it was.

Please don't let it be him...

Lila's Barbie-doll face came into view, peering down at me worriedly. Her blond brows zipped together at the sight of me awake.

"Tier!" She rushed to the edge of my bed, placing a comforting hand on my arm through the blanket. I guess she had swaddled me like she did Gennaro, like I was a human burrito. Now that I was noticing more things, I also had compression socks on, and my face felt like it'd been scrubbed clean.

"Hi,'" I croaked, sounding about a thousand years old.

"Sweetheart, you're awake." She couldn't stop stroking my face gently, so much warmth radiating from her eyes. "How are you feeling?"

"Like hell," I groaned. "Where am I?"

"In the hospital."

"Yeah, but...where?" I asked. "Europe? America?"

"New York," she said, dragging a chair by the door and plopping next to me. "You've been out for two weeks."

I groaned. "What happened to me?"

"A bullet to the head."

Trust Lila not to mince words. She was new to making conversations and often said things bluntly without regard for social etiquette. Came with the territory of finally stepping out of her mother's shadow and living life like a normal person after being sheltered for so many years by her parents.

"Okay, can you..." I winced, the headache mounting behind my eyelids. "Can you give me the rundown of what happened to me?"

"You got shot in Europe. The killer aimed for your head, but it turned out the bullet only fractured the back of your skull. It didn't touch your brain. You spent two days in a medically induced coma while they ran some tests. Tiernan arranged for you to be flown into New York so we could take care of you here. Are you feeling disoriented? Have poor eyesight? Confused?"

"I don't think so." I frowned. The simple action hurt like my forehead was about to split in half. "When did they take me out of the medically induced coma?"

"Two days ago. You took your time, but I guess you've had a very long few weeks." Lila rubbed my arm affectionately, but I couldn't feel much of it. "They're still worried about brain damage and hemorrhages. Do you remember anything?"

"I remember Achilles came after me. He was assigned to kill me."

Lila nodded but said nothing. My brows bunched together as something occurred to me. "Hey, how come your father let me come back to the United States? I thought I was banished."

Lila's eyes flared dramatically. "Oh, of course. You don't know."

"Know what?"

"He won't be bothering you anymore," she started to say, but before I could hear more, my body collapsed and I fell into slumber again.

CHAPTER THIRTY-EIGHT
TIERNEY

For the next four days, all I did was drift in and out of consciousness.

They pumped painkillers into me at a remarkable speed. Apparently, breaking your skull was no joke. Lila might have been a little gentle when relaying what happened to me. Because even though the bullet didn't reach the brain, it left one heck of a dent in the back of my head and created some balance and vertigo issues I was going to have to work on.

The doctors who treated me spoke directly to either Tiernan or Lila. I had zero agency. For the first time in my life, I didn't fight my own war, and even though I trusted Tiernan and Lila, I didn't like being in this position at all.

Two Irish soldiers stood on guard in front of my room at all times.

When I asked Tiernan about Vello, he vaguely assured me the don wouldn't be a problem anymore, but neither he nor Lila told me exactly what convinced him to drop his grudge. It worried me. Vello wasn't the kind of man to simply give up a vendetta and move on to other ventures.

"All you need to know is that you're safe," my brother assured me. "I should've never let that eejit Achilles run after you. Should've put a bullet in his head when I had the chance."

I took this as confirmation he was the one who pulled the trigger.

The gaps in my memory were consistently narrowing as more information trickled into my conscience.

Achilles had sent me off with maps, a fake passport, and a strategy for Prague.

I followed his meticulous plan, believing he'd tried to help me. It was the first time I'd put my trust in someone else, and it backfired spectacularly.

He cornered me in the apartment he'd instructed me to rent in Prague and killed me.

"Where is he now?" I asked.

"Achilles?" Tiernan twisted his wrist to glance at his watch. "Here in New York."

I was a little surprised Tiernan had let him live after what he'd done to me. Then again, Achilles *was* his brother-in-law. Still…It wasn't like Tiernan to forgive about something so egregious. He wasn't exactly the merciful type.

"I see." I was too exhausted to dig into the subject, so I changed it altogether. "And Tyrone?" I asked. "Why hasn't he visited me yet?"

My father was usually first in line to put on the saint act. I didn't buy his charade but respected the hustle. Almost everyone believed he was a levelheaded, good-intentioned man. Only I knew he didn't give half a shit about any of his children. Case in point—when Fintan disappeared out of the blue, he didn't so much as shed a tear. Tyrone cared about nothing and no one but his own reputation and image.

That he hadn't bothered visiting me once while I was in the hospital was puzzling to say the least.

"Tyrone…" Tiernan trailed off. "He's…away."

"Away where?" My eyes narrowed. "You make it sound like he's an elderly hamster Mommy and Daddy sent to the farm."

"Close enough. He's chained in the Ferrantes' basement."

At first, I just blinked, processing the information. I'd wager Tiernan was joking, but I happened to know my brother did not possess a sense of humor or any trait that could be interpreted as such.

"What?"

"He's in the basement of torture," Tiernan clipped out, jaw twitching in irritation. "And will remain so for the foreseeable future."

That made me sit upright. And *that* made me pass out from pain. It wasn't a figure of speech. I did, in fact, faint right onto the pillow.

Only to wake up a few hours later to the most terrifying surprise of my life.

My eyes fluttered open to a quiet, ominous presence in the room.

It wasn't one of the doctors or nurses. They always moved noisily and carelessly, bumping into stuff, causing a ruckus to see if I'd wake up.

I was still fuming at my body for fainting from just sitting upright. Apparently, I had some balance issues to deal with. Physical therapy was going to be a real challenge. I was bad at working out and even worse at following instructions.

Lila already assured me they had a room ready for me at their house. She'd been interviewing physical therapists around the area and ordered special equipment for occupational therapy in her backyard. I absolutely *loathed* the idea of being unloading onto them. Of being the second baby, next to Nero. I hadn't needed anyone since my days as an orphan in Siberia.

But… I didn't have much choice, either.

The worst part was that I didn't care—not about where I was going and not about getting better. Not much about anything, really, since I'd come to.

From the moment I first woke up from the coma, something fundamental had changed.

I woke up remembering.

Everything.

All the shit in Siberia that I'd buried in the back of my head so my life could resemble something normal had bubbled right up to the surface like an overflowing sewer.

The rapes.

The abuse.

The hunger.

The pain.

The despair—and the acute, bone-deep notion that humanity had stooped to places so terribly low—meant life was no longer worth living at all. Everything I'd run away from had caught up with me, and now I had nowhere to hide. I was stuck in a bed, forced to remember.

All the moments I wanted to forget.

All the trauma I drowned in parties and fake friends and lavish shopping sprees.

I didn't want to get better. I wanted to close my eyes and never wake up again.

The other presence flicked the light on, shifting closer.

"Lila," I groaned, blinking the world into focus. "How long have I been ou—"

The rest of the sentence perished on the tip of my tongue as soon as I opened my eyes.

Sitting across from me was Achilles Ferrante.

A wrathful beast of massive proportions. Imposing, scary, and dead in the eyes.

Our gazes clashed. My heart rode all the way up to my throat, and any lingering pain or dull ache disappeared from my body. My lungs scorched.

This wasn't happening.

Can't. Breathe.

He is here to murder you.

And considering you're bedridden, this time he is going to succeed.

Dying didn't scare me anymore. But I wanted to go on my own terms.

Still, I was me. So I decided to die with a smile.

"What, no flowers?" I tried to purr, but it came out all gruffy and wrong. "Oh well. Don't bother putting any on my grave. My first order of business will be haunting your ass into an early grave."

"I'm not here to finish the job." His voice was unbearably soft, and it made me angry because it reached a place inside me he had no right touching.

"You should." I plastered on my best airy-socialite smile. "Because once I'm back on my feet, I will certainly kill you."

His brows slammed together, concern and confusion fighting for dominance in his features. "Tierney…"

"Get out."

He stayed rooted in place, a war waging in his onyx eyes. He'd probably never gotten thrown out of anywhere before. If he had, he wasn't the kind of man to linger and try pleading his case. This solidified my suspicion he was here to kill me.

I scooted to sit upright, willing myself not to faint again. I searched for a panic button, so if he did finish me off, at least he'd get caught and spend his remaining days in prison, where he belonged.

How did he get past security anyway? Past the Irish soldiers at my door? Some things didn't click, but my mind was such a jumbled mess, trying to piece it all together made my head hurt.

Achilles's eyes traced my movements, and his face cleared, like a penny had dropped. *"No."*

"No, what? I didn't ask you anything," I attempted a weak, pathetic laugh.

"I wasn't the one who shot you."

"Spare me," I bit out. "I remember everything."

"You clearly don't," he growled doggedly. "Break it down for me." But again, the bite was gone from his voice, replaced with gentleness that made my chest tight. It reminded me of *my* Achilles.

The one I loved so hard and so deep, I was willing to take my own life to spare his. "Leave," I said.

"No, tell me," he insisted, tone leaking desperation. "Tell me what happened. Play it back for me."

He wasn't going to leave until we did this song and dance. Just as well, as I was eager to remember more than him.

"We got to Prague…" I licked my lips, rolling the film back in my head. "I opened a bank account under the new name like you told me. Then walked across the street to meet with a real estate agent."

"Yes?" The urgency in his speech was unmistakable. He leaned forward, like he was watching a soccer game, getting ready for his team to score. "And?"

"Uh…" His gaze on me felt like the first ray of sunshine I'd had in weeks, and I hated that it made me warmer than any blanket. "The real estate agent and I went to the apartment—the one you told me to rent…" A headache started to form behind my eyes again. I kneaded my temples with a groan. "But at the last minute, he said he'd gotten a text to pick up his daughter from school because his wife was stuck in traffic."

"Uh-huh." Achilles's tongue moved across his teeth in barely contained rage. It was the first glimpse of the Achilles I knew and remembered today. "Sure. Daughter. Traffic. Carry on."

"I took the stairs up because a man I didn't know entered the elevator just as I arrived at the building, and I felt…queasy about it."

The man in the elevator was a new memory. I guess my mind had skipped over that minor detail because it didn't feel important before. But maybe it *was* important. I remembered having the distinct feeling I didn't want to be in close quarters with him.

"What did he look like?" Achilles shot off.

"I don't know…" I squinted, desperate to remember. "Tall? Athletic build. Muscular but lean…" He wasn't unpleasant to look at. But he gave off the same vibe Achilles and Tiernan did when they entered a room, supercharging the air with violence and malice.

"Did you see his face?"

"No."

"Was he wearing a mask?"

I closed my eyes, feeling irritated, overwhelmed, but most of all useless. "I…I don't know."

When I opened my eyes, I caught his nostrils flaring with frustration. "Continue."

"So I went up the stairs and opened the apartment with the key the real estate agent gave me. I kept it ajar, remembering he said he was right across the street and shouldn't take long…"

I had looked out the window. Turned around. Saw Achilles…

But he wasn't the one who shot me.

Suddenly, the memory rushed back to me. The bullet had grazed the back of my skull. Not front. Not sides. The *back*. Achilles was a great shot, but he was no magician, and there was no physical way for him to reach that angle.

I cupped my mouth, tears distorting the world out of focus. "I thought…I thought it was you."

"Piccola Fiamma." He leaned forward and gathered me into his arms, stroking the back of my head. The bandages were off now. The back of my head was shaved, and Lila had cut the front in short pixie waves. She told me the black hair dye had washed out of my natural red hair. But I realized I had not seen myself once in the mirror since I'd come to.

I hadn't had time for vanity when I first saw Achilles here. I was too busy panicking about being murdered. But now that my face was crushed to his shoulder, him trembling with emotions, my pulse finally slowing to a normal pace, I realized I didn't exactly look like hot shit.

It wasn't the fact half my head was shaved—actually, that was adequately badass. It was everything else. The blue and purple bruises all over my face from the hit I took when I fell. The paleness. The flakiness of dry, air-conditioned skin. Not to mention the back of my head was stitched.

"Who did it?" I whimpered into his shirt. "Was it—was it my dad? Is that why you have him?"

"No." He dropped a kiss to my temple, and I could feel him struggling to contain his feelings, his movements, his need to crush me with his big body and swallow me whole. "It was Tristan Hale."

I reared my head back, staring at him in shock. "Your father sent him?"

He nodded. "He didn't think I'd have it in me to do it, and he was right."

"So Tristan followed us." I pulled away, pressing my knuckles to my mouth. I didn't know what the assassin actually looked like. No one did. Tristan Hale was half myth, half god. No one knew his nationality, his looks, his homebase; he was impossible to pin down. The only two people I knew who were able to hire him were Vello and, according to legends, Alex Rasputin.

He normally worked for corrupt politicians, especially overseas.

There were a million questions I wanted to ask, and I had no choice but to ask them one at a time.

"Did you…?"

Achilles shook his head with sorrow. "No. I had to choose between giving you CPR and killing him. He took off."

"And Vello is fine with me being here?"

He shrugged, and I marveled at how the scars made him even more beautiful than he had been as a teenager. Like he was carved from tragedy into something invincible that nothing and no one could ever break.

"H—how?"

"I almost killed him when I got home," Achilles confessed.

My stomach dropped, and I couldn't breathe.

"You did?" I croaked.

"Tiernan held him down, and I nearly beat him to death… Then fucking Enzo and Luca walked in and killed all the fun."

"Party poopers," I muttered through my tears. "And Tiernan's up to speed on it?"

"Everyone is. The Bratva and Irish took it personally, so let's just say Hale's going to stay well away from you."

Tense silence draped across the room. Heaviness settled in my gut. Why was he here? Probably to clear the air, make sure I knew he wasn't the one who'd tried to kill me, and move on with his life.

"I remember everything," I whispered.

He closed his eyes, pressing his lips together tightly. He didn't have to ask what I meant. He knew.

"And now that I remember," I choked out, my eyes burning with tears, "I know exactly why I worked so hard to forget. I can't live like this, Achilles."

His expression hardened, and he reached to squeeze my hands. Mine were cold and dry in contrast with his hot, giant palms. But I found no comfort, no solace in his touch.

I was back to being this fourteen-year-old girl. Tiny and angry and hopeless.

"How do I look?" I threw his words back in his face, after all those years I'd sat there, in a hospital room, trying to atone for my sins.

Achilles didn't miss a beat. "Still the most beautiful girl in the world. The one I walked through fire for and would gladly do it all over again just to win her smile."

His words, which I had craved for over a decade, brushed right past me. Like a stranger on the street. I couldn't bear the numbness.

"You lie," I croaked.

"It'd be my honor." He bowed his head.

"I'm sure your future wife won't like to hear it," I croaked out.

"There's not going to be a future wife for me, Tierney," he said quietly. "Unless it is you."

I closed my eyes. "I'm broken."

"I'm patient."

"Are you serious right now?" I peeled my eyelids open to catch him nodding.

"I told Don Vello I wasn't going to marry Katya sometime between breaking his nose and dislocating his jaw. It's you that I want. It's always been you. Fuck, Tier, it took me eleven years to come to terms with it, and watching you almost die to cement it. But I'm done fighting it. And I'm willing to wait."

"It's too late." My throat felt tight, and I clenched my teeth to keep my tears at bay. "Too much has happened. Separately, and between us."

"I made some mistakes—"

"No, Achilles! You made my life a prison of your own making for half of my existence. Even after I escaped the gulag, you made sure I'd never be truly free. You murdered my lovers, broke into my apartment, assigned bodyguards to tail me, and refused to allow me to move, date, or marry. To move on from this, from us."

"I know."

"You made me your *whore* for a weekend, knowing my past and what I'd been through. You fucked me every three hours on the dot for the privilege of not marrying me off to a complete stranger."

"I know," his voice cracked.

"And then, the cherry on the shit cake, you tried to *assassinate* me."

His eyes, so dark, so brutal, fastened on my own. No words left his mouth.

"And you think, after everything that happened, that I'm going to forgive you?"

"Yes," he said with conviction.

"Why?" I spluttered. Achilles was many things—shrewd, vicious, a prolific assassin, and an impeccable, unhinged mobster. He was not, however, delusional.

"Because I'll do anything to make you mine." Rather than

desperation, determination dripped from his every word. "Even at the price of obliterating my own life for your entertainment."

"Too much has passed between us to make this happen," I said.

"A lot more will happen, as you'll soon see." He stood, seemingly unbothered by my words. "Mark my words, Piccola Fiamma. By this time next year, we'll be married."

CHAPTER THIRTY-NINE
TIERNEY

In the ensuing days, more memories flooded to the forefront of my mind.

Every moment awake was excruciating, every recollection a deep slash in my already bleeding heart.

Lila and Tiernan came every day. I barely responded to them. The doctors wanted to run more tests. They thought they must've missed something. They hadn't. My body was healing just fine. It was my soul that was in critical condition.

I was retreating to a dark place inside myself no one was able to reach.

Achilles continued visiting me. He was the only person I communicated with, and even that was in order to hurt him for everything he'd done to me.

At first, I tried insults as a way to get him out of there.

"I don't need to see your ugly face while I'm recovering," I muttered when he walked through the door.

"Fair enough. I'll turn around." He stood and straddled the chair with his back to me. I watched his corded back through his olive-green Henley as he spoke. "Brought you some of that gross-ass fish soup you like, from the Russian deli on your street."

"Ukha. I hate that soup." I used to love that soup back when things still had flavor and meaning.

"I'll throw it out the window, then."

"I hate you, too. Can you jump out of it, as well?"

"Sure. But I'd probably choose a higher floor, just to be on the safe side."

No matter how cruel and dismissive I was, the asshole kept coming back. When it was clear I wasn't going to bully him out of my life, I pretended to be asleep every time he came by for a visit. It was the same strategy I used with Lila and Tiernan, and it worked like a charm.

Unfortunately, Achilles didn't mind at all. He would settle in on the chair, crack open *The Hitchhiker's Guide to the Galaxy*, and start reading me our favorite parts. He remembered all of them, of course, including the ones that made me roll on the floor like a madwoman as a teenager, howling in delight. Even when I tried blocking his voice from my head, I'd still catch bits and pieces, and sometimes, my lips would curve into a traitorous smile.

He never mentioned it, but every time it happened, he raised his voice, going the extra mile, providing me with a dramatization, exaggerated English accent included.

The days crawled by at a maddening pace. Tiernan and Lila were beginning to see that I was avoiding them. The doctors and nurses were catching on to the fact that my silence and refusal to speak had nothing to do with my fractured skull and everything to do with my fractured soul.

I was drowning in memories, rarely coming up for air.

I felt every assault, every cut, every slap like they happened yesterday, and not when I was a kid.

And though I always knew that it happened, I was now forced to either come to terms with it or take matters in my own hands and end this misery.

I was too exhausted to make the decision. Too lethargic to even care.

For a while, it was all the same, a never-ending string of hours full of misery and despair.

Then, one day, gruff voices seeped from behind my door.

"You must be out of your fucking mind, lad," I heard my brother growl. "I'm not letting you take her anywhere."

"I'm the only one she speaks to," Achilles argued back.

My heart picked up pace, reminding me it was still there in my chest. It was a strange notion, because in all the days since I'd woken up, I couldn't feel it beat.

"She hates you," Tiernan snarled.

"I know how to bring her back," Achilles insisted.

"Are you even listening? She *hates* you," Tiernan said again.

"Look, I'm not fucking asking," Achilles said, finally sounding like his old autocrat self. "I'm *telling* you I'm taking her somewhere to recoup. We can do it the nice, you-discharging-her-and-getting-updates way, or I can snatch her in the dead of night and make headlines neither of us wants. Either way, she's coming with me. Make the better choice, Callaghan."

"*Fuck*," Tiernan muttered.

There were no words spoken after that.

And I knew that, as always, Achilles had won.

CHAPTER FORTY
TIERNEY

Nights and days blurred together through the haze of my turmoil, so I wasn't exactly aware when it was that Achilles took me from the hospital.

At some point, strong arms fastened around me. I was put in a wheelchair. I kept my eyes closed, refusing to cooperate.

When he wheeled me out to a waiting vehicle, I let my eyes flutter open momentarily. It was dark outside. The whispers of autumn licked at my skin. I must've been hospitalized for at least a couple of weeks.

He placed my limp body in the passenger seat and rolled the window all the way down. Then he drove through the pitch-black night on desolate roads, passing woods, rolling hills, and even the ocean at one point. The brine from the water teased my nostrils, awakening something in me. A primal sense of being present somewhere beautiful.

The mystical silence, the gentle touch of a silvery moon, and the sharp fragrance of fall pleased me, bringing me back, even if momentarily, from my misery.

Fucker. How dare he?

He knew what he was doing.

Achilles didn't say one word the entire drive. I didn't ask how long it was or where we were going, but when we arrived, dawn broke across the horizon in gorgeous pinks and blues.

I wondered if this was a part of a meticulous plan. To show me the sunrise. To remind me that the world could be heartachingly beautiful, despite all the ugly things it harbored.

As always, he didn't ask. He took. That was all I needed in order to know Achilles hadn't changed. Not really. He still thought he could control every aspect of my life.

He parked in front of a solitary cabin so close to shore it looked like it could be swept away by one big wave. I didn't know what state we were in, let alone what town. It seemed remote, if not completely deserted.

Achilles rounded the car, opened my door, and lifted me up. My eyes were open, but he knew better than to take that as an invitation to talk to me.

Prowling the short walk to the house, he kicked the unlocked door open and marched inside. I couldn't muster enough interest to look at the place. I let him put me in a bed and turned my back to him.

Then I fell asleep, praying to never wake up.

I did wake up, despite my prayers.

I wasn't surprised nor disappointed. If there was God, He'd made it clear He did not take mercy on me.

I woke up crying to the memory of five men mounting me.

They were fully clothed, all unbuckled, and I was naked, on the snow.

I must've fought them in my sleep, same way I did in the camp, because my blankets were tossed to the floor and my limbs were in disarray.

I could feel the sharp bite of the cold against my back, even though when I looked around, the room was nice and toasty.

I couldn't remember the last time I ate or felt the sunlight over my skin and felt little desire to provide my body with either. But I did need to pee, so I kicked off the suffocating pressure socks Achilles had put me in and treaded barefoot around the small, one-story house. I found the bathroom adjoined to the living room and another bedroom down the hall. This must have been where Achilles was staying. As I shoved my underwear down my knees and squatted to pee in the toilet, I wondered if waking up to go to the bathroom was a positive sign.

I wasn't wearing the hospital gown anymore; now I wore comfy sweatpants and an oversized sweater, and I smelled of a basic soap and toothpaste.

That meant Achilles did wash me and probably cleaned my bodily fluids.

I waited for the shame and embarrassment to torment me, but they never came. Whatever consumed me stripped me of my pride, as well as my will to live, and I no longer cared.

When I finished peeing and flushed the toilet, I found no motivation to wash my hands, let alone make the journey back to my room.

Sitting on the cold toilet, however, didn't seem too appealing either.

I slithered down to the floor, curled into a ball, and cried into my chest until I fell asleep again.

CHAPTER FORTY-ONE
TIERNEY

He picked me up from the floor sometime later and undressed me. Put me into a bathtub full of warm water. Achilles then took a sponge and ran it over every inch of my body. He didn't dare touch my skin with his. Instead, he let the sponge do all the work. His movements were practical and impersonal. I wondered if he knew it was exactly what I needed—to soak myself in hot water and try to wash away the memories.

I stared at the small, dusty window in front of the bathtub, unresponsive.

"I made your favorite cabbage soup."

I didn't answer.

"And there's the rye bread that you love."

Nothing.

"You'll get out of this place inside your head," he said, his voice so sure, so full of conviction, I was almost tempted to believe it. "Just hang in there, Little Flame. I'm coming to get you." His throat worked with a swallow. "*Fuck*, baby, I should've never left."

I hated that he was trying to save me because giving up felt so much easier.

For the next two weeks, he spoon-fed me all my meals, brushed my teeth, did my laundry, and tucked me into bed. He read me my favorite books, and carried me outside to watch the sunrises, and the sunsets, and even the rainbow, once.

My favorite playlist was played every morning at a low, comforting volume, trying to lure me out of my room. Garbage and the Pretty Reckless and Yeah Yeah Yeahs.

I really wished he wouldn't try so hard. He gave me soul CPR every minute and every day, only to never find even the faintest of heartbeats.

His failures only made him more determined. They made him try harder.

Some days I wanted to die just to spite him—to be the one and only war he'd lost.

I told myself he'd give up eventually, return to his life, to his family, to his duties.

But it was a lie, and I knew it.

Achilles, like his namesake, would fight until death and beyond. Especially for the things he loved.

Three weeks after we'd first arrived at the cottage, I understood the term *cabin fever*.

I couldn't stare at these walls anymore. I knew every chip in the paint, every crack, and every smudge. It felt like I was trapped inside my head, inside my body, and now inside an unremarkable, dated house with a man I despised.

I stepped in front of the living room window to find that it was pouring rain outside.

"Where the hell are we?" The words ripped from my mouth like a Band-Aid, and I sucked in a breath. I hadn't spoken in so long, I hadn't even been sure I could produce words anymore.

"Maryland," Achilles's voice clipped from behind me.

Neither of us had stepped out of the house for these past three weeks. He had our food and toiletries delivered to us twice a week.

I turned around and headed to the door. I was still wearing my pajamas but no shoes. I didn't even think I had a pair here.

"Where are you going?" he asked from behind me.

I didn't answer. Just slammed the door in his face.

Rain danced across the rotten wooden banister of the front porch, but when I stepped into the storm, I couldn't feel its cold nor its wetness. I moved down the three steps until my feet touched damp sand, then continued walking.

The ocean was fierce, the waves crashing over the shore. My head felt especially wet, and when I moved a hand over it, I realized it was completely shaved, with only peach fuzz between my skin and the rain. I ran my fingers down the back of my head and felt the jagged bone beneath my flesh.

I played my entire twenty-nine years back in my head.

I was ripped from my mother's womb prematurely and snatched by my father's enemy to a Russian work camp.

Spent the first fourteen years of my life starved, beaten, worked to the bone, and sexually abused.

When I finally escaped, I found a family I had little to nothing in common with. My father looked right past me. My older brother didn't care about anything that wasn't his liquor, women, or gambling. And Tiernan, although a good brother, didn't have enough love in him to shield me from the awful truth—that I was all alone in this world.

Achilles had been the only source of light in my life, but even that got ruined. And the minute he thought I'd betrayed him, he'd made sure to hurt me in ways no other man could.

The rain poured down harder, and when I squinted ahead, I realized I couldn't see a thing.

I turned back toward where I'd come from, but I was dizzy and lightheaded from weeks indoors and no physical activity. I sucked in a breath when I realized all I saw in front of me was white and gray fog filled with rain.

Standing still, I hugged myself. A few moments later, Achilles stepped through the fog.

He'd followed me here.

He was wearing a short-sleeved shirt and his boots. Silently, he nodded in the house's direction. I followed him.

The walk back felt like it lasted a lifetime. I was weighed down by my soaked pajamas and my own frailty. I'd have rather died than ask to lean on him—let alone be carried by him.

When we got back to the cabin, the first thing he did was grab my shirt and pants at the door and tug them off me. The logical part of my brain knew that it was because he didn't want me to catch pneumonia. But the child who came back to life when I woke up from my coma felt the threat of his strong, capable hands and kicked into high gear.

"Don't fucking touch me!" I kicked and thrashed, pushing at him.

His steadfast hands continued wrestling the fabric off my body. My breasts sprung free. I let out an animalistic howl, reaching to claw his eyes out. He didn't step away. Let me scratch and claw at him as he continued his work.

"You have no right to touch me. I hate you!" I cried out desperately. Tears leaked out, hot and angry, and the ball in my throat felt impossibly bitter.

After he was done taking off my clothes, he turned around and walked to the bathroom. I heard him flicking the bathtub's faucet to life.

I knew he didn't take care of me out of the goodness of his heart. He took care of me because I was an integral part of him, a part he refused to lose and let go of.

Somewhere in the back of my head, I acknowledged that I poured some of my rage and misery into Achilles in a way that wasn't warranted. He wasn't one of those men who broke me when I was just a child. But he *was* the man who took away my agency for years and the man who fucked me just because he could, because I needed his help, and bartered the one thing I had promised never to sell again—my body.

I wanted revenge.

Grabbing the closest thing to me—a candlestick of all things—I hurled it at the wall. It dutifully exploded into two pieces before falling to the floor. To my astonishment, the act of breaking something else felt...liberating. It made the knot in my throat loosen a little bit. I could breathe better.

Next, I grabbed an ugly, old vase. Smashed it against the wall. Then came the plates in the kitchen. Then, the chairs. I was soaking wet and trashing the entire place.

And it felt good.

Achilles reappeared in the hallway when I was already in the midst of my frenzy. I managed to break a good amount of the cabin he'd rented, and I expected him to stop me.

He didn't.

He just propped a shoulder against the wall, crossed his arms, and smirked to himself.

This, naturally, pissed me off.

"What's so funny?" I seethed.

He shook his head enigmatically.

"No, really," I huffed. "Tell me."

"You're healing."

"Shut up."

"It's true."

"Fuck off."

"You have color in your cheeks," he pointed out. "And you're communicating again."

I hated that it was true. I hated that it was him who pulled me out of the hellhole in my head, the inferno I, myself, couldn't claw myself out of. More than anything, I loathed that the dark place I used to run away to in the hospital, and that first week in the cabin, was now unreachable. I had nowhere to hide. I had to face all of it. The past. The future. And the decisions they both dictated.

"Take me home to Tiernan and Lila."

"Soon," he said, unaffected. "Let's give you a bath. I ordered pizza."

Pizza sounded good. Actually, it sounded really good.

My stomach growled loudly, asking for garlic bread rolls, too.

I realized I was famished.

Famished like I hadn't been since Europe.

Hunger. I really was starting to feel again.

And this was bad news, considering the biggest threat to my heart was less than a heartbeat away.

CHAPTER FORTY-TWO
ACHILLES

One more month like this and she'd have loved me back.

It would have been Stockholm syndrome at its finest.

One more month, and she'd be mine.

But that wasn't the way I wanted things to be between us. Not anymore.

And so, despite my natural predatory instinct to use every dirty trick in the book to get what I want, I found myself driving her back from Maryland back to New York, to her cunt-bag of a brother.

She was alert the entire ride, staring out the window. Even though she didn't talk, I knew this wasn't one of her dark spells. The color was back in her face. Her eyes were shining again, her pupils responsive to what was going on around her.

It comforted me to know she was okay. For weeks, I'd watched her breathe while she was asleep, living but barely alive, acutely aware that her vulnerability was also my own.

I savored every fucking second with her in that car like it was my last on earth.

It wasn't fair that I was still losing her when I'd finally gotten my head out of my ass and done the right thing again.

Only it was.

It was fucking fair, and I knew it.

I had made her life hell, took the thing most important to her—her freedom—and then nearly killed her on top of it.

She had every right to forgive me at her own pace.

That pace could be tomorrow, in ten years, or never at all.

When we reached Lila and Tiernan's place, she flung the passenger door open without even looking at me. In fact, she waited until her back was to me and she was in front of their door before she spoke.

"Don't bother trying to contact me again. You're dead to me."

I floored the accelerator and was out of there before I had the chance to kidnap her back to the cabin.

CHAPTER FORTY-THREE
TIERNEY

"Tier! Have you seen the breast milk I thawed for Enni?" Lila burst into the kitchen in one of her ballroom dresses, readjusting her diamond earring. "I put it in a jug inside the fridge to defro—"

With the spoon halfway into my mouth, I choked and spat out my Reese's Puffs, gagging into my cereal bowl. "Lila! Oh my *God*!"

"What?" Her mouth fell open, and she slanted her head, taking in the scene of me, innocently enjoying my cereal at her kitchen island. Well, *I had been enjoying*. I knew that milk tasted funny.

"This is hysterical!" She clutched her stomach, giggling like a schoolgirl. "How did you not see the colostrum?"

"I thought it was just full-fat milk crust! I don't drink the reduced stuff because it upsets my stomach."

"It was in a glass jug."

"I thought it was one of those fancy glass bottles the milkman brings." My tongue actually burned with the realization I'd drunk my sister-in-law's breast milk.

"The milkman?" She looked alarmed. "What year are you living in?!"

I stood up and wobbled to the sink, flipping the faucet on and sticking my tongue under the stream of water. "Jesus Christ, I'm never eating anything from your fridge again. No one can know about this, Lila."

"No one can know about what?" My brother breezed into the kitchen, snatching my sister-in-law's waist from behind, planting a kiss on her head. He'd come straight from work and was going to take her to a charity ball.

Tiernan hated dancing. Hated people even more. But Lila loved dancing, and Tiernan loved Lila.

I was still a little shell-shocked to see my hell-raising twin all domesticated. It was bizarre. Like watching a hungry panther sniffing a catnip toy on its back, pawing it with its back legs.

"Tierney had Enni's breast milk with her cereal." Lila turned to lock her arms around Tiernan's neck, giving him a slow kiss. "And now she's pretending it doesn't taste good." She pushed her lower lip out in a pout.

"Don't listen to her, *Gealach*," he crooned, catching her lips in another kiss. He looked genuinely distressed by the prospect that Lila's feelings were even mildly injured. "Your breast milk is delicious."

Seriously, why did Tristan Hale miss? I thought he was supposed to be a good shot.

Jokes aside, I pondered that question every day. Something was amiss. Hale had shot me at point-blank range, hiding in the corridor in that Prague apartment. Even a terrible shot wouldn't have missed. Yet he did. It didn't make any sense, and it bothered me. I didn't believe in flukes, and I knew for sure Lady Luck wasn't with me.

"Enni doesn't have any complaints," Lila said. She was the only one who called my nephew that. Everyone else called him Nero.

"That's because he recognizes greatness when he sees it."

It had been two weeks since Achilles dropped me off at my brother's place after bringing me back to life in that cabin. I was still unsettled by the fact he did that for me but convinced myself it meant nothing. Fixing what he broke was the least he could do.

Now? Now I was feeling a different kind of suffocation.

I was grateful for everything Tiernan and Lila had done for me.

And at the same time, it was a lot.

All of it.

Sharing a roof with a loved-up couple whose love language was screwing on every surface in the house while their baby was napping (found that out the hard way). The way Lila was a busybody with good intentions, always on my ass about physical therapy, swimming as a form of occupational therapy, and eating clean. The way my brother barked at soldiers whose gaze lingered on me for a second too long. I didn't like being treated like a child.

On top of that, Lila insisted I shouldn't worry myself about Tyrone or Vello, so neither of them agreed to give me any information about the patriarchs.

They didn't mean to make me feel like a small child, but I felt like one all the same.

"Don't you have somewhere to be?" I groused, throwing the fridge open and plucking a Diet Coke from it.

Lila wrinkled her nose in disapproval as I cracked the can open and chugged it. "Tierney..."

"I'm not in the mood to be healthy. It's either this or meth. Your pick."

Tiernan and Lila exchanged glances.

Please. Just go so I can go back to staring at the ceiling, wondering how I went from New York's wildest socialite to this.

"Do you want some company?" Lila suggested gently. "We can just chill, maybe watch some Netflix and do a puzzle—"

The doorbell rang, and the kitchen quieted. Their eyes turned to me. We knew who it was. Achilles came here every evening at five, sharp. Every day, I turned him away. Actually, Lila, Tiernan, or Imma did. I wasn't in the mood to be seen by him. My hair was in a weird growing phase—there was still a bald patch in the back, where they'd operated—and the rest was growing unevenly. Plus, most days I rocked an unflattering two-piece pajama set and a grouchy frown.

The doorbell rang a second time. Then a third. Then a fourth.

A scowl knitted Tiernan's brow. "Should I tell him to fuck off?"

I nodded.

He left the kitchen, and I heard him telling Achilles I wasn't ready to see him yet. From what I'd gathered, Tiernan and Achilles were on good terms. Achilles did save me when I was shot, brought me back to the States, then spent those three weeks pulling me out of my dark fog. That didn't mean they were back to being friends. As long as I didn't forgive Achilles, neither would Tiernan.

"She's not ready to see you."

"No, she doesn't have the balls to face me," Achilles drawled mockingly. "She knows she can't resist me for long, and it's easier when she doesn't have to see me."

"Love your mental gymnastics," Tiernan chuckled venomously. "Who knew your ass could be so flexible?"

"Fuck you."

"Alluring proposition, but I prefer your sister."

"What a coincidence, so do I. Now let me fucking see her."

"No."

"Tiernan," Achilles warned.

"*Achilles*," Tiernan hissed back. "Take it from someone who went through hell and back to win his wife's trust—you can't rush that shit. When she's ready, she'll let you know."

After Achilles slinked away, Lila and Tiernan made their exit. Imma was with Nero upstairs. I heard my nephew's happy gurgles as I paced my way from the kitchen to the backyard. It was a beautiful rose garden. It was also boring as shit. I was feeling antsy. I hadn't had a drink in months. I hadn't met any friends, either, other than Frankie, who insisted on coming up from DC every week to check in on me.

I needed human interaction that wasn't fit for a five-year-old.

Drumming my fingers on the outdoor table, I grabbed my phone and opened my text box with Achilles. He was the only person who'd defy Tiernan and actually indulge me. Maybe it was time I faced him.

> Tierney: I want booze and a pack of cigarettes.

No niceties. Screw him. He had me bent over his private jet's bathroom and came in my hair.

The message was immediately accompanied by two blue checkmarks.

> Achilles: I'm sure the Callaghan household offers plenty of both.

I thought he'd fall to his knees and thank me for texting him, but I must have forgotten who Achilles was at his core. A cruel, callous man whose fondness for me was nothing but a nuisance to him.

> Tierney: They locked everything up.
> Achilles: Sounds like a you problem.
> Tierney: No, it's a YOU problem, because if you want my forgiveness, you can start with getting me wine and cigarettes. Leave them at my door.
> Achilles: I'm not your servant. If you want me to bring you a drink, you're having one with me.
> Tierney: You don't even drink wine.
> Achilles: I'd drink poison for the pleasure of your company, and you damn well know that.
> Tierney: Fine. One drink.
> Achilles: Give me ten minutes.

My lips quirked up. He was still in the area. He probably waited to see if I'd change my mind. Did he do that every day?

A short time later, the doorbell rang. I swaggered to answer it, taking my sweet time, and opened it with a face full of makeup and an emerald-green minidress.

Achilles stood on the other side, and he was right, because the minute our gazes clashed, my stomach flipped and the unmistakable rush of butterflies swarmed inside it. It wasn't a nice, fuzzy feeling but an uncomfortable reminder that the man in front of me had seen me at my very worst, several times, and still chose to stick around.

He looked like he wanted to strangle me for keeping him waiting all this time.

I flashed him a fake smile—the only kind I was capable of these days. "Miss me?"

"Do you enjoy driving me insane?"

"I'm surprised you'd even ask. Of course I do."

His eyes narrowed. "At least you're smiling."

"I'm doing better," I said quietly, suddenly a little embarrassed by the memory of him tending to a corpse version of me. Changing my sheets when I'd soiled them when I was too unresponsive to drag myself to the bathroom. Washing my hair. Shoving my limbs into pants and shirts. Feeding me with a freaking spoon when I had lost all willingness to keep myself alive. "So…thank you."

"Thank you?" he spat out the words in disgust.

"What's wrong with thank you?"

"If you don't hug me right the fuck now, I'm going to break both your brother's legs."

I frowned. "What does my brother have to do with anything?"

"Nothing. I just wouldn't lay a finger on you, and he shares most of your DNA."

I stepped into his open arms, a tremor rolling through me. He was warm, hard as stone, and smelled of something spicy and clean.

God. His *scent*. I'd missed it. It was no longer there, on my pillows, in my kitchen, in my closet. All the telltales he'd been to my apartment along the years, stalking me, *terrorizing* me. I'd always straddled the line between terrified and enamored with this man. He was the monster from the closet I'd always hoped would sneak into my bed.

The one I fell in love with, even though the fairy tales warned me not to.

"I drank your sister's breast milk today." My lips moved over his stubbled jawline as I spoke.

Achilles stiffened, his arms tightening around me possessively. "What kind of kinky shit are you two into these days? I don't share, Tierney. Not even with my sister."

"It was an accident." I forced myself to step back. "She put it in a jug in the fridge, with no label or anything."

"Only more reason not to touch it. Who keeps unlabeled milk?"

"Is everyone begging to be stabbed today?" I threw my hands in the air. "I made an error in judgment. I'm a little out of my depth here, all right?"

"You should come live with me."

"Achilles, I barely agreed to *one* drink with you," I groaned, aghast. "Anyway, did you bring me what I asked for?"

"Wine, yes, cigarettes, no."

"Why not?"

"It's unhealthy."

"*You* smoke."

"No shit. And I don't care about my life nearly as much as I do yours."

Deciding we had plenty of time to bicker, I stepped aside and let him in. Our first stop was upstairs, in Nero's room. Achilles always took a moment to nuzzle his nephew and speak to him in Italian.

"Gennarino, you rascal. Look how big you are!"

I stood at the door, hugging myself as Imma watched the scene from the nursing chair while Achilles blew raspberries on Nero's tummy. My nephew cooed happily, throwing clenched fists in the air and trying to bite Achilles's nose with his mostly toothless mouth. A deep, bone-crushing agony tore through me. Family was important to him. This had always been true.

He'd be a good father one day.

If he doesn't end up with you.

Clearing my throat, I stepped back. "I'll go open that wine downstairs."

"Now behave, *piccolino*." Achilles handed Nero back to the nanny and followed me silently down the stairs and through the patio doors. A server had already spread different cheeses, olives, and prosciutto on a charcuterie board. The wine waited for us with two tall glasses. Achilles opened and poured it, his silence buzzing in my ears.

"How's the war with Coppola going?" I asked, wanting to steer the conversation into a more neutral subject.

"In full swing." He took a sip of his wine. "He's been taking over our territory while we chip at his manpower, taking out his soldiers one at a time. Luca thinks we should give him concessions after what happened and eat the loss. I think we should off him."

"It's unlike you to listen to Luca." I popped a garlic-stuffed olive into my mouth, chewing slowly. "You usually do what you want and deal with the consequences later." *If at all.*

"Usually," he agreed blandly. "But everyone's riding my ass after I detonated the two-century Camorra Alliance structure to get my dick wet."

"I can imagine Vello's going to make you jump through hoops now to make you don."

"Nah, I blew my chance for the crown." He waved me off. "Got demoted. It's done."

My heart ceased to beat. A shot of pain zipped through it. Being the don was what Achilles had worked for ever since he was twelve. He sought his father's approval in a fierce, obsessive way. It was why I'd almost killed myself when we were young. I knew he'd regret the decision to marry me forever if he knew I couldn't give him heirs.

"I'd say I'm sorry, but none of it was my making." I fiddled with the stem of my wineglass.

"All right, Tier. Let's cut the crap. I love you. You love me. Everything else can be sorted. Get off your metaphorical high horse.

Say the word, and I'll announce our engagement in tomorrow's newspapers."

I choked on an olive, coughing it out into my fist. "That's the lousiest love declaration—"

"It's not a love declaration." He crossed his arms over his chest. "To declare is to announce new information. This is old news. I've loved you since that first night I found you bundled up in your bed like a little mouse when we were kids."

New or not, the information brought me to my knees. No matter how hard I tried to fight it, his affection and approval always mattered to me. But admitting it terrified me. He'd hurt me so much over the years, putting my trust in him felt like suicide. Putting my trust in *any* man felt like a colossal mistake.

"Well, I don't lov—"

"You do." His eyes were locked on mine. "Stop fucking lying, Tierney."

I tried swallowing the lump in my throat.

"I'm scared to love you."

"Why?"

"We've treated each other horribly. Your love is toxic, mine, barren; we've hurt each other too much to just move on like nothing happened."

"We never gave up on each other," he countered. "We never tapped out. That means something."

"I'm too haunted by the past."

"No, you're finally facing it," he said fiercely. "You've been ignoring who you were, your story, for most of your adult life. This is healing, Tierney. It's messy as fuck, but anything worth doing is."

I wanted to believe him. I did. Because the alternative was admitting to myself that I wasn't healing. That I was just stuck in an inferno of never-ending agony and vomit-inducing flashbacks.

"You're a controlling piece of shit." I sighed in despair.

He opened his mouth, likely to bite my head off, realized he was about to validate my accusation, and closed it with a scowl. "I'll do better."

"I need to see you've changed before I tie my fate to yours," I said.

"How can I do that?"

I licked my lips, meeting his gaze. "Show me you've changed your ways. No more stalking. No more overbearing rules. No more surveillance. None of that. *Freedom.* I want my freedom."

A muscle jumped in his jaw. He didn't like it. But he didn't have a choice, either.

"I can do that."

"Can you?"

"Ye—no." He scratched his jaw. Blew out a breath. "Fuck, yes. *Yes.* For you, I'll do that."

I wanted to throw up. Was I really giving him another chance?

Do you really have a choice?

He was a vital organ nestled inside me. With a pulse and a function—a living, breathing thing. If there were no him, there'd be no me.

He was the one person I knew would always be there, would always help, not because we shared a bloodline or trauma, like Tiernan, but because we shared a *soul*.

We stared at each other from across the table.

"I can't give you heirs," I reminded him. "So if this is something that's important to you…"

"*You're* important to me."

"And issues," I went on, ignoring his statement, eyes stuck on the table in front of me stubbornly. "I have a lot of them. I will put you through hell."

"I would choose hell with you over heaven with anyone else, any day of the week."

The panic inside me increased tenfold. We were doing this. Really. Weapons down. Just…letting ourselves succumb to our feelings. Over a decade after the fact but better late than never, right?

"How did you lose it?" Achilles cleared his throat. "Your…"

"Uterus?" I swallowed, pasting on a nervous smile. He was so careful not prodding, not asking anything about my past, not when we were kids and not at the cabin. But he deserved to know. "I was raped one too many times, by five too many men, at the work camp." I recited it as though it didn't happen to me but to someone else. Sticking to the facts. "I was twelve, and although being subjected to rape was a punishment Igor loved giving us, I did this one to myself." A grim smile found my lips. "See, the work camp we lived at in Siberia had a terrible food shortage. I was hungry all the time. Sometimes that hunger drove me to do stupid things. Like offering my body for a bowl of oatmeal or dry crackers. We'd go to the woods, and I'd let the older soldiers…*use* me, in exchange for food. My logic was that I was already being raped on a weekly basis. What did it matter if it happened a few more times or a few less?" I let loose a self-deprecating laugh. "Still, I didn't do it as often as I'd wanted to because Tiernan went ballistic whenever he found out, but it happened enough."

Achilles schooled his face to look unreadable. Probably so I wouldn't see the pity in it. I took another swig of my wine.

"I went to the woods that night with five boys. They said they had beef jerky, and I believed them. I think I was hallucinating from hunger at that point. Immediately when we got there, I knew that time was different. They were drunk. Very drunk. They stole alcohol from Igor. As soon as we were off camp, they pinned me down to the snow and started…experimenting with me."

I closed my eyes, rattled by my own admission. I hadn't told this to anyone. Not my friends. Not my family members. Not my therapists. Many filled in the details in their minds but I never outright spoke the words. "They stuffed snow into me until my body temperature dropped and I fainted. They cut me. They hit me. They bit me to a point that, when Tiernan later found me, he thought I'd been mauled by wolves. And they raped me while I was unconscious, including with the vodka bottle. So many times, I nearly bled out."

My body was wrecked with the force of the truth. I hated that I spoke these words but loved that, finally, someone else could carry the burden of them with me. "The broken bottle inside me tore me to shreds. Tiernan found me some time later, naked and wounded. He carried me back to camp, which was a forty-minute walk, hefting my injured body through the snow. When he got there, he didn't go to the camp's doctor. She was one of Igor's mistresses and knew how much Igor wanted us dead.

"Instead, he went to a woman named Olga who ran the camp. Threatened her with a kitchen knife. She called the local vet to come save me. The vet liked us better. He mostly dealt with the camp's animals—horses, hunting dogs, Igor's beloved cat. The vet operated on me. I was still unconscious, so I didn't feel anything. But when I woke up—a miracle in itself, I was told—he said he had to remove my uterus and that I would never be able to have children."

"Bear children," Achilles corrected.

I blinked. "What?"

"You won't be able to *bear* children. You will be able to have them. There's surrogacy. Adoption. There are many ways to become a parent that don't require a uterus. It doesn't make you less of a parent. If anything, going through the trouble, the angst, the bureaucracy makes you *more* of a parent. Means you fought for it, tooth and nail."

I'd never thought of it this way. I was so messed up about not being able to give Achilles what he was born to have—successors—that teenage me hadn't stopped to think there were other options.

"A teenager wouldn't process it the same way that we do now," I whispered. "All I knew was I wasn't good enough, and that if I let you marry me, you'd find out, be disappointed, and fall out of love with me."

"Not even you trying to kill me and handing me over to Agent Rothwell could make me unlove you." He stared at me like I was a complete dumbass. "And nothing ever will."

"I never tried to kill you." The truth tumbled out of my mouth on its own accord, making the ground slip beneath my feet. "I wanted to be gone before you got there. You were early. I never wanted you to save me, Achilles. I wanted to save *you* from *me*."

"You said you tried to get rid of me."

I pressed my lips together. It was time I came clean. About *everything*.

"I didn't want to." My entire body was trembling; he noticed, his palms immediately engulfing mine protectively. It gave me strength to push on. To confess. "Luca made me."

"Luca?" He scowled.

I nodded. "The first thing I did when I woke up was rush to see you. Luca was there. He only let me through on the promise I'd break things off. He said he'd kill me if I didn't. As much as I thought I wanted to die, I realized when I woke up I'd rather love you from afar and see you happy with someone else than die and not have you."

A low growl of pain ripped from his throat. "He did *what*?"

"A lot of time has passed." I pressed a hand to his chest.

He swatted it, standing up. "Why the fuck didn't you tell me?" He began pacing the backyard.

"He was right, Achilles."

"No, he was *wrong*." He stopped to roar into my face, snarling. "I'd have chosen you over the Camorra any day of the week. I'd have joined the Irish if I had to."

"Your family would have killed you," I said quietly.

"I'd have killed them first."

"Your entire family?" I shook my head in disbelief. "For me?"

"Minus Lila and Enzo. Pretty sure they're not shitty enough to make me choose."

I believed him. And still, at the time, complying with Luca's demand seemed like the best option. I was broken, devastated by all the things I couldn't give Achilles, and weak from the fire. I couldn't see us—two teenagers—standing against the entire Italian Mafia.

"Promise me you won't hurt your brother. He only wanted the best for you."

"Promising you I won't kill him is the best I can do, I'm afraid." He shook his head. "He *will* hurt."

I pressed my lips together, nodding.

"But, baby…" He rushed back to me, his face crumpling in pain as he took my hands. "Why did you start the fire in the first place? Why couldn't you just break up with me?"

"I knew if I broke your heart, a part of you would hate me. If I died in what was deemed an accident, you'd forever remember me fondly. You wouldn't take it personally, and you'd be able to move on with your life." Why was the truth so much harder to tell than the lie? My stomach was in knots. "You have to understand, I managed to suppress my memories, but the pain was still there. Always. I knew my father and older brother found me useless and disappointing, that I was a burden to Tiernan. You were the only reason for me to stay alive, and I was scared once you found out I couldn't be the wife you needed me to be I'd disappoint you too."

"You wanted to die for me?" His throat worked, and a flash of that humanity crossed his beautifully scarred face.

I nodded, struggling to swallow. "I thought if I died in a fire, you'd eventually move on. You'd know I always loved you. So many people let you down. I didn't want to be one of them."

He closed his eyes, drawing a breath.

"I'm so sorry," I croaked out, reaching to touch the jagged, coarse flesh of his cheek. The scars I had put there myself. "I was a coward and a fool." Tears streamed down my cheeks, hot and heavy. I'd been wanting to issue this apology for years. Had been convincing myself I hated him when really, I sought his forgiveness. "I have tarnished your beautiful face, and though you will always be the most gorgeous man in the world to me, I know it changed the trajectory of your life." I leaned forward and kissed those scars, every inch of them. He closed his eyes, his chest heaving as he tried to regulate his breathing, his pulse. He didn't move. Didn't waver. He'd been waiting for this, too.

"I'm sorry for your face," I whispered. "And I'm sorry for your heartbreak. But I'll never be sorry for putting you first. I'll just try to do better when I do it next time."

Those last words seemed to release all the pent-up emotions he'd been locking in. A guttural growl escaped him, primitive and elemental, and he reached to cup my cheeks, ripping me from his face, from kissing him, as he stared me in the eye. "I'd walk through fire every single day for you, Tierney."

My chin wobbled, and I nodded, accepting his words.

"You poor thing."

"Over the years, I tried to explain myself to you…"

"But I refused to listen," he finished for me.

"And I can't blame you." I shook my head. "My weakness, my insecurities, almost got you killed."

"Living without you was no life at all." He narrowed his eyes.

"But I want you to know, no part of me ever did anything to hurt you. All I ever wanted was for you to be happy. With or without me. You were my first friend. My first kiss. My first love…"

"Your last love too." His expression smoothed into something dark and impenetrable. He rapped the table. "Write down the names of the men who hurt you in the camp. I'll find them."

I waited for the terror to kick in at his words. I never wanted to think of them again, let alone come face-to-face with them. A few years ago, Tiernan had pledged to go back to Russia and deal with them. I'd made him promise not to. I wanted to bury that part of my history as deep and as far as I could. But these days, there was no escaping my past. It seemed to froth out of every corner of my thoughts, like an overflowing cesspool.

"They're probably in Russia," I muttered.

"They could be on Mars and I'll still find my way to them."

"I..." I hesitated. "I don't think that's a good idea."

"Why?" he growled.

"Because..." *Say it. You think it, so say it.* "Because I already told you, it was my fault that they did that."

The person who said those words wasn't twenty-nine-year-old Tierney. It was the girl I left behind in that camp, hungry, dirty, and so malnourished, she lost her uterus before she even got her period.

"*Your* fault?"

"Achilles I..." I trailed off again, forcing myself to push out the words. "I did what I always do. I bartered with them. Sex for food. For extra clothes. For whatever I could get my hands on."

The look on his face tore my gut like a hungry beast devouring it whole. Guilt dripped from his expression. After all, he, too, had benefitted from my barters not too long ago.

"Tier," he croaked, his voice snapping like a thin twig. "It wasn't your fault. Not with them. Not with me. It was *never* your fault. *Fuck.*" He kicked the earth, gripping the back of his neck and pulling in anguish. "You should never be put in a position to bargain your freedom and the food in your stomach. *They* were to blame. *I* am to blame. I'm sorry. I'm so, completely fucking sorry. You didn't ask for any of this. You were just a kid, trying to survive in a work camp, doing what you had to do to see tomorrow. They were the predators. And there was nothing, *nothing*, that you did wrong."

"That little girl in the camp didn't know that," I whispered, staring down at my shoes. For the first time, I felt like she and I merged into something whole, not two different entities. Her vulnerabilities hit roots somewhere inside me, and I gave her some of my fieriness.

"That girl is still going to be stuck there." He pointed sideways. "Unless you give me their names."

I owed it to that girl I turned my back on.

And I owed it to myself.

"Write it down."

He took his phone down and started typing, then, without further ado, swiveled and stalked toward the main house.

"Wait." I shot to my feet, almost enraged by the anticlimactic goodbye. "Aren't you going to kiss me?"

He shook his head. "I'm going to give you a little time to digest. Besides, when I kiss you again, you're going to be willing and *begging* for it, Piccola Fiamma."

I grabbed his wrist on his way out, looking up at him. "Now that you got all the answers from me, tell me one thing: Why is my father in your basement?"

"Tiernan didn't tell you?" His eyebrows shot up.

I shook my head. "He and Lila refuse to."

"He ratted you out to Vello."

I was surprised but not shocked. I'd never trusted Tyrone, just as I'd never trusted Fintan. Fintan ended up paying for his sins, and Tyrone would follow eventually. The only reason they'd accepted Tiernan and me into their family was because they realized we'd be beneficial to them. *We* built their empire. They watched from the sidelines and got rich while we hustled.

Achilles slipped his hand from my hold nonchalantly. "I've been keeping him alive for one reason."

"And what reason is that?"

"Breaking his body, then his spirit, so you could watch him die for what he did to you."

CHAPTER FORTY-FOUR
ACHILLES

My first stop was Luca.

I was already pissed Tristan Hale had slipped out of my fingers when I tended to Tierney in Prague, but I would deal with him later.

Meanwhile, I was waiting for my jet to fuel before I took it to Russia.

I had a list of motherfuckers who were going to pay for hurting her, and currently, my older brother was the closest to me geographically, so that was where I started.

Luca and Sofia lived in a swanky penthouse in Manhattan. I was sure Sofia would prefer a nice house in the suburbs like Lila did, just as I was sure Luca gave minus three shits what Sofia wanted.

I rapped on the door forcefully enough to break it down. Sofia answered it, Ciro in her arms.

She was pretty in the same way many Italian girls were—fresh faced, tan, with raven hair and soft features. Nothing wrong with her, so I couldn't understand why Luca was so goddamn opposed to trying to like her. Unless, of course, he wasn't capable of such feeling.

"Where's your husband?" I snarled.

She tightened Ciro to her chest protectively. A humorless laugh left her. "How should I know?"

"You live with him."

"If that's what you want to call it." She rolled her eyes like the teenager she was not too long ago. "All the same, he doesn't tell me where he goes, why, or when."

"Call him now and ask him where he is," I demanded.

"I don't—"

"We can do it with, or without a gun to your head, Sofia. You're holding a baby. Do as you're fucking told."

Jeremie bulldozed his way past her, getting in my face. He didn't say shit, but he didn't have to. His expression said it all, and it told me to mind my goddamn mouth if I was fond of my teeth.

I dug my fingers into my eye sockets. "The fuck are you doing here, vodka breath? You're on duty."

"I w-was in the area collecting payments from protection s-soldiers."

Did he just…stutter?

I'd never heard him stutter before.

His pasty-ass face was completely pink, his ears red. He was… blushing? Yeah. Definitely. Which was fucking wild. Jeremie wasn't the kind of person to blush or stutter. He was the kind of person to kill ten people before breakfast if they stole a drug shipment from us. Which was something he, in fact, did just last week.

I'd gotten it all wrong. Jeremie didn't erase footage from Luca's bedroom camera upon Luca's request.

He did it upon Sofia's request.

Shit. He was here for *her*. I glanced between them. Sofia looked distracted, if a little annoyed. Understandable, considering the asshole she was married to. Jeremie looked like a teenager who'd gotten caught sniffing his stepmom's underwear.

They were standing too far apart to exhibit the familiarity of a full-blown affair. So they weren't fucking…*yet*.

But after what Tierney told me about Luca, I was rooting for them to screw directly on my older brother's restrained body. Hell, I'd tie him for them myself as a gesture of goodwill.

"And?" I elevated an eyebrow. "Is the bastard here?"

"Fuck if I know. Just got here," Jeremie hissed, collecting himself. I wouldn't buy it if it weren't for the fact he still had his biker jacket and backpack on.

"I'm here." Luca strolled from the depth of the giant penthouse, tugging at his cuff links, face unreadable. "Jeremie, what did you want?"

To fuck your wife, idiot.

"To give you this." Jeremie unzipped his backpack, tossing the protection money he'd collected from our soldiers into Luca's hands. I had to hand it to him—the Russian appeared very businesslike. His deep blush and stutter disappeared, making way for his usual stoic expression.

"All right, now that you did, kindly fuck off."

Jeremie flicked his gaze to Sofia, searching. She looked confused but not alarmed. Jeremie pushed past me, looking none too pleased to be leaving.

"Now, you." Luca jerked his chin in my direction. "What crawled up your ass?"

"We're going for a drive."

Luca looked unimpressed with the idea, but apparently, spending any kind of time with his wife was even less palatable than potentially getting stabbed by me. He walked right past her, ignoring her existence. She slammed the door hard enough to rattle the entire building.

Once inside the car, I drove out of the city and toward the woods. I didn't bother telling him where we were going. What'd be the fun in that?

Luca waited it out for the first forty minutes, refusing to show signs of distress, before snapping when we slid into a thickly wooded area. "Who did you kill and what makes you think I care enough to help you bury them?"

"Don't be stupid, Luca," I said cheerfully, throwing my car into park and killing the engine in the middle of the woods. "You can't help me when it's you I'm burying."

"Huh?" He shot me a pissed-off glare. Oh, goodie. So he *was* capable of some kind of emotion.

I took my gun out and pointed it at him. "Get the fuck out with your hands in the air."

He did as he was told, looking annoyed more than scared. Bastard knew I wouldn't kill him. I didn't lack the will—rather, I lacked the way. Killing your own brother in the Camorra without a good enough reason resulted in death. And I was too close to having Tierney to give up my life.

Luca stood with his hands in the air, looking at me like I was ridiculous. "Care to explain your little tantrum?"

"Tierney told me why she broke up with me when we were eighteen." I aimed my gun straight at his forehead.

Luca's carefully contorted control snapped in the form of a sneer. "It's been eleven years."

"Exactly. Eleven years you deprived me of being with the love of my life."

"You're incapable of love."

"No, Luca, *you're* incapable of love."

"What are you talking about?" His eyebrows crashed together. "You can't feel anything, just like me. This is why we…this is why we do what we do." His olive skin flushed red, and I could tell that the revelation that I was capable of emotion rattled him.

He was jealous.

Angry.

Angry he couldn't feel a thing, and angry that it wasn't as common as he thought it was.

"I was in love with her, and you took away the only good in my life."

"Dad forced me to do it," he said coldly. "It was an order from above. Should I have defied him?"

"Yes," I said, unblinking.

"*Yes?*"

"A man worthy of the throne would. Sometimes you make executive decisions for the greater good. No one wants to follow a yes man."

He shook his head, exasperated. "Just do what we came here to do and get it over with."

It would be interesting, I suppose. To try to hurt this *stronzo*. Nothing ever did, and I appreciated a good challenge. Aiming my gun at his feet, I shot a bullet directly to the tip of his toes—not enough to blow them off but definitely enough to shave some skin. His nostrils flared as he stared at me calmly.

"Anything else?" he asked unflinchingly.

I shot him in the shoulder next. Again, narrowly missing all the essential parts, just enough to distribute pain.

His serene expression met mine. "You're wasting ammo for nothing."

I barked out a laugh. "I don't think I am. Watching you try and feel something—and fail—is entertainment enough. Must be miserable."

His jaw flexed and his fists clenched. "Are you done?"

"That depends. Are you going to get between me and my future wife again?"

"You know the answer to that," Luca drawled dispassionately. "I don't care about your personal life any more than I do about anyone else's. Marry her, fuck her, kill her, it makes no difference to me. I was executing an order. Trust me, I wasn't happy to inch you closer to the position of don by getting rid of her for you."

That, I believed.

I aimed at his other leg, blowing up the back of his foot.

Again, all I got was a muscle jumping in his jaw.

I sighed. "Put your weapon down and kick it over to me."

"With what feet?" he ground out.

I chuckled. "You're capable of walking just fine, but I'm happy to blow something up if you make me ask you twice."

He did as he was told, kicking it with the back of his foot. I dropped my gun and stalked toward him. When I reached him, I head-butted him. Blood gushed from his forehead. He stared at me in the same dead, unfeeling way of his. "I'm giving you two more minutes of this bullshit, then I'm fighting back."

"Better make the most of it, then."

Next, I threw a punch to his nose, breaking it in the process. He spat out blood sideways. I grabbed his healthy shoulder, pushing him to the ground, then mounted him to begin pummeling him all over.

Chest. Neck. Shoulders. Stomach.

He didn't groan, didn't sigh, didn't flinch, and didn't fight back.

Dead.

Inside. Outside.

It amused me that he thought becoming don would stir something in him. Nothing ever could. But I supposed if I were in his shoes, I'd chase any high I could, too.

When I was done, I stood up and spat on his face. "You upset my woman again, and you won't have an open-casket funeral. That's a fucking promise."

I got into my car and started driving.

He could find his way back home on his own.

CHAPTER FORTY-FIVE

TWO YEARS AND FIVE MONTHS AGO

It had been two weeks since Achilles dangled her from the bridge and declared her his property.

In those two weeks, life as she knew it ceased to exist.

Yes, she was still able to attend her luncheons, parties, and spa treatments with her fake friends. But now she had to walk around with a Camorrista bodyguard at all times. It cramped her style, not to mention reminded her of the dark period of her life where freedom was nothing but a faraway dream.

Every time she tried to shake her security off, Achilles appointed more manpower to watch over her. It drove her to the brink of madness. The suffocating reality of living inside the confines of someone else's decisions.

She saw Achilles at social functions the Camorra and Irish both took part in. He often had women on his arm. Rubbing his conquests in her face seemed to be his favorite pastime. He was hardly celibate.

So why should she be?

She would show him she wasn't afraid of him.

She was going to screw someone else and enjoy it.

Tierney had tried consensual sex for the first time when she was twenty-two. She couldn't remember the man's name any more than she could his face. She'd been drunk, numb to the world and to the dangers that lurked inside it. All she remembered was that the man hit on her at a bar and that she took him home. The act itself was tedious and awkward. But she continued to try drawing pleasure from sex anyway. She was so deep in denial about her past that she convinced herself if she tried hard enough, she'd be able to enjoy it.

When she was twenty-three, she had a one-night stand with a drunken Irish sailor. When they got to business, she suggested he might want to take a shower because he was sweaty. He slapped her hard across the face in response. She remembered the shock, the surprise...but no terror. He'd expected her to flee, maybe to cower and cry. She did neither. Instead, she tilted her chin up and said, "Harder now, you wuss."

He slapped her again. She tried scratching his eyes out. He threw her onto the bed, mounting her, muttering that she was a mad banshee. She laughed. Each time he hit her, she came alive. She liked fighting for dominance, and she liked losing. It got her hot and bothered, and though she knew it was probably ingrained in her fucked-up past, she had no plans to fix it.

She had a string of lovers over the years. All of them gave her pockets of pleasure, but none ever gave her peace.

It had been six months since she'd had sex.

The lucky winner was found at an Emilia Spencer exhibition in a swanky Upper East Side private showing. The penthouse belonged to the Spencers, and the man in question was delectable.

His name was Tucker, and he was tall, well built, and bore an uncanny resemblance to a Renaissance sculpture. He wore his suit like a second skin.

They enjoyed their martinis together, admiring a painting of a cherry blossom.

"Are you going to buy anything?" she asked, sliding an olive into her mouth. Her Camorra-assigned bodyguard stood only a few feet behind, hands clasped at his front, face impassive.

"Probably," Tucker sighed. "I'm trying to get Baron Spencer to invest in my new venture. Making a purchase might put me on his radar."

Baron Spencer was the billionaire CEO of Fiscal Heights Holdings and Emilia Spencer's husband. Also, the biggest asshole to grace this planet.

"You might want to buy the entire room, then." Tierney laughed. "I hear he's hard to impress."

"I'm not sure my apartment can accommodate thirteen pieces." He glanced around, grinning. "Can I buy you one?"

"Sure. I had my eye on that one." She pointed her martini in the direction of a gorgeous black-and-white painting of a man smoking. Emilia's son, Tierney guessed. Vaughn Spencer.

Tucker's lips quirked upward. "If I buy it, can I at least come and admire it on your wall?"

She shrugged. "I'll need someone to hang it up, anyway."

"Happy nailing, everyone." Baron 'Vicious' Spencer himself slid between them, his icy, pale eyes trained on his wife's art. "Just as long as we're clear that nothing of this sort happens on my property."

Tucker offered him his hand. "Mr. Spencer, good to finally meet you. I'm Tucker Reid."

"I know who you are." Spencer eyed his outreached hand like it was a warm bowl of shit, hands still linked behind his back. "I hear you came about your fortune because your ex's husband gave you a million dollars to evacuate their lives permanently after your stint in prison."

Tucker slipped his hand into his front pocket. "I didn't peg you as a gossip, Mr. Spencer."

Spencer's lenient smile was so mocking she felt the secondhand humiliation all the way down to her little toes. "Get off my property, Mr. Reid, before I exercise my Second Amendment rights—and those index and thumb muscles."

Tucker Reid sounded like a piece of work.

And that made him just perfect for Tierney's plan.

She didn't look for a boyfriend. She looked for a man corrupt enough to deserve a good beating, if Achilles decided to get territorial. This guy had served time in prison. He could hold his own.

"We'll be out of your way," Tierney chirped, throwing her dazzling smile at Mr. Spencer. As expected, it stirred absolutely nothing in him. He was a one-woman man, incapable of even noticing anyone else.

"You stay. I can take out the trash myself," Spencer drawled.

"No need. I was on my way out, anyway. Send your wife my warmest regards."

Tucker shrugged and followed Tierney to the elevators. He knew when to cut his losses. Spencer wasn't going to work with him. His ex's husband, Rhyland Coltridge, was as vengeful as he was influential. He had given him a million dollars to sign away any claim on his mutual spawn with his ex, but the bastard failed to mention it wasn't just his annoying kid he was giving up.

Tucker truly was cut off from polite society in every capacity now.

That he managed to sneak into this exhibition was a miracle in itself.

When a brawny man entered the elevator with Tucker and Tierney, the handsome man finally turned to his hookup. *"You know this guy?"*

"He's my bodyguard," she explained cryptically.

"Are you a big deal or something?" Tucker narrowed his eyes. *Maybe tonight wasn't a dud after all. If this woman was rich and influential, she could help him.*

"Or something." Tierney popped open a compact mirror she extracted from her bag and checked her makeup.

The trio entered a black Escalade. Tucker's spirits lifted. Having her own driver was a positive sign. But when the vehicle stopped in front of a gothic-looking church in a crime-ridden neighborhood, he faltered.

If she was so rich and famous, how come she lived in this shithole?

But she was beautiful, and her body was killer. If nothing else, he'd get a good lay out of it.

She led him into an Irish pub and up a flight of narrow stairs into her apartment. The bodyguard slipped into the one-bedroom property without a sound. Tucker made a face.

"Can you lose this guy? I don't want an audience."

"Marco will be staying in the living room." Tierney smiled sweetly. "Right, Marco?"

Tucker did not like this chick's sense of humor. Too aggressive. But he wasn't planning to stick around, anyway.

They slipped into the bedroom, and to his relief, she locked the door.

"I want you to be rough with me. Enough to hurt but not draw blood." Her tone was businesslike. She shimmied out of her dress, unclasping her bracelet and placing it carefully on her nightstand. This woman was a little frightening.

No matter. He wasn't going to marry her, just fuck her.

"Sure. Whatever." He pushed off his clothes.

Tierney felt a pang of regret. He seemed too eager and too sloppy to be a good lover. His first impression at the exhibition must've been a facade. But she couldn't afford to be picky. She wanted Achilles to know she intended to fuck men however she wanted and whenever she wanted—this was more than a one-night stand; it served as a lesson, too.

They met halfway across the small room, reaching for each other. Tentative, lackluster kisses followed. He got hard between her thighs, and she pushed through the taste of revulsion in her mouth, shoving him onto her bed and straddling him. She brushed her core against his erection, hoping the act would stir something in her. When it didn't, she grabbed his hands and put them on her throat. "Cut my air supply. Only for a few seconds."

She knew as well as he did that he couldn't kill her. She had an armed bodyguard sitting in her living room.

Tucker squeezed her neck for dear life. Her eyes rolled, and she reverted to that blank place in her head.

Wetness gathered between her thighs as she ground against him faster, rolling her hips. He grunted, squeezing harder.

She moaned, but no sound came out because of how tight his grip was on her neck.

Bright lights.
Birds chirping.

Warmth.

Somewhere far.

And pretty.

Where bad memories didn't have to be buried because they didn't exist in the first place.

She blacked out, falling to the side of her bed. When she came to, Tucker was above her, nailing her to the mattress, his sweat dripping onto her face, scorching her eyes. Her mouth was dry, and she wasn't sure if he was using a condom. A strangled sound tore out of her: half-laugh, half-sob.

Achilles was right. She was not equipped to be in a relationship, let alone have casual sex. She felt younger than her age and lost. Like her only way to feel any kind of control over what was happening was to accept pain and convince herself she chose it.

"Harder," she growled in Tucker's face. "I want you to leave marks."

"You're fucking insane," he panted, scowling. He picked up his pace, and her pubic bones screamed in agony each time he slammed inside.

A part of her hoped Achilles would burst through the door, rip this man off her, and save her from him and herself.

She wanted him to dry her tears and protect her. Wanted to know everything about his thoughts, where he spent his days, if the hate he had for her was real.

She wanted him to care, even though she didn't deserve it.

Time crawled, and Achilles didn't show up. Her disappointment turned into rage. Then, finally, to hollow resignation.

Tucker finished inside her. He pulled out too fast, causing her discomfort, and ripped off the condom he thankfully had the foresight to put on.

"Shit. That was insane." He wiped his brow with the back of his arm, chuckling to himself as he began to get dressed. "You got anything to snack on over here?" He shoved one leg into his pants.

"No." She wrapped herself in the duvet and sat on the edge, feeling unbearably cold all of a sudden. "Get out."

"Can I at least have your number?"

"No. Out."

She waited until he was out before she threw open the fridge and took out a drink. Grabbing the vodka by the neck, she shuffled back to her room.

Marco was still sitting on her couch, staring at the wall.

Three days later, she was out on a shopping spree with her friends. They were carrying their Chanel bags on Fifth Avenue when a fully tinted Hummer pulled up at the curb, blocking their way. The back door swung open, revealing Achilles's face, covered in aviators. "Inside."

One word, and yet it pierced through her breastbone and straight into her heart.

"Tier, do you know this guy?" Rosamund, a supermarket chain heiress, twisted her nose in disapproval.

"Unfortunately. He's my longtime stalker." Tierney tossed her bags into the vehicle and climbed inside. "I'll see you tonight at the gala."

They were still staring, shell-shocked, with their mouths hanging open, when the Hummer zipped into the busy New York traffic.

"Miss me?" Tierney cooed, plucking out her lip balm and dabbing it to her lips with her pinky.

Achilles texted on his phone, not sparing her a glance.

Even when he sought her out, he didn't give her proper attention. What kind of stalker was he?

She wanted to scream. Make a scene. The only reason she didn't was because she didn't want him to see how deep he burrowed under her skin.

"Whatever you need, it'll have to be quick. I have a hot date tonight." She yawned.

"We'll see about that."

"You're not my father."

"I know." His eyes were still on his phone, thumbs flying over the screen. "I'm much more involved in your life."

The rest of the drive was spent silently praying for his early and painful demise. They stopped in front of an abandoned warehouse in Brooklyn. She'd been there once before, when the Ferrantes attempted to broker a treaty between the Irish and Tatum Blackthorn, a local billionaire.

Achilles got out first and didn't spare her a glance, even though exiting his monstrous ride in heels was no easy feat.

They ambled inside. The place boasted a vast expanse of wooden floors and exposed brick walls. The only piece of furniture was a flimsy wooden chair.

Tucker Reid was roped to it, gagged and screaming into a red ball.

Her heart dropped to the bottom of her stomach. He looked like he'd been beaten so badly, the only reason she recognized him was that he wore the same black dress shirt as three days ago.

"What the hell do you think you're doing?" She dropped her shopping bags—which she could not remember why she'd brought with her in the first place—on the floor. "Untie him, you psychopath!"

Ignoring her rage, he strolled deeper into the room. "This the guy who touched you?"

She clamped her mouth shut, something between fear and rage dancing across her skin. She understood—even welcomed—a punch or two to the man who dared touch her. But kidnapping was a step too far.

"Is it him?" Achilles pressed, stopping a few feet from the man.

"Fuck y—"

"Answer me!" he roared.

She stared at him defiantly in a silent screw you.

"Come here."

She did because she was afraid he'd start chopping body parts off Tucker if she defied him.

Achilles studied her. His eyes dropped from her face to her neck. She wore a satin scarf. He tugged it free. It fell to the floor, revealing blue and purple bruises.

Achilles closed his eyes. His nostrils flared. Every single emotion ran through his body.

"Is. He. The. One. Who. Touched. You?"

"Y—yes." Her voice was small and frightened and drenched with shame. "But I asked him t—"

He turned to Tucker Reid, unholstered his gun, and shot him straight in the face.

She stared at Tucker's limp head tilting sideways. The blood oozing from his forehead. Shock and hatred swirled inside her, each fighting for dominance. She had so many things to say to him. All of them could send her to an early grave.

Achilles stepped forward, eating the space between them, so close their noses brushed. "Never again, Tierney. You hear me?"

She tilted her chin up, refusing to give him her words.

"If you let another man touch you, just assume you've sentenced him to his death."

"You're sick," she whispered.

"I know." He grinned, his coal eyes burning with hatred. "Every. Single. One. You can try to hide them. Protect them. I'll always find them, and I'll always kill them."

Her body trembled with rage. It consumed her so badly she thought her skin was going to explode. He pushed her into a corner. No one was going to defy him. He was Achilles Ferrante.

The joker of the underworld. The sadist everyone feared.

"Next time you bring someone home to get screwed, your bodyguard will kill him. That's an order from above. I meant what I said, Piccola Fiamma. If I can't have you, no one can. Stock up on those sex toys. Because you won't be seeing another dick for a long, long time."

CHAPTER FORTY-SIX
TIERNEY

The following weekend, we were invited to dinner at the Ferrantes'.

The last thing I wanted was to see Vello again, but Tiernan and Lila pointed out that for my return to become official, it would be good to put everyone in the same room. Send a message. Plus, I had a certain someone waiting for me in their basement I couldn't wait to reunite with—my traitorous father. I knew Achilles wanted him to marinate in his own misery longer, but knowing I was about to be on the same property as him and that he was suffering brightened my mood.

I sat in the back of Tiernan's Mercedes while he drove to his in-laws', staring out the window. Preppy Long Island mansions zipped past us, with their manicured lawns and German cars parked out front. I still couldn't believe I was back on American soil and that Vello had permitted it.

"What made him change his mind about me?" I asked, eyeballs still stuck on the view. "I mean, other than beating him up."

"Those weren't beatings. We got…carried away." Tiernan cleared his throat. "When Enzo and Luca finally tore us off him, they didn't kill us. That was my cue that Vello's power over his sons had dwindled."

"So… Luca and Enzo chose Achilles over their father?"

"Apparently, Vello was almost as shit a parent as Tyrone. It's common knowledge he's hanging by a thread and about to kick the bucket. That he hasn't chosen a successor yet is pissing everyone off. The Ferrante brothers decided to split the pie the way they see fit and appoint the don on their own terms."

"And he's agreed to that?"

I watched my brother through the rearview mirror. His mouth lifted at the corners derisively. "Let's just say he didn't have much choice."

"Does he know Tyrone's in his basement?"

"That would require him to use his functioning brain cells. And he currently doesn't have any of those."

"His condition has deteriorated?" My brows zipped together.

He just smiled serenely, the same smile he flashed his victims before decapitating them so he could have their skulls.

"Wait, but Achilles said he's been demoted," I said.

"He was," Tiernan confirmed. "By Luca and Enzo. He's ruffled far too many feathers, shitting all over Camorra operations twice in a row for you. The brothers have been calling the shots for the past ten weeks."

"And no one's asking questions?"

"They told the Camorra he's abroad for an experimental treatment or some shit."

This was a huge power shift that would change the fabric of the entire underground world. I couldn't believe it had happened. Moreover, I couldn't believe it had happened because of *me*.

I forced myself to relax for the rest of the ride there, knowing Vello was no longer a danger to me.

When we got to the Ferrante mansion, Enzo opened the door. My heart sank, but I kept my smile casual. I hadn't seen Achilles the entire week. Not since he brought me wine. I tried not reading too much into it. He had mentioned he'd give me time. And I still needed it. But I also needed someone who wouldn't treat me like I was a fragile little doll in need of saving.

"Tier-Tier, baby girl." Enzo offered me a one-armed hug, his Adonis body nearly crushing me to smithereens. "You look fantastic for a girl who had her head blown the fuck up."

I threw him a grin, strutting deeper into the lavish house. "And you smell amazing for someone who spews crap out of his mouth twenty-four-seven."

Enzo linked his arm in mine, leaving my family behind. "I missed you."

"Can't blame you. I'd miss me, too. When's dinner?"

"Soon, I hope. I'm starving. All I had today was twelve egg whites, chia matcha pudding, and some pussy."

I gave him a horrified glare. "You gotta stop doing that to yourself, dude."

"I know. But maybe one day I'll like it. I mean, my friends *love* eating pussy. What am I missing?"

"I meant your diet. It's unsustainable."

"Of course it's sustainable," he thundered. "It's how I sustain my six-pack."

We sauntered to the dining room. Tiernan and Lila loitered behind, unpacking her breast pump.

As soon as we slipped into the corridor, Luca and Sofia came into view, huddling in what looked like a tense conversation. Sofia shook off Luca's deadly gaze, flashing me a warm smile. She wrapped her arms around me in a quick hug. "Tierney, I'm so glad to see you up on your feet and well."

"Thanks."

Her swanlike features, her soft angles and elegant neck, and musical voice had a calming effect on me. I didn't know Sofia well, but she was very close to Lila. The latter had good judgment when it came to people, so I decided not to hold Sofia's marriage to her husband against her. It wasn't like she had a choice.

"Did you get the pies I sent you?" Sofia's lashes fluttered nervously. "Lila said you didn't want visitors. I didn't want to impose."

"I got them." My smile broadened. "They were great. Really made me push myself to the limit during all my PT sessions to burn those extra calories."

Sofia giggled.

"Tierney." Luca's voice dripped with disdain. His face was marred with faded purples and blues, and I had no doubt it was thanks to my revelation that he'd threatened to kill me. "The only reason your brain is not smeared all over this Italian marble floor is because of Achilles and Tiernan. And because that floor costs more than your life's worth. I hope you know that."

"Oh, I know." I smirked, sad I didn't have hair to flip to annoy him further. "And rest assured, Mr. Cold Fish, I don't care."

Enzo snorted, and we rounded the hallway into the dining room. Chiara, the matriarch, stood at the doorway, greeting her guests in her prim dress and coiffed updo. She, too, curled her nose in disgust at the sight of me.

"If it isn't the woman who handed my entire family to the feds."

"Are the feds in the room with us?" I squinted, glancing around the room. "I don't think so. I spared your family because of Lila and Achilles. Jury's still out if I'll extend the same favor to you, though."

No part of me wanted to win her approval. She'd been a horrible mother, to both Achilles and Lila.

I let my shoulder brush against hers, proud of myself for standing up to the she-devil, when I saw something that stopped me in my tracks.

Achilles.

His shoulder was casually leaning against the wall, and he was holding a glass of whiskey, conversing with a woman I *knew* was Katya Rasputin without ever seeing her face before.

She had the Rasputins' cobalt eyes, and the same composure of a cold-blooded serpent looking to sink its venomous fangs into an innocent.

A surge of dizzying wariness ran through me.

Tiernan lied. She wasn't average-looking. She had that Slavic-model look—with a svelte figure and a face where everything was small and neat and pretty.

She looked just like any college girl. Pretty and youthful, in a black velvet minidress and kitten heels.

They weren't standing very close, and the conversation seemed casual enough, but when he said something, staring at the bottom of his whiskey, and she giggled, demurely covering her mouth with her hand, an explosion of heat and anger detonated in my stomach.

Just having her in the same room with him made me want to shatter everything in my vicinity into dust.

Why was she here? Did he change his mind about marrying her? Did he have second thoughts after the dust had settled, and he realized he did want a little Mary Sue to pop out children for him?

I bled jealousy over the expensive floor, torn into a million pieces at the flirty gazes Katya threw Achilles from under her lashes.

She wanted him. And I wanted to kill her for it. If she didn't keep her hands to herself, one of us was going to get what they wanted. And it sure as hell wasn't going to be her.

I was so sick with rage that bile tickled the back of my throat. Not wanting to add vomiting on the dining table to my list of sins against the Ferrantes, I turned around with the intention of exiting the room, only for my sight to crash on Don Vello himself.

Or…what was left of him, anyway.

He was slumped in a wheelchair, a thin trail of saliva traveling from the corner of his mouth and down his chin. His pupils were blown, his expression blank. It was obvious he was out of it and couldn't register me, or anyone else, in the room.

"You're in my way," Chiara seethed from behind him, which was when I realized she was pushing his wheelchair. I stepped aside, my eyes following her as she positioned him at the head of the table. It was impolite to stare, but manners mattered little to me where he was concerned. Seeing the great Don Vello, who had ruled New

York with an iron fist for as long as I could remember, looking like a pale, ghostly shell of himself, sent a thrill down my spine.

My gaze trekked down to his armrests, landing on his pinky-less hand immediately.

I did that.

Satisfaction prickled my chest, spreading warmth across it.

"É pronto, venite tutti a tavola!" Chiara waved a frantic hand, securing the brakes on the wheelchair with her foot. "We have a big announcement to make tonight, and it cannot wait. Sit down and eat."

A big announcement?

I fell to the seat nearest to me, determined to pretend I wasn't in full-blown panic mode. Humiliation seared my skin. Why was I forced to sit here and watch Achilles flirt with his future wife? And why hadn't Tiernan and Lila warned me?

And here I thought getting shot in the head was the worst part of my summer.

Enzo plopped into the seat next to mine, patting my knee. "Will you let me sniff your lasagna?"

"Sure." I snapped my napkin and rested it in my lap. "If you'll give me a joint afterward. Tiernan and Lila are hiding all the tobacco, alcohol, and fun stuff from me."

"You need to get out of that house. My sister treats everyone like they're fresh outta diapers."

"I don't know how my brother lives like that." I shook my head.

"Well…" Enzo's eyes swept over the couple, who sat next to us. Lila was talking to Tiernan animatedly, moving her hands. His gaze was locked squarely on her bouncy breasts. "I can think of at least two reasons."

I gave his shoulder a push. "Pervert."

From the corner of my eye, I watched Sofia woodenly taking her place next to Luca. Jeremie settled on the other side of her, and Katya slipped into the seat next to her brother. I guess Jeremie was still here for the time being, but not for long. The tension from that side of the table made invisible spiders crawl along my skin.

Achilles scanned the room, his eyes finally landing on me. I fiddled with my phone, feigning deep fascination with an incoming message some scammer had sent me about getting my roof redone. He stalked toward me like a summoned demon.

"Hey, Enzo?" Achilles drawled.

"Yo."

"Fuck off."

"Nuh-uh. You can't talk to me like that anymore." Enzo flung his elbow onto the back of his seat. "I'm your superio—"

"If you don't evacuate your ass from my woman's vicinity, I'm going to cut out your larynx with a blunt spoon and feed it to my pet snake."

Enzo flashed Luca a look of disbelief.

Luca shrugged. "His woman, his rules. I'm not interfering in this."

"I'm not his woman." I fixed the napkin next to my plate, not bothering to keep the pettiness out of my voice.

"You have a pet snake?" Katya asked excitedly. "That's so cool."

Achilles ignored her, taking the now-vacant seat next to me, his eyes hard on my profile. "Hello to you, too."

"You seemed busy." I sounded like a jealous teenybopper, and somehow, I couldn't muster one damn. Between disappearing for a whole week and flirting with Igor's daughter, he wasn't winning any points with me tonight.

"It was just small talk."

I barked out a laugh. "Small talk, huh? Sounds like big bullshit to me."

"You're acting like a child."

"At least I'm not about to marry one."

Our conversation got cut off by a sea of servers who flooded the table at once, unloading savory Italian dishes and an unholy amount of wine. I tried focusing on the food, too distressed by the realization I was very close to stabbing a fork through Katya from across the table.

I told myself it had something to do with the fact she was the daughter of the dead Russian pakhan who'd abused me, but from what Tiernan had told me, all of Igor's spawn loathed their slain father with a passion.

Moreover, despite not seeing Alex, the new pakhan, for fifteen years, I had been fond of him growing up.

Fortunately, the food was mouthwatering and the conversation flowed. The women talked shopping, the men soccer. Vello just sat there, drooling as a nurse spoon-fed him a mashed version of our dishes. I had to admit, I liked this new version of him much better.

"Tier, are you okay?" Lila rubbed my back every five minutes, swinging her gaze from me to her father. "You're feeling comfortable, right?"

"Right," I muttered. God, I loved her, but she really needed to stop treating me like a baby.

After the entrees and wine were demolished, trays of champagne and dessert flooded the room. Achilles stood and clinked a flute with a fork. "I'd like to make a toast."

Everyone sat up straighter. My stomach churned, everything inside it threatening to pour back out. This was it. The big announcement. He and Katya were getting married.

He raised the champagne glass in the air. "To my brother Enzo and his new fiancée, Katya Rasputin. May their union bring the two families peace, prosperity, and continue our respective legacies."

My fork tumbled from between my fingers, clinking noisily on my plate. My gaze skated to Enzo, who sat still, face unreadable, fingers curled around the armrests to the point of white knuckles.

What? I mouthed to him in disbelief. Only I had confirmation of Enzo's secret—that he had an active profile on an LGBTQ+ hookup app called Queerdr—also known as queer Tinder—a location-based app for casual sex.

One day Enzo got matched with a good friend of mine, Calvin. And even though they never ended up meeting, it was enough for me to give Enzo a call and yell at him to change his profile picture, username, and other dead giveaways that could reveal his identity. Enzo swore up and down he wasn't gay—that he was just, and I quote, *conducting important research*.

The younger Ferrante brother tossed a careless shoulder in response.

"With this, we bury the Bratva and Camorra's feud," Achilles continued.

Katya blushed, still staring at Achilles with big, adoring blue eyes. It didn't take a genius to figure out neither the groom nor the bride was happy about this union.

"This also concludes Jeremie's time with us," Achilles announced pointedly, staring down the Russian with a glare as deadly as bullets.

Jeremie didn't balk as their gazes clashed. "I'm staying in New York."

"Says who?"

"Says *me*."

"You have no authority in this decision." Luca's rough voice knifed through the tension. My spine snapped to attention, my eyes ping-ponging across the table. "You're a mere soldier. A Rasputin but a soldier. Alex calls the shots."

Oh, goodie. I haven't even touched my champagne and already, they're serving tea.

"I do, actually. No New York, no Katya; no Katya, no alliance." Jeremie's brusque tone raised goose bumps on every arm in the room. His voice was so monotone, so assured, Satan himself wouldn't defy him. "And no alliance means war. Long. Bloody. And one that lacks any rules or regulations. Alex may be the decision-maker, but I can pull a lot of strings and cause a lot of trouble, given the time and inclination." A wicked glint ignited his sapphire pupils. "Don't give me both. It's either a full-blown war, or we do shit my way. Now, go call Lyosha and let him know I'm still needed here."

Jeremie's shoulder kissed Sofia's ever so slightly, and color shot to her tan cheeks. I blinked in disbelief. Fiery tension crackled between the two like live, uncontrollable fire. Even the silverware on the table could tell there was something going on.

Were they in love? If so, it didn't seem like Luca knew or cared.

Achilles and Luca exchanged frowns. Luca seemed exasperated but hardly bothered. He sighed, taking out his pistol and kicking back Sofia's chair in one smooth movement. She sailed backward, her back crashing against the wall. Luca now had a clear shot at Jeremie. Sofia yelped, her body jerked forward. She was itching to throw herself between them but stopped short.

Lila stood and rushed to Sofia to make sure she was okay.

"What the fuck is wrong with you?" Jeremie's eyes shot fire. "She's *pregnant*."

"My baby, my business." Luca pointed his .45 at Jeremie. "Now, you're getting the fuck outta here, either in a body bag or with an arm shot. Choose wisely."

"*Oh, Santo Cielo!*" Chiara tossed her napkin on the table. "Of course my children couldn't give me one decent meal without bullets flying around."

"How about a cig break?" I turned to Enzo after it was obvious Sofia wasn't hurt. He took one dispassionate glance at the dessert he knew he wasn't going to touch in a million years before pocketing his cigarette pack. "Sure."

We made our exit to the sound of Jeremie and Luca negotiating. I was over that entire screwed-up family. Not that my family was better—far from it. But at least there weren't so many of us.

When we reached the backyard, we settled on the lounge chairs by the pool. Enzo lit a joint and took a hit, passing it on to me.

"This marriage is not going to bode well for anyone." I inhaled until the smoke reached the bottom of my lungs, handing the joint back to him. "I'm worried you're trying to prove something to yourself by going along with it."

"Jesus, Tier." He shot me a *lower your voice* glare, even though we were clearly alone. "I don't even know if I'm...you know."

"Enzo..."

I didn't pretend to know him any more than he knew himself, but I did know that Enzo Ferrante was passionate about all things he did and touched—from killing his enemies, to protecting his family. Everything he did, he did fiercely. It made no sense at all that he'd be so dim, so disinterested when it came to love. Unless, of course, he'd been molded and forced to try to love the wrong people.

"It's true. I'm straight. *I am.* I'm just...intrigued. Variety is the spice of life, after all."

I didn't even bother answering him. Just shot him a *really?* look.

The tips of his ears, which were oddly perfect, like the rest of him, turned red. "I've never even kissed a man, let alone been with one. So far, I've only talked with them on the app."

"Well, what brings you to flirt with men online?"

"Curiosity. Boredom. My inherent tendency to fuck up my life and hurt myself. Exhibit number three thousand." He took a pull of the joint, jerking his chin toward his bare arms. Corded muscles flexed beneath skin inked to perfection. But beneath the beautiful art he wore on himself were jagged scars. "You know I like variety."

But he didn't. He'd had a steady girlfriend since high school before Achilles pumped and dumped her to prove to him that he wasn't straight. Everyone could see Enzo's blatant disinterest with the fairer sex. Just because he hadn't mustered up the courage to explore his sexuality didn't mean he wouldn't.

"Maybe I'm asexual," he mused.

I narrowed my eyes at him.

"It's possible!"

"It's not." That man loved getting his dick sucked more than

Abraham loved God. Every time I spotted him in an underground club, he seemed to have a head bobbing beneath his waist. It was easier to enjoy blow jobs when you could close your eyes and pretend the person servicing you was someone else.

"Fine." Enzo rolled his eyes. "I agree. I'm too hot not to fuck. God's sense of humor can't be that cruel."

"Put aside the damage it'd do to you to marry a strange woman you have no attraction nor affection for. What about Katya? She is young and hopeful. She deserves a man who would at least try to be a good husband." I couldn't believe he'd made me a Katya defender.

"I'll make her happy. I'll give her free rein and the option to take a lover. I'm not gonna be my father and Luca."

I believed him. He was just ferociously loyal and dedicated enough to his family to sacrifice himself for everyone else's benefit.

"But *you'll* be miserable." I jabbed my finger in his chest. "You'll live a lie. You'll never experience a great love, a truly sensational fuck. You deserve both, goddammit."

His jaw ticked, his heavily lashed whiskey eyes warning me to drop it. I couldn't. I cared about him too much.

"Why'd you agree to this?" I pushed.

"Loyalty, devotion to the Camorra…and power." His smirk was lazy, playfully decadent. "It was my one chance to push Achilles out of the race. I took it."

"What about Luca?"

Enzo shrugged. "The Camorra's closing rank around him. He'll likely become the don, but I'll still be the consigliere, next in line. Occupational hazards are common in our field of work. I'll be waiting in the wings—"

"Enzo, get lost," a brutally gruff voice commanded. One I knew perfectly well to belong to my own filthy god. Achilles materialized from the shadows, dripping menace and authority, arduous prowess poured into a Prada suit.

"I'm sensing a theme here." Enzo ran a finger over his jaw.

"You'll be sensing my knee on your windpipe next if you don't fuck off."

"I love it when emotionally constipated men finally let it all loose." Enzo passed me the half-smoked joint with a wink. "Sorry, sugar. Gotta go make sure I still have a bride in that bullet-infested room."

Achilles stared me down, waiting for an acknowledgment.

"Everyone okay back there?" I fixated on the birdbath across the pool, refusing to address my little jealousy fit from earlier.

"For now." He tugged me up by my elbow, grabbing the joint mid-suck and tossing it into the pool. "You thought she was here for me." His dark gaze fell to my mouth. That's all it took for my traitorous thighs to clench at the memory of him serving me with one earth-shattering orgasm after the other. Who said lust only made men stupid?

"I wouldn't care either way," I huffed, but the bite was gone from my voice.

"You're a very bad liar, Piccola Fiamma." His thumb brushed my cheek, leaving fissures of pleasure that made my spine tremble. "Admit that you're jealous."

"I can't admit something that's not true," I maintained calmly.

He produced a baffled, enraged snarl. I could tell he was losing his patience. Only this time, he was no longer able to punish me with a spur-of-the-moment idea that'd throw me into the arms of depression.

"Let me take you out after dinner. Somewhere fun," he ground out.

"I'd love to, but I can't."

"Why not?"

"I already have a date tonight," I lied. Anything to put more space between us. I wasn't ready to give up so quickly. Plus, if he really did change, he would let me have my freedom. We weren't together. I could date other people. Kiss them. Screw them. I wasn't his property, and he'd better remember that.

"That's a shame." His demeanor was still ice-cold, his tone dry and amused. "I'm afraid you won't be able to make it."

"Why not?"

He shoved me into the pool, going down with me. The splash reverberated in my ears as we pierced the water, sinking under the surface. His lips crashed down on mine underwater. Hard, demanding, relentless. Our limbs tangled, the water cooling our skin. We were in the deep end, both literally and figuratively, and I never wanted to come up for air.

Our tongues lapped at each other, devouring one another. I wrapped my legs around his waist as he pushed off the bottom of the pool. We broke the surface, still fused in this slow, drugging, erotic kiss. I ground against him, running my fingers over the scars on his face. "M—more," I panted, fingers curling over soaked fabric, clawing at sculpted muscles. "I want more."

"More what?"

"More everything."

A growl of satisfaction poured from his mouth into mine.

His words from last week ghosted over every inch of my needy flesh.

"When I kiss you again, you're going to be willing and begging for it."

"Admit that you were jealous."

"I wasn't—"

He reached between us and pushed his pants down, as he freed his cock, holding it by the root and dragging the crown along my slit through my underwear. "Admit it, Tierney."

My pride was eviscerated into smatterings in that moment, and all that was left was a throbbing, hot ache between my legs and adrenaline that made me tremble like a brittle leaf.

"I was," I growled, kissing him harder, sinking my teeth into his skin, and making the kiss about sex and not about emotions. "Next time I see her standing next to you, I'll break both her legs. Now, fuck me."

"Yes, ma'am." He tucked my underwear to the side roughly, pushing inside in one go.

I broke the kiss breathlessly, angling my head to the twinkling lights coming from the mansion. "Your family is ten feet away. They can watch me corrupting you through the window."

"Let them have their fucking fill." He devoured my neck, thrusting into me. "This is not sex, Little Flame. It is *ownership*."

The way he filled me made my mouth water, and I met him thrust for thrust, the golden gleam shining from the dining room our backdrop. All the people inside it could easily guess what we were doing in the pool if they turned to look in our direction, but I simply didn't care.

I raked my fingers through his wet hair, the orgasm building inside me. Achilles had one hand on the small of my back. The other was pinching and teasing my erect nipples through my wet dress.

"My jealous little flame," he teased, his lips finding my nipple and closing over it. The heat of his mouth against the coldness from the water gave me goose bumps everywhere. "You thought I'd give you up so quickly?"

"Sh—shut up," I grunted. We drifted to the shallow end of the pool, so I was able to ride him faster, with more desperation than I cared to admit. To make this about lust and not about love. About pleasure and not about submission. I couldn't be that girl anymore. The girl who wanted to die because she wasn't exactly what he needed.

His teeth closed in on my collarbone, hot tongue swirling over cold skin as he moved to my other nipple. "I'll *never* give you up, Tierney. If I can't have you, no one can."

His words were all I needed to fall apart between his arms, screaming his name to the sky, relinquishing control to the orgasm that ripped through me like a storm.

No decency lived in the way we climbed out of the pool afterward, soaked and flushed. Achilles threw a towel over my shoulders and stepped ahead of me to conceal me from view.

I secretly hoped Katya got a front-row seat to our antics in the pool. That should extinguish any inappropriate ideas she had about her future brother-in-law.

I was about to sit down on a lounge chair when Achilles shoved me against one of the walls in a hidden corner, crowding me with his impressive height.

"Move in with me." A demand. Not a request.

It must've been my head injury, but I actually didn't think it was a bad idea. Not that I could tell him that outright. "I just refused to go out with you, and now you're asking me to move in?"

"No, you *just* had mind-blowing sex with me. That cancels your rejection." He scowled. "You know you want to. My sister's driving you mad."

"That's not a good enough reason to move in with someone."

"Then do it for another reason."

"Such as?"

"That no one will ever take better care of you. No one will devote their entire fucking life to you the way I do. No one will go against their family, tradition, and self-preservation like me."

He was right, of course, but for some reason, that stunned me. I was so used to his love being laced with something punishing and cruel that I hadn't stopped to think that Achilles hadn't been the same person since I got shot. He tended to me without expecting anything. He nursed me back to life, even though he didn't have to. My broken pieces weren't his to pick up. But he still mended them.

But that wasn't the only reason I was considering moving in with him.

I knew it would soothe the aching part of his soul that I'd fractured.

"I started having nightmares again." My teeth munched on my lower lip. "I…I scream and cry in my sleep sometimes."

"I saw when we were at the cabin." He ran his fingers over his damp hair. "I can handle it."

"I want a different room."

He grabbed his own towel and ran it through his sooty, wet strands. "Done."

"No surveillance—I come and go as I please."

His lips gravitated to mine again, and we met halfway for a kiss.

"Done." His teeth clamped around my lower lip, and he sucked it into his mouth, releasing it with a pop before lapping it with his tongue to ease the sting.

"No sex, either, until I say so," I said. "Orgasms cloud my judgment."

"We don't want that." He nuzzled my neck, dropping addictive kisses along my sensitive flesh.

"And I want a one-night stand."

He ripped his mouth from me, glaring. "Why would you need a one-night stand with your future husband?"

"Not with you," I said boldly. "I've never really dated anyone else. Never had the privilege of living life as I pleased because of you. All I could do was hook up with people like a thief, hoping you weren't looking. If you've changed like you claim you have, you'll prove to me that I *am* free," I breathed out. "Free to choose you…or anyone else, if I wish to."

Sleeping with someone else seemed as appealing as getting shot in the head again, but I wanted the *option*. I craved some kind of a guarantee he wasn't going to treat me like an object he bought, like other made men. For the past few years, I had been sexually starved because Achilles couldn't handle me having a love life. All the while, he screwed women left and right without a care in the world, rubbing their existence in my face.

I needed him to prove to me he was a choice, not a decree.

"*No,*" he snarled.

"I'm not asking, Achilles," I said quietly. "This is not about sex." I shook my head. "You need to show me you can protect me from your own rage."

His foreboding glare would terrify anyone else, but all I saw in his face was the resignation of a man too far gone to back out of any arrangement, including one that could very well kill him, to have me.

"I'll do it whether you allow it or not," I clarified.

"One time," he growled under his breath. "*One,* Piccola Fiamma."

"One time," I repeated, my face so hot I fought the need to touch it to cool it off. "I want to know you mean it when you promise me that I'm free."

He searched my face, curling and relaxing his fist beside his body, trying to gain control over his fury. His pulse fluttered over the side of his neck. I licked my lips, trying to think of something comforting to say.

"And don't worry, I won't bring him home or anything…when it happens."

"You want no surveillance and to hook up with a random?" He bared his teeth. "You better know you're bringing him home, so I can save you if shit goes south."

My heart skipped a beat. How ironic it was that this man was going to finish me with his kindness after trying to destroy me for years with his malice.

"Does this mean you're game?" The only reason my jaw wasn't on the floor was because I was positive I was hallucinating.

He ran a hand over his jaw, tilting his face to the sky. "I swear to fucking God, Tierney, if this is some ploy to get me to lose my mind…" He didn't finish his threat, his jaw clenching tight. "*Fuck.* One time. One time. I can do it."

I stared at him in disbelief. Could he?

"And I want to be there when it happens," he growled.

"That's a terrible idea," I whispered, transfixed.

"You're a terrible idea." He patted his pocket, just to find out his cigarette pack was soaked and ruined. "I don't fucking care if it kills me. I'll always put your safety first."

CHAPTER FORTY-SEVEN
ACHILLES

I glanced at my Rolex. Five thirty-five. About half an hour until my brothers arrived for our meeting. Still plenty of time. I checked my phone again to see if Tierney had answered my last text. My heart did that weird stirring shit again when I realized that she did.

Tierney: Fine.

Fine? That's all I got? Jesus, she was cold.

I should've known she wouldn't let me breeze back into her life and put a ring on her finger the minute I finally succumbed to my Greek-tragedy-sized obsession with her.

It was inconceivable that a woman so beautiful, so bold, so sophisticated would deign to be with someone so scarred, so ugly, and as monstrous as me. She could marry a Tate Blackthorn, a Wolfe Keaton, a Baron Spencer. A dark, smooth stallion, gently bred, with billions in the bank. But no Blackthorn, no Keaton, and no Spencer would ever treasure her the way I would. If ever I could have her, I'd worship her so thoroughly, no man would ever fucking measure up.

My broken soul found her broken soul, and for the first time in my life, it felt whole.

Now I was on a mission to kill everyone who'd ever hurt her.

Well…except myself, obviously.

I was making good progress. In fact, the only asshole on my list I hadn't pinned down yet was Tristan Hale. Fucker fell off the face of earth before I had the chance to punish him. But I was going to find him.

And once I did, I would suck out his intestines with a fucking straw.

I reached for the portable faucet in my parents' basement, turning the valve all the way. It was linked to a dispenser. A stream of water turned into a one-drop leak.

The man tied horizontally under it ceased his tedious screams, darting his tongue out to lap the drops thirstily. What he didn't know was that after the waterboarding came the water torture. Which was a slower, more painful way to die.

"Hey, wanna hear some mad shit?" I cupped my cigarette, lighting up a smoke.

Apparently, Dmitri Pavlov did not, in fact, want to hear some mad shit. Because he started sobbing like a little bitch, like he didn't deserve it. I spoke over his cries. "So I sent my soldiers to help my fiancée pack up, and when I texted her to ask how it was going, she said 'fine.' *Fine.* What does that even mean?"

"*Pozhaluysta*," he begged, eyes squinted shut, the water drip-dripping down from his forehead into his ears. I made sure to change the rhythm and frequency of the pattern, as well as inserting a small amount of acid into the tank, for shit and giggles. "I'll do anything," he said in Russian. "Please, let me go."

"Can't do that," I answered back in his native tongue. Good thing I learned some Russian when Tier and I started out, so I could get to know her better. "You hurt my fiancée."

"I didn't! I—I couldn't! I don't even know American girls."

I'd fetched Pavel, Vitali, Vlad, Bogdan, and Dmitri from different parts of Russia and smuggled them into New York. I'd already killed the first four in spectacularly violent and slow fashion over the past week. In fact, it was why I had gone MIA on Tierney for a few days last week. Seemed like a good idea at the time, but I now realized I needed to be more present.

So instead of killing Dmitri by impalement as I did with the first four—watching as they starved to death while speared from their anus all the way to their mouths—I chose a relatively fast method for him. The acid should burn his brain clean in the next few hours. Oh well. At least he was going to feel every moment of it.

I'd always had a fascination with violent, gory deaths. Watching bad guys die soothed my soul.

"You knew this one. Tierney Callaghan." I puffed smoke into his face.

At the sound of her name, Tyrone whimpered from across the room. He was still bound by chains in a cage, shitting and pissing into a bucket, living on a can of beans and a bottle of water a day. Tierney deserved to see the bastard take his last breath. The only reason I'd waited was because I wanted to make sure she was feeling 100 percent, and I believed the time was near.

"Achilles, be reasonable. Let's talk about this! I had no idea—" Tyrone started.

"Shut the fuck up." I pulled my phone out again, thumbing the screen to answer my girlfriend.

> Achilles: Hey, beautiful. I have a meeting with my brothers in ten minutes, then I'll come home. Will you be there?

Three dots danced on the screen in front of me.

> Tierney: idk.
> Achilles: Want me to bring you a bite? Maybe dessert? 😊
> Tierney: idc.

Look at us. We were so fucking cute together. Me and my enthusiasm. Her and her dry acronym comebacks.

> Achilles: I'll pick up some takeout on my way back. Italian good?
> Tierney: w/e.

Sure, she wasn't the most talkative via text. But you could really feel the love shining through each word.

"Okay, this is getting boring." I tucked my phone into my pocket. It was ten to six, and I really needed to get this shit over with so I could take Tierney Dmitri's head, along with the rest of these fuckers', to heal her beautiful soul from what they'd done to her in that work camp. Yes, my gifts to her tended to be outside the box, but it was the thought that counted. "How about we speed things up a bit?" I winked at a lying, tied-up Dmitri.

"Nooooooo, nooooo, nooooooo!" He screamed and thrashed, arching from the bench press I'd used as a makeshift gurney while I unscrewed the water tank attached to the faucet and picked up the bottle of fluroantimonic acid. I poured it into the container. An unbearable odor of fumes immediately filled the air.

"I'd say I'm sorry for the smell," I told Tyrone over my shoulder, "but the stench is the least of your worries right now. Buckle up. What I've got planned for you will make shitbag here's death look like a euthanasia in a six-star Swiss resort."

I climbed upstairs, away from the racket of Dmitri screaming as the acid ate through his skin and brain, and from Tyrone, who rattled the bars of his cage.

The first to show up was Jeremie.

Peculiar, considering he wasn't fucking invited.

He was wearing his usual outfit of black combat boots, black tactical pants, and a too-tight Henley. Couldn't fault him for the Henley. He was the size of a kraken. I doubted they made human clothes his size. I was definitely a scary motherfucker, standing tall at six feet four inches of muscles, scars, and ink, but Jeremie was easily six feet six inches and more shredded than IRS forms at a Midtown hedge fund.

"This is a Camorra meeting," I informed him. "Ugly Bastards Anonymous is down the street."

"And yet here you stand, the chairman of the club." Jeremie pushed past me, his shoulder nearly dislocating mine. His deltoids were the size of his head. I threw the door shut with a frown. I wasn't in the mood to talk to anyone who wasn't my sweet angel fiancée.

Speaking of…

I took out my phone and checked my messages. None.

> Achilles: How are you settling in, fiancée?
> Tierney: Stop calling me that. I'm not your fiancée.
> Achilles: Yet*.
> Tierney: Ever*.
> Tierney: I'm at your apartment. You don't have any Diet Coke.

My lips quirked deviously. My little flame thought I was one of those amateur stalkers who didn't know the job.

> Achilles: The Diet Coke is in the cooler in your room, next to the fancy ice machine I got for you.
> Achilles: But if you don't feel like walking that far, I put one in the fridge behind your baby carrots and soy milk, JIC.
> Achilles: <3 <3 <3
> Tierney: Stop with the heart emojis. It's annoying.

She was looking for reasons to get annoyed with me. I refused to give her any.

> Tierney: Actually, I feel like a whole wheat New York water bagel with ham and cheese.
> Achilles: You only eat ham once a year. You think pigs are too smart and call it semi-cannibalism.
> Tierney: Your point?
> Achilles: No point. There's a whole wheat New York water bagel in the bread box for you, plus ham and cheese from your favorite deli in the fridge.

I beamed at my phone with satisfaction, giving exactly minus twenty fucks about leaving Jer waiting.

> Tierney: Fine. You win. I swooned. Happy?
> Achilles: I'll be happier when you fix the hard-on I've been walking around with since I saw you in that wet dress.

Before I could tuck my phone in my pocket, Tiernan's name popped up with a message.

> Tiernan: I see my sister is moving her things to your apartment. I want to remind you I know where you live. And I haven't added a new skull to my collection in a while.
> Achilles: YOU PUSHED A GUN INTO MY SISTER'S MOUTH ON YOUR WEDDING NIGHT.
> Tiernan: Don't change the subject.

Clicking my phone's screen off, I finally threw a detached glare Jeremie's way. "Oh. You're still here."

He stood in the same spot, unmoving. I knew the stubborn Russian would remain this way until I gave him what he came here for.

I groaned. "We'll speak in the office."

We went up to Vello's office. He no longer occupied the space, too busy drooling on his shoulder ever since we'd mixed up his medicine. The decision to get rid of him was a joint, albeit spontaneous, one. Once Enzo and Luca caught Tiernan and me beating him into unconsciousness, we decided we'd be better off with him out of the picture.

It was obvious Vello's next move would have been offing both of us.

And between Tiernan's family with Lila, and Luca and Enzo's loyalty to me, Vello had lost.

We still had time to sort out the don shit when he was officially dead, but I had agreed to withdraw my candidacy.

"You either get the pussy or the throne, but you can't get both," Luca had clarified. *"You made your choice."*

It was the easiest decision I'd had to make. Tierney came first. The rest of the world after.

"All right, asshole, what's up?" I landed on Vello's plush chair, stacking my ankles on his desk.

Jeremie assumed the seat in front of me. He looked as charming as a bucket of piss. What Sofia saw in him, I couldn't tell. I guess he was good-looking, if you were into the whole unhinged-motherfucker-the-size-of-a-football-stadium vibe.

"You're probably asking yourself what's going on."

"No, I don't really care, unless Tierney's involved." I slid a cigarette out of a battered packet, lighting it. "But go ahead. People bother me with boring crap all the time."

"Sangue Blu gunned down five of your soldiers in Naples last night."

I was aware. In response, we'd set up this urgent meeting.

"Enlighten me as to how my shit is your business?" I exhaled a thick stream of smoke to the ceiling.

"It's likely you and your brothers are going there in the near future to settle the score. It'll leave your family exposed to retaliation." He paused, waiting for me to put two and two together. I decided to play dumb.

"Leave Tierney's security detail to me."

"I'm talking about Sofia and Ciro. They need proper security."

"And?" I was going to make him spell it out for me, so he could hear for himself the level of deranged he'd reached.

"And I'm the only one who's fit for the job."

Silence followed. I waited for him to realize the error of his ways, but apparently, he was too drunk on my brother's wife's pussy juices to understand the gravity of the situation. He really was lucky I was still pissed with Luca for breaking up Tier and me when we were kids, or we'd be having an entirely different conversation right now. One where I did the talking and he did the falling off a fucking cliff.

"Are you asking me to give you the green light to fuck my brother's wife while he goes to war?" I stubbed my cigarette into an ashtray. The balls on this asshole.

His nostrils flared. "It's not like that. I've never touched her."

Chivalrous. Wasn't expecting that little twist. *Anyhow.*

"We're going to get rid of the entire Coppola clan," I said. Not a done deal but an educated guess. "So your services, though philanthropical, aren't needed."

"They could already be on American soil, waiting for the green light to hurt you," Jeremie drawled. "Every first-rank wife of the Camorra needs a bodyguard. I'll be hers."

That he'd lower himself to be the babysitter, the *help*, was enough to tell me everything I needed to know. Jeremie was a well-oiled killing machine, with combat and technological abilities that made him priceless to any organization.

"She is *pregnant*, Jeremie."

"I know."

"And you don't care?"

He flashed me an oblique smile. "I need to stay in New York because of my own reasons. Guarding Sofia is something I can do well and easily. Win-win."

"So you'll be content if I assign you to do something else in New York that doesn't involve Sofia Ferrante?"

"Yes," he said flatly. But he'd paused. I heard it.

"Are you fucking her, Jeremie?"

"No."

"Why did you delete the records from the CCTV footage in their bedroom?"

"Not because of that."

For the first time since I'd met the Russian bastard, his lifeless eyes glinted with fire and ice. *Alive.*

I believed him, but if Jeremie was half as good a liar as he was a hacker, that made him a world-class bluffer.

Fuck. *Fuck.* If this baby wasn't Luca's, we were going to have a lot of fucking problems. I wasn't going to let anything compromise the Camorra's already less-than-ideal position in the Northeast. Even if I had to take care of the damn fetus myself.

"He'll kill you if something happens between you two," I warned. "Her, too."

Jeremie looked unimpressed. "You're overplaying your hand. Make a decision, Scarface."

The only reason he didn't have a bullet-shaped hole in his forehead was that, strangely, I believed he cared for Sofia. And as a man driven by obsession and deeply fucked-up love, I recognized the same flame of insanity in myself.

If Tierney had a husband… Well, let's just say he wouldn't die of old age.

Still, I couldn't let Jeremie think it was okay to saunter into our territory and fuck our women. Our *married* women, at that. It sent a message that we'd gone soft, weak, and worst of all, prideless.

"Here's what's gonna happen." I opened the drawer and retrieved my father's old pistol, feeding bullets into it. "You're going to use the next sentence to convince me not to put three bullets in your fucking head for disrespecting a Ferrante and the Camorra, and I'm going to pretend to give it some thought, because apparently, I'm maturing into the kind of man my fiancée wants to marry." I raised the gun and pointed it at his forehead.

Bastard didn't even flinch. "If you convince Luca to assign me as his wife's bodyguard and extend my contract for six more months, the Bratva will give the Camorra everything east of Texas."

"Six months? That's all you need in New York?"

He nodded.

I arched an eyebrow. This was interesting.

Right now, we ruled the East Coast, which was the criminal powerhouse of America, but that left a lot of dead areas for the taking.

"You don't have the authority to give me shit," I drawled.

"Cleared it with the pakhan." Not a muscle in his goddamn body moved. "Don't believe me? Ask him."

Now I didn't know whether to punch his teeth in or take the bait. We *could* use more territory. If for no other reason than to put a buffer between us and the Bratva. We were still the largest crime organization in America, but Tiernan and Alex were gaining on us, fast.

What did Jeremie give to Alex in exchange for this solid? I had no idea, but it had to be big. The pakhan wanted his genius brother nearby.

"Luca doesn't care," Jeremie hedged, voice cold and flat. "See for yourself during the meeting. If he cares—if he so much as budges—let me know."

"And you'll back off?"

He gave me an incredulous look. "You and I, Achilles, we are not so different."

Asking what he meant would go against my religious belief of not giving a fuck. But Jeremie being Jeremie, he still volunteered the information.

"When we want something, even God himself cannot stop us from getting it."

I smirked. Life trying to win back Tierney was no picnic, but I had to hand it to Luca—he'd managed to put himself in an infinitely more screwed-up situation.

"I want weapons, too," I said.

"That could be arranged."

I snorted, shaking my head. "One man's trash is another man's treasu—"

Jeremie shot up from his seat, balling my shirt in his fist, his nose flat against mine. And there it was again. The adorable fucking *blush*. "Don't finish that sentence if you want to see your so-called fiancée in a wedding dress."

I laughed, pushing him off.

"I'll see what I can do," I drawled, just as I heard footsteps approaching down the hallway. "Now, get the hell out of here."

CHAPTER FORTY-EIGHT
ACHILLES

"We need to take Sangue Blu and his first-rankers out." I set my glass of whiskey down on the table. "This has been going for too long. Our business is suffering."

"This time, we're shutting down his entire operation." Enzo tossed his knife in the air, catching it with his fingertips. "I ain't hauling ass in and out of Naples weekly to deal with the Coppola clan. I've got important shit to do."

"Oh? Like what?" Luca folded his legs, the sharp crease in his trousers immaculate. "Hitting the gym twice a day and living off protein shakes and brussels sprouts?"

"For instance?" Enzo brushed off the dig.

My baby brother was an interesting creature. He'd die before making someone he cared for disappointed or sad but had no trouble taking down eighty men in the span of twenty-four hours.

"Enzo's right." I ran a hand over my tie. "We're going around in circles with them, and we have more pressing issues here in the States. The Bratva's getting bolder."

"The union between Enzo and Katya is supposed to fix that," Luca grumbled.

"That's not happening for at least four months," Enzo pointed out. "Katya has requested to finish her freshman year at college. A lot can happen in that time."

Luca ran a hand over his mouth. "You wanna wipe them out? Fine. We will. But if we want to keep shit in order in Naples, one of us will have to move there."

"I'll do it," I said without missing a beat.

"You'll move to Naples?" Enzo cocked his head sideways.

"Yeah."

"And Tierney?"

"She'll move with me."

She wanted to get away from all the hustle and bustle of New York, and this was a good opportunity to offer her that. Plus, I was tired of having to share her with all the clingy-ass people in our lives—Lila, Sofia, Tiernan, and the rest.

"All right, Achilles's in." Luca threaded his fingers together. "We need to be quick about finishing Coppola's clan, though. Our eyeballs should be on the Midwest. Alex has taken over Des Moines, I hear."

"Or we could wait until Alex is power-drunk and tries conquering Chicago. That'd pull the Outfit into our war." Enzo ran his knife shallowly along his palm. "The Bandinis won't let that happen, right?" Enzo searched Luca's face. They were his in-laws, after all.

"Hard to tell. President Keaton is breathing down their necks, wanting to take them down before his first term is over." Luca's tongue skated over his lower lip. "They're trying to keep their heads down at all costs."

"*Fuck*," Enzo muttered.

"There's another way around the Bratva." I pressed my fingers together. "It'll delay them, not stop them, but it could give us a couple years."

Luca curved a skeptic brow. "I'm listening."

Time to figure out just how much of a cold fish you are, Brother.

"Lyosha sent an offer through Jeremie. He's willing to give us everything east of Texas, Oklahoma, Kansas, and the Dakotas."

"That means they'll have to pull out of the newly conquered parts." Enzo shifted forward in his seat, lighting up.

I nodded. "They'll hand over some weapons, too."

"What's the tradeoff?" Luca drawled.

"Jeremie wants to stay in New York," I said tonelessly. "As your wife's bodyguard."

Not a flicker of emotion was present on Luca's face. His eyes were two dark pools of venom. No light and nothing behind them. *Dead*.

Jeremie was right.

He didn't give half a shit.

The silence stretched for another full minute before Luca spoke again. "Tell me about the weapons they're offering."

Holy psychotic shitballs.

I had a lot to aspire to. Yes, I was violent and murderous, and didn't have a drop of morality in my entire body, but at least I was capable of feeling. If someone wanted to touch Tierney—let alone babysit her while I was gone—I'd be killing them six ways from Sunday just to make sure the job was done.

Enzo and I exchanged looks. Our eyes said the same thing.

Luca was going to be the new don.

He deserved it.

He crossed every personal and professional line to get there, and he was pragmatic, cold, and calculating enough to make good decisions.

Clearing my throat, I went back to business. "Firearms, grenades, state-of-the art rifles—the kind that can pierce a row of refrigerators. You know, the works."

"Military issue?"

"With the serial numbers filed off beyond recovery," I assured him.

The Russians had a lot of weapons the Camorra could only dream of. They were prolific arms dealers, while our forte was drugs and money laundering.

"And what guarantees will we have about them honoring the new borders?" Luca rolled up the sleeves of his dress shirt.

I shrugged. "We'll figure out the fine print together."

"And Katya?" Enzo asked. "Do I still have to marry her?"

"Yes," Luca and I said in unison. We needed family ties with the Bratva. For our blood to mix with theirs. "Jeremie's babysitting gig is not gonna last more than a few weeks, until we're sure we've eliminated the Coppola clan," Luca added. "We still need to break bread with the Russians."

"Should I call Jeremie?" I asked.

"No. We're negotiating this directly with Alex," Luca snarled. "Get the pakhan on the phone."

I took out my phone, checking first to see if Tierney had messaged me again.

> Tierney: What's your weird fixation with me and coffee?
> Achilles: That's random.
> Tierney: So is the fact that you've always asked me to make you some.

Not recently, though. Not since our reconciliation. I cared too much to screw this up for a fucking Cup A Joe.

> Achilles: It symbolizes domestic bliss to me.

She typed, then deleted, then typed again. I should've lied to her. Told her I just liked caffeine because coke was too destructive a hobby. I didn't want to scare her away. But I also knew I couldn't keep this all-consuming hunger for her on a leash much longer. I'd agreed to stop the stalking. I'd never agreed to stop obsessing, though.

Fearing my answer would annihilate all the goddamn progress I'd been working on these past few weeks, I changed the subject.

> Achilles: There's a special edition of The Hitchhiker's

> Guide to the Galaxy in my office, if you're bored.
> Tierney: Already found/read it but thanks.

Phew. Although, it had to be said—I wasn't thrilled that a cup of coffee could throw our entire relationship into a crisis. Especially a hypothetical one. I mean, goddamn.

> Tierney: Do I want to know why the crown molding in your office has bloodstains all over it?
> Achilles: No...?
> Tierney: I cleaned them up.
> Achilles: I love you.
> Tierney: We should probably power wash the entire apartment.
> Achilles: I said I love you.
> Tierney: Shut up and take me to dinner when you're back.

I grinned like a lunatic.

> Achilles: You got it, baby. Put something slutty on. I'm in the mood to get in a fight.

After calling Alex and working over the fine print of the very generous deal the Bratva offered us—with me wondering just how much credit Jeremie had to use to wrestle his brother into this deal—we killed the call.

"Luca..." Enzo trailed off.

"Yeah?"

"Jeremie..."

"They're not fucking," he said dryly, but for the first time, there was some tightness in his voice. "He's a stammering fool in front of her. And she's frightened of his size, his presence. She doesn't trust humans, you know. Only horses. Nothing's going on between them."

"If you know she is scared of him, why are you doing this?" I asked.

"Because I don't give a shit how she feels," he said simply. "And he *will* keep her safe."

"What about pride?"

Luca ran a hand over his jawline, his wedding band catching the sunlight pouring in the window. "Pride is a sin."

Enzo choked on his vodka soda. "Bitch, so is murder, and I don't see you stopping your violent killing sprees anytime soon."

"Stay in your lane, Enzo," Luca said quietly. "Jeremie's the best the Bratva has to offer. He'll keep her safe. And me? I'll finally have my kingdom."

CHAPTER FORTY-NINE
TIERNEY

"Do you like it?"

Achilles's gaze clung to my face expectantly, like an eager child showing his parent his first work of art.

"It's…" My throat worked around my gag reflex. "Definitely interesting. What am I looking at, again?"

"The heads of all of your abusers." A blush crept up his sharp cheekbones. "Dmitri, Vitali, Vlad, Bogdan, and Pavel. I picked them up personally last week."

"From…Russia?"

His face was expressionless, but his eyes were all eager puppy, begging for scraps of love. I couldn't bear it.

"How did you find them?"

"Brennan."

Working with Sam Brennan was a status symbol in the underworld. He charged a lot and extra if you expedited the process.

"How much did it cost?"

He shrugged. "Doesn't matter. You're worth it."

We were deep inside the woods, and there was a pile of human flesh and bone in front of me. They had been tossed into a shallow grave. Now that he'd mentioned it, some of it did look like craniums.

I blinked, torn between gratitude and anguish. The girl I left behind in Russia didn't dare dream of getting revenge. She barely hoped to survive the memories she'd carried with her.

"Aw, *shit*. I fucked it up, didn't I?" Achilles laced his fingers together at the back of his neck, pacing. "I knew I should've just done the job and spared you the exhibition. Or… Did you want to do it yourself? I didn't mean to steal your thunder. I'm still new at thi—"

"No." I reached to put a hand on his arm to stop him from pacing. "I wanted to see it. I just wasn't expecting…*this*."

This grotesque and beautiful gift that cost more than any designer bag and took effort, time, concentration, and hunger for justice.

To my annoyance and horror, tears prickled in my eyes. I didn't let them loose, but I knew my eyes were shining. I forced myself not to break our stare. He deserved to see me vulnerable. Even if I couldn't bear to show my fragility to anyone.

Achilles cupped my cheeks. "Baby…"

I shook my head, sniffing. "I'm okay."

"These are good tears, right?" He plastered his forehead to mine. I breathed him in greedily, my head spinning with sorrow. How did I let us not be together for an entire decade? How did I give him up?

"The best." My words were delivered in a broken moan. "It's just that…no one's ever fought this hard for me."

Achilles forced himself to disconnect from me. He stomped to his gunmetal Ferrari, tossing the trunk open and taking out a tank of gasoline. He returned to the edge of the shallow grave and poured the liquid all over it.

"Where're the rest of their body parts?" I wiped at my nose.

"Evaporated," he said through a clenched jaw. "On that note, I need to buy my parents a new outdoor pizza oven." He took out a box of matches from his pocket, lit one, and handed it to me. "Wanna do the honors?"

"Certainly." I took the match and tossed it inside, watching what was left of my rapists' corpses go up in flames. The fire was so little but the distribution so big. It was my very own moth—the one I'd burned almost to oblivion—who served me the most precious gift of all: *Revenge*.

"Can I take you somewhere special?" he asked.

"Sure." I smiled.

He took my hand and led the way.

———

"Are you fucking kidding me?" I clutched my seat belt in Achilles's passenger seat, strangling it with fury. "When you said you wanted to take me somewhere, I thought you meant a restaurant."

"We can go to a restaurant after you're done." Achilles killed the engine, popping off his ball cap and running his fingers through his short hair. "I'll wait downstairs."

"I'm not going up there, you asshole."

"Dr. Andrews is the best therapist in New York," he said evenly, his impenetrable expression telling me I could kick and scream to the high heavens, but I was going up there. "Her waiting list is six months long. And I promise I won't have access to her records."

"How charitable." I narrowed my eyes. "Do you realize how condescending it is? To make *me* go to therapy? Twice a week at that."

"You need professional help."

"This is rich coming from a cannibal who just gifted me five corpses," I fired back. "If one of us needs professional help, it is definitely you."

"I'm seeing someone, too." He swiped his tongue over his lower lip. "I told you I'm serious about this, and I am. Sure, I don't tell him about my…*career* or about what certain business trips of mine entail. But I talk about what we've been through. About the stalking. I want to change."

This undid the tight lump of anger in my chest. I didn't have anything against therapy. On the contrary, I agreed we both desperately needed it. I just didn't want to do all the work while he sat there, making corpse pizzas in his family's backyard.

And…I had a feeling that, this time, I could have a breakthrough. In the past, my therapists had tried reaching a place inside me that I'd buried too deep in denial. Now, all the memories had resurfaced, the wounds reopened.

"Fine," I muttered. "I'll see this Dr. Andrews person." I glanced at my phone, heaving out a breath. "I guess I'll go fill out the paperwork."

I half expected him to tell me the paperwork had been taken care of—stalker Achilles had the tendency to overstep—but he surprised me by nodding. "Those are a bitch. I sat outside my therapist's office for goddamn forty minutes filling out that questionnaire. And lying about eighty percent of it."

I rolled my eyes, stifling a snort.

He munched on his inner cheek. "There's something you should know."

"Okay."

"I'm heading to Naples next week to tie up some loose ends with Coppola. Make sure he doesn't bother us again."

I nodded. I liked that he kept me in the loop. It was very rare for men in the Camorra, and I didn't take it for granted. "Thanks for telling me."

"You're welcome."

He studied me quietly. Expectantly.

He wanted me to show him that it worried me.

That I wanted him safe.

Considering our history, I couldn't blame him.

I put a hand on the door handle, struggling for words that usually came so easily to me. But they were derisive words, meant to hurt. I had to peel so many layers to show pain, loss, and vulnerability. To show love.

"Achilles?"

"Yes, Piccola Fiamma?"

"Truth?"

He paused. "Truth, baby. I'll always choose the truth."

"I spent my entire adult life regretting that fire. I couldn't bear how it hurt you, how it ruined *us*. Some days, the only reason I didn't finish myself was because I knew you wouldn't let me, and I would never put your life at risk again. With time, I got better. Better but never whole. I'm only whole when I'm with you. And if that's toxic, or unhealthy, then so be it. Because the truth is, there isn't me if there isn't you."

CHAPTER FIFTY
TIERNEY

I spent the first three days in Achilles's Manhattan apartment moving in my stuff, decorating it in the most feminine fashion, and trying to get rid of the suspicious stench coming from his otherwise impeccably clean and neat office.

I did find a secret passage from a cupboard in the office where Achilles stashed a profane amount of weapons but no human remains. The place *could* technically house a body, though, so I was sure one had been stored there at some point.

On the fourth day, Tom Rothwell arrived at Achilles's doorstep.

He'd been trying to schedule a meeting with me since I was discharged from the hospital, but with no warrant or a reason to issue one, all he could do was hope for the charity and goodwill of my brother. As it happened, Tiernan had none.

Now all bets were off. While I was sure Camorra soldiers patrolled the building, Achilles had issued strict instructions to let my visitors come and go as they pleased. No one knew Tom was not, in fact, a welcomed guest.

He stood at the threshold, a god among mortals, every inch and fiber of him demanding your attention and appreciation.

Elusive. Elegant. Malicious.

Too bad my heart belonged to a man whose face scared small children and was still the most gorgeous creature in the world to me.

I rested an elbow on the doorframe, yawning in his face. "Out of all the boyfriends you don't want to piss off, Rothwell, mine is probably at the top of the list."

"Nice haircut." His hands were stuffed into his front pockets casually, and he dripped nonchalance, like I didn't bail on his ass, ruined years of his work, and on top of that, got *shot* and had to shave my head as a result. Truly, Tom Rothwell was probably the only man on this planet who could rival Luca's coldness. "And why is that?"

"Why's what?"

"Why don't I want to piss off your boyfriend?"

I laughed at the blatant attempt to milk more information out of me. "Achilles could get here any minute, you know."

"Achilles is at the port, overlooking a shipment."

My stalker had a stalker. The universe really did have a twisted sense of humor.

"If that's true, why are you here instead of there, arresting him?" I challenged.

"Because if I catch him on drug trafficking charges, I won't be able to throw him in the can for the eleven homicides I have linked to him." *Jesus.* "Can I come in?"

"No."

"Thanks." He breezed past me, giving zero damns about my refusal. Tom peered around, cataloging the recently refurbished bachelor pad and burning every inch of it into memory. "Nice love nest."

"Isn't this considered breaking and entering?" I clenched my teeth.

"What'd I break?" He looked around in mock innocence.

"Trespassing, then."

He gave me a pitying look that assured me he could take a shit in the center of the living room without blowback from his superiors. "This'll be quicker if you cooperate."

I sighed in frustration. "Coffee?"

"Black. No sugar."

"Shocking," I muttered, shuffling to the coffee machine. His hawkish glare scorched through my skull as I busied myself with mugs and teaspoons.

"How've you been?" He reached for a vase, seemingly arranging it, and I made a mental note to throw it away when he was gone.

"Oh, you know."

"Can't say I do. You disappeared on me last we spoke, remember?"

"Vaguely. I had an unfortunate accident in Italy. Head injury."

"So I heard." He ambled closer, taking up much more space than his trim, athletic frame claimed in the room. "Funny, I couldn't find your passport in the database to confirm your flight to Prague."

"Hmm." I swirled my teaspoon in his coffee. "Governmental software is known to be glitchy."

"Tierney." He was so close now his breath tickled the nape of my neck, causing goose bumps. I swiveled on my heel, clutching the counter behind me. "Do the right thing. Give me those statements."

"What statements?"

"The ones on the USB."

"I can't confirm them."

"Why the hell not?"

"Amnesia."

I had very little to work with, and this seemed like as good an excuse as any.

Tom's brows dipped into a V. "I read your hospital report. You don't suffer from amnesia."

"Selective amnesia," I amended.

"Selective bullshit," he snapped back, his jaw clenching.

The air between us scorched with tension, but it wasn't sexual. More like we both knew he wanted to throttle me. The Ferrantes really were in trouble. This guy was a dog with a bone.

"You don't want to get on my shit list, Miss Callaghan."

"What happens to people who find themselves there?" I purred, making a show of shimmying my shoulders. Life was too short to be intimidated by egotistical men in positions of power.

His nose very nearly brushed mine when he whispered, "If they're lucky? I put them in prison."

"And if they're unlucky?"

He just smiled. Every bone in my body turned to ice. This bastard was more formidable than any mobster I'd come across.

Wanting some distraction, I turned back around and poured his coffee with shaking hands. By some miracle, I only spilled a few drops on the counter. I passed him his cup. "Here you go."

Tom took the cup from me, downed the hot coffee like a shot, and handed it back to me, leaning into my personal space.

"Don't keep me waiting, Callaghan," he whispered sardonically into my ear, his lip brushing my lobe. "Deception is not a trait I tolerate well."

CHAPTER FIFTY-ONE
ACHILLES

No part of me wanted to leave Tierney and go to Naples to deal with Coppola.

No part and *especially* not my cock. It'd been almost a week since she'd moved in, and true to her word, she slept in the spare room.

At least she was seeing Dr. Andrews. And I was seeing Dr. Clark. With a little luck (and a lot of fucking therapy), we'd be having a healthy relationship in no time.

"You'll take care of yourself, right?" Tierney tapped the wheel of my car, munching on her bottom lip. No one, including God himself, was allowed to drive my custom Porsche 550 Spyder. Which put Tierney above God tier. This woman was in the habit of making me break every word and promise I'd ever made to myself.

"Always do." I reached for my backpack, going over my stash of weapons and magazines.

For the first time since I was eighteen, I was reluctant to insert myself into a bloodbath. What if I didn't make it back to New York? The thought of being so close to having Tierney just to die a senseless death made my skin crawl. "Why? You worried about me?"

"Of course I'm worried. You're my nephew's favorite uncle," she snarled.

"If Tom Rothwell pays you another visit—"

"I'll exercise my Second Amendment rights. He won't break into our place again."

Our. She said *our*. My chest tightened.

A heart attack? Maybe. Still worth it.

"That's my girl. And you're sure I can't persuade you to have security, just until I get back from Italy?"

"Positive," she ground out. "You're not keeping me in chains anymore, Achilles."

I had no one but myself to blame for the fact Tierney didn't have security up the wazoo while I was in Italy, finishing a bloody war. I did this to myself, by pushing her for years and surveilling her every move. Now I had to remind myself she was a big girl, not an innocent, helpless damsel like Lila or Sofia. She could take down grown men without smearing her lipstick.

I was counting on it.

Tierney slid onto the tarmac of the private airport and turned off the ignition. She shifted in her seat to face me. The jet was already running, with Enzo and Luca waiting inside.

"Promise me you're coming back in one piece." She fixed her gaze on me.

Unfortunately for her, now *I* was feeling a little sulky. "What do I get out of it?"

"Not dying." She scowled. "Isn't that enough incentive?"

I shrugged noncommittally.

"You're ridiculous!" She pushed at my chest. "Promise me you won't die."

"You're making me promise you that I'm immortal and *I'm* the ridiculous one?" I cocked an eyebrow.

"What do you think you're doing, Achilles?"

"Negotiating."

"What are you negotiating exactly?"

"Affection."

She narrowed her eyes at me. "Okay. I'm listening."

"A kiss now as a deposit. If I come back in one piece…you let me fuck you."

Her eyebrows shot up to her hairline.

"And if I come back missing a few pieces, I can settle for oral."

She swatted my chest, laughing. I grinned, pleased I'd broken the tension. "What happens if you die?"

"You get everything in my possession."

"Your family will execute the will dutifully." She rolled her eyes.

"You *are* the will," I countered. "Everything goes to you."

"You changed your will before coming here?" She paled.

"No. You've been the sole heir to all of my possessions for a while now."

"How long is awhile?" The expression on her face teetered between puzzled and elated.

I had no choice but to answer. We'd promised each other to always tell the truth. "Ten years."

She did the math in her head, realized I'd chosen to leave her everything I'd ever owned even when we were bitter enemies, and cupped her mouth. "Achilles…"

"Deal or no deal?" I asked, businesslike.

"Deal."

We met halfway above the central console, and I dipped my head, capturing her lips in mine. She opened up for me, darting her tongue and touching the tip to mine. My throat produced a low groan. She tasted sweet. Toffee and cinnamon. And *mine*. She tasted like she was completely and wholly mine. Tierney threaded her fingers in my hair and deepened the kiss.

"Yo!" Enzo hollered from the plane's open door. "We all have a piece of ass waiting at home. Wrap it up, Romeo."

"Duty calls," I murmured into Tierney's mouth, stroking her face. "Wait for me?"

"Been waiting for eleven years. One more weekend won't kill me, I suppose." She pulled away, her brows furrowing when she remembered something. "Hey, who's feeding my dad while you're gone?"

"Jeremie's on pet-sitting duty. Why, are you worried?"

"Yes. Worried he'll die accidentally before I have time to give him a piece of my mind."

I smirked, stealing one last kiss. "I love you, Little Flame."

She didn't say it back, but she kissed me back with everything she had in her.

And it was more truthful than any words we'd ever spoken...and said one word.

Mine.

CHAPTER FIFTY-TWO
ACHILLES

"You're fucking kidding me." I let out a fiery breath.

Luca screwed his fingers into his eye sockets. "I don't know how it happened."

"You don't know how it happ... Turn the fucking plane around!"

"We're on it, dude. Chillax." Enzo dropped a hand on my shoulder. I swatted it off, darting to my feet and bulldozing toward the cockpit.

"Don't tell me to calm the fuck down."

Coppola was in New York and heading straight toward my apartment.

Luca just got off the phone with Sam Brennan, who'd put a tracker on Stefano's favorite Rolex for the measly sum of 400,000 euros. We'd been tracking him for weeks now. There was a slight chance the watch's location—which was currently between Newark and Manhattan—was a trick to lure us back to New York, but I doubted it. This particular Rolex belonged to Stefano's slain father. He'd part ways with his kidneys before giving up the family heirloom.

No, he was in New York.

And heading in Tierney's direction, while I was forty-five thousand feet above the Atlantic Ocean.

"He could be going to my apartment," Luca pointed out.

"*Your* apartment has Jeremie guarding it," I hissed back. "I'm not worried about your family. Plus, Coppola's beef is with me. Turn the plane around," I roared at our pilot.

"We're about to take the turn. It's been cleared with APIS." Our pilot flicked his gaze to the turn coordinator. "Forty minutes and you're there."

"You need to take a deep breath." Enzo plopped down on a recliner, lighting a cigarette. "You're probably going to beat Stefano to the apartment with the New York traffic. Have you tried calling her again?"

I had. Again.

And again.

And a-motherfucking-gain.

She wasn't picking up. It hadn't even been that long since she'd dropped me off.

"This can be fixed with one phone call," Luca mused from his spot on the upholstered lounger. "Carmine and Antonio are doing laps around your building. Say the word and they'll go up there." He flicked his wrist to check his Patek Phillippe.

Lacing my fingers at the back of my neck, I swore softly.

I promised her no security, but this was an emergency. If it was up to betraying her but saving her or following her instructions blindly and risking her life, I knew which one I'd choose.

Maybe she'd never forgive me, but at least I'd save her.

I dropped my head between my shoulders. "Make the call."

My phone started ringing. Tierney's name flashed on the screen.

Oh, thank fuck.

"Where have you been?" I growled.

"Easy there, tiger. It hasn't been a full hour." Her easy laughter filled my ears. "I'm driving. Must've gone into a tunnel when you called. What's up?"

"Sangue Blu is on his way to our apartment." I motioned for Luca to cut the call with Antonio and Carmine. They weren't necessary anymore. "We're making a U-turn now. I want you to drive to your brother's place and stay there until I come get you."

She bristled. "When's he gonna get there?"

"Did you hear what I just said?"

"Yeah. I'm just wondering if I have time to pee. I'm almost there."

"Don't go up." I managed to keep the desperation from my voice. Barely. The need to rip my skin apart for not being there to protect her clawed its way to my throat. "He should be there any minute."

"You prefer me in Irish territory?"

I'd prefer her in Bratva territory, too. Anything was better than Coppola.

"*Tierney*," I warned. "Don't fuck with me. I gave you an order. I don't do it often."

"Okay, okay," she sighed. "I'll go straight to Tiernan and Lila's."

I closed my eyes and forced my heartbeat to slow. "Thank you."

CHAPTER FIFTY-THREE
TIERNEY

I wasn't going straight to Tiernan and Lila's.

I was going to finish the bastard myself.

Served him right, for thinking he could buy me like cattle.

The fact he wanted the love of my life dead did not help his cause in the least. Stefano Coppola was my enemy through and through.

I'd spent my life pretending to be something I was not—the party girl, the socialite, the airhead. But the truth was, I was a soldier raised in a camp. A cannon fodder. A well-trained pawn.

Cold. Calculating. *Bloodthirsty*.

But sometime during the past few weeks, this pawn managed to reach the other side of the board. Against all odds, I'd promoted myself to a queen's position, and now, I was going to act like one.

It was time to quench my thirst.

I parked Achilles's Porsche in the underground parking and took the elevator upstairs. The apartment was locked, with no movement detected on the security app in or outside it for the last three hours.

Coppola hadn't arrived yet.

It gave me time to pee, then check out the secret stash in Achilles's office cupboard and choose myself a nice Nighthawk GRP with a suppressor. It packed a punch and was discreet.

Not that I was worried about waking up any neighbors—the

apartment was completely soundproof—but realistically, Coppola was coming with reinforcements, and I needed to take them out one bastard at a time.

As soon as I finished loading the magazine, a soft click sounded from the entrance, and I knew Coppola had entered the place.

With my back to the office door, I had no choice but to crawl all the way into the narrow passage and close it behind me. It wasn't an ideal spot, but it meant I could hide until he was in the bedroom or far enough inside that I could sneak out and ambush them.

I heard his soldiers filing into the apartment, the soft clicks of designer loafers hitting the floor. They spoke in Italian, their voices hushed and low.

Confusion and terror slammed into me. How did they get inside willy-nilly? How did they pass the security system, which alerted our phones every time someone walked through the door? And where were Achilles's soldiers? They were usually sweeping the area up and down, eliminating potential threats.

This was bad. I was officially outnumbered, cornered, and with no escape route. I'd have to take them all.

I heard footsteps edging into the office and peered through the narrow crack of the cupboard. All I could see were loafers and dark pants.

The person in the room rummaged through the documents on his desk, cursed in Italian, then broke whatever was within reach in frustration. A laptop, lamp, and picture frame came crashing down on the floor. I took advantage of the sudden noise to cock my weapon.

Come closer. I dare you.

For better or worse, the bastard decided to do exactly that. When he didn't find what he was looking for, he began throwing drawers open, emptying their contents to the floor. Anger shot through my spine. How dare he touch Achilles's things so carelessly? Who did he think he was?

When he reached my cupboard, I was ready. As soon as he

flung it open, I pulled the trigger, putting a bullet right between his eyebrows. The *pop* was soft, hushed by the suppressor. He went down, a surprised look in his beady eyes.

Since I didn't know what Coppola looked like, I didn't know if it was him I'd taken down. He seemed to fit the bill—thirtysomething, nicely dressed with a mustache.

It hardly mattered, though. I was going to clean this place up and kill all of Coppola's clan before Achilles had a chance to get here.

Crawling out of my hideout, I flipped the bastard face up on the floor. He was heavy and more than a little bloody. Swallowing down my labored breathing, I ripped his dress shirt open. As expected, he had a bulletproof vest.

"Gonna have to borrow that one. It's of no use to you now, anyway," I mumbled under my breath, aiming the gun with one hand toward the door while yanking the Velcro from his shoulders and adjusting the vest over my torso. Another figure passed through the hallway, and I had to duck under the desk. I eyed the person through the small gap under the paneled desk.

The man breezed through the hallway, realized there was a body lying on the office floor, and walked back into the doorframe. His face fell.

"Che cazzo succede...?" He took a step into the office.

I darted to my feet and shot him in the face. It struck true, though it wasn't the cleanest shot. His face detonated from the bad angle, making a sound of gory explosion. Did the others outside hear it? Even if they didn't, I knew I was running out of time. I needed to finish the job.

Keeping my back pressed against the wall, I slowly made my way out of the office, straining my ears to listen for movements in the apartment. I could hear two sets of feet—one from the main bedroom, the other from the kitchen. I decided to deal with the kitchen first. It was closer, and I didn't want my back exposed in the hallway.

Tiptoeing my way out of the corridor, I peered toward the kitchen and spotted a man ripping the art pieces from the walls, trying to find a safe or surveillance equipment. His back was to me.

Pop.

An easy, clean hit this time. He fell down. I had to be mindful of the number of bullets I had left. So far I had been able to aim straight at their heads, but I had a feeling Lady Luck was about to abandon me. I stepped forward, meaning to check the man's pulse, when a hand wrapped around my waist from behind.

It was accompanied by the cold muzzle of a gun, which pressed to the back of my head. Not too far from where Tristan Hale had shot me.

"Well, hello to my beautiful bride. We finally meet." Cold lips moved along the shell of my ear, the rugged Italian accent trickling into my system like icy raindrops.

I was captured by Stefano Coppola.

CHAPTER FIFTY-FOUR
TIERNEY

"You know, it is a shame, really, that things did not work out between us." Stefano was tying me to a kitchen island stool with a zip tie. "You killed three of my highly trained men in less than twenty minutes and with great accuracy. I find that quite enchanting."

I bit back a smart-ass response, knowing if I started running my mouth, it'd be game over for me.

Coppola tugged at the zip tie extra hard, almost cutting off the blood flow in my wrists. I pressed my lips together to suppress a yelp. He wasn't going to see my pain.

The mobster stepped back, admiring his handiwork with a smile. "Now, that's better, isn't it?"

"Is tying up women the only way you manage to keep them?" I bit out. So much for keeping my mouth shut. Guess some things never changed.

"Careful now." His leer widened. "If you talk back, I might do more than use you as a tradeoff."

"I'd like to see you try." I kept my tone calm. "I'll finish you o—"

The door burst open and Achilles stood on the threshold, panting.

I had the good sense to recoil in shame. I should've never come here. He'd asked me to go to my brother's house, and that's what I should've done. Instead, I'd defied him for the millionth time.

Achilles's dead eyes flickered with emotion at the sight of me, but he trained them back to their usual impassive pools of death.

Stefano had his gun aimed at him, and Achilles's weapon was drawn too, pointing at Stefano's head. A shotgun, of all things. A hunting one. A Mossberg or a Remington, I couldn't tell.

"Oh, good. You've finally arrived," Stefano greeted in English.

"Let her go," Achilles said evenly, his gaze purposefully homed in on Coppola, not me. "She's got nothing to do with it. It's me you're pissed at, so let's settle the score."

"I disagree. She has a lot to do with it." Stefano trailed his free hand along my cheek in mock affection, and when I looked up, I saw his canine smile widening. "She was mine, and you took her away from me."

"She was never yours," Achilles snarled, "and you should be grateful I had the good sense not to give her to you in the first place, because it earned you a few blissful months of life. It was only a matter of time before I snuck into your place in the dead of night and slaughtered you in your sleep to have her."

Achilles stepped into the apartment and kicked the door shut. The walls rattled around the room.

"If you fire that weapon, you're taking her with me," Coppola pointed out.

"It's my hunting shotgun. It's loaded with slugs," Achilles retorted twice as calmly and thrice as deadly. "So I get to blow your head off *and* keep the girl. Ain't that my lucky day."

"Don't you want to know how I deceived you into this position?" Coppola asked.

"Not particularly."

"I gave my Rolex to my consigliere. Dropped him off a few streets down and let him walk the rest of the way. Your soldiers picked up his track and followed him. You thought I wouldn't find out, huh?" Sangue Blu stroked his chin. "You've been getting too sloppy, Achilles. And for what?" He shook his head, gesturing to me. "This? This is what you started a war for?"

Achilles's jaw clenched, but he let his silence do the heavy lifting. He wore a mask of calm during psychological warfare. Meanwhile, I pretended to stretch my back, hiking my bound hands up and over my head. If I could bring them to my front, I'd be in a good position to wrap my arms around Coppola's neck when he was distracted and try to strangle him. For that, however, I needed Achilles to keep him engaged. My eyes searched Achilles's face, but he refused to look at me, his low-energy dominance electrifying the room.

"You know your little girlfriend here killed three of my soldiers?" Coppola huffed.

Achilles lifted his free shoulder in a shrug. He was buying time, and I wondered what his plan was. He always had one. A quick glance at Coppola clued me in. His arm began to shake. He'd been training his Glock on Achilles for too long. Achilles was counting on him getting tired. *He* could aim a much heavier firearm at someone for hours on end.

My gaze burned through Achilles's cheek, and finally, he spared me a neutral glance. I motioned with my chin to my hands behind my back. His eyes slid back to the Italian mobster.

"She's good with a pistol," Achilles conceded. "With other things, too."

"Is that why you decided to keep her?" Stefano tilted his head.

I raised my arms all the way over my head—slow, slow, painfully slow—bringing them to my front. Stefano still stood beside me, but he was fully immersed in the conversation.

"No," Achilles drawled. "I kept her because I'm in love with her."

Stefano snorted. "You cannot feel love, Achilles. You are a monster. Everyone knows that."

"Monsters can love, too. Harder than humans, in fact," Achilles assured him, not sparing me the smallest glance. "Did you not love your late wife, Stefano?"

"I did, yes." Coppola's throat worked. "She was the light of my life."

"And you thought Tierney could replace her in less than two years?" Achilles snarled.

I calculated the angle from which I needed to jump Stefano to strangle him. Luckily, I was on a stool. It gave me the height advantage—I could pull it off.

"No," Stefano said. "But I wasn't planning on loving her. Just to use her as a warm cunt and a mother to my child."

"Oh, well." Achilles sounded unbothered. "That's not happening anymore. But it's not too late to admit defeat. Give me your territories in Naples, and I'll save your kids from becoming orphans."

"Don't you dare talk about my kids, *stronzo*," Stefano spat. "I'll make sure you and your little slu—"

I jumped on Stefano and coiled my arms around his neck, squeezing for dear life. He jerked back, making a gurgling sound. But my angle was all wrong, and I flailed and fell to the side of his body. Stefano cursed, fumbling with his gun to try to shoot me. He managed to squeeze the trigger, the gunshot ringing in the air. The bullet grazed my vest, then continued its journey to the wall. Achilles pounced on us, ripping the man from me. He didn't use his shotgun. Likely, he didn't want a friendly-fire situation. Instead, he grabbed Stefano's neck with both hands and broke it in one smooth movement. Stefano fell to the floor like a sack of sand.

I dropped next to him and clutched my side where Stefano had shot me.

CHAPTER FIFTY-FIVE
ACHILLES

I tore the protective vest from Tierney's torso, numb fingers fumbling the side where the bullet had hit her. She lay on the floor. It appeared she wasn't seriously injured. In fact, the bullet hadn't even scratched her.

Coppola lay next to us, convulsing and foaming at the mouth. His heart would give out soon, but he still had a few excruciating minutes to suffer through.

"You hurt?" I cupped her face, my fingers trembling.

"Nope. The vest did its job." She shook her head, smiling dazedly at me. "I took out three of his soldiers," she bragged. "I could've taken more."

"You're insane," I snarled, bending down to kiss the shit out of her.

She looped her still-tied arms around my neck, arching and meeting me halfway, and I groaned into her mouth in approval. My cock throbbed through my pants, pressed against her sweet cunt, and I pried my Bowie knife from my boot and sliced open the fabric of her flimsy top. Her tits sprang out, small and perky and perfect. I reached down and flicked one nipple with the tip of my tongue. She shuddered beneath me, trying to reach me before realizing she was still tied. Coppola was still coughing out his last breaths, watching us through glassy eyes.

Let him watch and choke on it.

"Technically, I won the bet. I got back in one piece." I blew air on her nipple and watched it pebble. "Time to cash in my prize."

She threw her head back and moaned. "Well, a bet is a bet."

"We have an audience, though." I switched to her other nipple, wetting it enough to make the cold air tighten it into a hard diamond.

Her gaze skidded to the trembling figure beside us. "Who cares? Release me."

"Nah. I think I'll teach you a lesson." The tip of my knife trailed the skin of her belly, rolling south. Smooth, save for a jagged scar I now knew was from the loss of her uterus.

We both knew I'd never seriously hurt her. The shudder of anticipation and desire it sent through her made me even harder.

"Stefano, you have no idea what you're missing. She's so sweet." I tugged at the waistband of her pants. She kicked them down dutifully, revealing no panties. "So…" I dipped my head between her legs and took a leisured lick. "Fucking…" My mouth fastened around her clit. "Sweet." I gave it a good suck.

She cried out, thrashing as she tried to guide my head deeper between her legs with her hands, fumbling because they were still tied. "Please," Tierney bucked.

"Please what?"

"Please fuck me."

Coppola blinked once, and I knew he was registering everything. That this was the last thing he'd see before he died.

"Hear that?" I locked my eyes on his tauntingly. "She is begging for it. You could've never given her what she wants."

"Fuck me until it hurts," she growled.

She was a complete psychopath.

And I was so in love.

"Let's give him a show, Piccola Fiamma. A nice farewell." I winked in Coppola's direction. I flipped her to her stomach, but when she tried rising onto all fours in preparation for me, I pressed my knee on her lower back, restraining her flat against the floor. "I want him to watch my dick coming in and out of you." I unfastened my belt. My cock was ramrod straight and ready to plow into her, the tip glistening with the first drop of my cum.

"Watch," I instructed Coppola, propping Tierney by the hip bone so her ass was slightly in the air and guiding myself into her one inch at a time. A shudder rocked through her body. I relished every second of sweet torture I handed her, knowing full well this wasn't even the tip of what I'd been feeling for years, day in and day out, pining for her.

I leaned down and bracketed her with one hand on either side of her shoulders, then captured the back of her neck in a bite. "Watch how I hit her G-spot and fuck your little bride until she blacks out, Sangue Blu."

She gasped when I lost the remainder of my self-control and started plowing into her like an animal in heat.

I couldn't see straight as I rode her, fast and deep, feeling her walls milking the orgasm out of me. It had been too long since the night at my parents' pool. I'd teetered on the edge of insanity the entire time, waiting for another hit of my favorite drug.

My bite on the back of her neck tightened, and I felt the warm pressure of my climax gripping the base of my spine. I needed her to come soon, or I'd embarrass the both of us.

Forever my guardian angel, Tierney's gasps grew faster and more breathless. "I'm coming. Don't stop. Bite me harder."

I did, stopping just short of drawing blood. I couldn't fucking do it. I could never hurt this woman, even if the future of the entire world depended on it.

Her insides quaked around my dick, squeezing my pleasure. We rode our orgasms together, and I was seeing goddamn stars it felt so good.

When I threw a glance at Coppola again, he was dead. His lips began to pale around the edges, and the look of horror in his eyes hardened into something lifeless.

I pulled out of Tierney slowly, smearing the side of my cock on her ass to clean it of our juices, and stood up. She stayed lying down, her hands still tied.

"Up," I ordered.

She rolled to her back and pushed up. I grabbed my knife and cut the zip ties. Something inside me iced to a frightening degree. Now that the pleasure of the orgasm had faded, it reminded me that we hadn't actually made love yet. All we ever did was fuck. We'd had no connection beyond the physical. Nothing to cement those words I'd told her before I boarded the plane. Words I doubted she could ever say back.

"What did you think you were doing?" I untucked my dark shirt, zipping up my pants.

"Saving you." She massaged her wrists with a wince.

"I didn't need saving."

"Everyone needs saving every once in a while." She circled her arms around my neck and nipped at the lobe of my ear. "And I'm glad I took a bullet for you, because now you know that this is a two-way street. That I care for you just as much as you care for me."

Categorically impossible, but I wasn't going to burst her little bubble.

"Care or love?" I demanded.

She blinked in response, taken off guard. "They're one and the same."

"If that's the case, you wouldn't mind telling me that you love me back. Because I, Tierney, love the shit out of you. Have been in love with you since the first fucking day I laid eyes on you."

She physically recoiled, trying to step away from my embrace. I snatched her wrist, tired. Tired that we'd fucked instead of making love. Tiptoed around her feelings instead of forcing her to feel them.

"Say it," I hissed. "*Truth.*"

She swallowed. Stared at me like prey caught in a predator's clutches. She had nowhere to go. She had to face this. Us.

"I love you," she whispered. Barely an audible rumble, really.

The satisfaction was immediate and maddening. Still, I didn't let her off the hook.

"Louder."

"I love you," she grumbled between clenched teeth.

"Can't hear you."

"I love you, you bastard!" She pushed at my chest, heaving with anger. Finally—fucking finally—I was able to draw an emotion out of her. "Like you needed to hear it to know it to be true. It's always been you. There was never anyone else. You completely dismantled my life, and still, the brightest moments of each of my days were knowing you were there, lurking, watching, yearning."

I stepped into her face. "You liked driving me insane?"

"Yes!" She pushed me harder. "It was the only indication I had that you still cared."

"Of course I cared." I bared my teeth. "Every moment you weren't mine felt like trying to survive underwater. *I love you*," I asserted.

"I love you too, asshole."

"Are you ever going to listen to a simple instruction?" I clutched her waist. She melted into me immediately. I loved that she did that now. Let herself be vulnerable. Or simply not as tough all the time.

"Probably not." At least she had the decency to make an apologetic face. "It's ingrained in me. The need to rebel burns through me. I don't think I'll ever get rid of it."

I dipped my head to kiss her. "I don't know what I did to deserve falling in love with a woman so maddening."

She sighed. "Well, you *did* kill a bunch of people, traffic drugs, meddle in—"

I pressed a finger to her mouth. "Shh. It was a rhetorical question."

She grinned up at me, and I kissed her again.

I couldn't stop.

She was too delicious, too sweet.

And too temporary, unless I found a way to lock this shit down.

CHAPTER FIFTY-SIX
TIERNEY

The next day, I came home from therapy, and a feral need to do something nice for Achilles slammed into me.

I didn't know where it came from or how to stop it. It was like a volcano erupting out of nowhere.

I did kind things for people I loved all the time. I had nurtured Lila, my sister-in-law, back to health when she was starving herself during those first few months of her marriage. I had held Tiernan's hand, day in and day out, when he was feeling suicidal, watching his chest move every night to make sure he was still breathing.

But I never made a big deal out of it and never considered it a show of my loyalty and affection. I took care of people around me not because I wanted to be nice or kind, but because I loved them so much I couldn't bear the idea they were hurting or suffering.

This was different.

I *wanted* Achilles to know I was making an effort.

I wanted to show him that all of his hard work and efforts weren't for nothing. That I was cracking, melting, warming to the idea of being domesticated after years of acting like my only chance at freedom was to be as feral and combative as possible.

Since I was hardly traditional wife material, I was short of ideas. Pacing the living room, I tried to think of ways to make him happy that didn't include wrapping my legs around his waist.

I could shop for him, but Achilles had a unique style that wasn't necessarily predictable. Every piece of clothing he donned looked exactly right on him, even though he could wear a tailored suit one day and shorts and hoodie the next.

I could take a pottery or art class with him, but he'd hate every minute of it and just pretend to be happy to appease me, and I didn't want that.

There was only one stereotypical womanly thing I knew how to do and very well—cook.

I was very good in the kitchen. First, because I spent time in rather interesting places while Tiernan and I were on the run from Igor before we were reunited with Tyrone. Second, because I was the only female in the household growing up, and more than me caving to societal norms, I recognized that all the Callaghan men were simply awful at making food and didn't want everyone starving to death.

Knowing Achilles enjoyed home-cooked meals, I made sweet couscous with raisins and a hearty lamb and vegetable stew. Then, I realized he might want a bit of street food, so I fried some stuffed sardines.

When the clock hit seven o'clock and he still wasn't home, I decided I had time to bake him a dessert and made him my famous date cookies.

At eight thirty, he walked through the door. By then, I was surrounded by dishes and fragrances of spices and baked goods. I also looked a little disheveled from all the hard work. I grinned at him in welcome. "Hey!"

He shouldered off his jacket, sauntered over in my direction with the intention of giving me a kiss, then froze in his spot, taking in all the dishes around me. "What's happening?"

"Nothing. I made you dinner and got a little carried away."

"You made me…dinner?" he asked, as though the idea was unheard of.

And I guess it was. To him. Because I'd spent so much time trying to hate him and being deliberately rude to him.

"Yes," I said softly. "I know you like home-cooked food. But you don't have to—"

"I...need a second."

Abruptly, he turned around and stalked toward the bedroom. I stood in the kitchen, blinking in confusion.

Did I do something wrong?

Did I overstep?

I didn't think I did.

But maybe Achilles wasn't fond of trying new dishes. Or maybe he didn't want me to touch his things. Although, none of these options seemed even a little viable.

Itching to go to the bedroom and ask him if he was okay, I forced myself to stay in my spot. He needed a moment, and I intended to give it to him. I swiped my finger over my phone's screen, checking the time. I was going to give him ten minutes before I went there to check on him.

Achilles returned after eight minutes, just when I was becoming antsy enough to break my word and go after him.

He wiped at his eyes, and I noticed they were red-rimmed.

There was no way he'd cried, right?

Licking my lips, I didn't dare move or breathe.

"Are you okay?" I croaked, achingly sad for some reason.

Was it really that surprising, that out of the realm of expectation, that someone took care of Achilles and not vice versa?

I guessed the answer was yes. His mother never really liked him—his words, not mine—and his father was categorically incapable of emotions. Then there was me. I'd given him some affection, some love, something to cling to, while we were kids, then took it all away abruptly.

No wonder he'd hated me with such ferocious heat.

"I'm fine. I'm just..." He stopped in front of me and smiled a bit shyly. "I'm just really happy that you're here," he finished.

That was all it took for me to eat the rest of the space between us with two steps and twist my fingers in his hair, drawing him close for a heated, passionate kiss. I tasted the cigarettes and coffee on his breath and vowed somewhere inside me to take care of this man if he'd let me.

When I released him from my kiss, he still looked a little dazed.

"Are you hungry?" I asked.

He nodded. "Yeah…I think."

"You think?"

"I'm a little shocked you made all of this for me. But, yeah, I am. I am hungry," he said, stating the words to himself more than to me, trying to ground himself in the moment.

"I'm happy to be here, too, you know." I ran my fingers over the jagged skin of his cheek—along the scars I'd put there. "And I'm not going anywhere anytime soon."

"Yes, I know."

"How do you know?"

"I won't let you."

My heart sank. Was he going to keep me here against my will? Was he planning on meddling with my life again?

He must've read the wariness on my face, because he gripped my upper arms and said, "No, I won't let you leave because I'll do anything, *anything* to make you happy with me."

"Anything?" I scanned him from under the curtain of my lashes, the familiar warmth of his gaze filling my body.

"Anything."

"You must have some red flags." I smiled.

"When it comes to you? No."

"That's not possible."

He shook his head. "Trust me when I say, Tierney, that where you're concerned, I'm color-blind."

CHAPTER FIFTY-SEVEN
TIERNEY

"It's so good to finally hang out again." Lila picked a grape from the charcuterie board and popped it into her mouth with a content sigh. "It's been ages. I feel like I haven't seen you in forever."

"Because you haven't." I chugged half a glass of champagne, chasing it with a piece of cheese. "I was busy running away from your brother, screwing him, getting shot in front of him, and then moving in with him."

I left out the other juicy parts, like our showdown with Stefano last week. No need to add screwing her brother in front of a dying mobster to my list of never-ending adventures.

Sofia nodded, her eyes big as saucers. "You've certainly been busy. I'm just glad you're okay."

Doing something normal, after weeks of living life in the fast lane, was a relief. When Sofia picked up the phone and called to ask if I'd consider joining her and Lila for lunch, I did not hesitate. I appreciated her seeking out my company and including me, especially when I knew she had a lot on her plate right now.

"So tell me why you forgave him," Lila urged, reaching forward to pat my knee.

She was glowing and looking so much happier than when I first saw her. She and Tiernan brought out the best in each other.

"He was extremely persistent," I sighed. "And you were extremely overbearing. It was the perfect storm."

"I wasn't overbearing. I was looking after you!" She swatted my knee, turning to Sofia. "Tell her I'm not overbearing, Sof."

Sofia squirmed in her seat, turning red. She was painfully shy and sweet; it was hard to imagine her with a man like Luca, not to mention a man like Jeremie. "You can be a bit…much," she admitted softly. "But it's coming from a good place!"

"Totally," I agreed.

"You do look good together." Sofia beamed up at me, taking a sip of her herbal tea. Her pregnant stomach was starting to show. I didn't want to ask her anything about it because it was clear her marriage was a shit show, and I wondered if the new baby—or Ciro—were even the fruit of a consensual relationship. Knowing Luca, I wouldn't put it past him to take what wasn't offered.

I wanted to broach the subject, but I didn't want to embarrass her, either. If she'd come to me, though—if she gave me any sign of distress—I promised myself I'd finish her husband with my bare hands.

"You think so?" I asked.

Sofia nodded. "The way he looks at you reminds me of all the romance novels I used to hide under my bed so my mama wouldn't find them."

"Why? Were they dirty?" I wiggled my brows.

Sofia giggled, shaking her head. "Not too dirty, no. I think she didn't want me to read them because she didn't want me to have any expectations regarding marriage and men."

"That's horrible." Lila's light brows scrunched. "My mama was the same, though. She wouldn't let me read any romance books, only clean love stories with morals."

"Please," I sighed. "I didn't even have a mother. So I win. Sort of."

The three of us laughed quietly. We were sitting in Lila's kitchen, our respective beaus in the office upstairs, holed up and discussing God knew what.

"So…" Sofia looked between us, her teeth sinking into her lower lip nervously. "What does it feel like?"

"What does what feel like?" I asked.

"Being in love with the man you're with."

Lila and I exchanged looks. I wasn't sure I was one to talk about a steady and healthy relationship. Achilles and I were in a good place, but we still had a few hurdles to get past.

Yes, we were back to fucking. Emphasis on the word *fucking*. I still refused to give him what he wanted. My soul. Yes, I said the words. I loved him, and I couldn't deny him. But for me, letting go, having tender, intimate sex, was the last wall between us.

I wasn't going to make it easy for him to break.

He'd denied me pleasure with other people, and I couldn't get past that. No matter how deeply I felt for him.

"You take the lead." I cleared my throat, gesturing at Lila.

Lila smiled, turning back to Sofia. "It feels…like being in tune with the universe. But feeling secure and loved in a relationship is not a privilege, Sof. If Luca doesn't give you what you're looking for…"

"Then what?" Sofia's expression was defeated. "I can't divorce him. No one in our world is ever going to accept that outcome."

"You don't have to ask people for permission to live your life as you please," I thundered.

"Easier said than done. Even you had Achilles monitoring your every move."

She was right, and I could say nothing about it. In our world, women had to claw their way to freedom. Even that didn't always help. As much as I knew my brother loved Lila, I doubted he'd ever let her go. She was his, and he'd die before giving her up.

"Is love completely off the table?" Lila murmured. It was so Lila to ask such a thing.

Sofia bowed her head, twisting her fingers in her lap. "That ship has sailed. Luca and I have no positive feelings toward one another."

"And Jeremie?" I blurted out.

"Jeremie?" Sofia's brows knitted. "What about him?"

Lila and I exchanged glances. How could she be so blind to the way he looked at her?

"You seemed...close." Lila cleared her throat. "During dinner the other day."

"Really? He's super shy and completely disinterested. He wouldn't even look me in the eye!" Sofia let loose a self-deprecating laugh.

"So you've never...?" I frowned.

She tilted her head sideways innocently. "Never what?"

"You know..."

Sofia's eyes grew huge. "Oh, *never*. I doubt Jeremie is even capable of asking someone out. His social anxiety is worse than mine."

This woman had no idea what was going on in her life.

I opened my mouth, about to clue her in, when Achilles, Luca, Enzo, and Tiernan descended the stairway, making themselves known while conversing loudly. The three of us immediately clammed up.

Achilles stopped behind me, putting his hands on my shoulders and kissing the crown of my head. "Ready to go, sweetheart?"

I nodded swiftly, standing up.

Tiernan rounded the table, placed his index finger under Lila's chin, and raised her face to kiss her. The entire table watched as my brother took his sweet time showing his wife just how much he'd missed her over the last hour.

Only Luca stood a few feet away from his wife, glancing at his watch in boredom. "Sofia," he said tersely. "You'll be late to your obstetrician appointment. Stop loitering."

She deserved so much better.

I secretly hoped Jeremie would kill him.

Sofia stood, a blush flooding her cheeks as she straightened her sensible dress. "It's been such a pleasure spending time with you girls." She offered Lila and me quick kisses on the cheeks. "Let's do this again soon, okay?"

"Text us as soon as you finish your appointment." Lila squeezed her hand in solidarity.

We watched Luca and Sofia exiting the house, walking at least two feet away from one another, not sparing each other one glance.

"Can you imagine those two boning?" Enzo muttered, his eyes locked on his phone screen, per usual. "It's probably colder than a ski competition."

"We need to do something about your brother." I pinned Achilles and Enzo with a frown.

Enzo looked up from his phone. "I'll go see if Sofia needs help throttling him." With that, he walked out the door, following Luca and Sofia.

Lila stared at his back. "Enzo's been acting weird."

"*Everyone's* been acting weird," I sighed.

Achilles looked to be over everyone who wasn't me. He grabbed my hand in his and tugged. "Let me buy you dinner and then you can tell me why I need to punch Luca."

Tiernan shook his head at our antics. Lila smiled.

When we headed to the door, my brother called out after us, "Hey, her curfew is at nine and don't try any funny business, lad."

Achilles flipped him the bird as he dove to kiss me.

CHAPTER FIFTY-EIGHT
TIERNEY

"It is time." Achilles propped his arm against our bedroom's doorframe.

Three words, and yet, I knew exactly what they held inside them. I knew who he was referring to and what needed to be done.

Butterflies took flight behind my rib cage, reminding me that at my core, deep inside, a part of me was and always would be a killing machine.

"What makes you say that?" Clad in a black satin robe, I met his gaze through the mirror of my vanity. I was getting ready for a night out with Frankie. She was in town for an event, and we thought it would be a good idea to catch up over dinner and drinks. I no longer frequented parties, charity events, or lavish yacht trips with society's upper crust, but I still loved Frankie dearly. With her, I didn't have to pretend. Not much, anyway.

"He's broken." Achilles pushed off the door and strolled toward me. I put my mascara down and picked up my bronzer next, watching as he placed his palms on my shoulders. "Mentally and physically unwell. He's begging for his death. Willing to speak in order to get it. This is usually when they're primed to give you the truth."

His interrogation techniques were less than humane, but in my father's case, I didn't really care.

"Do you think he'll tell us why he did it to me?" I asked.

Achilles nodded, his gaze holding mine in the mirror.

"When do you want to do it?" I asked.

"Why don't you have your fun with Frankie and then swing by the Long Island mansion? I have a meeting with my brothers there anyway."

I nibbled on the corner of my lip. Was this really happening? Was I going to watch my father die? Contribute to his death in some way?

It seemed odd to even call him my father after what he'd done. But the truth was, a small part of me always held on to the hope that we could find a way to really be family.

After Tiernan killed Fintan last year, my twin brother was completely broken. He never said it in so many words, but I saw the way it altered him. Being betrayed by your own kin changed you in a fundamental way.

I had a feeling what was about to happen tonight would change me, too.

"We don't have to do it if you don't want to." Achilles wove his fingers through my short hair tenderly. "I will follow your lead on anything you decide. We can let him go and send him into exile. I could kill him and let you know it's been done. Or you can do it yourself. The choice is yours, and yours only, sweetheart."

I closed my eyes, drawing a deep breath. When I opened them, our eyes met in the mirror again. "I want you to do it, so I can focus on watching, and I want it to hurt. I want him to feel the pain I felt every single day as a child in a work camp, dreaming of the father who abandoned her. I want him to know, on his deathbed, how much I truly loathe him and that I'll never forgive him."

Achilles jerked his chin in a nod. "You know, Tier, once a promoted pawn is queen, she cannot be captured by a king. But she can put the king in a position he cannot escape. A checkmate, allowing another piece to capture the king and bring about endgame."

Licking my lips, I stared at him, understanding exactly what he was saying. "I'm ready for the endgame, Achilles."

"Your wish is my command, my queen."

A Camorrista drove me through the pouring rain from my hangout with Francesca to Long Island.

The Italian man behind the wheel couldn't have been much older than nineteen, with traces of acne still adorning his fresh face. He didn't look at me once and addressed me as *Mrs. Ferrante* when he opened the door for me, which must've been what my possessive roommate instructed him to call me.

I was getting used to the idea of marrying Achilles. Only so much love could be poured into a person before you allowed it to soak in and accepted it. Achilles drenched me with devotion, attention, and affection. No matter how hard I tried to fight it, I couldn't. Our souls clicked, like two pieces of an intricate puzzle, and I knew that no one, nowhere would ever fit me the way he did.

Still, my stomach was in knots. It had been months since Achilles captured Tyrone. A lot had happened in between. And though Tyrone's hands wouldn't be able to touch me, his words still could. I recoiled from guessing what they'd entail. What it'd take for a father to turn on his daughter like that.

"Mrs. Ferrante, we've arrived." The young driver parked in front of the main entrance, got out of the car, and opened the door for me, holding an umbrella to shield me from the rain. I stepped out, my Chanel jacket casually draped over my shoulders. I walked toward the doors, which swung open as I approached on the CCTV. Guess you could take the stalker out of the game, but you couldn't take the game out of the stalker.

Enzo and Luca emerged from the house, wearing designer peacoats with popped collars and sporting immaculately styled hair.

Luca breezed right past me, ignoring my existence. Enzo stopped to kiss my cheek. "Good luck tonight."

He knows.

I gave his arm a quick rub. "Thank you."

"All right, that's enough affection for a lifetime between you two," Achilles grumbled from the doorway. "Tierney, come."

When I entered, he peeled the jacket from my shoulders to hang it and kissed the side of my neck. "Had a good time with the First Lady?"

"It was nice to catch up. Why is your errand boy calling me Mrs. Ferrante?"

"Because he doesn't have a death wish," he answered in a deadpan.

"We're not even engaged yet."

"We've been engaged since we were seventeen," he corrected dryly. "I'll have you recall you promised to accept my proposal."

The wild fluttering in my chest increased tenfold. "You haven't given me a ring."

"Do you want one?"

I did. And that frightened me. I strutted deeper into the house. It was the first time I felt fully welcome in it. All the other times before, I was an extension of Lila and Tiernan, something the Ferrantes had to endure. "Which way to the basement of horrors?"

Achilles tilted his head to the left. "Follow me."

I did, walking past the crème columns and golden accents to a guest room on the far side of the mansion. Inside, he led me into a walk-in closet. Then, he opened another door, which was padded on the inside.

As we stepped down the steep, cobbled stairway, a shiver of terror ran up my spine. We descended into the bowels of the house, entering a massive basement that seemed as large as the entire first floor. The dark space was filled with devices of torture. A sinister smell clung to my nostrils, a mix of bleach, smoke, sweat, and blood.

A glass tank sat on a long, wooden table in the center of the room. When I reached the end of the stairway, I spotted a cage the size of a bathroom stall. Inside it was my father.

Or...what was left of him, at least.

Tyrone was shirtless, wearing what looked like pajama bottoms. His once salt-and-pepper hair was now completely white and in disarray. He looked gaunt, and streaks of filth adorned his cheeks and torso. When he saw us enter the basement, he rushed to his feet, tossing himself over the corroded bars, clutching them desperately. "Oh, Tierney! My sweet pumpkin. My little girl."

I stopped a good ten feet away from him, staring him down.

"Pumpkin, I can explain," he rushed to say. His upper lip curled over his gums, like he'd lost his front teeth, and his speech was off. "Everything. Trust me. This is all a big misunderstanding. Tell him to let me go."

I flicked my gaze to Achilles. He said nothing. He was letting me lead the way. I crossed my arms over my chest. "Sure, I'll hear you out."

Tyrone licked his cracked lips, his eyes clinging to my face. He was calculating his next words. Like they could make a difference.

"Are you going to deny collecting intel on the Irish and your own family and selling it to Vello?" I probed. "Because we've got receipts."

Vello himself blew Tyrone's cover the day I met with Tom Rothwell, so there was no way he could deny it.

"Well, no, but—"

"Are you suggesting, then, that Vello fabricated my meeting with Agent Rothwell on the same day I actually met him?" I proceeded.

Whatever little color he had in his face was gone now. "I'm not saying that."

"What are you saying, then?"

"I'm saying I never thought this would blow back on you this way!" He rattled the bars of his cage desperately, tears streaming down his dirty cheeks. "I thought—I thought Tiernan would take care of it. He always does. The lad knows what he's doing."

"You sold me to the Camorra," I said. "And the rest of your people, too. Why did you do that? Money? You've got enough of it."

The Irish's business was booming. The Callaghan clan was never as prolific as the Camorra—not in size and not in contracts—but Tiernan was doing very well for himself. He made sure to pay Tyrone a monthly cut. He lived in a lavish mansion and had luxury cars.

"I—I thought I was helping everyone!" he stammered. "I swear it. I thought if the Camorra knew they had an insider from the Irish operation, they would be less suspicious of us and do more business with us. All I ever wanted was to help."

I tipped my head back and laughed, a laugh that felt bitter in my throat. "How stupid do you think I am, *Dad*?"

"I swear—"

"All right, that's enough." Achilles cut in, taking a step forward. "Tyrone, any minute you're not giving us the truth is a minute I'm not spending inside your delectable daughter, and I'm afraid I'm running out of patience. You have one more shot before I start cutting organs." He flipped his knife open and angled it in my father's direction. "I'm going to go slow and make sure you feel every single minute of it. Help me help you. Talk and get it over with."

"You can't let him kill me." Tyrone's head snapped to me. "I'm your father!"

"Sperm donor," I corrected coolly.

"I took you in when you were broken—" he started, but I cut him off.

"Tiernan and I arrived at your doorstep after going through hell in Russia. You didn't even look for us."

"I tried, but—"

"And when we arrived on your doorstep, tied up with a fucking bow, you knew exactly what you were looking at: Two well-trained killing machines who could work for you. You made us your soldiers."

"I loved you from day one." He shook his head. "Both of you. I…I…I wanted to find you, was desperate to do it, but I was grieving my wife. It was hard."

"At least you got to know her!" ripped from my throat in a scream. "Now tell me why? Why did you betray me? *Us?*"

"Because you took her away from me!" It was his turn to roar in my face. The confession was filled with venom. He broke into tears, sliding down the bars to his knees. "You took Deidre from me. If it wasn't for you, she wouldn't have been alone in that house in Dublin when Igor got to her. She didn't want to leave. I *begged* her to," he growled. "I knew the Russians were closing in on us. But she wanted to raise you two in Ireland. Next to your family. You came first. And it killed me that she sacrificed herself and her happiness for you."

I burst out in tears. It felt strangely good to be validated. I always had a feeling Tyrone and Fintan did not really love us. Now I knew.

"You wanted to destroy me," I said.

"Not initially." He scratched his overgrown, greasy beard, using his shackled hands. "But… With time, I decided I'd kill both of you." A cruel smile painted his lips, his eyes bloodshot and wet. "At least your brother is a good mobster, a good son. He was a great investment. But you were always too broken, too traumatized. No one could reach you. I guess when Tiernan took Fintan's life, I realized it was time to make you both pay. That is when I went to Vello and offered to be his spy. I knew one of you would do something prideful and stupid to cause your downfall."

Achilles grunted but didn't speak.

"What were you hoping was gonna happen?"

"I thought Vello would do the right thing and kill both of you."

"Because Mom died?"

"Your mum. Fintan. My *real* family," he sniffled. "The one I knew and loved."

I waited for the pain to come, but it never did. Truth was, whatever he told me, I already knew or at the very least suspected.

Losing his patience, Achilles turned around and ambled toward the glass tank in the corner of the room. It was lit from the inside and quite spacious.

"I'd like to introduce you to a friend of mine, Tyrone," he said conversationally, grabbing a pair of chemical resistant gloves and donning them, businesslike. "Her name is Zelda." He picked up a serpent hook and unhooked the cover of the enclosure.

I watched, mesmerized.

"Zelda is a Russell's viper. Highly venomous. Illegal to keep, obviously, but just look at that face." Achilles used the snake hook to slowly lift the serpent and turn its head Tyrone's way. "Adorable. Wouldn't you say?"

Tyrone's eyes grew impossibly large at the sight of the brown-and-yellow reptile.

"I had to adopt her. I've always loved snakes. They don't bond with their mates, young, or in groups. Instead, they keep to themselves, preferring to live solitary lives. I consider myself much the same. Other than your daughter, I've no use for others of my species and hold them in low regard."

Tyrone sucked in a breath, crawling backward in his cage, trying to escape the inevitable.

Achilles's stride was slow and purposeful. Zelda's forked tongue slid out, but she looked otherwise comfortable in Achilles's care.

"What I love about the Russell's viper is their striking range. They never miss, and once they sink those fangs into you…" Achilles shook his head, tsking. "Let's just say it takes about thirty milligrams of venom to kill an adult human. An adult Russell's viper releases about a hundred. And while it's nothing in comparison to the king cobra's thousand milligrams of venom, one thing you should know about the Russell's viper is that it's a very, *very* aggressive snake."

Tyrone released a desperate sob. "Please! No!"

Achilles ignored him, continuing. "They don't like humans, bite them indiscriminately, and tend to hang on with their fangs for a long-ass time. So whatever you do, Tyrone, just try and keep still when I let her loose in your cage.

"Oh, by the way, my girl's hungry today. A little mix-up in the kitchen, I'm afraid. The freeze-dried rodents I usually feed her? I fed them to you."

Tyrone gagged uncontrollably, looking at the half-eaten, indistinguishable meal on the dirty plate in his cage.

Achilles stopped in front of Tyrone's cage. "You never should've hurt the woman I love, Tyrone." He shook his head. "Now you'll have to suffer through one of the slowest, most painful deaths known to man, and we're going to watch."

Achilles tossed Zelda into the cage, between the bars. She dropped to the ground.

"No, no, no!" Tyrone kicked and thrashed, squeezing into the corner.

"You're not making things better for yourself," Achilles muttered.

Zelda side-eyed my father, reared herself into an S shape, and lunged at him, striking his foot.

An ear-piercing shriek rang through the air.

I watched my father die with a smile on my face.

CHAPTER FIFTY-NINE
ACHILLES

Three days after I delivered Tyrone Callaghan his much-deserved demise, I sat in the office of Forbidden Fruit Club, tapping my phone over my desk.

Something was wrong.

I didn't know what it was.

Fine, yes. Yes, I did know.

What was wrong was the fact that I hadn't given Tierney much say in the decision to be with me.

As always, I'd bullied her into moving in, negotiated her love, and even lured her into a bet about having sex. I made everyone in the Camorra, save for my brothers, refer to her as Mrs. Ferrante.

Yes, I didn't stalk her anymore, but I was still a toxic, overbearing monster who didn't give her room to decide what she wanted to do with her life. And that bothered me.

What bothered me more, though, was my last loose end.

Tristan Hale, that motherfucker.

I needed to find a way to get him back on American soil so I could finish him off. Or at the very least, threaten him a little to ensure he knew never to mess with Tierney again.

Which meant I was now dialing the pakhan's number. It was still seven in the morning in Vegas, but if I had any fucks to give, they weren't in my immediate vicinity.

"Someone had better be dead," Lyosha greeted.

"Not at present, but I'm working on it. That's why I'm calling. I need a favor."

"I already did you ten this month alone. Were the territory and weapons not enough?"

I was sure the deal he and Jeremie had agreed upon put a dent in their relationship, to say the least.

"This has nothing to do with that deal."

"What do you need?"

"Tristan Hale," I said. "I need you to lure him to New York."

"Why?"

My silence told him what my mouth wouldn't. Hale wasn't going to survive his next trip to the Big Apple.

"And what makes you think I hold that kind of power over him?"

"You've worked with him before."

Hale only offered his services to people he deemed acceptable to work with, not vice versa.

"And what do I get in return for that favor?" Alex drawled.

"What do you want?"

"That Porsche looked nice. Is it custom-made?"

"You think I fucking go to the dealership and take what they have in stock like some kind of peasant?"

Alex snorted. "I'll have it, then. It'll look good in my collection."

The man had at least twenty-five sports cars. How small was that dick of his? "Have at it."

"And a month's supply of drugs, free of charge, delivered straight to one of my compounds."

"We don't have a contract with you," I said, balking, but only so he'd think he managed to negotiate a decent deal. "And that'd take a dozen trucks."

"Hmm." Alex mulled it over. "Sounds like a you problem."

"Fuck. Whatever."

"When and where?"

"Forbidden Fruit. Next Thursday."
"I'll be in touch."
I killed the call.

When I got home, Tierney popped out of the bedroom looking like a trillion bucks in one of those dresses that made me want to throttle the designer. "Should we go to the movies?"

I blinked back at her, stunned into silence.

The movies? That was normal-people shit.

We didn't go to the movies.

We went to underground clubs and Michelin-starred restaurants where the owners valued their organs too much to tell us we had to book a reservation, or on shopping sprees in places you could only get to with a private jet.

Movies were...well, *ordinary*.

Movies also meant a public outing. Together. This beautiful creature was going to be seen with my fugly-ass face. Tierney did not need to be reminded of the fact that I was hideous. No, thank you.

"I don't like movies," I drawled.

"You mean all of them?"

I shook my head slowly. Disappointment was written all over her face. I knew if I didn't go, I'd just prove to her I was still the old asshole Achilles. The one who'd pretended not to care what she wanted to do.

Fuck. I was going to do it, wasn't I?

"What did you have in mind?" I asked tersely.

"There's a new Henry Cavill movie out."

"What's it about?"

"Uh...Henry Cavill being hot?"

I flashed her a flat glare. "Really selling it to me. Wouldn't you rather I take you on a shopping spree on Crimson Key?" No one would dare whisper about my hideous face on my own private island. "Or eat at Casablanca's?" I knew the owner of the restaurant and was positive I could get an isolated booth, even at an hour's notice.

Tierney trotted over to me, coiling her arms around my neck. "I want to do something small and intimate. To share popcorn and a flat Diet Coke with you."

I stared her down, confused. "Why?"

"Because we never got to do it when we were teenagers. We were always so scared of our families. I want us to have these moments. Even if we have to make them as adults."

Don't be a fucking baby.

Just say yes.

Look how much she wants it.

So what if a few people stare?

I sighed, grabbing her waist and leaning down for a kiss. "Sure. We'll go see your hot-guy movie. Let me just hop into the shower."

She grinned up at me, looking genuinely happy for the first time in forever. Her hair was becoming redder—more hers—and even though it was still very short, she moussed it in a spiky, trendy way that made it look like a fashion statement.

"This is... I..." She struggled for words, her voice catching, and I knew it meant more to her than it did to my mother that I braved getting out there, taking a stab at normalcy. Tierney shook her head, chuckling to herself in wonder. "*Thank you*," she whispered. "Thank you so much for healing with me."

I never thought of it this way, but I guessed it was true. In helping her, I was helping myself get over our shared past.

Her eyes pinked, and I knew she was close to crying.

"Hey, are you sure you're okay?" I squeezed her waist.

She nodded. "I feel better than okay. Liberated, actually. Tyrone deserved to die."

It took him three days to kick the bucket. The kidney failure and internal bleeding occurred after twenty-four hours, just on track, but he battled it out, struggling for his last breath before he finally gave in.

The minute he was dead, I called Tiernan to remove his corpse from my parents' basement. Tiernan collected his enemies' skulls and he had been saving a special spot for his traitorous father's cranium after what he'd done to his sister.

"I'm sorry it had to come to this." I thumbed her cheek.

"I'm not. I never loved him."

"Not even a little?"

She shook her head. "Did you ever love your father?"

I gave the question some thought. I had wanted his approval and admiration growing up, and I was willing to go very far for it. So far, in fact, that the girl of my dreams wanted to set herself on fire before letting me know she couldn't give me heirs.

"Once upon a time, I suppose I did..." I brushed my thumb along her smooth temple, tracing the gorgeous face that was forever inked into my memory. "But the more I grew up, the more I realized nothing about our relationship was normal. And when he hurt you..." I closed my eyes, willing the fury bubbling inside me like lava to calm down. "When he hurt you, that's when I knew."

"Knew what?"

"The difference between love and obsession. I was obsessed with getting my father's approval, but I never liked much about him. He was a cold, angry man, driven by nothing but power and bloodlust. But you..." My forehead dropped to hers, and I breathed her in. "I realized that I loved you. Inside and out. Your sense of humor, your smarts, your resilience, your fight. I could name all the things that made me fall in love with you. I couldn't name one thing my father possessed that made me appreciate him."

She brushed the tip of her nose against mine. "See? This is how I feel about Tyrone. He was my family by blood only. His love and approval always felt conditional, so I never sought them. It was clear from the get-go that he favored Tiernan and Fintan. Strong, hungry sons who could further his own and the Irish clan's position in New York. I saw through his facade before Tiernan did, but only because I didn't have the luxury of his attention and respect. So don't you worry about my sensibilities when it comes to him, Achilles. Because I have absolutely none."

CHAPTER SIXTY
TIERNEY

It was a mistake to go to the movies.

I saw that now, when we were sitting in the theater, surrounded by teenyboppers and couples, all of them more interested in Achilles's face than the movie.

Achilles wore a baseball cap, the bill pushed low to hide his scars, but a jagged portion of his burned cheek was still illuminated by the giant screen's lights, bringing even more attention to it.

At work, Achilles's face was a weapon. But here, out in the real world, where no one knew who he was, he just looked…scary. And I knew that he'd had options along the way. Reconstructive surgeries he could've done. But rumor on the street was that Vello *liked* that his son looked like this. That he'd wanted his son's face to match the atrocities he was capable of.

I wanted us to start collecting memories other couples had, things we craved when we were younger, but I'd forgotten we were no longer those people.

A pimply college-aged girl with a pink hoodie and a haughty sneer leaned to whisper in her friend's ear in the row below us, her gaze flicking to Achilles's face in the dark. The friend's gaze traveled to the scarred side of Achilles's cheek, and she gasped. They both started to giggle.

Guilt and anger swirled in the pit of my stomach.

"This movie sucks." I swallowed hard, dropping a kiss to Achilles's shoulder. "Wanna get out of here?"

His pupils were glued to the screen, but I knew he was registering absolutely nothing.

He'd had very few brushes with civilian life outside the Camorra before today and preferred it this way. His soldiers, business partners, and other underground leaders did not recoil from his face and didn't judge him for it.

"No. It's fine. I'm watching it," he clipped out.

The girls' hushed whispers grew louder, with the words "fire" and "shame about the face" and "but his body's great" ringing through the air. I shifted in my seat. "Let's go."

"You wanted to watch a movie," Achilles insisted flatly.

"Not anymore. It's boring."

Another wave of giggles sounded from behind us. This was ridiculous. I didn't care that they were probably freshmen at some expensive Manhattan college. They were old enough to know better.

Shooting up to my feet, I swiveled around to face them. "Got something to say?"

The two stared at me, wide-eyed. Upon closer inspection, they looked like they could be twenty-three or twenty-four.

"Ah…are you talking to us?" The one with the perpetual sneer stubbed her chest with a pink, pointy fingernail.

"Yeah, I'm talking to you. You've been whispering about my fiancé for half the movie. He's taken, by the way."

The girls' mouth hung open.

Achilles sighed. "Tierney, leave it."

"No, I wanna hear what they have to say," I insisted. "What was so funny? I wanna laugh, too. And it had to be good because, instead of ogling Henry, they were staring at my man."

That made the brunette one—without the pimples—burst out in a laugh. "Trust me, girl, you can have him."

"I wasn't asking permission. You really don't want to see what I'm capable of if you look his way one more time."

"Is that a threat?" Pimply girl stood up.

The shushing theatergoers were now silent, and everybody was looking at us.

"Nah, it's a promise." I smiled.

"Okay, we're done here." Achilles stood and scooped me by the waist and tossing me over his shoulder. "You clearly aren't watching the movie, after all."

"Let me down. I want to fight them." I kicked my feet in the air while he sauntered to the stairs leading out of the theater.

"Why?" he asked.

"Because they were rude to us."

"No, they were rude to *me*. And I don't give a fuck."

"But I—"

"We're finishing this discussion later."

I had just enough time to look up and flip the two girls the bird before Achilles took us outside and placed me down on the sidewalk. It was chilly, but all I could feel was ire and heat for how they'd treated him.

"From now on, we'll only do Camorra and Irish functions. I'm so sorry I brought you here." I bit down on my lip.

"I'm not." He pinched a cigarette between his fingers, grinning boyishly.

"You're not?"

"When we were teenagers, I dreamt about a scenario where *you* were the jealous one. This was as close as we've ever gotten to one." He took a long drag of his cigarette.

I snorted, shaking my head. My heart rate slowed enough for me to take a breath and notice our surroundings. We were on a busy street. I grabbed his hand in mine and squeezed, heading toward an ice cream shop. "Is this…normal?"

"What? People whispering and snickering when they see my

face?" He puffed a cloud of smoke, looking unaffected. "Pretty much. I'm used to it."

My throat was thick with tears. "How do I make it up to you?"

"You already did." He lifted a devious eyebrow, his stride nonchalant.

"How?"

"By loving me despite my face."

The ache inside my chest grew.

"Besides, who says I'd have changed anything about what happened the night of the fire?"

"Of course you would have," I spluttered. "I would, too."

"Well, I wouldn't. The scars you left were a reminder you were once mine. And during the bad times, they were what I clung to. The evidence that I had you once and that maybe I could have you again."

"I don't deserve you," I said, and meant it.

"Maybe." He shrugged. "But you have me anyway. Forever."

CHAPTER SIXTY-ONE
TIERNEY

I loved Achilles, but I sometimes questioned his professional decisions, which seemed to directly cause bloodshed and underground wars.

"This is not necessary at all," I said for the millionth time as I jerked a dress from a hanger in my walk-in closet. A black bustier minidress that flaunted my assets…and my new tan from the mini-vacation he and I had taken in the Hamptons earlier in the week. "Meeting with Tristan Hale, with Lyosha of all people."

If I were being honest, I was more nervous about seeing Alex again than I was about seeing the man who'd tried to kill me. For Tristan Hale, I was nothing but a botched assignment. It wasn't personal, and he'd moved on to his next hit job. With Alex, it was different.

I'd managed not to meet him ever since he and Tiernan became friends again. Lyosha never treaded deep into the East Coast territory so as not to piss off the Ferrantes, and I never went to Vegas because…well, my taste ran more along the lines of French Riviera and less Sin City.

But Alex and I shared a childhood. A story. He knew things about me no one but Tiernan, Achilles, and Dr. Andrews were privy to.

"This is a recipe for disaster," I added when I realized I wasn't getting any response from Achilles. I slid into the dress, shimmying it up my waist and turning around for Achilles to zip. He did, dutifully. "Someone's gonna die," I warned.

"No one's dying tonight, Piccola Fiamma," he reassured me. "And we'll be having a family dinner, as well. Our first official outing with our families as a couple."

"Too many big egos in one room." I ignored his words. "And why does it have to be in Forbidden Fruit? Why can't we have a business meeting at the mansion or in one of your hotels?"

"Because I'm ambushing Tristan Hale."

Groaning, I stomped to my shoe rack and plucked out my red heels. "I still don't understand your need to see him."

"I want to make sure he never comes near you again." Achilles slid his watch-collection drawer open, clasping a Cartier on his thick wrist. "And I need to know why he missed that fucking shot."

My blood froze in my veins. I spun to him slowly, my mouth agape. "So you think it's weird that he missed too?"

"He never planned on killing you." Achilles's low growl rumbled between my hips, spreading heat along my spine. "And I want to know why. What was his plan, and what was he hoping to achieve?"

"You're never going to stop until you know I'm completely safe, are you?" I sauntered to him on my kitten heels. Suddenly, all I wanted was to make this man understand just how much I desired him.

His lazy gaze flicked along my body, taking it in. "You make it sound like a bothersome objective."

"Not bothersome." I unfastened his belt with one hand, eyes still trained on his. Next, I rolled down the zipper of his Armani dress pants. "But impossible. We both know some things are out of your control."

"Not when it comes to you." His vehement, soft tone made me tremble so badly I wanted it injected into my veins. How I thought I stood a chance against him, I'd never understand. I craved him like the night desired the moon. Like the desert longed for water. What we had, it was wild and chaotic. But it was uniquely ours. No love would ever match.

I dropped to my knees and circled my fingers around the base of his cock. It was already hard and throbbing, the tip shiny and purple, full of blood; shivers ran up and down my arms, and I tilted my head, giving his cock a long, lustful lick that made his hand wrap around my hair. There wasn't enough of it to tug yet, and the little I had was handled with surprising gentleness.

"What about sex, Tierney?" he drawled. "Regular normal people sex?"

"You're the one who said we're not normal people." Reaching forward, I covered his crown with my mouth, slowly taking him all in until the tip tickled the back of my throat.

I knew he wanted what other couples had. Missionary. Eye contact. Some kind of emotion. But I couldn't. Not yet.

"You want me to fuck your face?" he crooned.

"Yeah…" My voice trailed off, liquid heat rushing to my center. I could feel my pulse thrumming against my clit.

"Ask nicely."

"P-please?"

"Nice*r*."

I blinked. He smiled charitably, like I was an adorable, little puppy. Was he going to give me what I wanted? Was he going to finally degrade me?

"Open your mouth, Tierney."

I did so fast my head spun. There wouldn't be a second time, I sensed. Achilles did not like treating me the way I was used to being treated in bed.

He grabbed my jaw, peered inside with those dead, icy eyes, and spat into it. "Swallow."

A rush of warmth shot to my core, and my muscles squeezed against nothing. It felt so alarmingly good I thought I was going to implode. What we were doing was so sick, but nobody knew how to touch me like he did.

I tried closing my mouth to swallow, but his grip on my jaw tightened. "Nah. With your mouth open. You need to work those throat muscles anyway."

I tipped my head up, letting his hot saliva slide down my throat. It was gratifying and hotter than anything I'd ever done. Because it was Achilles who did it, and because away from me, from *us*, he was very good at being cruel. It wasn't his second but his *first* nature.

"Good girl." He grabbed the back of my neck and pushed all the way in until his cock followed the shape of my throat, stuffing it to the hilt, refusing to move. He pulled out of my mouth, only to thrust back in in one violent movement. I choked, coughing as tears prickled my eyes. "You're so pretty when you cry." He didn't stop. Only picked up his pace, fucking my face, humming to the sound of my gagging as I tried to keep my lunch down.

"Fuck, fuck, fuck." He thumped his head against the wall behind him repeatedly. "I'm coming in your throat, and I want to go so deep you're not even gonna taste it."

All I could do was nod. I felt the hot, thick liquid coating the back of my throat, and I had to breathe through my nose. After he finished, he let out a ragged breath and let go of my neck. I collapsed at his feet, giggling to myself.

"What's so funny?" He tucked himself in and fastened his belt before offering me a hand to stand up. I took it. It had only been three seconds, and he already looked as unruffled and clean-cut as though I didn't just suck his cock in the middle of our walk-in closet.

"I was just thinking about Enzo."

"Enzo?" His murderous glare silently informed me he was about to kill his own brother if I didn't explain myself.

"Enzo," I repeated, trailing a fingernail along the collar of his shirt. "I thought about how he's always so worried about his protein intake when eighty percent of mine comes in the form of your cum."

That *did* make Achilles bark out a laugh. He wrapped his arm around my neck and jerked me to him, kissing me hard. "Nice one, funny girl." His lips moved over mine. "Think about someone else ever again when we're together, and I'll chop off his cock."

Forbidden Fruit was the most exclusive underground club in Manhattan.

Arguably in the entire world.

No close second existed to the amenities and entertainment it offered.

With security and discretion guaranteed, it attracted some of the world's most prominent billionaires and royals.

What started out a few years ago as a brothel during the day and a club during the night quickly expanded into a gentlemen's club with a $450K-a-year membership fee and an invite-only operation.

Currently, it offered three gambling rooms, two restaurants, a bar, three lounges, a billiards room, and a high-end brothel. There was also a fully equipped, state-of-the-art gym, a sauna, an indoor Olympic pool, and two tennis courts.

I'd never actually been there before—Achilles had made sure to ban me from any establishment that his family owned—so I was a little giddy.

Of course, I was also frightened about coming face-to-face with Tristan Hale and nauseous about reuniting with Alex.

"Smoke on the job one more time and I'll shove the cigarette all the way down your throat." Achilles reprimanded the valet boy who rushed toward the Porsche, tossing his keys in his hands.

"S-s-sorry, sir." The kid wiped his mouth quickly, cringing in fear.

We walked into the club, which was painted black from floor

to ceiling, with golden accents on the grand chandelier and crown moldings. A sleek bar with golden arches and a waterfall greeted us.

A waiter in full attire glided toward us with a tray, putting in our hands Achilles's favorite whiskey and my drink of choice—a French 75. I took a big sip, feeling the champagne tickling the back of my throat. "Okay, I do like this place."

"Wait until you see the back rooms." Achilles placed a possessive hand on the small of my back, guiding me past lounge chairs filled with businessmen and their much younger dates. We took a flight of curved stairs up to the next level and walked through double doors leading to the gambling room.

I immediately spotted my brother and his wife standing by a blackjack table. Lila was wearing a tight, bubblegum-pink minidress, and Tiernan was staring at her like she'd just saved the world from exploding.

She was playing her hand, and he was watching. I ambled toward them, Achilles at my heels. "Hey."

"Hi!" Lila jumped on me with a hug, kissing both my cheeks. "You look so good. I'm so glad we're finally doing this. Dinner is supposed to start in about twenty minutes."

"How's the game going?" I gestured to the cards.

"Really good. I'm winning."

"She's always winning." My brother wrapped his arm around her waist, kissing her temple.

"The secret is in learning how to count cards." Lila grinned from ear to ear, turning her attention back to the table. "Oh, I wanted to ask you something."

"Yeah?"

"Sof and I are going up to the mountains for a weekend. You know, to recharge. Wanna come?"

My knee-jerk reaction was to tell her I'd have to find a way to sneak behind Achilles's back and whoever was tasked with being my chaperone this week. But then I remembered I no longer needed to ask Achilles for permission—or to dodge any unwanted security.

Swallowing hard, I said, "I'd love to."

I hung back to watch her play, and sure enough, by the end of the game, she won and scooped $50,000 into her fund. Lila and I jumped and cheered together. I was so happy for her. She had been deprived of human interaction for so long growing up, and I couldn't blame her for playing catch-up and enjoying her dances, gambling rooms, and parties.

"We'll see you at dinner," Achilles said to Tiernan and Lila, snatching my hand and leading me out of the gambling room. I was still giddy about Lila's win.

"Isn't that fantastic?" I took another sip of my champagne. "Lila's gotten so good at blackjack. She told me the other day she hasn't lost one game in three months."

Achilles looked at me like I was an adorable, dumb puppy.

"What?"

"She's good, but that's not why she hasn't been losing."

"Why, then?"

"*Tiernan.*"

"What does he have to do with it?"

"He cheats, threatens the dealer before every game she takes."

"But...*how?*"

"Easily. Who gets to play last in blackjack?"

"The dealer."

Achilles spread his arms as if to say "Voilà!"

Huh. "Why does he do that?"

"Says he can't take seeing Lila sad or disappointed, even for one second."

"Lila is a good sportswoman. I'm sure she's no more than a little bummed when she loses."

"Tier, he baby-proofed the house *before* Gennaro was born because she kept bumping into the corner of the coffee table and he couldn't see her with a blemish on her skin."

Good point. My brother was irrational when it came to his wife.

"Lila and Sof invited me to the mountains." Why did my mouth feel so dry when I said this? I didn't like that. If he had truly changed, I wouldn't have to fear his reaction. Damn him and his toxic, controlling personality.

His spine stiffened, but he kept his expression schooled. "Did they, now?"

"Yeah."

"They'll go with their security detail."

Fat chance that Tiernan and Luca would let their wives take a piss without a small army monitoring their well-being. "Probably," I offered noncommittally.

"What did you tell her?"

This was the big test. I licked my lips. "I told her I'll go."

A brief silence. A chill ran down my spine. A reminder I had been his prisoner before and possibly still was.

"Good," he said finally.

Achilles stopped in front of one of the doors in the hallway, leading to the dining room. "Stay here for a second. I need to see if our infantry room is stocked in case of an emergency." He kissed my cheek.

I leaned against the wall, checking my nails. A couple rounded the corner from the other side of the hallway, and I instinctively flung my gaze to look at them.

My heart dipped low in my stomach.

It was Jeremie and Sofia.

They didn't see me. I was standing in the darkened corner of the hallway. But I could see them. Both dressed in elegant black attire, walking side by side. She looked so tiny in comparison to the Russian. He was holding Ciro, confidently, calmly, like he claimed ownership of the child.

Ciro's strawberry lips pouted in deep concentration as he tried to tug Jeremie's nose off his face with pudgy fingers. Jeremie did not seem to care.

Their eyes met, and there was so much tension, heat, and desire inside, I knew the next thing they were about to do would change everything forever. They stopped at the end of the hallway, thinking they were alone. But they weren't. I was here, and soon enough, Achilles was going to join me.

Guess Sofia was catching on to the fact Jeremie didn't have social anxiety. He just had Sofia anxiety.

Before they took things any further, I stepped into the light, making myself known. "Hey. What's up, guys?" I asked loudly.

They immediately pulled apart, stepping back. Sofia snatched Ciro out of Jeremie's hands. "Hi, Tier. Sorry. I didn't see you." Her face flushed, but when I looked up to watch Jeremie, his eyes were threatening to kill me.

"Don't worry about it." I flung a dismissive hand her way. "Am I the only one who's super drunk here? I bet I'll remember nothing about tonight tomorrow morning. The hangover tomorrow is going to be a bitch."

I wasn't drunk at all, but I wanted to assure them I wasn't going to say anything.

Jeremie stared at me coldly. "Alex is already in the dining room. He is pleased to see you after all these years."

I gave him an airy smile, but zero words. I didn't like the Bratva, and I especially did not like the Rasputins.

"We were just going to send Ciro off with the nanny." Sofia smiled awkwardly. "I'd do it alone, but Jeremie is helping me with the stroller and baby seat…"

"Those things look heavy." I nodded, playing dumb. No stroller or baby seat was anywhere in sight. "Better hurry up, then, before Achilles comes out of the infantry room and starts playing with Ciro. You know how he is with kids."

The look on Sofia's face when she gave me a quick hug said "thank you."

And the wink I gave her back said she was very welcome.

Sure enough, Achilles reappeared a second after Sofia and Jeremie took flight.

"Who were you talking to?" he asked, locking the door and punching in a code that activated another lock.

"Just Sofia."

This was technically true. I hadn't said one word to Jeremie. Achilles cupped my neck from both sides, studying my face. "We still have a few minutes before dinner starts. Want me to eat you out in the meantime?"

I coughed out a laugh. "That sounds lovely, but I actually need to go pee." I didn't feel like sex right now because I was too on edge to meet with half the guest list. "Where is the nearest restroom?"

"You go back where we came from, first door on the right. Want me to walk you?"

I shot him a frown. "Please don't pull a Lila. I am perfectly capable of peeing by myself."

He smiled. "Okay."

But I didn't go to the restroom he directed me to. I took the stairs down to buy some time and allow myself to think.

Tristan Hale had spared my life.

He never had with any other victim—at least, none anyone knew of.

Why me? And why did he take the job if he hadn't planned to finish it?

Aimlessly wandering through the dark corners of the establishment, I looked for signs of restrooms. I was now somewhere between one of the restaurants and the bar. The place was buzzing, with dozens of well-dressed people, mostly men. The silver sign for a bathroom finally twinkled from the other side of the venue. I headed in its direction into a narrow alcove, slowing my steps when I detected a large, muscular form standing by the door.

Squinting, I tilted my head to study the vaguely familiar face.

Relax. It's not him. It can't be.

There wasn't a chance in hell the Ferrante brothers would let this person walk into their establishment without a warrant. Besides, my luck wasn't that shitty. Alex and Tristan Hale in one evening was more than enough without meeting this asshat.

But the closer I got to him, the more I was convinced it was Agent Tom Rothwell, his arm propped against the wall, waiting for someone to leave the restroom.

I stopped, shrinking behind a wall, and watched him.

I naturally assumed that if he was here, he'd be here for me, since I was the only person in the Ferrantes' inner circle who ever gave him the time of day. But it appeared he was waiting for someone else.

The door unlocked from the inside, flinging open. Out came Enzo, dressed to the nines and pissed into oblivion. Their gazes clashed, and my heart jumped to my throat. Every small hair on my body stood on end. I couldn't understand this reaction, especially as I had no skin in whatever game these two were playing.

"Agent Rothwell," Enzo purred finally. "I hope you have a warrant because you sure as fuck don't have an invitation."

"Not that it's any of your business, but I do have an invitation. And from a founding member, no less."

"Is the founding member in the room with us?" Enzo faux scanned the hallway. I ducked my head lower.

"Luca invited me."

"Luca invited you?"

"That's what I said."

"Why the shit would he do that?"

"To save your ass," Tom deadpanned. "Or at least try. Now, I want to take a piss. Step back, kid."

"Kid?" Enzo's neck flushed under his elaborated ink, and he didn't budge from the door. "Dafuq, man? You don't even know how old I am."

"You'll turn twenty-six on November thirteenth," Rothwell

said without missing a beat, fastening his cool gaze on Enzo's firelit warm eyes. "Born at 5:33 a.m. in Cardarelli di Napoli hospital," he continued, fixing Enzo's collar nonchalantly. "Weight 6.8 pounds. The smallest of the four siblings. You live at 1215 W 46th Street. A modest one-bedroom, but you like the neighbors and it's close to your fancy gym. I know your A/B plan. Your cardio routine. Who you fuck, when you fuck, and how much you come each time. Down to the milliliters. I know who you killed last week and how. I just need a shred of evidence to prove it. The things I know about you, *kid*, you haven't even begun to learn about yourself."

Enzo's reaction was similar to my own. His jaw was on the floor. For the first time, I saw my happy-go-lucky friend completely speechless.

It wasn't just Tom's knowledge about Enzo's life that rattled me. In fact, I wasn't completely shocked that he knew so much regarding the mobster he'd been studying for years now. What blew up my senses was the palpable, knife-edge attraction between the two. The air between them sizzled. And just like that, I realized why Tom Rothwell had no girlfriend or wife to speak of.

He was gay.

And he could be hating Enzo from today until his last breath—but he was attracted to him, too.

"Out of my way, peasant." Tom shouldered past Enzo robotically, slamming the restroom door in his face.

Enzo stood there for a full ten-second stretch before spinning on his heel and crashing his palm against the door. "Hey! Peasant is even worse than kid."

"File a complaint with internal affairs," Tom drawled to the sound of his piss.

I turned around and found my way back upstairs before my bladder exploded. The journey to the restroom upstairs was drama free, an achievement in itself. After relieving my bladder and washing my hands, I dried them with a towel and slipped back to the hallway. It was a straight shot to the dining room. I hoped to make it in one piece. Something about tonight felt different, devious, like all our sins were catching up with us and everything was coming to a head.

When I reached a point in the hallway that forked, a body slammed into mine. I tumbled back a step before shooting an arm to the wall and righting myself. Luca stood in front of me. Our eyes met. It was the first time I was alone with him since Achilles found out what he'd done all those years ago.

"Watch where you're going, asshole," I muttered.

"Call me asshole one more time under my roof," he dared quietly, blocking my way.

"Asshole," I said cheerfully. "Now what?"

He took a step in my direction, his eyes shooting fire, and for a fraction of a moment, I saw it: the humanity behind them. It was dimmed, but it existed. And I wondered who'd put it in there. Because it couldn't have been Sofia. Sofia didn't even try.

"Are you gonna hit me, big guy?" I got in his face, laughing. "Threaten me? We both know you can't do that."

"You're wrong." Luca clutched my jaw between his fingers, tipping my face up with a sly smile. "Being with Achilles doesn't make you immune from me. Nothing does. When I want to kill, I kill. It's what I do. You're a bad influence on my brother, always were, and eliminating a mere pawn from the chessboard is not something I'd hesitate to do."

His eyes told me he wasn't bluffing. His body language was languid, relaxed.

I believed him.

"You'll have to kill him if you kill me," I said quietly.

He didn't blink. "The Camorra comes first. Family after."

"Even Ciro?"

His eyes narrowed. "Don't talk about my son."

"Who put the light in your eyes?" I tilted my head.

His tight jaw twitched with surprise.

"Who made you feel? Made you smile? Made your cheeks flush?" I interrogated him. "I've never seen you this alive. Is she here?" I elevated an eyebrow. "Does Sofia know about her?"

Luca's nostrils flared at the sound of his wife's name.

"You have no idea what you're talking about." His jaw locked again. "There's no one, and if you—"

"I'm a socialite, Luca." I drummed my manicured fingers over his collar. He had good form. Very lean, very muscular. Shame about the shitty personality. "I have my ways to extract information from anyone. I will find out your secret and use it against you. It is the least I could do after what you've done to Achilles and me," I promised with a sweet smile on my face.

Luca grabbed my throat and pinned me against the wall, snarling in my face. "I have no idea what the fuck you're talking about, but I'm only going to say this once—snoop around me, and you'll regret the miserable day you were born. I'm not Tiernan or Achilles, sweetheart. I do not have a heart with strings you can tug on or compassion to spare. I *will* ruin you. And if any of the assholes protecting you stand in my way… Guess what. I'll ruin them, too. This is the last time you bother yourself with my personal life, *capito*?"

His grip on my throat tightened to the point that he cut my air supply. I knew he wouldn't kill me. Not here. Not now. But I knew that he could. And that was enough to confirm he had someone in his life I wasn't supposed to find out about.

Challenge accepted, fucker.

"Let me go," I hissed through pursed lips. "Before I make sure you'll never be able to have children again."

He let go of my neck and I dropped to the floor. I gasped, massaging the sensitive flesh over my throat.

Slowly, I stood, smoothed my dress, and wiped the moist residue from under my eyes.

Then I straightened my back, put a smile on my face, and marched into the dining room to have dinner with the man who was contracted to kill me.

CHAPTER SIXTY-TWO
TIERNEY

I was the last to enter the dining hall, which meant everyone had the opportunity to have their fill of me as I entered.

Smiling broadly, I swaggered to my seat next to Achilles and plopped down on it. He kissed my cheek softly. "Everything okay?"

"Perfect." I snapped my napkin open in my lap. "What's for dinner?"

His gaze halted on my neck. Luca probably left red marks. Since things were already strained, I wasn't in the mood to share my little talk with his older brother.

"What's this?" Achilles brushed his thumb along my neck.

I shrugged. "Allergic reaction."

"To what?"

"Assholes."

"Did someone—"

"Yes, and I handled it. Don't worry."

The menus were brought to the table, and it gave me a second to catch my breath and study the room. I took in Tiernan and Lila, Sofia and Luca, Katya and Enzo, Jeremie…and Alex.

The minute my sight landed on him, his pale blues caught mine in a vise. A ragged breath rattled in the back of my throat.

Lyosha.

Aristocratic and princely, with his blond curls and frighteningly chiseled face. He still looked younger than his years. Like our lifestyle, and all the death in it, couldn't touch him. Not really.

"Tierney," he rasped.

"Alex."

"How have you been?" he asked in Russian.

And though I hadn't spoken the language in many, many years, the answer slipped past my lips naturally. "It's been a long, pleasant walk in the park. You?"

He grinned. "Same."

"Don't flirt with her," Achilles barked at Alex, hammering his whiskey glass on the table.

"How do you know I'm flirting?" Alex raised his vodka to his lips, one side of his mouth curling in amusement.

"Your goddamn eyes are an open invitation."

"Don't worry, honey." I patted Achilles's lap. "I have a strict no-Russian-men policy." I leaned to kiss the tattoo of my lips on his neck.

Ignoring me, Achilles reached for his whiskey and gulped it in one go. I quirked an eyebrow. It was unlike him not to pace himself, but I guessed everyone was on edge today.

"Where's that fucker Hale?" Achilles turned his attention back to Alex.

"Running late." Alex flicked his wrist to frown at his Cartier. "But he'll be here for the after-dinner drinks."

"With his mask off?" Achilles poured himself a second glass of whiskey.

Alex smiled leniently. "I suggest you put that whiskey down. You're not Russian, Achilles. You lack the capacity to hold such a drink."

"And I suggest you stick to your business," Achilles retorted in the same pleasant tone. "That's a nice face you've got there. I'd hate to ruin it."

"What the fuck is Rothwell doing in the club?" Enzo turned to look at Luca, breaking the tension between the other two men. "He said you invited him?"

"I'm trying to recruit him." Luca handed his menu back to the waiter.

"And you think he'll bite?" Achilles snapped his head to his brother.

"I think we can't afford not to try." Luca cocked an eyebrow. "With Dad out of the picture, we need a new wave of dirty feds to do our bidding."

The rest of the dinner was relatively pleasant. Or at least, pain free. The food was delicious—bourbon-glazed salmon and truffled salads—and the alcohol was great. Conversation flowed, and I actually managed to relax. Dessert came and went, and still no sign of Hale.

Achilles did hit the whiskey bottle harder than I'd ever seen him before, but I couldn't fault him for it.

When everyone retired to the bar, Achilles squeezed my thigh and leaned to whisper into my ear, "I'm going to check the security footage. See if Hale is planning a surprise."

I nodded and joined Lila and Sofia on their way to the bar. The entire length of the way, I felt Alex's gaze heating my skin from behind. I threw a glance behind my shoulder. He was walking with Luca, Enzo, and Jeremie.

At some point, he broke away from them and joined us women.

"Tierney, may I have a word?" His English was crisp and lightly accented with Russian.

"You may have a few, but I doubt any of them would interest me." I yawned into the back of my hand.

Sofia and Lila giggled and headed to the bar, leaving us standing at the threshold. Traitors.

He wore a navy suit, the first buttons of his shirt undone, revealing smooth, bronze skin and sculpted pecs. He looked like a movie star, always had, and never made a big deal out of it. When I left

Siberia at fourteen, he was already a big hit with the girls. And even though I'd been too busy surviving to pay him my full attention, even I wasn't immune to his charms.

He was still not my type, though. I didn't trust men who were prettier than me.

"What's going on?" I parked my hands on my waist. I didn't want Achilles to see us together. He'd made it quite clear he was jealous.

"Don't you think we should catch up?"

"No," I said flatly. "There's no reason to."

"Well." Alex shifted his weight from one foot to the other. "I still feel the need to apologize for what my father did to you."

"Why?" I asked, genuinely perplexed. "I don't feel the need to apologize for what my father did to your mother."

Tyrone—accidentally or not—killed Lyosha's mother before Tiernan and I were born. This was why we were kidnapped to Russia in the first place.

"Many of the things you went through happened right in front of me," Alex said in a clear, confident voice. He didn't let my hostility affect him one way or the other. "And I want you to know that, after a sufficient mourning time when you and your brother escaped, I eventually rooted for you, and I'm glad to see you happy and settled."

Finally, a twisted smile curled my lips in distaste. "Is that what you think I am? Happy and settled?" I turned to him fully, narrowing my eyes. "Do you know, Alex, that I've had thirty-three therapists in my lifetime? Only the last one stuck. With all the others, I simply couldn't get there. The minute they wanted me to seriously open up, I failed. Someone I'd once been close to advised me to forget everything that'd ever happened to me. Bottle it in. Turns out it was bad advice."

He watched me silently.

He'd meant well and was just a kid himself, but that mattered little. His face, his existence, his last name were still a bitter memory for me.

"Do you know what it's like to have your innocence stripped from you layer by layer? To reach the brink of starvation and be tipped beyond it? To watch your humanity slip between your fingers and not even know what it means, because you are too tired, too hungry, too beaten to think?"

Alex's eyes never wavered from mine. "I was there, too."

"Yes, as the heir and successor. You didn't go through all the bullshit."

He nodded. Well, at least he was honest. "I fantasized about saving you sometimes, you know," he drawled. "When you were going through those things, I was desperate for your approval. With Tiernan, I had it from the get-go. We were always thick as thieves. But you never gave anyone your trust, your sympathy. Only to Tiernan." He took his hand out of his pocket and reached for my face, running his thumb over the exact same spot he'd wiped a tear from fifteen years ago. As though it were still there. "I wanted your affection. Wanted to be seen by you. But every time I tried to come to your aid…"

"I pushed you away," I finished quietly. "Yes, I know. You were a boy. I didn't like boys. Boys hurt me a lot."

He inclined his head. "When I told you to bottle it up, I meant it as a coping mechanism."

"You were only a child," I whispered. "You don't have to explain yourself."

"Under any other circumstances, I think we'd have made good friends. Don't you?"

"Sure." I smiled. "And in a way, we still are, everything considered."

"Are we?"

I nodded.

"Last we spoke, you wanted me to kiss you," he reminded me.

"I wasn't spoken for at the time," I said. "You and I will always be unfinished business."

"Well, I'm here now. Let's finish this fucking business."

I shook my head. "I'm a taken woman."

"I know." Lyosha put his hand on the junction between my cheek and neck, using his thumb to angle my jaw up. "Achilles offered you to me."

My entire body iced over in shock. "W-what?"

"Achilles," Alex rasped slowly, dragging his gaze from my eyes down to my lips. His hand a necklace on my throat, loose but heavy. "He told me you were in the market for a no-strings-attached hookup. A one-off in a controlled environment. Something about proving something to you."

That fucking fucker, I seethed. *How dare he confide in Al—*

"He told me because I already know too much," Alex explained, reading my mind. "I'm discreet, can take a rejection like a man, and will never judge you."

This was why Achilles had been drinking so heavily tonight.

He was preparing himself for what was to come.

My heart cracked open and warmth poured out, giving my belly a fuzzy feeling.

He is killing himself. For me.

While I understood exactly why he'd done what he had, I couldn't see myself fully going through with the plan I'd weaved myself. Touching someone else—touching someone at all—felt... wrong.

But another part of me knew that if I didn't put Achilles's promise to the test, I would forever live in fear of what he might do. He'd maimed, murdered, and abused every single man I'd tried to be with since he'd taken control over my life, over my future. He'd psychologically destroyed me and had taken away all of my decisions when it came to sexual partners. He exhibited complete lack of self-control where my freedom was concerned.

This was my emancipation.

And I knew, as sick as that sounded, that Achilles needed this as much as I did.

The confirmation that he had changed—that he was better.

"You wanna fuck me?" I dragged a nail along his neck, up to his mouth. He captured it in his hot, gorgeous mouth with a come-hither smirk.

"You know the answer to that question." He spoke around my finger. "You're Tierney Callaghan. Everyone wants to fuck you. You'll be a gorgeous notch on my belt."

I forced myself to laugh as Alex plucked a champagne flute from the bar next to us and handed it to me. I took a sip. "How long is the belt?"

His smoldering gaze slid down my body. "Almost as long as something else of mine."

"Subtle." I pushed more alcohol between my lips. "I'll consider it, but only if he joins us."

"You think your little boyfriend wants to see his girlfriend get railed by the man who is about to take over his business?"

The cockiness of this man was almost as breathtaking as his appearance.

"I didn't say watch." I smirked coolly. "I said *join*."

A pitiless sneer touched his mouth, and he reached to caress my jaw softly. "No man is ever going to fucking touch me."

"He'll be touching me only."

"Hard pass." He stepped back, eyes narrowing on my own. "Temptation" by New Order reverberated against the walls of the bar, and I couldn't think of a more perfect song.

Alex was calling my bluff, waiting for me to back down from my ultimatum, but that wasn't going to happen.

Either I was including Achilles in this, or I wasn't doing it at all.

I parked my elbows on the bar behind me. "Turn around and walk away, pretty boy. I'm not doing this without my fiancé."

Alex did exactly that. His movement was swift and uncaring, as he spun on his heel and ambled off. I watched him take five steps before turning around and slicing through the crowd back to me.

"He isn't going to touch me," he warned through clenched teeth.

I grinned. "I know it might come as a shock to you, Lyosha, but not everyone wants to fuck you."

"I'm only agreeing to this because I know you fucking need this to move on."

"Hey." I held up a hand. "I haven't even agreed to do it yet. There's one more piece we still haven't talked about."

"Enlighten me." He was losing patience, and I couldn't blame him. Achilles asked him for this, and while he agreed to the act, he never consented to my never-ending roasting.

"Tiernan won't be happy," I said.

"Tiernan's never happy. Any other objections?"

My smile widened. "No."

Achilles chose this moment to reappear. He looked drunk as hell, eyes red-rimmed and hair in disarray. He looked beyond pissed, but as soon as he spotted us, he smoothed his expression over to something blank and businesslike.

"Had a nice chat?" Achilles kissed the side of my neck.

"An interesting one for sure." I slithered under his arm and burrowed into him.

Achilles leveled his glare on Alex. "Hale's not here yet."

"All the better. You cannot face him in your state."

Achilles's nostrils flared. "You better watch your mou—"

"Who wants to skinny-dip in the indoor pool?" I asked, smiling brightly. "I've heard all about it. It's supposed to be pitch-black, right? With benches overlooking the skyline?"

"Oh, I want to see the pool too!" Katya said excitedly, inserting herself into our conversation.

"Absolutely not." Alex turned a slight shade of green.

"Maybe Enzo can show it to you some other time." I patted her shoulder, stifling a laugh. "We have a business meeting to conduct."

Katya skulked to the far end of the bar with her tail tucked between her legs. I made a mental note to extend an olive branch to her. She hadn't actually wronged me in any way or capacity, and she was young. We women needed to stick together.

"Are you sure about this?" Achilles turned to me. "You don't have to, if you don't want to."

I grabbed his face and kissed him hard in front of the entire bar. When we disconnected, I whispered, "We're doing this together, and we're smashing that invisible wall that's stopping us. Now, lead the way."

He snatched my hand, and we slinked out of the bar, Alex matching our pace. We poured into a dim hallway and toward a second set of doors leading to the recreational center.

"Are *you* sure about this?" I whispered to Achilles.

"You wanted to be sure I'm a choice," he said. "This is how you'll know."

We reached the gym first—it was decorated with dark tiles and blond wood accents—then passed the spas and sauna. Elevator music and eucalyptus scents entwined around my body. The temperature kept rising the farther we ventured away from the club.

"The heated pool's closed to the public from ten at night until ten in the morning. We'll have privacy there." Achilles stopped by a frosted-glass door, punched in a code, and it swung back automatically, revealing a dark-palette pool with a floor-to-ceiling window overlooking the entire city.

Vapor rose from the glasslike body of water, curling up like cigarette smoke. A soft click sounded from behind me as Achilles fastened the lock on the door. "You touch her wrong, you bruise her, you make her feel unsafe, and—"

"You and I both know that'll never happen." Lyosha shrugged off his navy jacket, folding it neatly over a black concrete bench which sat flat against the wall. "This is why you turned to me with this *particular* request." He undid his cuff links meticulously. His eyes never wavered from me as he undressed. A hunger lived in them—some malice, too. Lyosha wasn't the worst of the mobsters I'd met, but he was still Igor's son. And he still had an unsatiable appetite for whatever didn't belong to him.

That included me.

Achilles lowered himself to the bench, a safe spot for him to watch, while I unzipped the back of my dress.

"Don't bother. You'll be joining us." I let the dress pool around my feet, stepping out of it and kicking it against the door.

"*Tierney*," Achilles warned.

"I want to feel you too when I feel him inside me." I unclipped my bra, then shimmied down my panties. "Besides, he is game as long as you two don't touch."

Achilles and Alex exchanged looks. When I turned to watch the pakhan, he was already fully undressed, his magnificent, bronze six-pack on full display. He was hard, pumping his long shaft lazily, eyes licking me from head to toe. "Come and join the fun, Ferrante. I'm in a charitable mood."

To my surprise, Achilles sprawled against the wall, spreading his muscular thighs, one hand resting on his knee, and smirked. "Why don't you two start and I'll join in on the fun if I see you can't please my woman, *Lyosha*?"

He'd never called him that before.

Alex flashed him a wolfish grin. "Challenge accepted."

He reached to his folded trousers and produced a condom. Ambling in my direction with the confidence of an undefeated warrior, he knew he was formidable and delectable, even stark naked. His hand palmed my cheek. My breathing became hard and labored. I didn't know what turned me on more: the fact this gorgeous, powerful creature, the head of the Bratva, was touching me or the fact that the love of my life was watching and letting it happen.

"*Ognennaya krasotka.*" Fiery beauty. "The boys at the camp crowned you the prettiest every year." His hand slid from my jawline, his thumb capturing my chin and tilting my face up to look at him. "You're still the prettiest of them all."

I opened my mouth to bite out something snarky, but he smashed his lips against mine.

I gasped, stumbling backward. My knee-jerk reaction was to fight him off, but then the pleasant taste of vodka and desire flooded my mouth and senses, and my muscles relaxed, letting him do what he wanted.

Alex deepened the kiss, his tongue flicking mine playfully, exploring the corners of my mouth as he pushed his body against mine until I could feel all of him. His thick cock pulsated against my stomach, leeching onto it hungrily. I tried to keep my pleasure restrained for Achilles's sake, but when Alex's hand traveled from my thigh up to my waist, clutching it as he crowded me onto the first step of the pool, I let out a moan.

"You're delicious." He bit my bottom lip, sucking away the pain before I could feel it. "Now I know what all the fuss is about."

My breasts felt heavy and full, and I ground them against his pecs, which were defined and smooth. I parted my legs just an inch, enough for his thigh to do the rest and slide between them. He pressed hard against my clit, my arousal for him already dripping all over his skin.

"I think." Alex moved his lips from my mouth to my neck, licking a warm path down to my collarbone, biting softly. "I'll have no trouble satisfying your fiancée judging by how wet she is for me. Put my condom on me." He deposited the slippery item between my fingers.

I reached for his cock with shaky hands, refusing to be the one to back down from this.

"With your mouth."

Halting, I darted my eyes to Achilles. Alex quickly captured my chin, bringing my attention back to him. "Don't ask for his permission. He's been killing every single motherfucker who dared to give you pleasure. This is yours. Own it."

Swallowing back a gasp, I pushed the condom between my lips

and dropped to my knees, taking in Alex's huge cock. Pale, veiny, and uncircumcised but just as monstrous as Achilles's. Shifting forward on my knees, I wrapped my lips around his tip, using them to roll the condom along his shaft. I hadn't done it before, and when I pulled back to examine my work, it was only halfway done. Alex gave it a rough tug to sheath himself completely with a satisfied groan. "Up."

I stood and elevated an eyebrow. "What now, big guy?"

He gripped my ass and hoisted me up. My legs instinctively wrapped around his waist, and the ridge of his dick was now rubbing right against my clit. I threw my head back and moaned. "Jesus."

"Hmm. What were you going to say?" Lyosha's fingers dug into the flesh of my ass. He descended the stairway into the heated pool, his mouth traveling across my upper body, exploring, biting, and licking.

"D-don't talk to him like that."

"Such a good little girlfriend, aren't you"? Alex crooned. We were now waist-deep in the pool. The water sloshed over us, nice and warm. His cock was still grinding against my clit, providing delicious friction. "Defending your lover. Look what you've made him do, though." Alex gripped my jaw and forced me to look at Achilles as his head dipped down. He took the tip of my nipple into his hot mouth, first giving it an almost painful suck, then swirling the tip of his tongue along my areola gently to ease the pain. The air became humid and thick with sex. I panted hard, feeling every thread of thought in my brain, in my muscles, dissolving into nothing. I melted inside his arms, the pleasure taking over.

My eyes locked with Achilles's. His chest moved up and down to the rhythm of his labored breaths, but he remained completely still. "You're beautiful." His voice cracked. "So fucking beautiful."

I closed my eyes, tears springing to them. The pleasure was too much, and I couldn't stop myself from coming even if I wanted to. Alex's cock against my clit—teasing, swirling, rubbing—along with his mouth on my tits was too much.

"Please…I…" I started, then stopped. I couldn't get the words quite out of my mouth. Not when Achilles was there.

"Make her come," Achilles demanded. "*Now*."

A low growl escaped the back of Lyosha's throat as he dove underwater, hoisting my thighs around his shoulders, squeezing the backs of my thighs in a death grip, and pushing his tongue into my pussy, his nose rubbing against my clit. I exploded, clutching his tongue between my muscles, throwing my head back and crying out. I gripped the back of Lyosha's head, riding his tongue while he was still underwater. He rose up with me still wrapped around his head and walked us back to the shallow end, where my feet reached the floor. "I think I'll take my prize now, if you don't mind." Alex smirked, his lips deliciously pink and swollen from eating me out.

I tossed a searching look at Achilles.

His face was bricked over, and I knew he had retreated to the place where no one could reach him. The same headspace he used to take a life. A place far removed from where we were and what we were doing.

He gave me a slow nod. "Take it, sweetheart. It is your pleasure."

I closed my eyes, nodding at Alex without looking at him. Alex gripped my waist and slid into me inch by inch. Slowly. Teasingly. Perfectly.

My knees buckled and my hips began moving on their own accord. Alex thrust into me, and I returned the favor by arching and meeting him halfway.

"God, you feel so fucking perfect." Alex's mouth latched onto my neck, sucking hard. "*So* tight. You're incredible."

His head dipped toward me, but I turned away, unwilling to kiss him again. Kissing felt intimate. Sex—not so much. Alex let a low chuckle loose, pounding into me, hitting the elusive spot inside me that made my entire body throb.

I was trembling all over, but I couldn't get the image of Achilles watching me out of my mind. I squeezed my eyes shut harder, but the look of him—resigned, serious, tortured—kept popping behind my eyelids.

Suddenly, I felt a bare, warm chest plastered against my back.

"Shh." A familiar rough palm wrapped around the front of my throat, tilting my head back. Achilles's eyes met mine. "Let go, sweetheart." He leaned down and shoved his tongue inside my mouth, erasing Alex's vodka taste with his whiskey flavor.

I arched back eagerly, kissing him and moaning into his mouth, while Alex dipped his head and devoured my breasts, running his stubbled chin over my flesh, and leaving marks.

I was ready to explode.

"Please," I begged, rolling my hips, riding Alex's cock harder.

"I think she wants more," Lyosha groaned, and when I unlatched my mouth from Achilles, I saw that his chest was glistening with sweat and waterdrops.

"My queen gets whatever she wants." Achilles spat into his index and middle fingers, reaching down, slowly prodding my ass with them. I squirmed and moaned, instinctively squeezing against both his fingers and Alex's cock.

"Oh God."

Achilles removed his fingers, then angled the head of his throbbing cock into my ass. I shifted slightly to allow him a better angle. He slowly guided himself inside, the pressure on me from behind mounting, my tailbone tingling with his uncomfortable girth.

"You know, I always find it so funny that people say God's name in the bedroom. He has nothing to do with it and probably wouldn't approve of the sins we commit." Alex reached between my legs, opening them wider to help Achilles slide inside me.

"Oh fuck," Achilles groaned, dropping his forehead against my shoulder as he slid into my ass, filling me to the hilt. I'd done this before but not with someone this well-endowed. Alex stopped fucking me but stayed inside me. They both let me take a moment to adjust to the position. I was pretty sure their balls were probably touching, I was sandwiched so hard between them, but considering I'd never been this turned on, this full, this *alive*, I wasn't going to point that out.

"This okay?" Achilles pulled my face to kiss me from behind again.

"Perfect." My lips moved over his mouth.

They started moving at the same time, slamming into me in the same rhythm, in punishing strokes that felt almost competitive in nature. The dirty thwacks of skin slapping echoed through the walls. Our bodies were covered in mist. My pleasure was so acute, so real, it took over my entire being. I felt it everywhere.

"Look at her," Alex groaned, staring at the space between us where he entered me. "She's taking it so well."

"She's amazing."

"Might ask to borrow her sometime."

"This is a one-off. Next time you touch my woman, you'll be filled with lead."

My orgasm coursed through every inch of my body, from toes to the top of my head, and I threw my head back, overcome with the incredible sensation of falling apart in the hands of the two most powerful men on this earth.

They continued plowing into me while I rode the high of my climax, with Alex coming first, and Achilles reaching his orgasm a few seconds later. Achilles pulled out first, grabbing my jaw to tilt my head up and give me a reassuring kiss. "You did amazing, Piccola Fiamma."

Alex slid out of me slowly, while Achilles propped me to sit on the first step of the pool.

"You good?" Achilles asked.

I nodded, still trying to catch my breath. This was the best sex I'd ever had. And yet I knew I'd never do it again. It served the purpose of proving to me that Achilles was done controlling my sex life, but I wasn't in the market for anyone else.

Alex reached between my thighs, prying them open and taking a good, humiliating look. I followed his line of vision. My cunt was pink and swollen from the inside. "Your pain is beautiful." He kneeled between my legs, kissing my pussy. "Thank you for putting your trust in me."

"Thanks for putting your dick in me," I retorted, giving him a playful shove with my toes. "Your work here is done, Alex."

He grinned and tipped his head down in a bow as he removed his condom, tying it in a knot. "At your service."

Nonchalantly, he climbed up from the pool, leisurely walking toward a stack of fresh robes and plucking one to dry himself off. He pocketed the used condom, because Alex, nice or not, was still a sociopath at his core. A sociopath who did not want any surprise heirs somewhere in the universe. Achilles still sat behind me, bracketing me with his legs. He kissed my shoulder. "You sure you're good?"

"Yes. Are you?" I looked up to search his face.

He nodded. "It was needed. Did it help?"

"Yes," I said honestly. "I think it did."

No one could ever know what had happened tonight, but I trusted all three of us to never breathe a word about it. Too much was riding on it for the truth to come out.

Even if people found out, I couldn't find it in myself to regret what had happened between us. It was the closure I needed to a horrifying period in my life.

Achilles proved to me that he put me before him. Before his obsession. Before his jealousy.

Swiveling my entire body so I was face-to-face with Achilles, I smiled up at him. "Thank you for this."

His eyes never wavered from mine as he barked, "Rasputin. Get fucked."

"Been there, done that, even got the shirt." We both turned to look at the pakhan fastening the last button of his crisp dress shirt.

"And way ahead of you. I'm wholly disinterested in the cuddling portion of the event. Tier." He sauntered to the lip of the pool, his mouth twisting in a smirk. "It was good seeing you again." He leaned down, touching his lips to my forehead.

"Same here." I pulled away. "Next time we catch up, we'll be wearing a lot more clothes."

He winked and found his way out of the pool.

Turning to Achilles, I put a hand on his cheek. "How much does it hurt?"

"Not enough to fuck this up." He covered my hand in his.

And I knew, in that moment, that we were going to be okay.

CHAPTER SIXTY-THREE
ACHILLES

How did the saying go? If the mountain won't come to Muhammad, then Muhammad must go to the mountain.

I was going to the fucking mountain, and if I had to move it, so be it.

Tristan Hale had bailed last night at the Forbidden Fruit Club.

But he was still in New York—my home, my playground, my turf.

He wasn't getting out of here without a little chat.

My first step? Shut down New York's airspace. Well, sort of. Every private airport in the tristate area reported to me about incoming and outgoing flights, and all commercial flights were monitored by Jeremie, who was once again at my disposal.

My second? Fermanagh's, Tiernan's pub.

Alex was still in the city, conducting business with his Irish bestie. I hated to interrupt their little makeup-and-gossip sesh, or whatever the fuck they were doing, but I had pressing matters to discuss.

Parking my Ducati in front of Fermanagh's, I popped my helmet off, tucking it under my arm, and sauntered right in. I strode past the drunken crow, and into Tiernan's back office, where two Irish soldiers greeted me with a stern look. They blocked my path to the ajar door.

"If you don't move right this second, I'm smoking your ass like you're a fine Cuban."

Tiernan's husky chuckle sounded from the office. "Liam, Tadhg, let him through."

They parted ways, and I bulldozed inside, finding Alex and Tiernan enjoying a joint and a drink together. Two peas in a shitty-ass pod.

"Hello, brother-in-law." Tiernan puffed smoke in my direction.

"Hello, asshat."

"The fuck you pouting about now?" Alex elevated a brow. "Problem with the missus?"

"Almost." I grabbed a seat and joined them. "Problem with a certain bitch-ass boy who promised me Tristan Hale and didn't deliver."

There was zero awkwardness between us.

Yeah, he'd fucked Tierney as a favor to me. But that was where it ended.

I'd chosen well—a Rasputin man, a last name Tierney wouldn't take if she had to die a thousand deaths.

A good-looking motherfucker whom she trusted and had shared history with but one who'd never occupied her thoughts or left her craving more. She'd had plenty of opportunities to meet him again over the years and had chosen not to.

All in all, it was a good deal, and one I didn't regret.

Sure, it killed me. I threw up multiple times before and after the act. And yes, a part of me died last night.

But a part of her resurrected, too. I saw it in her eyes. In the way she looked at me afterward, with *real* trust. With ease.

It was worth it.

Tiernan drummed his fingers on his desk, tilting his head. "Actually, Hale arrived. Couldn't find your ass anywhere, though."

Alex and I exchanged a quick look before I spoke. "Was he wearing a mask?"

"Naturally," Tiernan said. "Where were you?"

"With Tierney."

"You went with my sister?" His green eyes turned impatient.

"Uh-huh."

"You blew off a meeting with the most elusive contract killer on planet Earth for a...for your fiancée, who you live with?" he asked again.

I cocked an eyebrow. "I'm sorry, am I speaking to the same motherfucker who stood in the middle of a goddamn birthday meal at my parents' house to screw his bride after she ground all over him at the dinner table?"

His jaw flexed in annoyance at the mention of *that* debacle.

"And you?" Tiernan turned to Alex.

"Important phone call." Not a muscle in his face moved. He lied well and often. "I'll call him now. I bet he's still around."

"You do that, while I go check on Lila." Tiernan stood and grabbed his phone.

"Check on her?" I glanced up. "Is she okay?"

"Fine. Just a little nauseous."

"You knocked her up already?" My voice tightened. "Nero's not even a year old, for fuck's sake."

"Mind your own business, asshole." Tiernan flashed me a cheerful smile, exiting the room.

Alex reached for his phone, punching in a number, then a few sequences of numbers to connect to Hale. Eyes on his screen, he asked, "Tierney okay?"

"None of your fucking business," I hissed out. So much for keeping my shit in check. One more look from this fucker and I was going to wipe Vegas off the fucking map.

An indulgent smirk tipped the corner of Alex's mouth. "I was glad to help yesterday."

Scratch my earlier comment about shit not being awkward. It was about to get pretty damn weird when he lost all of his teeth.

"Aren't you in the market for a bride as well?" I shot back. "A single pakhan is a weak pakhan. Time's a wastin'. You need an heir."

He snorted. "Got anyone in mind for me?"

"What's your taste?"

If he answered *Tierney*, I was going to kill him. I didn't care that Tiernan liked him. He could find himself another pet. I'd get him a fish or something.

"My taste for women tends to run toward hellions with the potential to ruin my life."

"Sounds healthy."

The line connected, and a deep voice grumbled, "Hale."

"Tristan, this is Alex."

No answer from the other line. Conceited, little shit. He was waiting for more.

"Achilles Ferrante is ready for your meeting."

"Is he, now?" He sounded amused.

"Yes. He is right here with me."

"And where are you?"

"Fermanagh's. Need the address?"

"I got it." He sounded American, but that didn't mean jack shit. Conflicting reports had surfaced about him throughout the years. Some said he was Italian, some from Scandinavia, and some insisted he was from an undisclosed country in Africa. "I'll be there in fifteen minutes." He hung up.

Interesting that he didn't ask for any guarantees on his life. Then again, if he couldn't keep himself alive, he was a shit assassin to begin with.

Tiernan returned, looking very much like the cat who ate the canary. I didn't ask him if Lila was pregnant. I wasn't in the mood for anyone else's good news.

"Hale's on his way." Alex stood and collected his gun and phone.

"Leaving already?" I drawled. "I thought you and Tiernan had a slumber party scheduled."

"No sense of humor, no looks." Alex stopped midstride on his way to the door to clap my shoulder. "Hold on to Tierney as hard as you can because you're punching way out of your league."

I was fully prepared to stand up and go after him, but Tiernan stopped me when he rounded his desk and turned his screen to face me. "There's something you need to see."

Fermanagh's CCTV footage was on display. In the grainy alleyway, I spotted a tall figure donning their mask.

Tristan Hale.

He was getting ready, putting on elastic, fake finger pads to disguise his prints. The little shit was good.

"You can probably catch him if you hurry up," Tiernan said.

"Which way?" I grumbled.

"Take the back door from the kitchen and break right. He's locked in. A mountain of trash blocks the exit from the other side."

I stood up and charged in the kitchen's direction. Cooks and waiters bustled across the small space, and I shouldered through them, the heat and scent of deep-fried bar food assaulting my nostrils. I elbowed the door open, slamming it so hard against the wall it rattled. Tristan twisted his head in the direction of the noise, but I had the element of surprise working for me.

That and my alluring personality.

And by alluring personality, I mean, of course, the cocked and ready gun I pushed straight to his forehead with a smile. "Thanks so much for coming." I walked him back to the opposite wall of the alleyway. "Very nice of you, Mr. Hale."

If he was surprised or rattled, he didn't let it show. His posture was relaxed, his breathing even. "Your charitable greeting doesn't go unnoticed," he drawled back. "But if you're looking to hire someone, you're out of luck. You can't afford me."

"One thing you should know about me, Hale." I gave him a pat down with my free hand, my gun still shoved to his forehead. As expected, whatever weapon he carried was well concealed. Not in his pockets, waistband, or shoulder holsters. "I enjoy the killing requirement of my job."

"And yet, here I am." I could hear the smile on his face. "Why?"

"You shot my woman."

He shrugged. "It wasn't personal. Your father gave me a job, and I took it."

"You *missed*."

A beat of silence reigned before he spoke. "So I heard." He trained his gaze on mine. He had the cynical, steely eyes of a man who had seen everything and loved nothing. "Those things happen from time to time."

"Maybe. Not to you, though."

I wanted to rip the mask off his face, but I also knew that every fiber in his body was alert and ready for this. One wrong movement, and he could break my wrist. We were both trained enough to know the risks and consequences of every move we made.

"Thank you for the compliment, but I assure you—"

"Why'd you miss, Tristan?" I cut him off. "It was a clear, easy shot. You wanted her to survive. What do you have with Tierney Callaghan?"

He said nothing. I wanted to strangle him. I couldn't. Any sudden movement could be the end of both of us. I'd shoot. He'd snap my neck. And we'd both lose.

One of us needed to make a mistake.

That someone wasn't going to be me.

I had too much riding on this.

I decided to switch gears. "You came to the Forbidden Fruit Club yesterday."

"Yes."

"Why, if you weren't going to take any potential job from me?"

He said nothing. I pushed.

"It's a long way from Africa, and I hear that's where you live these days."

Again, he didn't answer.

He was curious. About the club. About our family. About the Ferrante legacy. Something drew him to us, and it wasn't money. He accepted our father's business but not ours. Money was money, though. And mine was just as green as Don Vello's. It made me wonder if maybe he had a soft spot for the don.

"Have you heard from my father recently?"

He gave out a low chuckle. "I do not discuss my clients' business. Ask him yourself."

"Oh, I would..." I slowly ran the gun from his forehead down his nose, all the way until I reached the base of his throat. "But he is...shall we say, *indisposed* these days."

Tristan didn't say anything, but I'd known I caught his attention. I kept twisting that screw, knowing he would snap sooner or later. I always managed to find people's pressure points.

"He's on his deathbed currently. Sad, really."

"That so?" His voice was scratchy. *Bingo.*

"Hmm." I nodded. "I did it to him myself. Well, Tiernan Callaghan and me. For sending you to kill her. We were...less than impressed with the both of you."

If I needed to guess, I'd say he was licking his lips behind this mask.

"What's the damage?"

"He's not lucid anymore. Eats through a straw. Shits into tubes. Mercy killing is the humane option. Too bad he's surrounded by coldhearted bastards."

"And you kept this mum all this time?" he hissed out. "I don't believe you."

Anger. This was good. He was close to snapping.

"Told the Organization he's abroad for medical treatment," I said. "But for all intents and purposes, he's dead, and we've taken over."

"With what authority?"

"Our own."

Tristan pounced on me, but I sensed it seconds before he'd even moved. He was acting out of pure rage. I had the time to step sideways and watch him tumble through his own momentum, and that was when I pushed him to the floor and straddled him, leaning my entire weight against his arms, which were pinned between our bodies. Making sure he was neutralized, I snapped my elbow against his collarbone, fracturing it for good measure. A soft groan sounded from behind the mask.

"You're a big boy. You'll manage." The level of sympathy in my voice was minus a fucking thousand.

I ripped the mask from his face, not knowing what I expected to see.

Whatever it was, it wasn't...*this*.

He was about Luca's age—perhaps a little older, around thirty-two or thirty-three—with dark brown hair—shaggy and unkempt—and baby blue eyes. A handsome, ordinary-looking man, for all intents and fucking purposes. One with a chiseled jaw and bedroom eyes. All he needed was a pair of goddamn Calvin Klein briefs and a horse. He had olive skin but his features were European. I couldn't place him anywhere on the map. I shook my head, grabbing him by the head and jaw, ready to snap his spine. It didn't really matter why he'd spared Tierney. If he wasn't going to talk, I wasn't taking any chances.

"You don't want to do this," he croaked, voice flat and even, as though we were discussing the weather. Danger crackled in the air. I could feel it. *Taste* it, even. We were both on the edge of chaos.

"Oh yeah? Why not?"

"Because I'm your blood, your brother." A taunting snarl found his lips. "I'm Vello's *Il prediletto*."

CHAPTER SIXTY-FOUR
ACHILLES

"You're my secret half brother?" I pushed off him, up on my feet in a flash.

He stood and picked up his mask, then shoved it into the back pocket of his jeans. He threaded his fingers into his shaggy heap of hair, tugging. He looked like a lot of things—angry, annoyed, in pain from his swelling fucking collarbone.

What he *didn't* look was like my half brother.

Other than our skin tone—mine a few shades darker than his—we looked nothing alike.

"Yeah," he said around thickness in his throat. "That's me."

"Not another word." I held up a finger. "I'm calling my brothers."

I wasn't in the mood to recite all this bullshit to Luca and Enzo. We needed to sort out this mess together.

Luca and Enzo arrived at Fermanagh's twenty minutes later. I thought about chaining Hale to something before realizing there was no need to. He wasn't going anywhere. He'd kept his identity secret until now because it served a purpose. With Vello practically dead, that purpose was gone.

"All right." Enzo rubbed his hands together. "I'm ready for my Jerry Springer moment. Who's announcing the DNA results? Tiernan?"

"Sit down and shut up." Luca smacked the back of our baby brother's neck.

My older brother took one look at Tristan and I immediately saw the displeasure on his features. Tristan was simply more competition.

"How old are you?" Luca demanded.

"Thirty-three."

"A year younger than Luca." Enzo poured himself a whiskey with a groan. "Good to know. Dad was in his *dipping his dick in whatever moved* era."

"Who's your mother?"

"Name's Rita." Hale looked calm and composed. Tiernan slid a glass of water in his direction, and he reached to take a sip. Suddenly, he looked unbearably young. I once again was reminded that the allure of the faceless and unknown often hid something painfully ordinary. "She was a hooker from Philly."

"How'd it happen?" Luca demanded. "Vello's always been careful with his whores."

"He enjoyed this one just a bit too much," Hale said aloofly. "And by the time I was born, it was too late. Rita died of an overdose a few years later, and I was sent to be raised in a village in Georgia, with Vello checking in a few times a year."

"Georgia as in the state?" Enzo asked.

"Georgia as in the Caucasus region of the Black Sea."

The three of us exchanged looks. That sounded exactly like something Vello would do.

"And your accent?" Luca asked.

"Fake," Tristan Hale spat out. "Just like my Italian, Russian, Spanish, and Romanian. I can adapt almost every accent if need be." He said all of this in perfect Neapolitan-accented Italian.

Luca scratched his jaw, one hand on his waist. "What's your real name?"

"First, tell me what you intend to do with me."

"Bold of you to assume what's happening here are negotiations."

"You're safe," Enzo cut in, giving Luca a chiding glare. "You're a Ferrante. We take care of our own."

"I saw how you took care of our father." His voice caught again.

Jesus. Did he really love Vello? In a way the three of us never could?

"Vello overstepped," I said slowly. "As long as you do not betray us, you're safe."

"Gurgen." He pressed his lips together, staring at the floor. "Gurgen Ferrante."

"Why'd you come yesterday?" I boomeranged a pack of cigarettes his way. I felt bad for the boy. He was obviously mourning our father, something none of my brothers, me included, was capable of.

He didn't touch the cigarettes, but his scowl cleared, somewhat. "I hadn't heard from Dad in a while. I thought he was mad at me for what happened with the Irish girl. I wanted…" He swallowed. "I wanted to see what was going on for myself. And something else was bothering me."

"We'll get to that something in just a moment." I held up a finger. "First, why did you spare Tierney?"

He lifted his gaze to mine, malevolence burning in his eyes. "Isn't it obvious?" He smirked. "She's your Achilles' heel. Your weakness. She'd have been no good to me dead. But alive? She's damn useful. She took you out of the race. You chose her over the kingdom.

"For as long as she is alive, you can never be don. I wanted to hurt her just enough to put her in your care—to knock you off the pathway to becoming the don—without actually eliminating her from the game."

"From the game?" Luca bared his teeth.

"Our chess game, of course." Our half brother sprawled back in his seat. "I'm sure you've seen it on our father's desk. He'd been sending me a picture with his weekly progress since I was in diapers. It is a telltale sign of who he sees as his successor."

We did.

We just didn't know who he'd assigned to what piece.

We'd had our speculations, of course. We'd watched him move the pieces along the years as he played against himself.

We deduced Enzo might be a rook and Luca a king.

Hale, however, knew with certainty who each of us was.

Who *he* was.

None of us had the stomach to ask him.

"Fine." Luca extinguished his cigarette in an ashtray, smoke skulking out of his mouth as he spoke. "You're here, and you're Vello's son. What the fuck do you want now?"

"What I've been promised." Tristan opened his arms wide. "The throne."

"The throne?" Luca repeated dully.

"That's what Vello had in store for me. He *did* call me his golden boy."

"Golden or not, you're a by-blow. An accident." Luca was direct but calm. We all knew that if push came to shove, we'd get rid of the little fucker in no time. "As legitimate as a three-dollar bill. No one in the Camorra will take you seriously."

"And yet here you were, chasing me halfway across the world." Hale seemed unfazed by the truth bomb that had just exploded in the room.

"I can't believe you're almost Luca's age." Enzo bristled. "That bastard Vello was busy." He tapped his lip, mulling this over. "We could've been raised together. We could've had fun. These two fuckers are such party poopers."

Tristan flashed him a disinterested look. "Sorry. I was busy becoming a killing machine to pay my way through life."

"Yeah, man." Enzo tossed gum into his mouth, handing him a piece as well. "Because I was out here living my best life as an inspiring fashion influencer. What do you think we've all been doing?"

"If your plan is to infiltrate the Camorra, you'll have to start from the bottom," I said, steering the conversation back to topic.

"You're not going to cut any corners just because you're Tristan Hale or because Don Vello couldn't keep it in his pants."

Tristan shook his head. "You'll carve me a role fitting for my talents and expertise. You don't take a trained assassin and have him collect protection money from laundromats."

Luca and I exchanged looks.

"We cannot afford to pay you what you're used to for your work," Luca clarified.

"That's fine because I don't intend to quit my day job," Hale drawled. "But I want in on the operation. And I want to see Vello for myself."

"I guess we can always use another pair of hands." Enzo shrugged.

"You can see Vello, supervised," Luca said. "We'll want a DNA test, though."

"Be my guest."

"And we want your details. Address. Real paperwork," I listed. "A direct line to you."

"I don't give those out, but you can have my direct phone number. That's more than I offer anyone." Tristan stood up. "Anything else?"

"Yeah." Enzo stepped in his direction. "Welcome to the fam, motherfucker." He threw his arms around him in a big bear hug.

Tristan just stood there, unimpressed. Much like Luca and myself. Why was Enzo always so goddamn sweet and kind? It was becoming a real issue.

"If you need anything, you give me a call." Enzo disconnected from him, punching his chest lightly.

"You can start by escorting him out," I said. It was time to wrap this shit up. Tierney was waiting for me at home, and this had taken longer than I'd anticipated. "We'll be in touch, Hale."

When Enzo and Tristan were out of the room, Luca turned to me.

"Can he be trusted?"

I shrugged. "Can anyone?"

"He seems like bad news."

"We don't have much choice in the matter," I said pragmatically. "If he is Vello's—and you and I both know that he probably is—he can stir up a lot of shit if he works against us. Blow up this secret, recruit an army, go against us. He has the capital and the charisma. Best to keep him close."

Grabbing my shit from Tiernan's desk, I turned around and headed to the door. Luca shot a hand in my direction, wrapping it around my arm.

I swiveled my face to him.

"He wants to become don."

"He can only dream about it," I assured him.

"If he tries…" Luca trailed off.

"We take him down," I said, not missing a beat. "And we make an example out of him."

That didn't mean I was handing Luca the title, though.

Fuck that.

A few months ago, I'd screwed up. But I'd paid a hefty price for it. In the meantime, Luca had managed to fuck shit up by inviting a goddamn fed into our club, letting his wife screw the help, and dropping the ball.

Being don was no longer my chief objective, but if it played into my hands, I damn well wasn't going to hand it over to him.

"Oh, by the way." I snapped my fingers. "How'd it go with Tom Rothwell?"

"Working on it."

"You think he'll turn?"

"I think something about us piqued his interest." He rolled the sleeves of his dress shirt up to his elbows, leaning against the desk. "And if I can't turn him, I'll eliminate him."

Whatever Agent Rothwell was after, he was going to need to pry it out of the Camorra's cold, dead hands.

CHAPTER SIXTY-FIVE
TIERNEY

I wasn't in the habit of freaking out.

Had managed to stay relatively calm and collected when I'd escaped the Camorra, crossed borders, and took off Vello's finger.

But the unease I felt right now threatened to drown me in anxiety.

Achilles had been gone all day. He wasn't answering his texts. Wasn't calling to check on me, either.

This was different from what I'd been used to in the past few weeks. The constant doting and affection disappeared today, and in turn, I paced our apartment like a lion in a cage, wanting to rip the walls apart.

I should be going out. Shopping. Visiting friends. Living.

But I wanted to stay home instead, to make sure that we were okay.

Only one thing happened between yesterday and today that could cause his sudden withdrawal from me—Alex Rasputin.

It had been a mistake to have the threesome.

In my defense, it wasn't even my fault. I hadn't initiated it. Admittedly, I enjoyed every second of it, but had I known Achilles would react this way…that he'd give me the cold shoulder all day…

Where the hell was he?

Picking up my phone from the marble slab in the middle of the kitchen, I opened our text thread.

> Tierney: Hey, when will you be back? I'll book us reservations at Maggiano's.
> Tierney: Have you seen my AirPod charger?
> Tierney: ?
> Tierney: I'm worried. Please call back.

Those were the normal texts. Unfortunately, the subsequent ones were completely unhinged and gave strong *Fatal Attraction* vibes. I didn't have the stomach to read through them.

I wanted to throw up.

Were we over? Was he giving me the silent treatment to teach me a lesson? Was the threesome a test? Had I failed?

After the club, we had gone back home, and everything was fine. Normal.

Maybe it took time for things to sink in.

I was clawing at the bars of my enclosure.

I couldn't lose him. No matter what. I'd make it right. Do whatever it takes.

What would it take to bring him back?

Restless, I shot Lila a text.

> Tierney: Have you seen Achilles today?
> Lila: No. Why, what's up?
> Tierney: I can't reach him.
> Lila: Have you tried Tiernan?

No, and I didn't want to. My brother would demand an explanation for all of my questions, and once I came clean, he'd blow a gasket. He'd barely come to terms with Achilles and me as a couple. Throwing Lyosha into the mix would be practically suicidal.

Luckily, Lila knew her own husband and his psychotic ways because another text appeared on my screen.

> Lila: I can ask Tiernan on your behalf, if you're not in the mood to be interrogated.
> Tierney: Thank you.

Putting the phone down, I walked over to the closet for the millionth time. All of his things were still there. At the very least, he was coming back to take them.

I didn't recognize myself in this desperation, but I couldn't help it.

I loved him.

I loved him, I loved him, I loved him.

From the very first moment when he entered my room and took the nightmares away.

My phone pinged in the living room. I went back to fetch it.

> Lila: Achilles was at Fermanagh's earlier. They had a meeting with Alex. He mentioned Achilles is pissed.

I couldn't breathe.

Grabbing my head, I folded in two on the floor and began to sob.

The loss felt impossible to digest. He'd slipped between my fingers once, when I was young and stupid, but I was given another chance. Another shot at happiness.

Of course, I blew that, as well.

Maybe I didn't deserve good things. Because whenever they came my way, I was so good at letting them slip between my fingers.

"I didn't want to do this…" I choked out, my tears dampening my face and the collar of my shirt. "I should've never…agreed…to this…"

The mechanical turn of the lock started from the entrance door. I whipped my head up just in time to see Achilles step inside. He hadn't seen me yet. Instead, he tossed his phone and wallet onto the kitchen table and peeled off his jacket, looking exhausted.

"Tier, baby?" he called out. "You here?"

Baby...?

Wiping off my face, I slowly rose up to my feet, making myself known. "Hi," I squeaked.

He turned to look at me, scowling. "Have you been crying?"

"No." I rubbed at my eyes pointedly. "Hay fever, I think. What's going on?"

"So... I have a half brother." He stared at me, wide-eyed, letting his words sink in.

Shamefully, my first thought was *THANK FUCK*.

So this was why he was upset.

Not because of the threesome and not because of Alex.

A secret half brother I could deal with.

"Vello's son?" I blinked.

He nodded.

I sprang into action immediately, rushing to the kitchen and pulling out a chair. "Sit down. I'll fix you a drink. Tell me everything."

He did what he was told, a telltale sign he was shocked. Achilles had never taken one direction in his entire damn life. I rushed to the liquor cabinet and pulled out his favorite whiskey, pouring three fingers into a tumbler and putting it in front of him. "Drink."

He tossed it back in one go. "It's Tristan Hale."

"*What?*"

"I went to Fermanagh's to ambush him. Wanted to see why he spared your life. Well, I found out."

"Why?"

"Because he knew you were my weakness and that as long as you live, you'll be my priority. I won't become don."

"That's—"

"Completely true," he finished flatly. "The Camorra's going to work with him."

"Oh." I put my hands on his shoulders, pressing a kiss to the top of his head. I didn't know what to say to this. I was glad Hale hadn't killed me, but I was more concerned with what this revelation did to Achilles. "How do you…feel about it?"

"Pissed," he growled. "Vello should've had the foresight to use a condom when he visited his hookers."

"And…about your new family member?"

"We'll see about that. He's an annoying motherfucker."

"Did you see his face?"

"Yeah."

"What does he look like?"

"A one-dimensional football hero who cheats on his girlfriend so that she falls for the nerd in a bad chick flick."

"First of all, that sounds like a great chick flick." I squeezed his shoulders. "Second, I have a feeling this is going to be a fruitful collaboration. Tristan Hale is a capable man."

"He is also undoubtedly a cunt if he has Ferrante blood running through his veins." A frown touched his face, and he picked up his phone for the first time since he'd gotten back to the apartment.

"Have you been blowing up my phone?"

Fuck my life.

"No…?" I cringed.

His eyebrows shot up as his thumb scrolled through the texts.

"*Please answer your phone, I swear I didn't even come from him, all I could think about was your dick in my ass?*" He read from one of the less palatable text messages I'd sent him, tilting his head to examine me.

Feeling my blush burning through the first layer of my skin, I tried snatching the phone from him. He pulled his hand back and stood, a devious grin on his face.

"Give me that," I huffed. "This is personal."

"You texted it to *me*."

"And you haven't bothered answering," I muttered bitterly.

"Hold on one second." He put his finger up, frowning at the screen. "*Please, baby, I'm willing to do whatever it takes to make it better. I love you so much. You're the only one for me.*"

I rolled my eyes. "You ghosted me the entire day."

"It's been five hours since I left."

"You always check on me." I recognized my bratty tone and was past caring.

"I do." He put his phone back down, taking a step toward me and tilting my head up to look at him. "I got caught up with the Tristan situation. And when it was over, I was eager to get home to unpack it with you, so I didn't check my phone."

My lower lip trembled. I messed with the collar of his shirt. "I may have…overreacted because of yesterday."

Achilles studied me closely. "Why?"

"Because you don't like sharing."

"I'm not going to anymore. That was a one-time thing to prove to you that I've changed."

"And how did it feel?"

He pressed his lips to my forehead, his mouth moving over it in a whisper. "Like death."

Something like darkness spread over my bones as he cupped my shoulders and walked me back toward the bedroom. I didn't resist. I needed this—to feel his skin against mine. Him moving inside me.

I'd made good progress with my therapist. We'd dug into some of my decisions…and preferences. I could now identify why I liked to be hurt in bed. It was because my expectation from my partners was so low, so incredibly nonexistent, letting them hurt me was a way to reclaim my control and convince myself that I'd wanted it.

I didn't have that problem with Achilles. I knew he was incapable of hurting me.

He parted my lips with his thumb slowly, meticulously, making my pulse thrum between my legs with excitement. My lashes fluttered, and he pushed his entire thumb between my lips. I clasped my mouth around it, sucking hard, my vision clouding with a thick mist of desire. My legs hit the base of our bed.

"I want to suck you off."

"No."

"Excuse me?"

"No." His voice, brash and low, made my insides tremor, his darkening gaze caressing every cell in my body. "I'm done playing games."

He shoved me to the bed, and I fell with a bounce. My heart fumbled like a bird trapped in a cage. His weight came down on me, and he pinned me to the mattress, the softness in his eyes threatening to rip me to shreds.

Intimacy.

Not sex.

This was what he wanted and what I was so scared of.

It was one thing to admit to him that I loved him.

And another to follow through on these words and show him with my body.

Desperately, I reached for his cock, trying to set the mood and the pace. He slapped my hands away and bunched my wrists together. *"No."*

I thrashed and kicked, trying to release myself from his grip. My pointy fingernails slashed at every exposed sliver of inked flesh. I drew blood and kept going, hoping to hit bone.

Achilles slammed my wrists above my head, covering my entire body with his. He was panting hard, and I knew it wasn't from paralyzing a 110-pound woman. He dropped his forehead to mine, growling, "I'm not doing this shit with you anymore, Piccola Fiamma."

I thrust my pelvis between us in answer, meeting his hot erection through our clothes. "Of course you are. That's what we do. We hate fuck."

"No more hate fucks."

"No?" I purred mockingly, arching my back so my nipples grazed his muscular chest.

"No." His voice sounded surprisingly somber. "I'm going to make love to you, and you're going to make love to me."

I ignored the traitorous way my heart sped, careening behind my breastbone like an out-of-control vehicle.

No one had ever made love to me. I accepted long ago that I wasn't worthy of any kind of normal love. My father tolerated me out of civilized necessity. My brother cared for me because of our shared past and trauma. Both their affection was laced with pity.

Achilles studied my face like he could read my entire stream of consciousness through my eyes. Normally, it'd unnerve me. Surprisingly, I found myself not caring if I bared my soul to him. He'd seen the ugliest part of me long ago and still thought I was the most beautiful woman in the world.

"Little Flame," he rasped, in English now, which felt unbearably intimate and whimsical. "Let me love you. Show me every jagged, ugly piece of you, and watch me stay anyway. I *will* stay. But you have to let me."

I stared at him, defenseless and tired. So, so tired. Of fighting this. Of clinging to habits that meant to defend me from a man I no longer needed protection from.

I burst into a sudden sob. Dr. Andrews had cautioned me that grief would pay me more frequent visits, now that I was finally facing my trauma. Still, weeping during foreplay wasn't exactly the height of seduction.

But Achilles didn't seem to care.

"Let it all go." He slowly freed me from my shirt, jeans, and underwear. After removing my clothes, he kicked off his slacks, keeping the pressure of his body on mine, anchoring me in place.

I shook beneath him, my body wrecked like a ship caught in a storm in the middle of the ocean. He let go of my wrists, cradling the back of my head with one hand and wiping my tears with the other. He caught one tear between his index and thumb, rubbing it together into evaporation.

"Look at you," he rasped, kissing the column of my neck so tenderly, it robbed me of the last of my self-preservation. *"Chelovek."* He fed me back the word I gifted him all those years ago, and just like it brought him back to life, it revived me, too. "Human after all. Flesh. Blood. The full range of emotions. They didn't break you, baby. Nothing could. You went through it. You remembered. You faced it. And you came back."

Our eyes met as he moved over me, and for the first time in my life, I didn't want to run. To lose myself in carnal desires. I wanted to be present, to see this moment through. He slid into me, a hiss of pleasure rumbling from his chest. I forced myself to loosen my muscles, to stop my body from going into fight-or-flight mode, where I was ready to slit his throat at any moment.

His movements were slow, leisured, tender strokes. I felt like I was falling into a dream.

He touched and caressed me everywhere, taking great care of every curve and part of my body. Kissed my tears, my mouth, my eyes each time he entered me. And though I felt his touch, what made this time different from all the others was how I felt his *soul*. Our souls clicked together, fusing into a whole. We needed this so badly.

For him to break the final wall between us and make me submit fully to this relationship.

I clung to him desperately, like a child seeking comfort in the arms of a safe grown-up, and he never let me go. Not even when we shifted and changed positions.

"Is this okay?" His lips moved over mine.

"Y-yes."

"I can feel you in a way I never have before."

The rush of dopamine to my veins made me tremble like a leaf. "I feel like you're injecting your DNA into my system or something."

He pulled slightly back and stared at me, his expression wonderous. My words had hit him somewhere deep.

Because this was what he always wanted.

To engrave himself in me the way I was seeded in him.

The pleasure of my orgasm started with a tingle at the base of my spine, spreading all over my body quickly. Achilles let out a grunt, coming at the same time. We stared at each other the entire time, arms braced, like we were holding on to each other in a storm.

And I knew in that moment that if eighteen-year-old Tierney could've experienced this just *one* time, this connection, this love which passed between one body to the other, she wouldn't have tried to take her own life.

And she wouldn't have let Luca bully her into breaking Achilles's heart.

When Achilles rolled off me, he was silent. I imagined the same whispers of surprise and emotions crawled over his body as well. Because I was the farthest thing from okay. This whole making-love ordeal rocked my world and tipped it over.

Instead of talking, I offered him my hand. He took it. Our fingers clicked like two pieces of a puzzle.

"Thank you for making me face my biggest fear," I whispered. "And thank you for…everything."

He squeezed my hand, still staring at the ceiling. If I didn't know him so well, I'd think he was going to cry.

Fifteen years of love and hate and everything in between boiled down to this.

We made love. And we survived.

"Achilles…" I turned in the bed and pressed my hand to his jagged cheek. "I want you to know that from now on, I am going to try to be the best wife that I can be. I will devote my life to you."

Silently, he pulled our joined hands to his face and kissed my knuckles.

I think maybe, in that moment, even he didn't have the words to describe what was happening inside us.

"But we'll never have biological children," I croaked, running my fingers along his face. "And you'll never have a traditional wife. Someone who stays at home, cooks a meal every day, and knows how to knit a sweater. A woman like Lila, who'll be content to simply stand by your side and watch you lead."

"No," he agreed. "But I'll have something else no man I know possesses."

"And what's that?"

"Enough." He pressed his lips to my temple. "You're enough for me, Tierney."

ACHILLES

Rolling off Tierney felt like crawling out of a battlefield after winning a war.

Injured.

Exhausted.

Scarred.

Triumphant.

It wasn't going to be easy, but it was going to be worth it, and the worst of it was behind me.

The final wall had detonated.

It was just us now.

Me. Her. And the love we shared.

CHAPTER SIXTY-SIX
ACHILLES

"This is a bad idea." Tiernan handed me his sister's passport.

He'd told her he'd keep it for her when she was on the run from me, and he kept his promise—until this moment anyway.

I ignored his observation, tossing her passport to the bottom of a moving box and filing through her old apartment above Fermanagh's. Tierney never had the chance to grab the things she loved.

"Aren't you going to ask why?" Tiernan followed me from the living room to the bedroom.

"No, I don't care."

"You're going to make me look bad," Tiernan snarled.

Hardly. He had taken in my sister's bastard son, from when he was still in her womb, and raised him as his own. The entire family had vowed to never let Nero know who his real father was. And that was arguably more than I could ever offer Tierney.

"It's not a competition." I tossed her favorite ball cap into the box, sauntering over to her closet.

"And Lila wants my sister around," Tiernan pressed on. "They're close."

"Do you expect me to make every decision in my life with your wife's preferences in mind?" I ground my teeth together.

"Naturally." Tiernan narrowed his eyes. "I think the entire world should bend to her will."

I shook my head, chuckling as I packed Tierney's jewelry box next. "I intend to make your sister happy."

"You already do." He propped a shoulder against the doorframe and crossed his arms. "Still, we'll hate to see you move."

I knew very little about proposals. Every person in my vicinity came into their matrimony through an arranged marriage. And while I didn't know much about romance, I knew more than enough about Tierney.

Her likes. Her dislikes. Her *dreams*.

I remembered everything about her. Every single damn thing.

Every freckle, every eyelash, the exact number of crow's feet, and the shape of her hairline. I knew what made her laugh and what made her sad and what made her body sing.

And it was time to put all of this information to use.

"Is there anything else I'm forgetting?" I set the box down and looked around her bedroom. I'd already filled four other boxes, which were sitting in the hallway, ready to be picked up by my soldiers.

"Nope. That was everything she ever cared for."

I jerked my chin in a nod. "I'll catch you on the other side."

Tiernan quirked a brow, watching me heading for the door. "Achilles."

I stopped and turned to face him.

"What if she says no?"

"She won't."

"How do you know?"

"How did you know Lila loved you?" I shot back.

"When she almost took a bullet for me," he answered, unblinking.

I thought about eighteen-year-old Tierney trying to take her own life just to clear a way for someone else who might be able to pop out babies for me so I could be don.

"Tierney did much more for me. That's how I know."

CHAPTER SIXTY-SEVEN
TIERNEY

"This is honestly exasperating." I sighed my frustration, itching to pull off the blindfold Achilles had wrapped around my eyes. For one thing, it was ruining my mascara. For another, I didn't like surprises. My life had enough twists and turns to last a millennium. I was perfectly content being informed what was about to happen in the next day, week, month, and decade from now until my demise. "Why do I need to be blindfolded?"

"Because I said so." Achilles's flat answer emerged from my right.

My short hair swirled in the wind, dancing in every direction. The humming sound of a plane's engine filled my ears. Everything told me we were boarding a jet. But I didn't know where to or when we'd be back.

"Hurry up."

"I can't see where I'm going," I hissed out.

The solution to that predicament, apparently, was lifting me up honeymoon style and carrying me at the speed of light up a short flight of stairs. I heard the metal under his feet and knew for certain we were on the jet.

Next, he buckled me up, like I was a toddler, and popped my AirPods into my ears. "What do you want to listen to?"

"An explanation as to where we are—"

"Music or audiobook."

I really wanted to strangle him. He was lucky he was attached to my favorite dick, or he'd be in serious trouble.

"Put on *Hot Girl Bummer*," I grumbled. It was my favorite true crime podcast. "'The Gnarly Case of the River Murderer,'" I specified. "I already have it downloaded."

"My sweet, delicate flower." His mocking tone ran straight past me because he still did as I said.

I dozed off twice during the long flight, and he had to feed me at some point, when he heard my stomach grumble loudly. It didn't sound like anyone other than him, me, and the staff on the plane. A rarity in itself. The Ferrante clan enjoyed moving in packs of threes and fours, minimum.

Finally, we landed. Achilles picked me up again and led me into the back of a car, giving the driver instructions in a language I didn't know but sounded like Latin.

"This is kidnapping," I groused.

"You came here willingly."

"I thought we were going to Maggiano's down the street!" *I still had clothes in the washer, dammit.* When he didn't answer, I added, "How'd I even get past customs?"

"Tiernan gave me your passport."

"He's a traitor," I mumbled, but I wasn't angry.

I'd go to hell if it meant being with Achilles, and my brother knew that.

"Do we have a long drive?" I prodded.

"Please just shut up and let me be romantic for once in my fucking life."

"Well, since you asked so nicely…" I sulked, crossing my arms.

The vehicle pulled over after a short while and the back door swung open. The air was mild and tinted with brine. I recognized the scent instantly; it was uniquely Mediterranean.

My pulse quickened, and I tried to calm it down, but it was hard.

"Careful, there's a step." Achilles's rich, low voice grumbled as his roughened palm clasped my wrist, guiding me down a pebbled pathway. Birds chirped and water gurgled. It was daylight—I could feel the sun on my skin—but since I wasn't able to track the time during the flight, it meant little to me.

We stopped when the front of my legs hit a concrete barrier. Achilles's scent wafted into my nostrils from the side—woods, whiskey, smoke, male—and he slowly pulled at one corner of my blindfold. I'd gotten so used to the dark, I felt lightheaded from the prospect of seeing again.

"You said if you could do things all over again, if you got your second chance, you'd retire by the Mediterranean Sea. Choose a good man. Crochet and drink a good cocktail while staring at the horizon." His words skulked into my ears, soaking into my body, and settled somewhere so deep it was etched into my entire existence. "I can give you all of it."

The blindfold fell to the ground, and I stared at the azure, sparkling water of the sea, vast and endless under a cloudless sky, twinkling at me playfully.

"I'll give you a quiet life, away from the hustle and bustle of New York. I will manage the Ferrantes' business from here in Naples, and you will be left to your own devices, to do whatever you want, however you want, as long as you're by my side."

I turned to look at him. Behind him was a stunning villa. Beyond it was greenery I recognized as an olive grove. It was a handsome property, and yet not gauche or over-the-top, with soft yellow arches and an inner court with roses and a fountain. I recognized the place as Posillipo, from the heart-stopping view and proximity to the sea.

"If you want kids, we'll have them. If you don't, we won't. If you want to rule this city with me, we'll share the throne. If you'd like to spend all your days crocheting and shopping, that's okay, too." He gestured to his side, and I realized we were standing on a patio overlooking the beach, with lounge chairs, a small round table with yarn and knitting accessories on it. A delighted shiver ran through me.

"The world will be your oyster by my side. I'll fulfill all your dreams. Every single one of them. All I ask is one thing—you."

His volatile gaze landed on me. Longing. Yearning. Unapologetic hunger. My breath caught in my throat as he lowered himself to one knee…

And then the other one.

He was on both knees now, staring at me, steadfast, with a gaze that promised fighting my every war, winning my every battle, never wavering from my side.

"I thought long and hard about what ring I wanted to give you."

Of course he did. I wouldn't expect anything less from this man.

I wanted to throw a smartass remark his way, to ask if the diamond was as big as my head, but I couldn't find it in me. Not sarcasm and not empty flirtation. I was speechless and completely anchored in the moment with him.

So I licked my lips instead and said, "Whatever you chose—"

"Legacy," he cut me off.

"Huh?"

"Money doesn't impress you. It never did. You like legacy. History. You said you wanted a home. Roots. Something that meant something." His black eyes shone as he produced something from his pocket. A small, black velvet box. He popped it open. "This ring has all of it."

It was an antique signet ring, made from gold, the intricate design on it no doubt used as a stamp at some point in its long history. It had an agate cameo depicting a skull and a snake. It wasn't lavish or pretty. It was bold and magnificent. And I loved it even more for it.

"Any rich man can buy his wife an expensive ring. I don't think there is much to it, really. But to find this ring, I had to visit every reputable antique shop in southern Italy. This ring dates back to the early nineteenth century. I wanted it specifically because it belonged to Queen Maria Carolina of Austria. She was the wife of

King Ferdinand IV and one of the baddest bitches in the history of Naples."

This earned him a little nervous giggle from me.

"Maria Carolina had spice and defiance; she called Napoleon a wicked bastard and meddled in her husband's business relentlessly, not giving half a shit what everyone around her—and in their kingdom—thought. At some point, she became the de facto ruler of her husband's two kingdoms. She was an absolutist and she was unstoppable." He took a breath. "And she still didn't hold a candle to you."

"You're insane," I whispered, giving his shoulder a small shove. He didn't budge. "You got me a queen's ring?"

"The queen is the most important piece in chess," he said gravely. "This was never a game to me, Little Flame. It was always a matter of life and death. Still is. Be my wife, Tierney, and I will dedicate my entire life to making you happy. What do you say?"

"Yes, you bastard. Of course. Yes."

He slid the ring onto my finger, and my entire existence clicked into place. He stood up and grabbed my face roughly, pressing an urgent kiss to my mouth.

"Truth?" he asked.

"Truth," I whispered into our kiss.

"I loved you long before I even met you. You came to me in a dream when I wasn't even ten yet. With your red hair and bright eyes and indomitable spirit. And you bewitched me. When I entered your room all those years ago, when I saw your hair, your face, I immediately recognized you." He ran his thumb along my cheek. "And I knew."

"Knew what?"

"That somehow, someway, *someday*, we'd end up here. Exactly like this."

EPILOGUE
ACHILLES

TWO WEEKS LATER

The water glimmered like diamonds under the weak October sun. Fucking beautiful, almost like the woman next to me.

We married a week and a half ago in Naples' city hall. A small ceremony, consisting of our families and a few friends. We didn't want to wait any longer than we already had. We'd wasted an entire decade pretending to hate each other.

The bride wore red and a badass smirk. The honeymoon was scheduled for next month. We were renting a vintage car and touring the French Riviera for a month. Phones off. Just her and me. My current role as the leader of the Ferrante clan in Naples allowed it. The position was a slower pace, for sure, but I didn't mind that shit all that much.

If she wanted quiet, I'd give her that.

And if she ever decided she wanted to go back to New York, I could provide that, as well.

I'd already resigned myself to the fact I was going to spend the rest of my life making sure this woman was happy and could think of no better role I wanted for myself.

"Your coffee's ready, honey." My wife swaggered from the depths of our home to the patio, where I was sprawled naked on a lounge chair, holding a steaming cup and placing it on the round table next to me. The scent of freshly ground coffee hit my senses, releasing orgasmic quantities of dopamine.

This.

Every morning.

Tierney, making me coffee.

Nuzzling into me.

Bliss.

Reaching a hand to caress her cheek while she was still standing, I smiled at her. And though I was the ugliest bastard my eyes ever saw, under her gaze, I felt beautiful. A fucking god.

"Andare in brodo di giuggiole." I cupped her palm, bringing it to my lips and kissing it softly.

Her smile broadened. "What does it mean?"

"To be in a state of rapture. The joy you give me, sweetheart... If I could translate it into drugs, I'd be the richest man alive."

Pouting happily, she nudged me back and settled against my bare chest, snuggling me under the sun. She had taken a break from her crocheting to make me this coffee.

She made me coffee at least three times a day these days. I hoped caffeine poisoning wasn't a thing because I was well on my way to getting it.

I set my newspaper down, already feeling myself hardening as her long, bare leg curled around mine. Our days consisted of very little work—mainly me checking on our operations and conducting business in lobbies of hotels—and her reading books, crocheting, and walking along the shore. Healing. She still saw Dr. Andrews twice a week via virtual call.

A visible light danced in her eyes now. Something I'd never seen before.

"This is nice," she murmured into my skin.

"Hmm."

"Do you want to go out and grab a bite later?" She kissed my neck. "Maybe catch a street performance?"

I want to fuck you right here, right now, in plain view, even though there are dozens of joggers and tourists under our balcony.

"Whatever you want, baby."

"I want to try that place down the street. And maybe we could take a long walk afterward." Her hand trailed down my abs and cupped my cock. "The weather's so nice."

"Sounds perfect." I ran a hand down her back and grabbed her ass. "Let's work up your appetite in the meantime."

She rolled on top of me, lips fusing with mine. A rush of heat coursed through me. I could never have enough of this woman. Never. And though children were an option, I hoped she didn't want them soon. I wasn't nearly done having her to myself. Not even close.

My phone buzzed with an incoming call on the small table next to us. I let it go to voicemail. It rang again immediately. This time, I scowled at it.

"Who is it?" Her mouth feathered across my six-pack. She was kissing a path down my body, going south, to the place that begged for her attention.

"Enzo," I growled.

"Answer him."

"Nah." I spread my legs open to give her more room to settle right where I wanted her. "He can wait."

She sat back on her knees and laughed. "It's your brother. It might be important."

"The only pressing matter in my life right now is getting you out of this ridiculous bikini and into my bed." I hooked my index finger into the string of her red bikini top, pulling, then releasing it teasingly to brush against her skin.

My wife shot me a chiding look. *"Achilles."*

"What?"

"Answer your poor brother."

I made a show of sliding my finger over the screen of my still-ringing phone. I pushed the speaker button. Anything Enzo had to say could be said in front of my wife.

"The fuck do you want?"

"Hey…" Enzo's voice sounded strained and hoarse. Like it suffered from many cigarettes and not enough sleep. Not his usual perky self. I sat up on the sunbed, alert. He always greeted me with a stupid, frat-boyish "yo."

"What's going on?"

"Are you sitting down?"

"Do I look like the fainting kind?" I ground out.

Enzo didn't laugh. Shit. Enzo *always* laughed. That couldn't be good.

"It's Dad," he said.

"What about him?"

"He's dead."

I said nothing.

"He was found unresponsive this morning in his bed."

I said nothing.

"The clans know. They're sniffing around to find out who the new don is."

Still, nothing. There were too many suspects to count, too many people to gain from Vello's death. As for me, I felt nothing but mild relief. He was a shit father, and he'd cost me valuable years with my wife. The only part of me that mourned him was the part that wanted to resurrect him so I could kill him again.

"You need to come home. We're crowning Luca. He's taking over. The new king of the underworld."

No answer.

"Are you listening?" Enzo hissed out.

"He'll be there," Tierney said, loud and clear. "We wouldn't miss his funeral for the world."

We shared a private grin. A grin that said no amount of therapy could heal the fuckery that went on inside our heads.

I hung up and kissed her forehead. "Pack red for the funeral."

"Red?" She reared her head back to study me. "Why?"

"It'll stain less than any other color, and we're walking into a bloodbath."

ACKNOWLEDGMENTS

This book is the actual inception of Society of Villains. It was the first story I had in mind when I came up with the idea for the seven-book series, but my gut told me that Tiernan and Lila's story needed to come before Achilles and Tierney's, in order to set the scene just right. *Bad Bishop* turned out to be one of my favorite books I've written, so no harm done, but it was hard to wait to tell Achilles and Tierney's story, and I'm so glad it's out in the world now.

As always, and in no particular order, I'd like to thank my alpha readers, Bryanna and Claire, for the amazing feedback and attention. I am so grateful for your initial input. It always puts things in order and perspective.

To my beta readers—Tijuana, Vanessa, Lena, Aisling, Veronica, Dr. Claire Reed, and Liah. You ladies are a tour de force of honesty, devotion, creativity, and love, and I am so happy to have you holding my hand through this crazy ride. I appreciate you all so, so much.

To my editors—Annie Meagle, the one, the only. I love the way you can be brutally honest and ruthlessly kind at the same time. Mara White—I am not above begging when it comes to your expertise. Sarah Plocher—you are such an integral part of my process! Thank you so much for everything. And Silla Webb—thank you so much for everything (I'm still reeling from the chapter numbers, IYKYK), and Gretchen Stelter for the copyedit. And to my Bloom editor—Christa Désir, who has changed the trajectory of my entire career and did it with such humbleness. Thank you so much for simply being you.

Many thanks to my UK editor, Lucy Stewart, for working relentlessly for this series. I get such a kick when I see my books at Waterstones and the Works!

Bloom and Hodder superstars: Madison and Siena (from Bloom)—thank you! For your kindness, dedication, and expertise. Same goes to Charlea and Kallie from Hodder. Thank you from the bottom of my heart.

Big thanks to Kimberly Brower, my agent, for everything she does every single day. I don't say that enough, but I am so grateful to have you in my life.

To the Author Agency, specifically Becca and Shauna, for the wonderful PR and the tours, and to Tijuana, for managing my life, and Emily, for managing my social media accounts. You're the GOAT and I know you know it because I tell you every week.

Thank you to Jay Aheer at Simply Defined Art for the covers, and to Julie at Bloom for the inside cover art and for making sure everything looks just perfect.

Finally, thank you to my team! TJ, Emily, Vane, Marta, Yamina, Gabby, Susan, Leslie, and Liah. I love you and I love you and I love you.

And to my readers, who show up, be it if I write a fluffy best friend's brother or about Mafia lords killing each other in the goriest ways. You make my dreams come true.

Thank you.

All my love,
L.J. xo